THE 7 STAGES OF GRIEF AND LOVE

Name: Chmura, Nicole (author)
Title: The 7 Stages of Grief and Love
Identifiers: ISBN 9798992779103 (paperback)
            ISBN 9798992779110 (ebook)

Cover art by artbysolange
Cover design by Sandra Pavleska

This is a work of fiction. The characters, places, and events portrayed in this book are used ficti-
tiously. Any similarity to real persons is entirely coincidental and not intended by the author.

First Printing, 2025

The 7 Stages of Grief and Love

Nicole Chmura

For anyone who has been left torn and scarred by the claws of grief--especially all the grown up little girls who just miss their mom. She's proud of you, I promise.

And for my mom. You would've been mortified that I wrote sex into this book but hyped it up anyway. Forever my biggest fan. I miss you. Love you, mean it.

Dear Reader

Thank you for picking up this book. Whether it just arrived on your doorstep or it's been on your shelves for a while, I hope you find that it's the perfect time for you to jump into Maggie's story. I beg you to please be patient with Maggie. She can be frustrating and irritable and make decisions that will drive you absolutely mad. She's also only human.

This story, although fictionalized and romanticized, is at its core *my* story. Losing my mother turned me into a version of myself I didn't recognize and I mismanaged my grief for a very long time. I'm not proud of everything I did while grieving, but I am proud of the woman I was for doing everything she needed in order to survive what felt like a cataclysmic pain. Maggie's story in this book takes place over the course of about 7 years–not including the epilogue. My grief story continues to stretch on. There are portions of this book inspired by life and there are portions of this book that my characters created all on their own. I will never confirm nor deny which events were inspired and which were entirely created from the chaos of these characters having their way with my keyboard.

If you know me and see yourself in any of these characters, I hope you smile. I thank you for sticking with me through this messy life of mine. If you know me and see yourself in any of these characters and aren't particularly happy with their portrayal... well, maybe you should sit with that for a minute. In the end, though, none of these characters–with the exception of Maggie–are based on any one person. Each character you meet has been strung together by hundreds of interactions and a whole lot of creativity.

Reader, I'd like to warn you of a few things. This book is a mix of many emotions. You'll find heartbreak and devastation alongside laughter and love. I do want to make sure you're not jumping into anything less than fully aware. In sections of this book there will be allusions to alcohol abuse and depressive thoughts. There will also be on page emotional and physical abuse in some scenes. Please take care of yourself if these are things you'd prefer not to read about. Also, *if you are related to me* and would rather not acknowledge that your little sister, cousin, niece, or whatever knows what sex is, please text me so I can tell you exactly what pages to skip. Otherwise, as you read I'd love to see your reactions, so please tag me @readsandrescues so I can live vicariously through your first read.

I truly hope you find value in and enjoy my very first novel. Again, I ask you to not judge Maggie as she goes through *our* grief journey. This is your not so gentle reminder that grief is messy and can be all consuming. No two grief journeys are the same and they are never linear. If you're currently on one of your own, I hope you feel seen in Maggie. I hope I did this story justice. And, I hope you fall a little bit in love... with her, with her man, and with life again.

Love always,
Nicole

P.S. My characters love to curse. You've been warned.

Shock

Playlist

birthday cake / Dylan Conriqué
How Do I Say Goodbye? / Dean Lewis
Not Like I'm In Love With You / LEW
Nightlight / We Three
You Are In Love (Taylor's Version) / Taylor Swift
I Just Killed A Man / Catie Offerman

1

Shock

Maggie stared at the strange, stark contrast of the brightly colored flowers against the gray slab of stone. The two didn't seem to fit together and yet there they were. The vibrant oranges and purples of the fresh birds of paradise against the gloomy gray of the headstone marking her mother's grave. The opposites created a paralyzing effect on her brain. Her thoughts focused on how and when those two would ever naturally mix together as they did here.

But they wouldn't. She knew that because this wasn't a natural circumstance. This was the only circumstance she never thought she'd have to live through–at least not yet. Her mom wasn't supposed to die. Her life wasn't supposed to tip like this. Her future wasn't supposed to be so irrevocably altered and unrecognizable. This couldn't possibly be her new normal.

As she stood frozen, her thoughts shot from the impossibleness of the situation back to those damn flowers. She couldn't decide if the flowers made the headstone more beautiful or if the headstone made the flowers uglier. Or maybe it was a bit of both. She couldn't decide if the placement of the birds of paradise bundle at this site of sadness made her hate them or love them more. Seeing them here felt wrong, even if they were her favorite flower.

"Who brought these for you, Mom?" Maggie asked out loud, knowing she wouldn't get a response. She also knew the answer: one of her aunts. It wasn't her or her brother and she knew no one else was going through the hassle of getting birds of paradise–also her mom's favorite flower–this time of year. In general, they weren't cheap flowers and in the winter on the East Coast they were even harder to come by.

"Probably Aunt Agnes. She mentioned she'd be visiting this morning when I talked to her," Maggie said aloud to no one in particular as she rearranged the plants around her mother's headstone to fit in her own bouquet. It always overwhelmed Maggie how many flowers were constantly surrounding her mother's grave. Her mom was just an immigrant factory worker, but based on the floral array around her headstone you would've thought she was a celebrity or town hero.

Thinking of this sweeping amount of love reminded Maggie of the funeral home owner who handled her mother's service. It felt like an endless stream of people had come to say their final good-bye. He hadn't realized how many would be in attendance and the disbelief on his face was almost comedic–almost. He even had to open a secondary space within the funeral home to accommodate all who arrived. She thought of his bewildered expression as he came to her unsure what to do with the amount of floral arrangements that had been delivered from friends and family. Her heart ached thinking about how loved her mother had been without ever fully realizing it. It was this ache that shook her out of the memory and back to the present.

She stood up, pulling her jacket tighter around herself and nestled the lower half of her face into her scarf. The bitter cold proved it was determined to stick around even though nearing the end of March should've meant the start of spring and warmer days. She took one last look at the contrast of colors and darkness before turning to walk back to her car. Back to her new reality. A reality she still couldn't believe existed. And to her thoughts. Thoughts she couldn't keep focused. Thoughts that went from too many one moment to empty in the next. She took one last glance at the flowers and chose empty. She liked the emptiness the best.

Maggie bustled into the bar like the hurricane she typically was and threw her jacket onto the stool next to Rosa.

"Sorry I'm late Ro! Traffic was a bitch getting here. I swear the construction is just never ending in this state," Maggie said as she started unbundling the rest of her layers.

"Mags, you act like I don't know you. You're late to life. I'm used to it after this many years," Rosa laughed as she motioned to the bartender and he placed a drink in front of Maggie. These were the moments that made Maggie appreciate her friendship with Rosa most.

They'd been best friends since high school and had since learned the nuances of each other's personalities. Each other's habits, quirks, loves, and dislikes. Maggie didn't have to worry about impressing Rosa or toning herself down around her like she did with most other people. This friendship was easy. This friendship reminded her of what normal could feel like. She could be herself fully and unapologetically. Rosa would always understand and love her because of everything *and* in spite of anything. Not to mention, Rosa always made sure a drink was ready for her whenever she showed up–both on time and late. Usually late, though.

Taking a sip from her drink, Maggie relished the slow burn of the bourbon as it went down and warmed her chest.

"Mmmm. Basil Hayden. You know me too well Ro," Maggie said, taking another sip and smiling.

"Or maybe you're just a bit predictable? I mean come on Mags, you get a whiskey or bourbon neat *everywhere* we go. And it's *always* this one if they have it. It's always the same with you," Rosa scoffed teasingly.

"Says the girl who exclusively drinks tequila. Really?" Maggie retorted, smirking. Rosa giggled and shook her head. Happy hour was coming to an end and the crowd was starting to thin with checks being requested and tabs closing out. The two friends settled into a comfortable silence for a moment enjoying each other's company and the people watching. The commotion of those wrapping up their happy hour began to settle as they eased back into conversation.

"So, when do you head back to Baltimore?" Maggie asked, picking up her glass and trying to keep her sadness from seeping into the question. Rosa had come back to New Jersey for Maggie's mom's funeral. She somehow managed to get off of classes for two weeks but had to head back to Baltimore to finish her last semester before graduation. Rosa had been there for every moment. The loss. The planning. The burial. She had been a rock to lean on and the one wiping those very first tears away.

Maggie remembered the first phone call she made after she got the news. She knew things weren't good after her mom got moved to the Intensive Care Unit at Sloan Kettering, but never suspected it could turn so horribly so quickly. After weeks of staying at the hospital with her mom, test after test, and treatment after treatment, her mom had finally convinced her to head back to her dorm to shower for the first time in days and sleep on her own bed. Maggie refused time and time again, but somehow her mom convinced her to leave that night. She still can't really remember how.

The next morning, as the sun was just starting to rise, she woke with a start. Not to her alarm but to a sinking feeling in the pit of her stomach. At her core she knew something was wrong. She had multiple missed calls from the hospital. Something told her this was it, but she refused to believe it fully until she heard the words from a doctor. Grabbing whatever clothes were closest, she got dressed, jumped into a cab, and called her brother as the cab drove across town.

She sobbed on that phone call and didn't even know the truth yet–at least nothing that had been confirmed. She sobbed into the phone that he needed to come to the city now. She had never asked her brother to come into the city for any of the medical tasks before, but this time she could feel in her bones how they would need to be together. She refused to speak to any doctors until he was there. In her core, she knew that whatever news she was about to receive, she couldn't bear it alone.

Somehow her deepest fears were confirmed. Something had shifted overnight. With all of the medical jargon, she couldn't fully understand everything, but she could understand that her mom wasn't breathing on her own anymore. That her mom was asleep and living on medications and machines. That her random good-bye the night before would be the last relatively lucid one she would ever get. She understood this was the end no matter how badly she didn't want it to be. No matter how much she willed it, this would not change. Her brother offered to call their family and deliver the news while she went to the ICU waiting room and made a phone call to the first person she could think of–Rosa.

That phone call is tattooed on her memory. Maggie barely spoke. Rosa answered, and all Maggie could muster through her sobs was, "my mom... not good... Ro..." With a friendship like theirs, though, that's all it took. Rosa started rapid firing into the phone, "I have one midterm I have to take in person tomorrow but after that the rest are submitted online and then I have a break. I'm going to get on the first bus I can into the city after tomorrow's in person exam and I'll go straight to the hospital. I'll be there as soon as I can. I promise. As soon as we hang up I'm going to get my ticket. Until then I need you to do what I know you do best: be as strong as you can. I know you can do that. You always have." The quiet sobs on Maggie's end told Rosa all she needed to know. She waited a few moments before finally saying, "Mags, I'll be there as soon as I can and we'll figure this out together. Love you, mean it."

Staring at her drink, replaying that memory in her mind, Maggie began to think of the second phone call she made immediately after. He answered on the third ring. They always answered each other on the third ring. She was pulled from her reminiscing when Rosa repeated herself, "Mags, did you hear? I leave in two days. Saturday night."

"Oh yeah. Sorry, got lost in thought there for a second. Are you excited for the rest of the semester? To finally finish and graduate? And you're graduating *early*! What a freaking accomplishment. I remember our little freshmen high school selves. When we both first thought the other was a bitch. Universal best friend experience! I don't think we ever thought we'd actually make it this far, do you?" Maggie prompted with a massive smile plastered on her face looking into her best friend's eyes.

She saw the look in Rosa's eyes shift. The quick scan she did of Maggie's face. The urge to push her to open up. Then, the understanding. Rosa could tell she didn't want to be prodded about whatever memory had overtaken her in that moment. She could see her sadness but could also see that talking about it was not what she wanted or needed right now. So with that one look and her understanding, Rosa gave Maggie what she needed in this moment–a conversation not on the topic of her mother's death. A fleeting distraction from the chaos and confusion of her feelings that consumed her entirely the rest of the time.

"I am. I wish I could stay longer, though. Honestly, the semester is basically done. By the time I get back, I have just over a month left. Finals shouldn't be too bad and then I'll be back here right after graduation," Rosa offered.

"What about you and Max?" Maggie asked flirtatiously.

"Oh, who knows? He has another year left and you know I don't love the whole distance thing. That one is a play it by ear situation. What about you and Kameron? I've seen you two these last few weeks. Anything rekindling there," Rosa asked playfully, wiggling her brows and revealing a devilish smirk.

"Ro, there's nothing to rekindle. We've never been anything like that to each other. He's an amazing friend, you know that. He's been there for me and I appreciate that more than I can put into words, but we've never had the romance in our relationship. Just great friends and I–"

"Oh shut the fuck up," Rosa interrupted. "You two just need to get over yourselves and bone already."

"RO!" Maggie shouted as she looked around to see if anyone near them had heard her blunt best friend.

"Mags, I love you but open your damn eyes. You two love each other–or could. Sure, maybe it started as a friends thing but that is not what it is anymore. It's just what you two pretend it is. You've got chemistry coming out the asshole. You're both hot as hell and flirt without shame. You fit perfectly together. You have fucking sleepovers for crying out loud. Who else just sleeps over their guy friend's house, hanging out, cuddling, and *getting to know each other*? To literally every other person in the universe that is a date or relationship. I don't get why you two don't just do it already," Rosa finally finished her tirade and took a sip of her drink. She stared at Maggie expectantly.

Maggie couldn't deny most of what Rosa was telling her. It's true, there had always been a semblance of something there. But, their friendship meant too much to her. She didn't want to screw it up. Any attempt at romance just wasn't worth losing Kam as a friend. Not to mention Kam was basically her right person, wrong time. When she was single, he wasn't. When he was single, she wasn't. In the rare occurrences when they were both single, neither of them were in a headspace where they could be in a decent relationship. And so, the friendship continued. That was absolutely enough for her.

"I don't know what you want me to say here Ro. Other than that we need another round," Maggie finally responded. As if on cue, the bartender came over to give them just that. With fresh drinks, Rosa continued to stare at Maggie. Maggie knew that look. Rosa may have let her avoid talking about her mom, but she wasn't going to give up on this topic as easily. Sipping on her tequila, Rosa gave her one more stubborn, pointed look that forced Maggie to continue.

"Okay, you're right," she sighed. "There's always been *somewhat* of a thing there for us. But our friendship is too important to me, Ro. You know I'm fucking terrified of opening up in that way. Can you imagine me dealing with the potential rejection? What if it's one sided? What if it's just me? And what if I ruin everything by even suggesting something like this? I can't risk that. With where my life is right now, his friendship is more important to me than the potential of something else. Not to mention, I'm kind of a fucking mess right now. Got a lot of shit to work through in case you forgot? I'm not exactly in a place to be with *anyone* right now."

"Well it's not one sided, anyone can see that," Rosa started, "But, you're right about the rest. You're probably gonna be a disaster for a bit. More than usual at least. Best to sort your own shit out first. It doesn't hurt to keep the potential alive, right? You know I love you and just want you to be happy, right?"

"I know, I know," Maggie said, staring at her very best friend with gratitude. "How did I get so lucky? An amazingly perfect best friend AND apparently I'm hot as hell and have chemistry with someone else who is also hot as hell? What did I do to deserve so much?"

"You're probably one of God's favorites," Rosa responded without missing a beat.

"Well then, cheers to being God's favorite," Maggie laughed, holding up her drink. Rosa tapped her glass to Maggie's and they laughed as they ordered some food. For a moment, in *this* moment, Maggie felt content. This is what her life was supposed to consist of. Not whatever she was about to face outside of this bar. That couldn't possibly be her life. It still didn't feel entirely real most of the time.

As much as she wished this could be true, deep down Maggie knew that her life was now a distorted disarray of both. Her life was a combination of what she had always imagined and the unexpected mess she never thought possible. But for right now, drinks with Rosa were all she wanted to think about. This was the reality she wanted to stay in.

After an endless stream of conversation that always felt easy, Rosa and Maggie said their last goodbye before Rosa headed back to Baltimore. Although neither of them were much for physical touch, this hug was necessary. The embrace they both needed in order to reassure each other they'd be okay until the next time they could be together. At the very least as okay as they could hope to be.

"Text me when you get home, Ro!" Maggie called out, walking across the parking lot.

"Will do! Love you, mean it!" Rosa shouted back, getting into her car. The smile on Maggie's face as she dropped into the driver's seat felt confusing. Like it didn't belong there. Like she didn't belong here anymore–in moments that feel this happy. She started the car for the heat and without meaning to, let the paralyzing emptiness kick in. She sat staring blankly at the Honda emblem of her mom's car–her car now.

She wasn't sure how long she sat there but it was easier than driving. Easier than moving forward. Heading home. Well, to her aunt's house. She didn't have a home anymore since the apartment she used to share with her mom felt off limits. Would she ever sleep in what used to be home for them ever again? Would she even be able to step into that apartment to clean it out? The thought of it was too much, so she cleared it from her mind as she put the car in reverse to pull out of her parking spot.

As she turned onto the main street of her hometown, her car phone rang. She checked the name that flashed across the screen, allowed herself a small smile, and picked up on the third ring.

"Well, speak of the devil," she said.

"Oh? And who might I ask was speaking of me?" Kam's voice asked through the speakers of her car.

"Ro and I were out for drinks and dinner. You might've come up here and there," Maggie said playfully.

"Only good things, right?"

"Oh no, only the worst," she jested.

"Lemme guess, you talked about my excellent ass?" Kam boasted.

"Of course, especially about that nasty mole you have on it. In detail. You should really get that looked at." She smiled as she heard his boisterous laugh on the other end. His laugh felt like sunshine and honey—warm, smooth, and sweet. She knew he never laughed like that unless he truly meant it, and she always felt a small sense of pride when she was the one behind it. She could imagine him shaking his head, smiling gently as he called her a smartass. There was a comfortable pause as his laugh dwindled and she waited to hear why he had called. Except he didn't say anything. Just the light chatter of the tv he had on in the background came through her car's speakers.

"So-," she began.

"We're going to a party next weekend," he cut her off, blurting it as if he just needed to get it out, knowing it wouldn't be received well. Maggie froze, hands rigid on the steering wheel. She said nothing. Not a single sound escaped her as she sat almost entirely still, focused on the road ahead of her. Why would he even suggest a party? What was he thinking? Her mom had just died and he was one of the few people she let see—no matter how briefly—how truly shattered she was. How could he think that a party would be good for her? She couldn't believe he'd even suggest it. Not yet, at least. And now he sat silent on the other end waiting for her response. Expectant.

Except she couldn't say anything. Didn't know what to say. The idea of having to pretend to be fine in front of that many people. The confusing dichotomy of feeling nothing but a pit of pain internally while making jokes and being the life of the party that everyone expected externally. It was too much. It was too big an ask. Even from Kam, who she'd do just about anything for.

As if he could sense everything running through her mind through that silence, Kam said quietly, "Mags, you need this."

"Kam, a party is too much right now. It's too soon. But I appreciate the invite," she forced out too tightly.

"Mags, I know–"

"Kam, I cannot," she cut him off, more sharply than she meant to. She'd never spoken to him like that before and his surprise was clear from the quiet that followed. Not the comfortable silence that was typical for them. This one was tense and he had no idea how to respond to her tone.

"Mags," he finally started cautiously, "it's Mitch's birthday. Everyone wants to see you. They're worried about you."

"I'll just send a gift with you, okay?" she tersely responded.

"Mags..." was all he said as he let the silence after her name linger. She knew they were all concerned. She knew she hadn't been keeping up with all of her messages. She knew she shouldn't have snapped at Kam. She knew a lot of things, but knowing didn't change her reality or how she was feeling.

"I can't," she whispered.

"I'm asking you to do this for yourself, Mags," he continued. "If you won't do it for yourself, do it for me. I can't watch you sit there, paralyzed by life. It's like you're refusing to do anything other than go through the motions. Wake up, work, classes, repeat. You've just stopped moving forward entirely. You don't go anywhere. You don't do anything. You don't talk to anyone. You don't answer anyone else's texts or calls. Unless it's your family, Rosa, or me. I know you stopped doing all of the post grad apps you started in January. I'm not saying you should be moving on entirely, it's only been 3 weeks–"

"Yeah, Kam, it's ONLY been 3 weeks. I think my mom deserves, and I'm allowed, a little more grieving before I start going to parties and getting wasted again and acting like my life isn't entirely fucked," Maggie fumed into the car phone. "A fucking party Kam? With our friends? Really? This was your best idea? Did you even *think* about how hard this would be for me? Did you think of me at all?"

"You're all I think about," he said, sounding defeated before she could continue yelling any longer. The words sliced through Maggie's anger. She knew he meant it. Once their friendship really deepened a few years ago, it's what always came first for both of them. No matter who he was dating or what was going on with his family, Kam always dropped it for Maggie. She did the same for him. So why wouldn't this be any different?

"I'll think about it," Maggie answered him in a way that sounded more like a petulant toddler than an adult woman.

"I knew you'd say yes," Kam said and Maggie could hear the smile in his voice. She hated how being able to make him that happy made her feel.

"I said I'd *think* about it, asshat," she giggled lightly, a smile starting to replace the angry furrow she wore a few moments ago.

"That's as good as a yes. Listen, I know you're driving so how about you Facetime me when you get home and we can work on those apps I know are due soon that you put on pause?" he tested.

"Kam, one thing at a time, please," Maggie meant for it to sound stern, but Kam heard her undertone. The plea for him to back down.

"Okay, okay, then Facetime me and we'll talk about that nasty mole on my ass. You can tell me exactly how you described it to Rosa and how exactly you knew it was there in the first place," he answered her plea.

"You're the world's biggest loser, you know that, right?" she chuckled.

"Only to you. And you love it, you know it. Seriously, Facetime me when you get home? I don't care what we talk about. Okay?" Maggie heard the strain in his voice. The concern seeping through every word. The same concern she saw and heard from everyone else around her. As if she was a glass house littered with cracks, ready to shatter with just the tiniest shift of the wind. As if she would let herself break in front of anyone. As if she would let them see any of that.

"Of course, Kam. It shouldn't take me too much longer. I wish you were here today," Maggie's voice lowered on the last part. Kam and Maggie lived about an hour from each other on a good day's traffic. Not absurdly far, but still inconvenient. He had driven back and forth so many times during the week her mom was in the ICU and the weeks after. It was a miracle his car hadn't given out. They still talked every day that he couldn't be in town because of work or school, but his physical proximity was always the most comforting for Maggie. Physical touch was not her love language, but his hugs made her feel safe. Safer than she'd felt anywhere else over the last three weeks.

It's what she craved to be driving home to. Him on the couch, ready to watch some tv. Or them cooking in the kitchen. Or just reading in the same room together. Not the house she knew was empty at the moment since her aunt worked nights. Her aunt wouldn't be home until after Maggie was asleep. Or, more accurately, after Maggie would pretend to be asleep. Her aunt knew she was faking. Maggie knew her aunt knew she was faking. Neither ever spoke about it.

The quiet was always the hardest. It's when her brain went into overdrive with confusion. Opposing thoughts splattering every inch of her brain. The pain. The joy. The fear. The strength. The uncertainty. The truth. All of it collided whenever she was alone.

"Me too," Kam started, "and I will be whenever I can. For any other time, Facetime will just have to do for now. I'll see you soon, okay?"

"Yupp! Get that ass mole ready for me baby," she joked to lighten the mood.

"For sure," he laughed, "anything for you... only for you, Mags." Maggie couldn't help but feel the extra meaning conveyed in his words, even in the midst of a joke. She couldn't decide what scared her more: that he meant every word or the way that made her feel.

She walked through the front door and stared at the light her aunt had left on for her in the kitchen. Everyone knew Maggie was scared of the dark and although her aunt liked to complain that it would run up the electric bill, she always left a small light on when she went to work. The small kindness brought a fraction of a smile to Maggie's face. The tiny tug of her lips upward was immediately followed by the sudden burst of a sob. The tears came quickly and ferociously after that.

Her first real moments of reprieve from the world were spent this way everyday. While commuting, while working, while in class she was able to keep it all forced down. She had things to focus on. She had people around her counting on her. No one would see the full extent of her pain. She would never let anyone see that. But in these moments, she could unleash it all.

Every second of pain she felt and pushed down throughout the day came rippling out of her. It was like a tidal wave every time she was finally alone. She was only three steps into the house when she fell to her knees. Her bags fell at her sides as she let the tears fall unrestrained and the strangled sobs fly free. She folded in on herself, bringing her forehead down to her knees as she shook with the force of her crying.

A few minutes passed like this, until Maggie knew she had to reign the pain back in. As much as she wished to remain curled up on the floor releasing sob after sob, she knew Kam would start to worry if she didn't call soon.

Maybe it was the fantasy reader in her, but it always helped her to imagine her pain as a burst of black shadows she released only when alone–exploding from her in tendrils but always attached to her being. This gave her something to imagine pulling back into herself. She focused first on regaining control of her breathing. As slow steady breaths replaced ragged sobs, she could feel a few of the shadows curling back into her.

Next were the tears. The flood slowed first to a trickle as she collected her bags around her, and then stopped entirely. She slowly brought herself up from her knees. With her shadows now locked back in the pit inside of her, she went into the kitchen to turn on the rest of the lights. After getting her things unpacked and in order, she went to the bathroom to change into sweats and call Kam.

One look in the mirror and she knew she was screwed. He'd know she hadn't called immediately. That she'd sobbed without abandon. Maggie immediately looked around to try and figure out how she could cover up the wreckage of the explosion of her pain. If she texted him some weak excuse, he'd know something was up. Damn him for knowing her so well. She had to call him soon or else he'd call her first. If she didn't answer on the third ring, he'd know something was wrong. It was almost bedtime, so putting on more makeup made no sense.

She went with the next best thing she could come up with on the fly. She threw her hair into a messy bun and grabbed a makeup wipe. If she couldn't make herself look better, she'd make herself look worse. She wiped off any streaked mascara before propping the phone on the shelf next to the bathroom mirror. Makeup wipe in hand, she went to his contact and pressed the video call icon. As the Facetime call started to go through, she looked in the mirror and started slowly wiping off the rest of her makeup.

He answered on the third ring, like always. His face filled the screen, with his smile spreading at the sight of her. Deep down Maggie knew that friends didn't look at friends that way. How many times had she looked at him that way? The kind of smile you can't hold back from the joy in your heart that only one person can bring you. *Your person.* From seeing them. Knowing them. Knowing you get to be a part of their life. She knew that kind of joy would never truly be hers again, even if Kam used to make her feel that way. She didn't believe she was meant for that kind of happiness anymore. Even if it was right there in front of her.

Her full face wasn't on the screen yet, just an ear and her hair, but she could see all of him. His piercing, dark hair against his pale skin. The dark brown eyes she used to mistake as cold but now knew every nuance of after years of friendship. Eyes that reserved their warmth for the ones he truly cared for and trusted. The sharp jawline that was peppered with stubble. She didn't think she'd ever get sick of that smile–the smile he reserved for her: full, bright, and unforced. Real.

"I hope you don't mind, but I wanted to start taking my makeup off," she said leaning back a bit so he'd finally see all of her. She hoped he wouldn't notice anything as she worked the makeup wipe around her face. The second he saw her face, she knew she wasn't so lucky.

His smile faltered ever so slightly as concern flooded his features. It was no more than a few seconds, but she saw it. He tried not to let it show because he knew she hated people worrying about her, but it was impossible for her to miss the microexpressions. He knew her all too well, but that went both ways for them. She knew every inch of that face and every expression–no matter how small. Before he could say anything, she made her smile even bigger as she said, "So, about that nasty mole..."

The smallest of shifts, but she could see his disappointment. So quick and minuscule, any other person might have missed it. But they weren't any other person to each other and there was nothing about his expressions that she could miss. She'd spent too long learning them, earning enough of his trust for him to show her all of them. Slowly, over time. Of all his expressions, small and big, disappointment broke her heart most. But she saw it there: his hurt.

That she wouldn't let him see all of her anymore. That she wouldn't fall back on him. That she was hurting and lying about it. Kam shook it off and brought back his camera ready smile, the fake one. Maggie hated that smile. It was the one he reserved for the rest of the world but rarely for her. She knew she couldn't be upset. She had been the one faking it first after all.

So they continued their call. Both refusing to acknowledge the other was hiding their feelings–one of concern and one of pain. Both refusing to acknowledge that any other feelings existed between them.

Despite her best efforts to get out of it, a week and a half later Maggie found herself in the passenger seat of Kam's car. She couldn't believe she'd actually agreed to this. Granted, Kam was so adamant, Maggie was almost certain that even if she continued to refuse, he would've thrown her over his shoulder and walked them to New York on foot if he had to.

They had planned for him to pick her up so they could drive into the city together. He would nurse his drinks so that they could leave at any point if needed–the only reason Maggie even humored the idea of going to a party. They'd drive back to her aunt's house and spend the night there and he'd head home in the morning. Easy. Simple. Unlike the rest of Maggie's life at the moment.

She sat there in all black, staring out the passenger window at the bright lights on the George Washington Bridge as they crossed into the city. The lights contrasted the darkness of the night, her clothes, and her thoughts. Kam had picked her up from her aunt's house about thirty minutes ago and she wasn't entirely sure he had stopped talking from the moment he walked through the front door.

While Maggie was typically a hurricane–all untamed chaos and strong rains of emotions traveling in swirling winds–Kam was like lightning. His energy was infectious and spread to everyone around him without him even trying. He'd flash into your life with flailing limbs when telling a story and thunderous laughs when he hit the punchline. But you had to earn it with Kam. His lightning didn't strike casually. Once you did, though, you could expect to laugh a little harder and smile a little brighter without even meaning to. It was something he considered a talent. It was one of the few things he loved about himself.

Which is why it bothered him more than he'd like to admit to see Maggie unaffected by his usual shenanigans. She exuded an uncharacteristic timidness that had been growing over the last month. Where her hurricane would normally match his lightning, ever the chaotic (but entertaining) duo to their friends, he saw a muted version of the storm he'd grown so fond of. The eerie calm you see at the eye of a hurricane. The kind of quiet that tricks people into believing the worst is over. The kind of stillness that eventually breaks into all out destruction. Kam, typically not a religious man, silently prayed this wasn't some kind of foreshadowing for what was to come of her.

As Maggie stared at each light, she wondered how she got here. To a point where being in a car with one of her best friends, who she adored, felt uncomfortable. Where she dreaded going to a party she normally would have been the life of. Where everything felt wrong. She felt stiff. Frozen. Confused by who she was becoming and what was happening around her.

"Hey! Are you even listening to me? I'm saying very important things here," Kam shrilled at her. Maggie was pulled back from her thoughts. She gave herself one more quick breath before schooling her features and turning back to Kam with a playful smile.

"And what were these very important things this time? Back on your rant that pigeons aren't real?" He rolled his eyes at her, but she saw it. The way he took his eyes off the road for just a moment to not only roll them but also check on her. His need to bring her back before she was too far gone. She knew he'd do anything to always bring her back. She hated herself for also knowing he'd probably destroy himself in the process.

"First of all, you know I only think *some* pigeons aren't real. They mix real and fake pigeons to trick us. But the fake ones are absolutely government surveillance devices. Second of all, no that's *not* what I was saying. What's a man gotta do to get and keep your attention these days? I can wear a candy thong if that'll do it," Kam fumed back with fake frustration.

At this Maggie's smile grew a fraction of an inch wider and more authentic. She knew he wasn't serious about his frustration—or the thong. Though, the thought of him in a candy thong wasn't the worst thing she could imagine. Her cheeks flushed as her brain diverted from the conversation yet again but with *different* thoughts this time. Luckily, she was able to bring herself back after a split second of indulging.

"How's a girl to focus with that kind of temptation right in front of her? Only pull out the candy thong if you'd like me irrevocably distracted," Maggie replied. Kam's brows shot up in surprise. This kind of explicit flirting didn't happen often when it was just the two of them. This kind of flirting between them was typically reserved for the safety net of a big group. Or, with the freedom that came after a few drinks. If Maggie wanted to play, he would absolutely join the game.

"Well shit, now I absolutely have to buy an expansive collection of candy thongs for us to see just how distracted you can get," he said, trying to sound casual and failing miserably.

He shook his head, as if to clear it, and stared ahead at the road with a laser focus she'd never before seen him use while driving. This *truly* made her smile. The effect that this back and forth they played from time to time had on him. That she could do this to him after all the years they'd known each other. That after everything he knew about her, he could somehow still get so flustered by some simple flirting.

"Candy thongs off–" at this he turned to her abruptly, shocked, and she just winked in response, "–the table. Candy thongs off the table, dumbass. I wasn't suggesting anything else...yet. What were you saying that was so very important?" She bit the corner of her lip, suppressing a smile at his reaction. Even so, she felt bad about ignoring him because she was lost in her own mental spiral. He deserved better than that.

"I was asking about your spring break. I know you have your service trip for the first half, but what were your plans for the second half? You could come stay with me. Or I could try and get off work and try to stay with you? Your choice," he said and waited. She hadn't thought that far ahead.

"We've got like a month until then, Kam. We've got some time to figure it out. We can talk more about it later," she mused, clearly confused.

"Maggie, it's the week after this coming one..." he said drifting off at the end of his statement as if he wasn't sure if she was serious or messing with him. Maggie's brows furrowed. Was it really coming so soon? How had she confused her timeline so badly? She was normally so on top of her schedule. She may have been late to just about everything, but she never messed up actual dates. She pulled out her phone to double check her calendar.

"Oh shit! You're right. Fuck, sorry. Not sure where my head is at right now," she said, scrolling through the next few weeks and trying to ignore Kam's look of concern. "I can just come to you, honestly. It's so soon, I don't want you to have to stress and try and get off from work. We're already staying at my aunt's tonight, and I'm already predicting my niece will shmooze you into staying most of the day tomorrow too. That would make it my turn to head out there anyway. What do you want to do while I'm there?" Maggie prompted.

"I have a few fucking fantastic ideas that involve a candy thong," Kam grumbled under his breath while turning up the music a notch or two. He continued at a volume Maggie could actually hear, "Well, you know that my mom will want to have coffee with you—"

"Is she upset with me?" Maggie winced. "I haven't talked to her since... I know I haven't been the best at answering her calls. Any of them. I- I- I don't mean to ignore her. She means so much to me and I don't want to hurt her feelings, it's just..." she trailed off.

"It's just that being around moms feels hard for you right now," he finished for her. Of course he'd know. Of course he'd understand. Of course he'd never make her say it herself. She was beginning to wonder if there was anything she could actually hide from him.

"She knows," he continued, "She gets it. My mom fucking adores you. Mags, please don't worry about that of all things. She just doesn't want you to forget that she's there for you. And that you are very clearly her favorite between the two of us." At this he winked and smiled so brightly his dimples made an appearance. She couldn't stop the smile that spread on her own face in response.

"Thanks," she said, and without thinking put her hand on his forearm that was resting between them. It was a gentle touch but conveyed all the gratitude she needed. A few seconds passed as they appreciated the connection. Maggie realized the intimacy of the touch and pulled away abruptly. It was an intimacy she could no longer offer. She returned her hand to her own lap, interlacing her fingers.

"I figured," Kam cleared his throat as he continued, "that there would also be a lot of relaxing. Some movies. I'm sure my sister will want to steal you for a while since apparently having a big brother isn't enough. We can really play each day by ear and see how we're feeling. We can check out that bookstore you've had on your list if you want. I'll get you all the books you want—"

"Careful there. That's a dangerous statement when it comes to me and books. The limit does not exist," Maggie interrupted. Kam chuckled knowingly. She truly had no self control when it came to books.

"Okay, fine. I'll get you all the books my bank account will currently allow. Better? We can just enjoy the time. No need to plan anything too extensive right now. It's enough for me to just know you're agreeing to come out to me," he said a bit tightly.

"What do you mean?" At her question Kam bristled a bit, clearly uncomfortable and regretting his phrasing and tone.

"Well..." he took a moment to compose his response in a way that wouldn't absolutely piss her off. Kam knew he was already pushing his luck by getting her to go to this party. After a few seconds he finally continued, "I mean this in the best way possible, but you've been a bit dodgy lately, Mags. Even with me. I know you're dealing with a mound of shit right now, but it feels like you're frozen in time. I wasn't sure if you'd want to come out and actually do things. I kinda assumed you'd want to just stay at your aunt's and..." he didn't particularly want to finish his sentence.

"And what?" she pushed.

"And I don't know... exist, I guess. I just don't want you to be paralyzed in this moment, Mags. I know you're hurting. And I know you're going through a lot more than I could ever imagine right now. But, I also know you need to keep giving life a chance and you haven't been. It's like you've conceded that this is it and there is no more. I've never known you to be one to concede. *Ever.* So it's scary to see you do it," he finally stopped and waited for her response.

At first there was nothing. What could she offer him? He had read her like a book, and he was hoping to write an alternate ending for her. But, was she?

"I get it," she finally sighed, turning away and looking back out the window. She wasn't sure what other response she could offer him at the moment. She couldn't face the vulnerability he was offering and asking for in return.

"Hey, don't do that," he said, grabbing her hand and interlacing it with his own. She turned at the physical contact. Again, not unusual for them entirely but unusual for them when alone. It was never a spark with Kam. His touch struck like lightning–a sudden, vibrant flash that electrified her skin. She almost couldn't focus on his words from the sensation of his touch. "Please don't turn away from me because you don't know what to say," he continued, "or what to do. Or how to respond. I know I just laid some serious shit out for you. I know this will all take time. But please, never turn away from me and give me some half assed response. I'd rather you face me and say nothing. I'd rather you face me and we figure shit out together, than you turn away from me and kill yourself doing it on your own."

He meant every word and she knew it. In that moment she could feel it. His willingness to do anything to ease her pain. Anything to support her and show her how much life still had to offer. He would walk into the fires of Mordor with her if she asked. She just wasn't sure if she was willing to ask that of herself.

For a long moment she just looked at him. Maggie wasn't sure where to take this. They were just friends. But this? There was something forging here beyond friendship. Something she wasn't sure she could foster and continue at this point in her life. Or, maybe their friendship had evolved a long time ago without either of them ever acknowledging it. She wasn't sure she'd be able to give him the kind of love he deserved, but she couldn't possibly bring herself to ruin this moment either.

"Okay," she finally offered, noting her hand was still in his. "I won't ever turn away from you, promise." He released the breath he'd been holding this entire time and his shoulders relaxed as his tension eased.

"Good. Because in addition to everything I just said, your face is much better to look at right now than the back of your head." Maggie giggled at the backward compliment as he continued, "It's not that you're particularly pretty right now. It's more that the back of your head is a fucking mess. Please don't make me look at it every time you look out the window," he teased.

At this, she truly laughed. Fully, like she used to. Maggie was fairly certain the last time she laughed like this was the night her mom died. That night her family was still in the deepest of shock and making ridiculous jokes as they all spent the night together. The worst night of her life and they had spent it making the most absurd jokes, all hoping to avoid what was their new reality without her mom for just a little longer. Too shocked to acknowledge what they'd be stepping into with the sunrise.

She couldn't believe it, but she also couldn't stop. She pulled her hand from his and slapped his shoulder playfully. She laughed so hard her eyes closed and she tipped her head back, face to the roof of the car, Kam laughing along with her.

When she finally stopped and reopened her eyes, her heart fluttered at the wonder in Kam's gaze. The hope after seeing the glimpse of her old joy. Her heart broke for him. Maggie knew this was a fluke. A one off. A rare occurrence. But, the look in his eyes made her feel like she'd just lassoed the moon for him. And who was she to take that hope away from him? So she smiled broadly, leaned in to him, and turned the music up. Tonight. She could feed his hope tonight. She could give him the old Maggie for one night.

Kam parked in the only spot he could find down the street from Mitch's house. He cut the lights, turned off the car, and took a deep breath. While he breathed deeply to steady himself, Maggie's breath hitched as her anxiety peaked. She shouldn't have agreed to this. She should have fought Kam harder. She should have—

"Hey, we can leave at any point," Kam said quietly, resting his hand gently on her knee and turning his body to face hers. "But I really think it'll help you to just try. And I think you're the strongest person I know right now and will probably ever know. And I know what people think of you has never mattered to you before, but I think you are amazing." His voice was barely louder than a whisper, but his words and the heat of his hand on her knee were enough to shake Maggie from the full panic she was about to enter.

She turned to him, her breathing still slightly uneven. He was staring at her with a level of gentleness she had only seen from him once before.

She was thrust into the memory of a sterile hospital with beeping machines. There, he had gone into her mother's room with her to say his final goodbye. At this point her mother wasn't conscious and they weren't sure what she could and couldn't hear, but the gesture was still important to him. In that room, Maggie broke down as Kam held her and told her mom he would make sure to take care of their girl. He would look after her. He would push and protect her. He would love her with all he had to offer. The way he looked at her as she sobbed and told her mother the kindest things was the same look he gave her now. As if he were also remembering those promises he had made and was doing his best to keep them in this moment.

With each silent second focused on his gaze, Maggie's breath slowly regulated. As they stared at each other she replayed the words he had said and used them as a tether to this moment. As a reminder of what she was capable of. As a reminder that she would be the old Maggie. For Kam. For tonight.

Once her breathing had stabilized and her panic had mostly passed, she finally looked down at his hand. Still on her knee. The heat of his touch burned through her tights and into her skin. A burn she enjoyed more than she'd like to admit.

Kam followed her line of sight, realizing where her focus had landed. If Maggie were looking at his face, she would've seen the small blush that crept up his neck and into his ears. He squeezed her knee before releasing it and reaching into the backseat. As his arm swept over her head, she breathed in his scent fully and deeply. The first real deep breath she'd taken in minutes. It was a combination of bergamot and mahogany. She thought it could very well be her favorite smell in the world.

"You carry the gift and I'll carry you, deal?" Kam asked, handing her the bag with their gift in it. They had gotten Mitch something for the audio system of his car. She had no recollection of what it was called or what it did exactly. All she knew was that he really wanted it and it cost her and Kam more money than she'd put into her own car for the last year. Well, her mom's car. No, *her* car now.

"Deal," she replied, with a single nod as she grabbed the gift. As she turned to reach for the door handle, Kam grabbed her arm turning her back to face him again.

"Seriously, though, the moment it becomes too much you tell me and we're out. I'll say I have explosive diarrhea or something," Kam reminded her. He meant it. He'd make any excuse up so that their exit was on him and not her. Maggie smiled at his willingness to make her feel comfortable. Make her feel safe. If only he could see that Maggie didn't know what safe was anymore. Was anything in her life safe? She didn't believe it was, but she still appreciated his effort. His desire to give this to her, regardless of her own disbelief.

"Let's do this. And I'll absolutely let you know if I need you to shit yourself for me," she joked. She turned away to open the door and the frigid night air hit her immediately.

Her outfit, although perfect aesthetically in her opinion, wasn't very useful against the cold that still clung to the night air as everyone anticipated the warmth of spring. Her black tights were sheer and chosen for their look and not practicality. Her fitted skirt did wonders for her curves but nothing for the cold. Her black turtleneck in theory should've kept her warm, but the thin fabric proved otherwise. She did have a coat on, but again she chose aesthetics over practicality. The only real warmth she felt came from her knee high boots.

She rose from the car, gift bag in hand, and pulled her poor choice of coat tighter around herself for a futile attempt at warmth. She closed the door and leaned back against the car, looking ahead. Although they were down the street from Mitch's house, she could see a few people outside on the sidewalk smoking. It hit her again how much effort this would take. How much work she would have to do to convince everyone she was okay. How many excuses she'd have to make and lies she'd need to tell. She froze, again doubting whether she should've ever let Kam's idea get this far. She felt paralyzed. How was everyone moving forward so easily when she couldn't even manage a single step?

"Don't forget about my diarrhea! Always an option for you, babe," Kam called to her from a few feet up the sidewalk. "Now hop on! You're carrying the gift and I'm carrying you," he said, setting up his stance as if he was about to give her a piggyback ride.

"Kam, you cannot be serious. I thought you were speaking figuratively," Maggie said back.

"Mags, you of all people should know I have no clue what figuratively means, let alone how to speak it. Now get your ass on my back."

"Not a chance. I don't think you can even physically carry my ass. Even if you could, do you see my outfit? This skirt? Not exactly made for piggyback rides," she countered.

"Mags, I have *literally* carried your ass before. Up stairs… while you were passed out drunk and nothing but dead weight I might add. And yes, I have seen your outfit. The moment I saw it AND how you looked in it, I had to remind myself that my goal for today was to get you around people and not to keep you entirely to myself for the night. You look fucking perfect, except the back of your head," he winked before continuing, "Whether that skirt was made for piggyback rides or not, I must keep my word. You wouldn't make a liar out of me, would you?"

"Kam, you can't possibly be serious," Maggie sighed. But she knew that look. She knew this game. She knew his persistence. She knew no matter what she said or did, once he got a ridiculous idea in his head, it was happening. He was the king of "hold my beer" moments, and she was usually his partner in shenanigans.

Mumbling a set of expletives that would make most grown adults blush, Maggie walked over to Kam and twirled her finger signaling him to turn around so she could hop on. He turned, crouched, and as gracefully as she could, she jumped on to his back.

"Please don't let anyone get a free show," she said as he straightened out to his full height.

"Copy that! I'll make sure to charge them first! Shit, maybe you are heavier than I remember," he teased.

"You fucking–" but before Maggie could continue, Kam took off in a jog down the sidewalk. She squealed at the sudden movement and clutched their gift and him tighter. Without meaning to, she started to laugh again. At the utter ridiculousness. At the fleeting freedom. At the man holding her up right now as the cold air rushed past. She laughed fully and freely. For the second time that night Kam showed Maggie a glimpse of what was and what could have been.

"Look who it is!" someone shouted as they walked inside. Kam was still carrying her as Maggie held on for dear life, still caught up in residual giggles.

"These two! Always making a fucking entrance," someone joked. It was Mitch shaking his head and smiling as he walked over to them. "Listen, I know how touch starved you are Kam since not a single woman wants your scraggly ass," at this Kam winced dramatically, as if he'd been deeply wounded, "but do you really plan to carry her like that the entire party? Or, are you going to put her down so I can give Maggie a proper greeting?"

"Does Maggie get a say in any of this?" she asked sarcastically from Kam's back. She quirked a single brow in surprise as she felt Kam's thumbs begin to move lightly back and forth in a small motion along her legs while she was still in his grip. He truly *did* want to play today. Well, if there was one thing about Maggie you could count on, it was the fact that she could never let Kam win this particular game. Ever.

"My lady, do you desire to be put down or to continue this ride?" Kam asked in his most stately (and ridiculous) voice. Maggie leaned forward slightly, positioning her mouth close to Kam's ear so that only he could hear.

"As much fun as a ride would be," Kam's thumbs stilled and she felt him tense slightly, "I'm not much for an audience, so you should probably put me down," Maggie whispered into his ear. She saw the bob in his throat as he swallowed, but he put her down smiling knowingly and shaking his head. With both feet finally on the ground, Maggie adjusted the parts of her outfit that needed fixing–mainly the skirt as predicted.

She couldn't help but notice that Kam kept a hand gently resting on her lower back as if he wasn't ready to break their physical connection just yet. Maggie finally looked back up, mostly pleased with her appearance again and noticed Kam was staring at her with a little bit of playfulness and a whole lot of yearning. Not a look she was used to seeing from him. Mitch was shaking his head and rolling his eyes as they managed to ignore everyone around them.

"For fuck's sake, Kam. Cut the McSteamy bullshit and give the rest of us a chance to hit on Maggie before you sweep her away to do whatever it is you two do," Mitch complained jokingly.

"We don't do anything," Maggie responded, "unless you count the things Kam dreams about."

"Oh and what fantastic dreams they are," Kam smirked. "I'll get us some drinks. That gives you at most 4 minutes to woo her. Better make 'em count," he said and finally removed his hand from her lower back as he moved away.

Even though Maggie resented admitting it to herself, the coldness that replaced where Kam's hand had been was uncomfortable. For someone who hated physical touch, she sure did miss his.

Mitch pulled Maggie in for a massive bear hug before she could even get a word out. The hug lasted a little longer than was usual and Maggie knew it wasn't Mitch's attempt at flirting. It was his attempt at consoling. This was the part she was looking forward to least. She had learned quickly over the last few weeks that either people weren't really sure how to act around her and tried to escape as quickly as possible or they overcompensated their condolences. Mitch was an overcompensator.

"Happy birthday, Mitch," Maggie exclaimed when he released her. "I hope this year gives you everything you wish for. You really deserve it. Here's a start to the wishlist," she said as she handed him their gift.

"I'm happy you could be here. I know you weren't sure if you could make it for a little while. You didn't need to bring me anything, your–"

"Presence is enough?" Maggie finished for him. "Come on, don't get so cliché in your old age Mitch." Old age. The two words rattled through her.

Aging wasn't something she had spent much time thinking about before. The fact that her mom wouldn't see old age, though, was something that consumed her brain regularly now. Her mom who wanted to see her graduate college. Who wanted to see her get married. Have kids. Babysit those kids. Live to be wrinkly and sarcastic, saying the kind of old people shit that people just shake their heads at and laugh. She wouldn't get any of it. And now, Maggie wasn't even sure she wanted any of it for herself. Not without her mom. She couldn't believe this was it. This was her life now.

Not realizing how badly those two simple words would affect her, Maggie tried to redirect the conversation. She had no clue where to take it, though. So, she reverted back to what the old Maggie would suggest at any moment at any party. She looked Mitch in the eyes with a smirk and said just one word.

"Shots?"

🌱 🌱 🌱

Maggie was surprised by how easily she could turn it on–the charm, the smiles, the life of the party attitude. As her and Kam walked back to his car, arm in arm, she rested her head on his shoulder replaying the party.

There were certainly a fair share of awkward moments with friends who weren't sure how to act around her. Or, moments with friends trying to check on her at the most inopportune times–like in the middle of chugging a beer. Once she showed everyone the old Maggie, who didn't have a mountain of grief on her shoulders, they eased back into the old rhythms of their friend group.

Dumb shit was done. Ridiculous shit was said. Laughs were had. Memories were made. And, Maggie was entirely certain she could not handle another party any time soon. Tonight she learned that it was one thing to contain her grief all day while she was at work or in classes. It was another thing entirely to contain her grief *and* put on a show. She was utterly emotionally exhausted.

"What?" Kam asked in response to the sigh Maggie hadn't realized she had let out. She looked up at him, ready to be honest and tell him exactly how she was feeling but stopped short when she saw his smile.

It wasn't his big, dimpled smile that she loved so much. She did love this one almost equally as much, though. It was simple. Content. Like this moment was enough for him. Like he had accomplished his goal and he had hope again. For her. She knew she couldn't destroy this feeling for him. So, resting her head back on his shoulder, she simply shrugged.

As they approached his car, he stopped walking and turned, cutting her off from getting into the car so they were face to face.

"What is it? That felt like a heavy sigh," he pushed. She looked up at him. At the face of the man she couldn't deny loved her anymore, no matter how much they avoided it. She wished in that moment with every fiber of her being that she could be who he deserved again. She wished she could believe that woman was still salvageable. That she wasn't entirely wrecked by her grief. Damaged. Ruined.

She had no clue what to say. How do you tell a man he doesn't actually love who you are? That instead, he loves who you were. How do you tell him you wished you believed you could be that person again? That you wish you believed in things like love and hope and joy still. She didn't know. So she did the only thing she could think of.

She took the half step to close the distance between them. She wrapped her arms around his waist and buried her face in his chest, taking in his bergamot and mahogany scent again.

And she lied.

"I'm just really tired," she said. "Thank you for tonight. I think you were right. I really did need it." His arms wrapped around her and they simply stood there embracing each other. Kam finally pulled back and took her face in his hands, forcing her to look up at him. She stared into his eyes as they searched her face for any hint of what was going on inside her head. Any clue to help him figure out what she was thinking.

When they couldn't find what they were looking for, his eyes finally locked on hers. She saw something in his gaze she didn't recognize for once. Something new. Different. Then, she saw something else that concerned her. The split second dip of his eyes to her lips. Quick. Easy to miss if she hadn't already been staring at him. His eyes locked back onto hers. They were somehow frozen and on fire. As if neither knew how to proceed.

As badly as she had wanted that kiss in the past, she couldn't bear it now. Couldn't bear the idea of them starting like this. She couldn't handle the thought of their first kiss happening immediately after the first outright lie she'd ever told him that he seemed to somewhat believe. It felt like it would taint a beginning that was already destined for doom.

So, she exaggerated a shiver, using the cold as her cop out. She knew his desire to take care of her would outweigh any others right now. This time, he sighed but didn't release her just yet. With his hands still on the sides of her face, he leaned forward and kissed her forehead.

"It'll get better," he almost whispered, resting his forehead to hers. He took one more deep breath and then turned to open her door. As she got into his car, she heard those three words he uttered over and over again in her mind.

It'll get better.

He meant them. He believed them. The only problem? Maggie didn't.

Maggie couldn't remember when she had fallen asleep. All she knew was that she was now being gently awoken by Kam and they were already in her aunt's driveway. She must have knocked out shortly after she got into his car because she didn't even remember crossing back over the bridge.

"You really were tired, huh," Kam mused as he helped her out of the car. They walked up the driveway silently as Maggie searched for her keys.

"It's kind of late, so we should probably be quiet going in. We don't want to wake my niece up," Maggie said as she unlocked the front door and was promptly greeted by a shouting six year old sprinting towards them.

"MAGGIEEEEE! KAAAAAAM! YOU'RE BACK!!!!" Maggie and Kam chuckled. They knew Maggie's niece should've been asleep. They also should've known better and realized there was no chance she was going to sleep until they got home.

"June! Shouldn't you be in bed, you menace?" Maggie teased as she lifted her niece into her arms.

"She insisted on staying up to say goodnight to you two. She said it wasn't a *real* sleepover unless she did," Maggie's aunt shouted from the living room. June was already reaching out for Kam. When he was around, Maggie might as well have been invisible. Maggie passed June off to him, who took her happily. She walked into the living room and plopped on the couch. Her aunt was watching some Lifetime movie.

"Well, looks like it's time for that *real* sleepover to happen now that we can all say goodnight," Maggie commented.

"NOOOOO! You just got here! Can't we play just one game?" June begged from Kam's arms offering her best puppy dog eyes.

"We already played a little before Maggie and I left. We're really tired. If we go to bed now, we can wake up earlier to play a game in the morning," Kam tried to offer as a compromise. June thought long and hard. Her little wheels turning as she tried to decide if this was an adequate offer.

"Okay, but if we go to bed now, we play TWO games in the morning," she finally replied. Kam nodded as he handed her over to Maggie's aunt. She added quickly, "And we all sleep in here!"

"June, don't be difficult," Maggie's aunt scolded, but it was futile. There was no arguing with a six year old whose mind was entirely made up. She was determined for this to be a proper slumber party and they were thus forced to comply. They set up a makeshift bed on the living room floor by the tv for June and Maggie's aunt. Maggie and Kam grabbed pillows and blankets to sleep on the two ends of the L shaped couch.

They put on a kid's movie quietly to play while they got ready for bed and drifted off. June and Maggie's aunt were the first ones to fall asleep. Once Maggie was changed with her make up washed off and nightly routine done, she sat back on the couch and stared at the tv, zoning out a bit.

She didn't move. Not even when Kam finally joined her, sitting at her feet on her left. He rested his head on her knee and wrapped an arm around her leg, stroking it gently in his best effort at silent comfort.

They sat like that for a while and watched the tv screen as the princess tackled challenge after challenge and journeyed through her own tragedies–determined to rescue her people and herself.

Kam couldn't help but imagine Maggie as the princess they were watching. She'd been dealt so much shit in life. She had already tackled so much. She'd walked through hell and he wasn't entirely sure that all of her had made it out the other side. He couldn't help but wonder if Maggie had enough determination left to rescue herself. He couldn't help but solemnly think she believed the answer was no.

Meanwhile, Maggie couldn't help but think these movies they were fed as children were bullshit. Sometimes the challenge *was* too much. Sometimes the princess *didn't* succeed. Sometimes the tragedies were more accurate than the fairy tales.

Without a word, Maggie pulled her legs up to lay down. She was ready for this day to be over. She was tired of thinking. Tired of realizing how fucked her life was. Tired of being torn between her reality and her disbelief that this was her life now. Taking this as his cue, Kam got up to walk over to his side of the couch.

Before he could take a step Maggie grabbed his hand. He turned back to her and felt as if his heart were caving in on itself. Her timidness was one thing that concerned him. The emptiness she exuded throughout the day was quiet and startling, but this was a different kind of hurt. He saw everything she hid in the day in this late night moment with nothing but the tv illuminating her face. The concerned lines in her forehead, the panic in her eyes, the gentle curve downward of her lips.

He took it all in. The shit she hid from everyone all of the time, including him. He was hurt. But not because she hid this from him–he expected as much from her. But because for once, he had no clue what to do or how to help. She was drowning in an ocean he had no clue how to navigate. Even if he swam with her to keep her afloat, he had no clue in which direction to paddle. No idea where to lead her. And if he swam blindly with her long enough, would they both end up drowning?

He wasn't entirely sure what scared him more: not being able to save her or drowning along with her? That was something he'd have to decide eventually. Was there a point at which he would tap out?

But, after the night they'd had. After hearing her truly laugh again. After playing like they had. After seeing her with their friends and her niece. After seeing flashes of the woman he had fallen in love with again. He placed a hand on her cheek and nodded.

He let go to grab his pillow and blanket, placing them on the floor next to where she lay on the couch. He laid on his back and felt her hand fall gently to his chest. He wrapped both his hands around hers. She was on her side looking down at him, while he was looking up at her. She took a deep breath–the deepest he'd seen her take all night and finally closed her eyes. As if this were the first moment of solace she had experienced in weeks. As if her soul could finally rest for just a single night with him beside her. His heart swelled at the comfort he could offer her.

He stared at her for a long while, watching her sleep. He loved seeing her finally at peace, unburdened by what her life had become. There was a level of calm on her face he hadn't seen in a long time. He finally shut his eyes to try and fall asleep with one final thought: he'd happily drown a million times over if she'd just let him swim with her.

The next week passed uneventfully. Maggie went to work, night classes, home, and repeat. She ate because she knew she needed it. She cried in the car on her commutes home. She Facetimed Kam when they could. Everything seemed to be flowing in the boring, tragic routine that had become her life. Until Thursday.

"Bitch, we're getting fucked up tonight. And I'm not taking no for an answer," Lara said to Maggie. Lara was Maggie's old roommate turned college best friend. Lara was also someone Maggie had been using work and classes to avoid as much as possible. Friendships felt like too much work for her right now. She preferred the quiet loneliness to watching all of her friends move on.

"But–," Maggie tried to interject.

"No! You have no excuses. We haven't seen you in forever! We allow it because you're busy as fuck with work and classes, but I know you have tomorrow off so you can have some time before going on your trip. You don't have to worry about driving home because you can stay at my place since my roommate just moved out and their bed is just a spare at the moment. We are going to have a bunch of people get together. We are going to get trashed.

We are going to be hungover in the morning. And you'll nurse your hangover while traveling to go do good things and be a good person. I will not accept any answer other than yes," Lara barely gave Maggie a chance to get a word in.

For once, Maggie didn't feel like arguing. She didn't feel like remembering. She didn't feel like navigating. She didn't feel like *feeling*. So, Maggie shrugged her shoulders and finally answered, "We're going to need a bottle of Jack."

Lara squealed with joy and squeezed Maggie so tightly she thought she might pop. They ran off to grab some food and head to the liquor store. While Lara sent a flurry of text invites to their friends, Maggie sent one, lone text to Kam letting him know that she wouldn't be able to Facetime tonight and that she'd call him tomorrow.

"Have fun." She read his response and then threw her phone into her bag determined to forget everything about what her life had become tonight.

☀ ☀ ☀

Maggie knew a few things for certain at this moment. She knew it was Friday morning because the sun was managing to somehow sear through her eyelids exacerbating her growing headache. She knew she had no idea how much she had drunk last night. She knew she also had minimal recollection of last night's events. She knew she was not in her own bed. And as she rolled over, crashing into something solid, she learned she was not the only one asleep in this bed.

What the fuck had happened last night? One moment she had been on a table dancing with Lara and then... blank. At least she had accomplished her goal of not remembering. A small piece of her regretted that goal this morning, along with the massive hangover she knew was coming. She silently prayed it was just one of her girlfriends who also got too drunk sleeping next to her. Something in her gut told her that wasn't likely.

She finally braved the pain the sunshine would cause and opened her eyes just a centimeter. In doing so, she confirmed that she was not sleeping next to a girlfriend. Next to her, Aidan snored like a hibernating bear. *Aidan?* Shock consumed her. She couldn't believe this. She looked down slowly, wincing at what the motion did to her head. Thank fuck. They both were fully clothed, so nothing that scandalous could have happened.

She laid her head back down, covering her eyes with the back of her hand. She tried to force any recollection of last night to come to her. As she thought, she saw bits and pieces in flashes. A lot of shots were taken. A lot of drunken dancing and singing. And... there it was. Aidan and her making out sloppily. This was not a problem she needed to add to her plate. What the fuck was she thinking? Oh right, she wasn't. Jack Daniels was.

"Mmmunnnghhhh," Maggie grunted a garble of sounds.

"That bad, huh," Aidan grumbled from beside her.

"Mmmmm. Don't open your eyes unless you have a strong desire to be assaulted by the sun," Maggie replied, voice hoarse and eyes still closed. She felt the bed next to her shift as Aidan turned onto his side and slid his hand onto her stomach. Fuck. This she *really* didn't need.

At that exact moment she heard her phone ring–a sound that felt devilishly loud and split her head in two. She grabbed her phone from the bedside table it was sitting on and inched one eye open ever so slightly to see who it was.

"*Fuck!*" Maggie half groaned, half shouted. She scrambled from under the sheets and out of the bed, banging her knee and elbow in the process. The second ring started as she sprinted–hobbled like a bridge troll being a more accurate description–across the room. She simultaneously closed the bedroom door behind her and answered the Facetime call on the third ring. As she did her best to steady herself, Kam's face filled the screen.

He took one look at her and erupted into booming laughter. She slowly dragged herself toward the living room as she listened to his fit of giggles. She couldn't quite figure out what he was laughing at, but she didn't exactly care at the moment. She inspected the damage in the living room–quite clean, honestly, for how drunk they had all been. After finally slinking onto the couch, she looked back at the screen to see what Kam found so comical.

It was then that she finally saw herself in the tiny rectangle in the corner of her phone. She tapped her own image to enlarge it and even she had to giggle. She looked like the stereotypical image of someone who had just had a shit show of an evening. Her hair was in utter disarray. Half of it was a knotted mess and the other half of it was plastered to the side of her face that she had slept on. Her mascara had smudged into dark, raccoon-like circles around her eyes. Her lipstick resembled what a toddler might draw onto someone's lips. And for a reason she could not fathom, FBGM was written across her forehead in something she was praying wasn't permanent marker.

"Fuck bitches, get money?" Kam asked, barely able to huff the question out in between laughs.

"Fuck if I know dude. Still trying to piece together my night if I'm being honest with you," Maggie mumbled in reply. Now that her surge of movement was over, the full impact of her hangover embraced her. Her stomach felt like it was on fire. Her head felt as though it might split in half. Her legs were sore, as if she'd run a marathon. Her hair even hurt. How in the flying fuck was that even possible? She was in desperate need of a Dr. Pepper.

"Have fun?" Kam asked as he tried his best to compose himself, failing completely.

"Again, I'll let you know once I piece my night back together," Maggie mumbled. Was it possible to die from a hangover? If so, this was it. Everyone should say their final goodbyes, because this would be the one to take her out. She let her head fall back onto the couch as she heard Kam chuckle again. And then, she heard the bedroom door crack open. The one she had just come out of. The one she had left Aidan in.

"Hey, if I don't die from this hangover, I'll call you when I get home. I really need to get my shit together and make sure I'm ready for my trip. Sorry," Maggie blurted in a rush, hanging up the Facetime as she finished. At that very moment Aidan came around the corner.

He leaned against the corner with his shoulder, crossing one foot nonchalantly over the other. She took a moment to take a real look at him. Aidan and Maggie were in overlapping social circles, but they had never really spent much time together. Maggie had to admit that he was relatively attractive, but what the hell was she doing drunkenly making out with him? Where in the world did that come from and how did it even start?

"Any chance you've seen my glasses?" Aidan finally asked. She chuckled at the casualness of his demeanor. Of course she'd drunkenly make out with someone who would not give a single fuck about it. Thankfully, that was exactly what she needed. An awkward conversation would not help this hangover or the state of her life in any way. She did a quick scan of the room and pointed to the counter near the window where his glasses sat. He stumbled over, put them on, turned back to her, and immediately started laughing uncontrollably. "Fuck bitches, get money."

"Yeah, yeah. No fucking clue where that one came from. Any ideas?" Maggie groaned, closing her eyes as she rested her head back again. She heard his steps as he walked across the room toward her.

"Yes, and I truly don't think you actually want to know," he said as he sat down next to her. At this, Maggie groaned, slapping her palm to her head. What the hell was she doing? Her life was already a shit show. Why was she adding to it? How would she tell Kam? Would she tell Kam? They weren't actually dating but they were clearly something. Right? He deserved to know, didn't he? Here was more proof that she simply didn't deserve his kindness, his care, his love. Him.

Her mom would be so disgusted with her. She has a good man in her life who loves her and treats her like the damn sun and the moon, and she's over here getting black out drunk and making out with a guy she's had maybe seven conversations with. Ever the disappointment. But, did it really matter what her mom *would* feel seeing as it wasn't something she *could* feel anymore?

"Penny for your thoughts," Aidan said, breaking up her self condemnation. She finally removed her hand from her face and opened her eyes. He was just sitting there looking at her.

"Believe me, you don't want to know. How are you not dying?" she replied.

"Oh, I am. But, seeing that FBGM on your forehead is worth every second of pain," he said, poking fun at her. She groaned, covering her eyes again. Apparently, words were too hard for Maggie today and another guttural groan was the only response she could muster.

"Hey," he softened, grabbing her hand more tenderly than she expected. Granted she barely knew the man, so she couldn't really know what to expect. Even with this in mind, she felt like the touch was too intimate for two people who barely knew each other–even with a drunken makeout now in their past. "You good?"

"Yeah, just a lot of shit to get through today and this hangover is not going to help." She heard him get up and walk away. She was genuinely hoping he was making his exit and she wouldn't have to endure some awkward dismissal. A few minutes later she heard a throat clear from in front of her. She looked up and he was standing there with some ibuprofen and a glass of water. She took them, mouthed a *"thank you,"* and downed them both. He turned, grabbed his coat, and headed toward the front door of Lara's apartment. Enough time had passed that Maggie assumed he had left.

"Enjoy your trip. I'll see you when you get back," he called from the front door. She jumped at the sound of his voice and then heard the front door click closed. What the hell was she doing? This was not something she needed to deal with right now. So, she decided she wouldn't. It never happened. She would go on her trip. She would come home to Kam–her not boyfriend. And she would at least try to doggy paddle through the confusion surrounding every area of her life.

The four days of her trip came and went. She did her best to participate with the team. She did her best to mask her grief as their leader. Her personas shifted with the sky. In the light of day she was the smiling, bubbly, life of the group. A charming, fearless leader. In the quiet, dark moments of the night she would release the pain. She would become the shattered mess she truly was deep down.

Each day was the same. Her team would wake up and share breakfast. They'd head to the worksite until it was time to come back. They would have dinner and listen to their voicemails. The voicemails were special. The team itself had agreed to give up technology for the four days of their trip. This meant no phones, no tablets, no computers, no social media, and no communication with loved ones. Except the voicemails. Each member had shared the phone number to their team's voicemail box. People could call in to hear that day's updates and leave a message for someone or the team as a whole.

It was special sharing the messages from each other's loved ones. But all Maggie could think about was who wouldn't be leaving a message for her. Who would be missing. For their part, Kam, Maggie's brother, Rosa, and Maggie's aunts left messages for her every night. Overcompensating. She appreciated the gesture, but it almost made her feel worse. Hearing how much they wanted to make up for the massive hole now torn into her life. So she smiled through the voicemails each day and saved the tears for the darkness each night.

Although she enjoyed the four days of her trip as much as she could, she realized pulling into Kam's driveway just how ready she was to be here with him. As she got out of her car, his dog was the first one to greet her. She crouched and gave the massive ball of fluff every ounce of attention and affection she had. She heard the crunch of gravel behind her and didn't need to turn to know it was Kam coming toward her.

"I hope you enjoyed your trip, but remember, no matter how many good deeds you do, you're never earning your way back into heaven. You're in hell with the rest of us heathens!" he shouted from across the massive driveway. Maggie chuckled to herself, rising from the dog who was now offended his ear scratches had ended. She turned and the sight of Kam knocked the breath from her.

There was nothing particularly special about the way he was dressed–just jeans and a t-shirt now that the cold had finally broken. Everything about him was the same. Familiar. She realized now, though, just how much she had missed his steady presence in her life over the last four days. Not seeing his face. Not having him to call and check on her. Not having him keep her in check. She was taken aback by the sheer tug of her heart as he looked at her with nothing but joy and admiration.

Before she realized what she was doing, she found herself running towards him. She saw the flash of surprise on his face. Maggie had never been one for outright emotional gestures, but in this moment she didn't give a fuck. She ran to him and jumped up, wrapping her arms around his neck and her legs around his waist.

As always, Kam was ready to catch her. She buried her face in the crook of his neck and breathed him in. She grounded herself with his presence. To his credit, Kam simply continued to hold her and she could feel the vibrations in his chest as he chuckled. He would have held her there all day if she needed it.

"Shall I carry thee inside or does this majestic display of affection end if I move us out of this spot?" Kam finally joked after a few minutes.

"Apparently it ends the moment you run your mouth. Release me, peasant," Maggie quipped. He did as he was told and they stood there for a few more moments smiling like fools at each other. Maggie still didn't necessarily believe she could have the kind of life she thought Kam deserved. In this moment, though, she felt a flicker of hope that she could maybe try to give it to him.

They got her things from her car and took them up to his room. He was currently living with his family but none of them were home at the moment. Kam had this goofy grin on his face as they sat in the living room.

"So, are we going to do anything, or are you just going to sit there and stare at my endless beauty all day," Maggie poked, posing dramatically on the couch. As she posed, Kam mouthed *"get over yourself"* while looking her up and down hungrily. She had to bite down her smug smile at the gleam she saw in his eyes that told her exactly how much he appreciated that endless beauty.

"My mom works late tonight, so she was hoping we could swing by whenever we go out to eat. This way she can get a quick hi in before we fall asleep by the time she gets home tonight. Otherwise, I genuinely don't care. Whatever you want to do," Kam said.

"*Whatever...*," Maggie mused provocatively, sketching a brow. Kam nearly choked on his water at her outright flirtatiousness. First the exuberant display of how much she had missed him outside and now this? What was going on with her? She continued, "Well, I am hungry. So I'd be down to go say hi, eat, and then come back here and just hang. Movies. Dinner with your sister maybe? Shoot the shit with your dad. Maybe we could read a little bit?" He nodded at everything she said. She took this as her cue to get up, grabbing her keys as she did. To which Kam responded by slapping her keys out of her hand. Maggie's face shifted to playful shock and dismay.

"You're with me for the next few days. That means passenger princess privileges ONLY," Kam responded to her fake shock. "Now grab what you need and get your 'endless beauty' into my car." Maggie giggled and grabbed her purse as Kam grabbed her hand, leading her to the garage. Yes, for him... maybe, just maybe she could *try.*

Seeing Kam's mom was a lot harder for Maggie than she had thought it would be. Since her mom died, Maggie had made it a point to avoid watching mothers with their children–especially with their daughters. It hurt too much to watch what she would never experience again.

She had been blessed to have a mother, who despite having her own past to work through, loved her fiercely. They had laughed and loved harder than the typical mother daughter relationship. Their closeness had always astounded people. Maggie's mom had quite literally been her best friend but not in the cliché ways movies portray.

Maggie genuinely loved spending time with her mother. Her mom had been her first and last call most days. She never told anyone, but she still called her mom's phone–which she hadn't had disconnected yet–everyday in order to listen to her voicemail. She knew it was depressing, but hearing her mom's voice made her death feel less real. It was almost as if as long as this little piece of her existed, her death didn't.

So, seeing others with their moms made her think of how she used to be with hers. And what she would never get again.

The inherent love some mothers look at their children with. The natural fussing that happens in some familial relationships. The jokes. The smiles. Because of all this, unfortunately, dropping by his mom's work shifted from something she was looking forward to into something she had to bear with a forced smile comprised of gritted teeth.

Kam noticed. At this point, Maggie was beginning to wonder whether there was ever a moment he didn't notice every change in her mood. He grabbed her hand, pulling her ever so slightly closer to him with the motion. A motion his mother made sure to happily point out, making both of them blush. Maggie and his mother agreed to have coffee together in the morning if they didn't get a chance to talk over a glass of wine tonight. Or both, if they could manage it.

With those plans in place, Maggie and Kam left to grab lunch before deciding what to do next. Every step away from Kam's mother eased the tension that had been building in Maggie's body. By the time they were back in the parking lot, Maggie was back at relative ease, laughing and smiling more authentically. She couldn't help but notice, though, that Kam kept ahold of her hand until the moment he absolutely had to let go in order for her to get into the car. She *also* couldn't help but notice that she didn't mind this a single bit.

🌿 🌿 🌿

The next two days passed mostly peacefully. Maggie got to shop with Kam's sister and share laughs with his father. She got to be a part of a family dynamic that was equal parts dysfunctional and delightful. When Maggie and Kam weren't with his family, they were simply enjoying each other's company. They read together, watched movies, went on hikes, and shared enough laughs to momentarily counterbalance Maggie's deep grief. She was surprisingly happier here for the most part.

When Kam was at work and Maggie was left in the house on her own, she would use that time to release that pit of pain she kept leashed internally. In the solace of solitude, she'd sob and scream. This way, by the time anyone came home she would be ready to play her part as the slightly muted version of who she used to be. The girl with the big laugh and bright spirit. The girl everyone else needed to see but that she didn't believe in anymore.

On the third day, though, Kam came home early and almost caught her in the depths of her despair. She hadn't been expecting him, so when she heard the garage door opening, she sprinted up the stairs. Thankfully, Kam was none the wiser when she came out of the bathroom and feigned surprise at seeing him home so soon.

He had come home to take her to the bookstore on her list and buy her all the books his budget could afford, just as he had promised.

As they pulled into Kam's driveway after an amazing post book shopping dinner, Maggie was overwhelmed by the goodness she had consistently felt over the last few days. The pain was still there in the quiet moments she spent alone. Overall, though, things felt as normal as they could. The smile she had on her face in public wasn't as forced and hadn't been since that first moment of anxiety with his mother days ago.

They walked through Kam's front door and into the kitchen and Maggie's heart stuttered. The scene before them was wonderful, but for her it was absolutely gut wrenching. The kitchen was an utter mess–flour and sugar and eggshells everywhere. Music was blaring loudly and Kam's mom and sister were jumping up and down to the beat while cookies baked in the oven. They were screaming the lyrics of some song while using a spoon and whisk as microphones.

Maggie's heart felt like it might explode and implode at the same time. Her heart loved to see this mother and daughter share such a joyful memory, a moment that probably felt perfect for them. Her heart wanted to explode from the beauty of it. From what these two still got to experience with each other.

And then the pain overwhelmed her, putting her heart at risk of crumbling in on itself. It felt as if all the air had been sucked out of her. How many times had she danced in the kitchen with her mom? How many laughs and silly moments had they shared this way? How many of those times did she take for granted? Always assuming she'd get more of them. She never fully cherished those moments. She never fully respected the memory they would make one day. Because now, memories were all she was left with.

It hit her like a semi truck that she'd never get another one of those with *her* mom ever again. That the joy she was creating here would never be anything like what she once had. She was ready to turn and run up the stairs, but the exact moment she started to do so was also the exact moment Kam's mom noticed them.

Before Maggie could retreat, Kam's mom was putting a wooden spoon in her hands and dragging her into their baking dance party. Maggie knew she meant well; that she was trying to include her in their joy. It only caused her more pain. Looking at their expectant faces, smiles full and real, Maggie knew at this moment she'd have to revert back to the one thing she'd become a professional at recently–faking it.

So she did. She danced and scream sang and gave these two people who loved her what they needed. All while shattering on the inside. The song ended and she was out of breath. She couldn't figure out whether that was from the jumping or from the pain still strangling her heart. She hugged the two women and told them she wanted to shower before the movie night they had planned for later. The movie night she assumed the cookies were for.

She grabbed her bags and her freshly bought books and headed straight for the stairs, glancing at Kam for only a moment. She saw his smile full of joy and hope and love and it broke her even more. It broke her to see how real he thought this was and how much he truly believed this could be their life. It broke her to know that the last few days had been a fluke. That she couldn't handle the kind of joy these people deserved–that Kam deserved. She saw his smile falter from whatever he read in her face as she passed. And it broke her even more to know the pain she was causing him by not being able to be what he wanted, needed, deserved.

She picked up her pace, dropping her things and heading straight for the bathroom upstairs. She shut the door behind her, turned on the shower, and as if the pain couldn't be contained any longer, she broke. Not just internally but also externally this time.

She had been tricking herself into believing she could do it. Could be the person she used to be. Could give her people what they needed. Could move on. She couldn't. Whether it was because she wasn't strong enough or she simply didn't believe she was worth it, she wasn't sure. But she was sure that she simply could not do it.

So she sat on the toilet, sobbing while the shower ran, hoping it muffled the sound of her cries. She wasn't sure how long she sat there. She knew she wasn't close to done, though. She knew she had no clue how to reign in her pain this time. The shadowy tendrils of her grief had come loose with no intention of being pulled back in.

She heard the bathroom door open, but couldn't force herself to care enough to look at who it was. Damn her for forgetting to lock it. She learned it was Kam who was now turning off the shower and on his knees in front of her. She couldn't make out his expression through the blurred vision of her tears, but she could make out his features. The dark hair and sharp jawline she loved so much.

She felt his arms go to her legs and wrap them around his waist. She felt one of his arms go under her thigh and the other go behind her back as he lifted her up. He carried her to his room and sat down on his bed with her still wrapped around him. A long time passed as they sat there. He simply held her and she sobbed. Neither of them said a word.

❧ ❧ ❧

It wasn't until she woke up in the middle of the night in her pajamas to darkness that she realized her sobs must have exhausted her. They had missed movie night. He was laying next to her and staring at her. Watching her. The look in his eyes felt like too much. He didn't have to tell her he loved her; she saw it. It was the kind of look you can't explain but can feel.

She stared at him and let her heart break one more time, because at this point what was it to carry around more shattered pieces of yourself. She looked at him and knew that she loved him, deeply and fiercely. As she continued to look at him, she knew she couldn't let herself *continue* to love him. She wouldn't let him drown with her. She wouldn't let him cut himself on her shattered parts. She wouldn't let him miss moments with his family because they were too much for her. She wouldn't ruin his life with her ruined self.

Maggie took a deep breath and prepared to say goodbye to a man she loved. She took a deep breath and prepared to give him the memory he deserved and a moment they'd never share again. She took a deep breath, leaned forward, and kissed Kam.

The surprise on his face was clear. This was the last thing he expected Maggie to do at this moment. Especially after the breakdown she had earlier. He started to say something but Maggie put a finger to his mouth and wet her bottom lip. He was distracted into silence.

She leaned forward and kissed him again. This time with less gentleness and more purpose. Kam was kissing her back with an equal fervor. As if this were a moment he had imagined many times, but was never sure he'd get to experience. As if he wasn't entirely sure this was real. Maggie felt his tongue on her lips seeking permission for more of her and she parted hers, ready to give him everything he wanted and needed for tonight.

As they moved closer, Maggie could feel the warmth of his body on her own. His touch sent electrical currents sparking through her.

"I've thought about this for so long," he whispered against her lips. She pushed him from his side so that he was flat on his back and moved to straddle him, all without their lips breaking contact. As if now that they had started they couldn't be separated.

Maggie wore her usual pajamas–a baggy t-shirt and shorts–and Kam was only in sweatpants, no shirt. As she straddled him the heat of his bare skin on her knees singed. Every point of skin to skin contact felt like a blazing fire. Maggie was almost certain that if she were to raise her hands from his chest, she'd find scorch marks in their place.

She began to move her hips against his, her hands moving from his chest to his shoulders to the sides of his head. At this, Kam's fervor increased exponentially, deepening his kiss and squeezing her hips even tighter. He had his fair share of late night romances in the past but none of them had ever felt like this. He needed a moment. He needed to make sure this was real. He needed to make sure this was what they *both* wanted.

He grabbed Maggie's shoulders pushing her up and finally breaking the contact their lips had maintained this entire time. Both of their chests were heaving from their ragged breathing. Maggie was surprised by the sudden disruption.

"Mags, are you sure?" Kam asked, panting the question.

"I am," she responded as she began lowering herself once again. He stopped her.

"No, Mags. I'm serious. Take a second. Are you sure about this? Right now? Is this what you want? In this moment. Are you sure you want to do this? All of this? I need to hear you say it," Kam said. Maggie looked at him and took one more deep breath. Kind Kam. The man who loved her and would do everything to protect her—even if it went against his own desires.

"I'm sure about this," she said, but she could see the doubt in his eyes. He was still wary of whether this was the right time for them.

Her face softened. Slowly, she grabbed his left hand off her shoulder, kissing his palm, and placing it on her hip. She repeated the process with his right hand, maintaining eye contact with him the entire time. As she stared at him, she crossed her arms at the bottom edge of her shirt. He watched her every move, entirely still. In one motion, breaking her gaze on his face for only a moment, she pulled her shirt over her head. His intake of breath was sharp as his gaze dropped to her chest, entirely bare before him. Maggie pushed his shoulders back down, resting both her hands at either side of his face. She could feel every single inch of where their bare skin touched. It was a fire that gave her the confidence to keep going and say what she needed to say and what he needed to hear.

"I want," she leaned down and kissed him, "every moment of this." She kissed him again before continuing, "I want you." Kiss. "Tonight, I want this moment for us to have forever." Kiss. "And I want you to stop ruining the moment by doubting me *right now*." She could still sense some hesitation in his eyes. She flipped her hair over one shoulder and pushed her hips into his with a fraction more force. That was enough to shake away his lingering uncertainty.

Kam pushed himself up to a seated position taking Maggie with him and holding her tight. She was still straddling him and the sudden full contact of their bare chests made her gasp. He searched her face one more time for any hint of uncertainty. She made sure he found none. She was long past doubt when it came to Kam. She was certain of what she needed to do now and what she would need to do next.

"Fuck it," Kam finally said with a roguish grin letting go of any restraint he had left. He brought his lips to hers, taking charge of their connection now. He reached between them to untie the strings of her pants and pushed them down as he hungrily said, "I have to see you. All of you." A shiver ran up Maggie's spine at his tone. They had flirted before and pushed certain boundaries. But this? This was entirely new. This was a side of him she had only ever imagined and never had the pleasure of experiencing.

With a new sense of assuredness, Kam braced himself with one arm and wrapped the other tighter around Maggie's back. One second they were chest to chest as she straddled him and the next he had masterfully flipped them so her back was to the mattress and he was hovering just above her. She couldn't help the giggle that escaped her at the sudden and surprising movement. Regaining her composure, she looked back at Kam's face and stilled at what she saw.

His smile was *heartstopping*. One she had never seen before. Her gaze became reverent as she looked up at him. He was offering her yet another piece of him that she had yet to collect and admire. Without thinking, her hand reached up and her thumb trailed across his lower lip, stopping to rest on his cheek. Her own lips were parted slightly and Kam could see the awe on her face.

He realized in that moment that this wasn't a time for haste. This was a time for *worship*. For them to exalt each other in new and unknown ways. Gently, he turned his head to the side and kissed her hand as it rested along the side of his face. He slowly brought his face to hers and pressed a tender kiss to her forehead. Then at the corner of each of her eyes. Then her nose. Along her jaw. He worked his way down her neck and chest, pressing featherlight kisses that made goosebumps spread along her skin.

He sat back and looked at her once more. She was breathtaking. Every single inch of her skin was more exquisite than the next. His eyes struggled to take her in fast enough. He needed to burn this image into his memory. This new first of theirs. He cursed her for ever saying anything negative about herself and her body. How dare she? Staring down at her bare skin he knew she was a masterpiece that he'd never get enough of.

Minutes had passed with him taking in every inch of her that he could before he realized her body had tensed below him. He looked up and saw her face turned away, staring out his window. He knew that look. *Shit.*

Kam knew her better than this. What to him was adoration, to her was scrutiny. Every moment he had spent soaking in the perfection of her was a moment she spent assaulted by her own insecurities. He vowed to work on that with her later. There would be a later.

"Mags, look at me," he whispered gently. Her only response was a slight shake of her head. How had he let her get so far into her own mind without noticing sooner? Granted, the distraction of her body underneath his was enough to block out an apocalyptic event if he were honest with himself. He didn't get it. There was absolutely *nothing* for her to be insecure about. He still couldn't find any of these flaws he had heard her complain about so many times before.

"It's okay Kam," her voice was no more than a breath. Absolutely not. He would not let her become this small version of herself that he knew came out when her self doubt spiraled. Not when the woman was a fucking goddess in human form. A growl of frustration grumbled in his chest.

"Eyes here," he said forcefully this time. Her head whipped up and her eyes met his. "Good girl," he smirked. Her lips parted and her eyes flared. So that's what she enjoyed? Kam should've known. The woman who always had to take care of everything and struggled to accept a compliment. The woman who relied on no one and struggled to believe in herself even with all she'd accomplished. Of course she'd want someone else to take charge. Of course she'd need reassurance. Of course she'd want to be praised.

Praise would be the easiest of all to offer her. She was exquisite. He had already fallen for her mind and heart a long time ago. Her body was just another piece in the perfect puzzle that was Maggie.

"You're perfect," he continued as his hands moved reverently, and shakily, down her body. His control was paper thin at this point, but he knew he needed to keep bringing her back from whatever self conscious ledge she'd been teetering on a few moments ago. As his hands cupped her breasts, she arched into his touch and closed her eyes.

"Eyes on me," he ordered again. Her eyes flew open at the command and he smiled mischievously before continuing, "You will keep your eyes on mine the entire time, you understand?" She nodded shakily in response as his hands made their way lower. He chuckled. "This may be the first time you've ever listened to me without putting up a fight. I want you to see just how amazed I am by you. By all of you," he finally said, spreading her thighs wider with his own.

Maggie's breathing was ragged as his hands stopped briefly just below her belly button. Kam's breaths came in barely restrained heaves. Their gaze was electric. The next thing she knew, his hand dipped between her legs and she almost threw her head back, eyes closed before remembering his command. Maggie shouldn't have been surprised that he had figured out what she enjoyed so quickly. It was Kam after all.

"So ready for me already," he whispered. "Perfect." Kam moved a single finger expertly inside of her, as if he already knew exactly what she needed. Maggie's hips moved in sync with him and a small moan escaped her lips as his thumb teased her clit. "Fuck, you feel amazing," he said, letting a second finger join his first. Maggie wasn't sure if it was the words or the added pressure, but her back arched at the sensation of the combination of the two.

She never took her eyes off of his. Kam made sure that each of his feelings was on full display for her to read easily. He opened himself to her entirely. She could see the adoration. Kam had found his church and was ready to worship. Her heart swelled with dozens of emotions. She knew she wasn't worthy of this devotion, but she couldn't find it in herself to stop him.

He continued a teasing pace, constantly murmuring words of affection and praise. She clenched around him. It all became too much and simultaneously not enough. His words. His touch. His gaze.

"Please Kam, I need more," she whimpered.

"Anything for you. Always for you," he whispered. He made quick work of grabbing and putting on a condom and recentering himself between her legs. "You're more perfect than I could have ever imagined," he said before slowly sliding into her. Had she had a moment to internalize what he said, the words would've shattered Maggie because deep down she knew they weren't true.

She didn't have time for any of her spiraling thoughts, though. The feel of him inside of her took over any lucid thought she was capable of. She was officially lost in Kam. The idea of him. The feel of him. The love of him.

Their bodies moved slowly together. Tenderly. Both in astonishment of the other. As they moved and shifted and intertwined only one constant remained. Her hazy green eyes never left his adoring brown gaze.

Maggie woke to the sun rising the next morning, her head on Kam's chest. Both of them were still entirely naked. She tilted her head to look up at him and a sad smile crept onto her face. At least they would have last night. She felt a tear trickle down her cheek. She knew how much today would hurt, but she knew it was also necessary. She was hoping to leave before Kam woke up.

Gently, she unraveled herself from his body. Every inch of her skin longing for the comfort of his touch again as she moved. She moved silently around his room. She was used to this. She had left while he was sleeping so many times before, she knew exactly how to avoid waking him up. She hadn't brought much, so it was a quick job getting dressed and packing her bags. She stacked the books he had bought her on his desk with the receipt and a note on top:

> Kam,
> I'm so sorry. I have loved you for so long, but I can't love you any longer. I can't be who you want. Who you deserve. You deserve more, but we will always have last night.
>
> Love,
> Mags

Maggie crept down the stairs with her things silently. She took one final look around the house she had grown to love so much. In another world and another life maybe it would have worked. But, Maggie only had this world and this life she had been dealt. In this one? She couldn't burden them with her pain. She couldn't burden them with her downfall.

She had made it to her car and gotten her bags in the trunk before she heard rushed footsteps on the gravel of the driveway behind her.

"What the fuck is this?" his voice was angry, desperate, confused as he spat the question at her. Maggie took a deep breath before she turned around to face Kam. Her heart shattered at the devastation in his eyes. She couldn't bear the way he was looking at her.

"Mags, what the fuck is this?" he repeated. It was then she noticed he had her note in his hands. She took another steadying breath.

"Kam, we can't do this," was all Maggie could muster in response. He took a step toward her and she threw her hand up halting him.

"Of course we fucking can. What are you spooked after last night? Was it too much? I asked you! You said–" he sputtered out before Maggie cut him off.

"Kam, last night was perfect. Beyond perfect. You are the best thing that has probably ever happened to me. You have been everything I needed and more these last few weeks. These last few years, honestly. But Kam," it was here her voice cracked, "I can't be everything *you* need anymore. I'm broken. More than you can imagine. I'm not who you knew. I'm changed and I don't think I'll ever go back to her. I can't be who you deserve. I can't give you the love I used to so desperately want to give you. I just... can't." Every word was harder and harder to say, but she knew they were true.

"You don't get to decide what I deserve, Mags–" he started, but she cut him off again.

"In this moment, I do Kam. You love me *so much*. I know that. But you're blinded by that. You love a girl who doesn't exist anymore. I wanted us to have last night so that we could have experienced it at least once. If we keep going, you'll grow to resent me. Or worse, you'll drown with me. I can't let that–"

"Mags," it was Kam's turn to cut her off as he pleaded, "It will get better. I believe that. You'll want to be happy and love and live again." He stared at her full of a final bout of hope.

"That's the problem, Kam. You believe that but I don't," was all Maggie could muster in response. She turned to walk to her car door.

"Hey!" She could hear the despair in his voice and she swallowed the sob that caught in her throat. "You promised you would never turn away from me!"

"What are you talking about?" she asked, turning back to him and immediately wishing she hadn't. The pain was etched all over his face and it took all of her strength not to run to him to make him stop hurting. In the end, this was all she would do. Hurt him. Better to end it now before she dragged him too far down with her.

"In the car. On the way to Mitch's party. You *promised* me you would never turn away from me," he said. And the way he said promised tore Maggie's heart entirely from her chest.

"I lied," she said simply and got into her car. Kam didn't move. Stunned into silence. It wasn't until she started to pull out of the driveway that she saw him start to move again. He started jogging after the car, pulling his phone from his pocket. His name came up on the screen of her car as he was calling and chasing after her. As she watched him in her rearview mirror, her heart broke into even more pieces–something she thought was impossible at this point.

She looked back at his name under the incoming call and she let it ring once... twice... three times... It was on the fourth ring she saw him stop short in her rearview mirror. Frozen. She could see the shocked anguish behind his tears.

They always answered each other on the third ring. They had promised each other that years ago on a dark, cool night after swapping stories and leaning into each other's friendship. This was the one promise they had both kept. Always. This was the one promise that meant the most to both of them all these years. She had now broken her second promise to him in one day.

Denial

Playlist

Do I Make You Nervous? / Lilyisthatyou
Dress / Taylor Swift
Please Please Please / Sabrina Carpenter
Hold Back / Miles Hardt
Scared To Be Lonely / Martin Garrix, Dua Lipa

2

Denial

The first few moments of the morning were always the hardest for Maggie. In that blurred state between dreams and real life, it was easy to forget her mom was dead. It was easy to confuse her facts and believe that she could roll out of bed and call her mom for their morning update. These were both her favorite and least favorite moments in each day. She loved being able to believe no matter how briefly that her mom was still here.

It never lasted long, though. Soon enough the clarity of morning light would settle and bring her crashing back into her reality. The weight of her grief would suffocate her. It was like a fresh hell every day having to remind herself that her mom was in fact dead and her life was in fact unequivocally altered.

It was the moment that this realization settled every morning that Maggie sprung out of bed to get her day started; to busy herself and her mind. It had been a month since she last spoke to Kam. Since she vowed to herself on that tumultuous and painful drive home that she was done with shattering hearts and hurting. From that day she had denied the pain that swelled within her. Except for during these first few moments every morning.

So, as she lay there with the grief beginning to settle on her chest, tightening around her permanently shattered heart, she sprang into action. Pushing the covers back, she threw on a hoodie and went downstairs to start breakfast for herself and her aunt. Her mornings tended to veer on the chaotic side. Maggie was a seven alarms every three minutes and still not necessarily awake kind of lady.

After the alarms and the grief, she would pop out of bed and begin the chaos that was her mad dash to work. Never giving herself enough time, because time was where the pain had a chance to creep in. She would only ever give herself an hour to get ready. In that hour she had to make breakfast and coffee, get dressed, do her makeup, pack her lunch, chat with her aunt, and rush to her car to drive into the city.

With where her aunt lived, her commute was always a toss up. There were days she could get into the city unscathed by traffic in forty minutes. And then there were days she would be stuck in a slow crawl and the commute would take hours. That was the thing with New York City, you just never knew what to expect.

Luckily her bosses understood the situation she was in and went easy on her. They never pressed her about being late since she always made sure her work was done either before she went to classes or when she got home that night. And if she was being entirely honest, her work at the moment wasn't life or death. She was just an assistant whose duties mainly revolved around office maintenance and organization.

Lately, she had grown to prefer the days where she had to take her work home with her. It gave her less time to think about anything and more time to grow so exhausted she passed out the moment her head hit her pillow.

As she sat there basically parked on the highway between a Toyota and a Mazda, she knew today would thankfully be one of those days. She was absolutely certain she would be late seeing as it was already 9:05 (she started at 9) and she hadn't even crossed the bridge yet.

The bridge. The only part of her commute that always caused her anxiety. The one part of her commute that reminded her each morning of a promise she had made and broken. That reminded her just how awful she was. That reminded her of part of the reason she stayed so busy every day.

An hour later, she walked into her office and got right to work. She had missed the office morning meeting, but her boss had texted her all of the top priorities that needed to be done by end of day for their next event before heading to a meeting across town. She liked this job. The pay wasn't great, but she worked with good people, they were flexible around her class schedule, and it was pretty easy work for her.

As she sat down to get started, her phone buzzed with a text from Rosa.

You haven't called in a while. I'm back next week and we better have something planned bitch.

The tiniest smile worked its way onto Maggie's face. Rosa was graduating but had zero desire to actually walk. This meant she was coming back earlier than initially planned and Maggie was so ready to have her best friend back in the same state as her. She typed up a quick reply apologizing for being absent and planning a sangria dinner date for just the two of them.

As she went to pull up the office website to make updates, her phone buzzed again. This time it was Lara.

**End of year party tonight. You're my date. No is not
an option. Meet at the dining hall for lunch to
figure shit out.**

Maggie rolled her eyes. She knew she wasn't getting out of this
so she gave Lara a simple "okay" response and jumped into her
work.

❧ ❧ ❧

"Who is hosting this party again?" Maggie asked as she waited
for her chicken parm panini to be done.

"Honestly, I'm not entirely sure. I just know it's a rooftop party
really close to here that is beach themed. It's also our last chance to
really hang out before I head home for the summer. So, we
obviously have to go," Lara answered as she popped a french fry
into her mouth.

"Ugh, you're impossible to say no to sometimes, you know
that?" Maggie teased.

"I know. But it's only because you love me so much," Lara said,
winking before she continued, "Listen, this place is packed. I'll go
pay and find us a table while you wait for your food, okay?"
Maggie simply nodded in response and then turned back to where
the staff was making her panini.

As she checked her phone for any updates or messages from
work she felt someone stand uncomfortably close to her. Had
she been taller, their shoulders would have practically been
touching. She tilted her head ever so slightly diagonally to the
left and saw Aidan right next to her, staring straight at the menu,
smirking.

"I couldn't help but overhear that you're getting dragged to tonight's rooftop party," Aidan said half as a statement and half as a question.

"Didn't anyone ever teach you that it's rude to eavesdrop?" Maggie answered, turning to face him. He chuckled before responding.

"Come on Maggie, you and I both know it isn't eavesdropping when Lara is talking. I would've been able to hear her from across campus," he quipped. She simply scoffed and nodded because he wasn't wrong.

She took a moment to truly take Aidan in. She thankfully hadn't bumped into him much since their last... encounter. She had never noticed how tall he was. Maggie was pretty tall herself and still had to turn her face up at a sharp angle to face him fully. His curly hair was a mess, but a messy look that definitely worked for him. He had ridiculously blue eyes that were framed by his round, wire-rimmed glasses, which made him look academic but not obnoxious. His skin was extremely pale, even though spring was in full swing and most people were starting to glow with fresh sunkissed tans. His smile was sandwiched by dimples. For a drunken make out she definitely could have done worse, she thought.

"So, are you actually going? Or are you just trying to appease Lara?" he asked when she didn't say anything else.

"Aidan, if you know Lara at all, you know there is no simply appeasing her. Once she's decided, we all have no choice. It would seem I am at her mercy tonight. I'm just praying she doesn't make me wear some bullshit coconut bra or something to match the theme," Maggie joked. He laughed and she noted that she liked the sound of it. It was deep and uninhibited. It flowed and filled her and made her feel like she wanted to make more jokes just to hear that laugh again. The moment that feeling started, she clamped it back down. She had promised herself no more of this. She wasn't putting herself through anymore of *these* kinds of feelings. And she definitely wasn't putting anyone through *her*.

"Oh, you definitely can't wear a coconut bra," he answered at the tail end of his laugh. At her furrowed brow clearly displaying her confusion he continued, "well, obviously that's what I'm wearing and I wouldn't want to show you up." The laugh that sprung from her mouth surprised her. When was the last time she had laughed like this? She didn't want to think back on those memories.

The kitchen staff, as if on cue to save her from her own mental spiral, came with her chicken parm panini at that exact moment. She grabbed it from him and thanked him. She turned back to Aidan to try her best to exit the conversation as naturally as possible, but when she turned she noticed that he was looking at her in the most curious way. She didn't know him well, so she couldn't place exactly what the look was or meant.

"Well, I guess I'll see you tonight. Promise not to steal your thunder with a coconut bra," Maggie finally said as she started to turn away and head to the registers. Before she could take a full step away from Aidan, he had grabbed her elbow. His touch was gentle, but also had enough force to turn her back to face him. He leaned forward, coming close enough to whisper in her ear.

"You know, I wouldn't mind you wearing a coconut bra," he took a breath she could feel against the shell of her ear before he continued, "but only if I can be the one to help you into and out of it." He straightened, winked at her, and turned back to the kitchen staff to order. She stood there frozen, flustered, and completely caught off guard. After a beat she finally turned away to go pay and find Lara.

He had made her laugh for the first time in weeks. She ignored what that could possibly mean. And the way he looked at her. What was that about? She ignored whatever that could mean too. And well, if she still had goosebumps from the shiver his final words had sent cascading all over her body, she definitely ignored whatever those were trying to tell her.

Eight hours later, Maggie was exhaustedly walking down the stairs to where she promised she would meet Lara. After lunch, work had been chaotic with phone calls about the upcoming event her office was hosting. Her last night class of the semester, though it was a final exam, had been relatively painless. She enjoyed the class and knew she would do well. She also loved having a final to throw all of her focus into. It left no room for her to think about anything or anyone else.

As she walked toward the front entrance of the building she saw Lara there and couldn't help but snort her laugh. If there was one thing you could count on Lara to do, it was commit to a theme for any party. She stood there as people in plain clothes walked by dressed in a shoulder to ankle surfer body suit and holding a boogie board.

"You are utterly fucking ridiculous, you know that?" Maggie asked as she stopped in front of Lara.

"And you love every second of it. Now here's your outfit, go get changed," Lara ordered.

"Lara, I told you. I'm changing there. There is no chance I am going to change into a shark onesie in the building I take classes and work in," Maggie argued.

"Fine, fine. Then let's get out of here. It should only take a few minutes to get there." Maggie was suspicious at the lack of argument that Lara was putting up. Normally, Lara was one who would never give up until she got her way. Maggie knew that making her walk through the building in a shark onesie was something Lara would give just about anything to see. Lara was already turning away holding the bag with her costume in it, so Maggie shrugged off her suspicions and followed her friend who would never surprise her with an outfit change. Never.

Lara was right. The rooftop the party was on was only a few blocks from campus. They made a quick stop at the bodega to grab some beers and then started the walk up the stairs because of course there was no elevator. New York is known for its walk ups after all. Before they made their way up to the roof entirely, they stopped in the apartment of the person hosting the party. Luckily, Maggie did know them, making it slightly less awkward. It was someone she had taken a random class with last year.

Maggie and Lara headed toward the bathroom after saying their hellos so she could finally change. As Lara handed her the bag with the shark onesie in it, Maggie couldn't help noticing the mischievous gleam in her eyes. Suspicion crept back up as Maggie went into the bathroom and locked the door. She reached her hand into the bag and as she pulled out the outfit, she realized that she was most definitely not holding up a shark onesie. She turned back toward the door, furious, and glared at Lara who was standing right outside happy as a kid on Christmas morning.

"What the fuck is this?" Maggie questioned.

"Your outfit, obviously," Lara stated as if it was the clearest thing in the world.

"We agreed on a shark onesie, Lara," Maggie argued.

"Well actually, you agreed on a shark onesie. I decided rather than going for your typical ridiculous look tonight, that I wanted you to make every he, she, they, and gay drop their jaws and drool," Lara said in the most confident tone. Maggie just stared at her. Lara was absolutely infuriating. As neither of them made a move, Lara finally continued, "Mags, I love you but you lean way too much into your goofy side and are so uncomfortable with your feminine side. You are quite literally one of the hottest bitches on our campus and it is infuriating to see you cover it all up, brush it off, and not believe it. So tonight I am forcing you to revel in your glorious goddess energy. I will literally tackle you if you try and walk by me in what you're currently wearing because you know how seriously I take themed parties. So get your ass back in that bathroom and put on what is in the bag."

Maggie stared at her for another moment and realized her best, but obviously most annoying friend was not budging. With a huff of annoyance (followed by a shrill of glee from Lara) Maggie turned back to the bathroom and changed.

A few minutes later, Lara and her were walking up the final few flights of stairs to the rooftop. Lara still in her skin tight surfer suit and Maggie in one of the tiniest bikinis she had ever worn in her life. She did have to admit that Lara found the perfect cut for her body. The suit itself was a mint color that contrasted the slight tan she had started to work up now that the weather had warmed. The top was cut in a way that held her boobs magnificently in place and miraculously made them seem curvier than they really were. The bottoms were cheeky enough to accentuate the muscular curves she'd worked on for the last few years, but thankfully not cheeky enough to be anything too scandalous. And tied at her waist was a black cover up that was long enough to just barely brush her ankles but sheer enough to still let everyone see everything the suit highlighted. The weight she had lost over the last two months definitely didn't hurt the look, either. But that weight loss was something that probably should've concerned Maggie and not pleased her.

To top it all off, Lara had tied Maggie's hair into the perfect messy bun atop her head, because of course every inch of her skin needed to be exposed for this outfit. She added a body chain down her front and a ridiculous pair of wedges that no one would ever actually wear to the beach.

Lara's smug smile annoyed the living shit out of Maggie. As she stepped onto the rooftop, it was a miracle she didn't turn around and punch the friend she loved so dearly. There were *so many* people here that she knew. People she would see regularly in classes next semester. Other students that she would pass in the hallways at work and in the dining hall. And guess what? Not a single one was in a bikini. Thankfully a few of the guys were in swim trunks with shirts unbuttoned. But it would seem that all of the ladies decided shorts and cover up dresses were the best route for tonight's theme. Here Maggie was, almost naked and probably looking utterly ridiculous.

She started to doubt everything as panic began to settle. Her thighs were still too big and jiggled when she walked. Although she'd lost some weight, her stomach definitely should not be exposed like this. And don't get her started on the cellulite that was definitely now on full display for people she'd have to see over and over again. Maggie started to reach for the bun on her head to release her long hair and at least somewhat cover up, but Lara grabbed her hand before she could reach the hair tie.

"You're making that face that tells me you're saying a million and one mean things about your body and probably going to puke at any moment from panic and not alcohol. I need you to cut that shit out so we are going to go take a shot and then drink our beers. You are going to stop being so infuriatingly mean to yourself. You're fucking gorgeous right now and you should not be saying anything otherwise to yourself," Lara scolded, staring into Maggie's eyes.

"Everyone is staring," Maggie said shyly.

"Because they're probably thinking about how they would fuck you," Lara said matter of factly. Then she dragged Maggie by the hand to the table with all the alcohol on it. As they walked, Maggie could feel everyone's eyes on her. Was Lara being serious right now? She felt exposed, but maybe she was overreacting?

As Lara turned to pour them two shots of Jack, Maggie tensed as she felt a presence behind her as someone leaned forward and whispered in her ear, "Someone sure does know how to make an entrance." Lara turned back around and her eyes widened ever so slightly and the smugness of her smile multiplied.

"Aidan! Love the coconut bra. I think you should consider adding it to your daily attire. Shot?" Lara greeted the man standing so close to Maggie that she could feel the heat emanating from his body.

"I'd love one, Lara. Thanks," he answered, prompting Lara to turn back around to pour a third shot. As Lara poured, Maggie could feel Aidan leaning forward from behind her again, his mouth dangerously close to her ear. She felt his breath before he spoke and it again sent a shiver down her body. "You seem a little uncomfortable with your outfit choice right now, but I want you to know..." he paused and she could hear him swallow before he continued in the quietest whisper, "every single man, and even some women, are currently wondering how you look under that bathing suit. And, they're wondering exactly what they would need to do in order to be the one who takes it off of you. I'll have you know, I plan on that being something only I get to experience tonight," he finished, straightening back to his full height and moving from behind her to beside her.

As he moved, he caressed a gentle touch along her back, leaving goosebumps along the path his hand traveled. He finally rested his hand gently on her opposite hip, lazily draping his arm across her lower back. It was a soft touch, but she could feel the command in it. The message he was sending to anyone watching them. The message that if she decided to leave with anyone tonight, it would be him and only him.

Normally, the possessiveness of this moment would piss her off. Right now, in this circumstance, it felt... sexy. She was shocked by her own response. Lara turned around to hand Aidan his shot and immediately noticed his hand on Maggie's hip. Her smile turned into an all out Cheshire Cat grin. She raised her shot glass saying, "To being young, sexy, and somewhat reckless." Aidan was the first to bring his shot glass to hers in cheers.

Maggie looked at them and realized that for the first time in weeks she didn't have to work to ignore her pain. Lara, the outfit, Aidan. They had all worked seamlessly to help her ignore the grief, the pain, the destruction that was her life. Rather than forcing herself to dive headfirst into work and classes and cooking and overwhelming herself with tasks, they did the forgetting for her. The denying. At that moment she decided that she liked it. This was easier. So she raised her shot glass in cheers and slammed the Jack, vowing to use every single distraction around her. Vowing to deny every last ounce of pain the last few months had caused her and let everything else take its place instead.

A few hours and many shots later, Maggie found herself pressed against a bathroom wall with Aidan pressed firmly against her. His hands were exploring every inch of her body and her hands were wrapped around his neck. She grabbed the hair at the nape of his neck and tugged. Not too hard, but hard enough it pulled Aidan's mouth from hers and angled his head back, exposing his neck to her.

Ever so slowly she dragged her tongue up his throat, stopping only to gently graze her teeth in the spot where his throat met his jaw. Her move had the desired effect on him because what had previously been a building erection against her leg was now fully hard as she heard him whisper the word fuck.

He turned his head back down to face her and the heat in his eyes was enough to let Maggie know exactly where this was going. He leaned forward, pressing kisses along her jaw and coming in close enough to tug on her ear lobe with his teeth. The sensation sparked through Maggie as she threw her head back against the bathroom wall, giving him perfect and complete access to her throat. He alternated between gentle kisses and tugs with his teeth as he worked his way slowly down. Maggie moaned softly at the touch. He continued to work his way down to her chest, stopping level with her breasts.

Using his tongue and teeth, he slowly worked the fabric of her bikini top to the side. He started with her left breast, making quick work of taking her nipple into his mouth once it was free. He swirled it with his tongue and tugged gently, causing Maggie to arch into him even more. She could feel him chuckle against her skin as he moved his mouth across her chest to the other side. The cold air against her nipple contrasted the warmth his mouth had just provided, causing her to shiver. As he worked his tongue along her body to her right breast, he brought his hand from the side of her head down to the space where his mouth had just been. He took her nipple between his fingers and twisted it in the most torturously delicious way.

It was almost too much for her. Her body was now reacting naturally and she knew she wouldn't stop this. Aidan really called his shot earlier in the night. For just a second, she questioned whether she should be doing this. She didn't need someone else in her life right now. She was also a little tipsy. But when Aidan finally looked back up at her with nothing but lust for her body, it made her forget everything else.

If she was being entirely honest, all she wanted to do was forget. She didn't want to be the girl with a dead mom who broke a good man's heart last month. She didn't want to be the girl who had to throw herself entirely into her work in order to distract herself from the grief. She didn't want to be the sad girl who had no clue what she was doing with her life and who wasn't even entirely sure she wanted a life anymore.

So as Aidan went back to work on her breasts, Maggie made a decision. She decided she wasn't any of those things. Her mom wasn't dead. She wasn't broken. Her life wasn't ruined. No.

She decided she was just a girl in a bathroom having a sloppy, drunken hookup with a hot guy. She decided to pretend that in the morning she'd be hungover and call her mom trying to hide her hangover, and life would be the same as it was.

As she made this decision, there was a knock on the bathroom door and both Maggie and Aidan froze. Aidan smirked and quirked a brow at Maggie. She looked at him and decided she was done acknowledging the pain. She decided he would be her denial. He would be her greatest distraction.

"Just a minute," Maggie shouted toward the bathroom door. She turned to face Aidan and whispered, "You have exactly two minutes to get both of us off and then hide in the shower while I walk out. Think you can handle that?"

He didn't need to verbalize his answer. Faster than Maggie thought a man could move after the amount of shots they had, Aidan had pulled down his shorts, finally freeing his erection, put on a condom, and grabbed her by the ass, lifting her onto his hips. As she locked her ankles behind his back and tightened her thighs around his waist, he moved the fabric of her bikini bottoms to the side and slid into her. She gasped as he slammed every single inch into her. She pressed her back against the wall behind her and her hands into his shoulders, trying to alleviate some of her weight and get better leverage.

It didn't matter, though. Aidan had taken her words literally. He thrust into her roughly and quickly. Going deeper and deeper with each drive. It was almost impossible to muffle her moans as he filled her up. It was a quick fuck. It wasn't love. It was a rough and ready job he was getting done.

And with every thrust that rode the border between pleasure and pain, Maggie was thankful he was filling her up with everything but the things she was avoiding. She was so close. Almost there.

There was another sharp knock on the door and breathlessly, Maggie shouted, "coming!" Aidan chuckled at her choice of words. As if using her response to the person waiting outside as a command, he gripped her even tighter, pushing down on her while he thrust into her one more time with his full force. It did the job. Maggie tensed around him and bit his shoulder to muffle her shout of pleasure as she shut her eyes. Nothing but black and stars filled her vision as she worked through her orgasm.

As she was tensing around him, she knew it was his turn. She may have been using him as her distraction, but she'd make sure he'd be rewarded for his efforts too. She tightened the lock of her ankles and the grip of her thighs around his waist as he continued pounding into her. Timing it perfectly, she used her ankles to push against him, forcing him deeper than he had been this entire time. For her, it caused a twinge of pleasure filled pain. For him, it did exactly what she needed. He stiffened and then spasmed as he came.

As soon as he was done, she unwrapped her legs from around him and straightened out her bikini top and bottom. She used some toilet paper to clean up, passing some to Aidan too and then pointed at the shower. He dutifully got in as she made a show of flushing the toilet and washing her hands. As she opened the bathroom door, she looked at the person waiting and apologized, making up some excuse about maybe drinking a little too much.

As she sauntered across the apartment to make her way back to the roof and find Lara, wearing a freshly fucked smile, she thought that this was a much better way to spend her time. The alcohol. The sex. It was much easier to fill herself up with those things than with the grief and the pain. So as she made her way up the stairs to the rooftop, she decided she would continue to drink and fuck her way to this glorious numbness rather than acknowledge the clusterfuck her life had become.

Maggie enjoyed working the summer months. Although it was a pain to still have to make the drive onto campus every day, she enjoyed the calmer feel of everything. Not as many people took summer classes, so it was really just staff and a few students there. She could grab lunch at peak times with no lines. She could work from her laptop at various spots around campus that would normally be crowded with someone studying.

Like today, for example, Maggie had brought her laptop out onto a shaded portion of the lawn and was proofreading various emails and updates that needed to go out for work by tomorrow. She loved her coworkers, but holy hell was their grammar awful. As she worked her way through the first few sentences of an email blast, she scrunched her face at the misuse of just about everything. She realized this particular blast was probably a wash and she should just start from scratch.

"Penny for your thoughts," she heard someone say as a mop of curly hair flashed past and sat on the lawn beside her. Aidan. What the fuck? He was the last person she expected to see on campus during the summer months.

"I'm thinking that I love my job and coworkers, but their writing is fucking awful... making my job slightly more difficult," Maggie answered, working through her confusion.

"Ah! In that case, remind me to never show you my writing," he responded. She chuckled but still wondered why in the world Aidan was here.

"What are you doing here? Classes ended last week," Maggie puzzled.

"I got some part time work on campus and decided to take a summer class while I was here," he offered. "What? Don't want me around? Afraid you won't be able to resist my charm?" Maggie rolled her eyes in response.

"Of course not," Maggie scoffed. "I'm just not used to seeing many people in the summer months. It usually gets a lot quieter around her. Calmer. More boring." At this Aidan leaned toward her, tucking a strand of loose hair behind her ear.

"Oh, I promise to keep it interesting for you," he whispered. Her body froze at the closeness. She was both caught off guard and intrigued. As she was about to respond, Aidan looked past her and tensed, noticing something behind her. He let his thumb drift down her jaw as he got back up and abruptly walked away. Maggie couldn't help but notice that his pace was just a bit faster than was normal. What was that about?

As she was about to turn back to drafting a new version of the email blast, two of her friends sat on either side of her. What in the hell? Did everyone decide to stay on campus for the summer and not tell her? As they chatted, she learned that both of them needed to take summer classes in order to graduate on time. Made sense. She realized that she would get no work done if she stayed on the lawn so after a few minutes, she excused herself and decided to head back to the office.

As she was walking to the parking garage later that day, someone came up beside her matching her stride. Aidan.

"Twice in one day? How could a girl be so lucky?" she asked by way of greeting. He laughed at her sarcasm and smiled.

"How about a drink? Happy hour just started and I know a great spot," he suggested with no other conversation.

"I already have happy hour plans with some other people. You actually know them, I think. Jack, Kate, Amber, and Max," Maggie replied.

"Oh," was all he answered as they continued walking. There was a weird silence that filled the space between them before Maggie finally continued.

"I mean, you could come with me if you want. I'm headed to my car now, and I'm just going to drive into Brooklyn to meet them at a spot we love. It's nothing fancy, but it's fun." She didn't necessarily want him to come, but drinks and a reenactment of their night in the bathroom felt like it would be a welcome distraction. The thoughts had started to creep back in.

Although she enjoyed the quiet campus and workdays, it also meant she had more time to let her reality sink in. That was one thing she was avoiding with all her might: her reality. Most days she denied any of what had happened from February through April was real. It was easiest to do that when she had work and drinks and guys to distract her. She thought the offer was nice and could end well for both of them. When she looked at Aidan, though, she second guessed herself. The look he wore made it clear that he loathed this idea. As if suggesting a happy hour was the last place he wanted to be. But hadn't he just asked her to go to a happy hour?

"You know what, how about I text you where I'll be and if you and your friends finish earlier than expected, *you* can come join me," he recovered. The tension was still clear in his tone, but his body had eased a bit. The way he had said "you" made it clear that this invitation was only for her, not her friends. Who were also his friends. Weird.

"Sure. No promises since I haven't seen some of them in a hot minute. But if I'm still up for it, I'll let you know," she offered. He pulled out his phone to text her the name and address of the bar and mentioned he'd be there for a while. As he went to leave, he pulled her in, kissed her cheek gently, and walked away.

※ ※ ※

An obnoxious and traffic filled drive later, Maggie walked into the bar her friends were already at and ordered her usual–bourbon neat. They spent a good chunk of time catching up and swapping ridiculous stories. She loved spending time with them, but because of their differing majors and her chaotic class and work schedule, they didn't get a chance to overlap much.

An hour had passed and Maggie had laughed at all of their ridiculous stories and jokes, wiping cheerful tears from her eyes. This was perfect. Not a single moment to think about anything else. At least that was true until Jack and Max went to get everyone another round and Kate turned to Maggie.

"How are you really doing Maggie?" she asked. She genuinely wanted to know.

"I'm great! Work is good! I'm keeping busy," was all Maggie wanted to offer. Could offer.

"Are you? Really? You know you can open up with us," Amber pressed. Maggie could feel her muscles slowly begin to stiffen as she did her best to plaster on a smile. The fake one. This was not what she came here for. She came here for a drink. For a good time. Not to acknowledge anything else going on in her life. And definitely not to talk about it with anyone. You can't deny things you speak into existence.

"I really am. Things are better and life is good," Maggie forced out through her smile. Maggie grabbed her phone, pretending she had received a notification. "Oh fuck," she continued, "my aunt just texted me. She needs me to head back to her house because she can't remember if she locked the door. Sorry, y'all. She's paranoid about this kind of shit," Maggie lied.

Amber and Kate gave each other a look as if they could see right through the lie. They both knew better than to push Maggie, though. So, they let her drop some cash on the table and promised they would let Jack and Max know she had to leave. As she walked out of the bar, Maggie sent a single text:

Still there?

She told herself if he didn't answer she would just grab some beers on the way home and drink to some Marvel movie or something. As she plopped into her driver's seat, her phone buzzed.

Have been saving the seat next to me since I got here.

That was all Maggie needed. She plugged the address he had given her into her Maps app and made her way back out of Brooklyn. She was prepared to do whatever she could to distract herself.

As she walked into the bar, she couldn't miss him. How was he so tall? Even seated on a bar stool, he towered over everyone else. She could easily see his untamed curls over everyone else's heads. She made her way over to the stool next to his. His smile was sexy and confident as he took her in. His expression confirmed that it would be extremely easy to get what Maggie wanted right now.

She propped one elbow on the bar, resting her head on her hand. She knew exactly what her cleavage looked like right now and she knew exactly what leaning forward ever so slightly would do. There it was. His eyes couldn't resist dipping down to take in the view. The view that had been in his mouth not too long ago. He bit his bottom lip as he raised his eyes back to hers.

"How about a drink? Do you know what you want?" he asked, trying his hardest to maintain eye contact and not let his eyes drop back down to her chest. Maggie decided she would steal his own move from him. Leaning forward, she put her hand on his leg and brought her mouth to his ear.

"I know exactly what I want. Sadly, though, I don't think I can get it here," she said as seductively as she could muster. Reinforcing her point by sliding her hand up his thigh under the bar. Her face was still next to his ear, but she could feel him stiffen in surprise before relaxing at her touch.

He recovered quickly, taking a hand and sliding it up the inside of her leg. He took his time working his way up in lazy circles as she slowly pulled her face away from his. She had prepared for this. Had assumed he would want to tease her the same way she teased him. She was ready. As he inched higher and higher his smile grew sultry. They both knew where this was going.

He had finally reached the edge of her skirt and was moving his finger along the hem, tapping each of her inner thighs as he skated back and forth. Maggie smirked. This was the game he wanted to play in public? Oh, she could play.

"*I dare you,*" she mouthed silently as she stared right at him, challenging him. Aidan couldn't resist a dare. He began his lazy circles again as Maggie turned her body to face the bar, shielding what was happening from anyone around them. He made sure to take his time and she made sure to open herself up just enough so he could play all he wanted. She had never been this bold before. And definitely never in public. It was sexy wondering if she'd have to order from the busy bartender while his hand was up her skirt.

Thinking about his finger being inside of her while people talked around them was thrilling in a way she hadn't experienced before.

His fingers stuttered a second as he noticed what she had been waiting for him to notice. Before Maggie had gotten out of her car to enter the bar, she had made sure to prepare a special surprise for him. She had taken off her underwear. He tilted his head toward her and raised a brow in surprise. Her only response was to ever so slightly scoot herself forward in her seat. Forcing his finger to feel her and how ready she was. She looked at him and looked down. She could see his growing erection now and was excited to be wrapped around it as soon as possible.

He took just a single finger and slid it gently into her. Her quiet gasp and his gentle groan was all it took for him to hurriedly get the bartender's attention, pay his tab, grab Maggie's hand, and walk her out of the bar.

Maggie parked across the street from her and Rosa's favorite Mexican spot. She sent up a silent prayer that Rosa wouldn't be in the mood to push and pry into her life too much. Maggie had given her the simplified version of what had happened with Kam and had already mentioned her flings with Aidan. She had no desire to talk about either of them. Or her feelings. Or the dumpster fire that was her life.

She wanted to ignore all of that right now and just enjoy a sangria night with her very best friend. She had arrived first so she got them a table on the patio and ordered a pitcher of sangria. She was already one glass in and refilling her cup as Rosa arrived.

"Look who is the late one for once," Maggie joked as Rosa sat down across from her.

"I missed you too," Rosa snarked back, smiling. "Now fill up my cup!" Maggie did just that after refilling her own glass. Then, Maggie raised hers in a toast.

"To the magnificent, beautiful, intelligent woman sitting across from me. Congratulations on graduating early. Congratulations on finding a job. I hope I can be like you when I grow up," Maggie toasted in Rosa's honor.

"You're literally like three months younger than me," Rosa responded.

"Can you just shut the fuck up and accept my toast to your accomplishments?" Maggie rolled her eyes, still holding up her cup. Rosa scrunched her nose but clinked her glass to Maggie's and drank as directed.

※ ※ ※

Two pitchers of sangria and four appetizers later, Maggie and Rosa were caught in a laughing fit at some silly joke Maggie had made. The evening had been perfect. They talked about everything Rosa had accomplished and what her next steps were. They talked about Maggie's work and the classes she'd be taking in the fall. They reminisced on their chaotic and ridiculous high school shenanigans. There was not a single second of conversation wasted on men or grief or anything of the like.

They split the check and planned their next dinner date. Now that Rosa was back in town, Maggie was going to see her as much as she could. With Maggie's job and classes and Rosa starting work soon, their schedules might not allow them to get together as much as she hoped, but she would take what she could get.

And so Maggie spent her entire summer keeping herself busy. She picked up extra projects at work. She scheduled as many dinner dates and brunches as she could with Rosa. She went to every happy hour she was invited to. She made sure Aidan was a regular presence in her life. He never came out with a group. They never had any real conversations. But, the sex was enough for Maggie. So she let herself sink deeper into her denial. She reveled in the sex, alcohol, and busy schedule. She ignored the fact that there was anything else to deal with in her life.

The fall semester kicked up and it was getting harder and harder to keep up with everything. With her working close to full time hours and attending four night classes a week, it was becoming almost impossible for her to make time for dinners with Rosa, happy hour with friends, and seeing Aidan.

She found it interesting that Aidan only ever showed up around her when she was alone. Almost like it was planned. He'd pick her up at the parking garage by campus every morning and then mysteriously disappear with some excuse or another as soon as they were in the building. He'd offer her a smile when they passed in communal places but only stopped to talk to her if no one else was around. If she did join a group he was already conversing in, he'd ignore her or find a reason to leave the group immediately after she joined it. He'd walk her back to her car at the parking garage after her class every night but would only ever meet her on a corner just off campus. Again, when no one was there or would see. And repeat.

It was on one of those nightly walks back to the parking garage she finally decided to ask him about it.

"Why do you avoid me when people are around?" Better to just say it than to beat around the bush.

"What are you talking about?" he laughed off her question.

"You haven't noticed?" she prompted. He just stared at her blankly. "Aidan. You've never joined me to hang out in a group even when it's *your* friends I'm hanging out with. You never stop on campus if I'm in a group. And if I join a group you're in, you act as if I'm not there or leave. I've never really thought about it before. But now that my schedule is so much more chaotic and I have to figure out how to make everyone fit, it's become pretty obvious," Maggie explained.

"Has it?" he asked. "Maggie, I think you're imagining it. I literally pick you up from your car every morning and drop you off every night."

"Yeah, and you leave as soon as we're in a place where anyone can see us and meet me on a corner across from campus. You don't think it's weird?" she pushed.

"I *think* you're making something out of nothing. We're busy people. We're getting the time where we can find it," was all Aidan offered in reply.

"Okay, then why don't you ever agree to go to happy hours with me when other people are around? I always have to choose between you or my friends or I have to meet you afterward. You never just come with me," Maggie pushed back.

"Maggie, seriously? Why are you harping on this? Most of the time when you're meeting your friends for happy hour I'm busy or meeting other people. You're being crazy right now. Stop making a big deal out of nothing," he said as if that was the end of the conversation, but Maggie wasn't done just yet.

"So you're too busy for drinks with *our* friends, but you're never too busy for me to meet you somewhere after and fuck you? Interesting," she commented. Aidan stopped in his tracks.

"What the fuck is your problem?" he asked.

"My problem is that you deny my existence when anyone else is around and make scheduling my life infinitely more difficult. My problem is that it's as if I'm not even a person you know when we're in a group, but then you fuck me senseless when we're in private. Just acknowledge that I'm right," Maggie fumed. She hadn't realized how much this had been bothering her. Aidan closed the distance between them and Maggie had to angle her head to maintain eye contact.

"I would... if you were right. I think you're just stressed with work and classes kicking back up. I think you're making something out of nothing to compensate for that stress. And I think there are much better ways I can help you alleviate that stress," with those final words he grabbed her hair, wrapping it around his hand and pulled so her head tilted back.

He nipped at the spot where her jaw met her neck and then feathered kisses along her cheek until he met her mouth. When he made it to her mouth, her lips were already parted from the gasp she had released at his grip on her hair. He kissed her and slipped his tongue through her parted lips. At the same time he tugged a little more on her hair, opening up more of her, allowing him to slip his tongue deeper. Maggie was helpless against this side of him. So she grabbed the loops of his jeans and pulled him closer to her–closing the distance between their bodies entirely.

If he wanted to deny what she saw plain as day, who was she to argue? She was clearly denying her own shit in life. She couldn't be one to judge.

He slowly dropped his hands from her hair and moved them down the sides of her body, sliding them under her t-shirt and resting them on the bare skin at her lower back. She wasn't sure how long they stood there pressed against each other, their kiss deepening and their hunger for each other building.

"Get a room," someone shouted from across the street. That was enough to snap Maggie from the hypnotized heat and remind her she was in fact still in the middle of a New York City sidewalk. They pulled apart and Maggie wondered if maybe she *was* imagining some of what she had brought up. She wasn't sure. The only thing she was sure of was the fact that she needed to be on top of Aidan as quickly as physically possible. So they walked the rest of the way to the parking garage, paid for Maggie's parking, got in her car, and followed the advice that the stranger had screamed at them.

A few weeks had passed and Maggie's life hadn't gotten any less chaotic. Work had a major event coming up that had all hands on deck and was taking up most of her time. Classes were kicking her ass and she wasn't sure where she was going to find the time to get all of her assignments done. Happy hours with her friends were still a struggle to coordinate and Maggie still had the nagging feeling that Aidan was pretending she didn't exist when anyone else was around.

He still had never gone to a group happy hour with her and he still never gave her a second glance when they were on campus in a group of people. Maggie wasn't looking for a relationship by any means, but with how intimate they had been, she had to admit to herself that his denial stung. So, she did her best to focus not on his denial but her own. Until she couldn't any longer.

It was Labor Day weekend and Maggie was finally excited to have a long weekend. For once, she needed a break from all of the things she had been using to distract herself. She just wanted to go to the beach, tan, drink, and enjoy the sound of the waves crashing. Aidan and Maggie had gotten a hotel down the shore for the long weekend, and it was the first time they were going to spend more than a few hours together.

Her work day was coming to an end and they had already decided she'd skip her night class so they could head down the shore early. Her bags were in her car and Aidan was planning on meeting her at their usual corner with his stuff. She shut down her computer, grabbed her purse, and told her bosses to have a great weekend. This was the most excited she'd been about something in a while. The excitement felt different from the numbness she normally forced upon herself.

As she walked to meet Aidan and saw him on the corner, she couldn't help the smile that spread on her face.

"Hey hot stuff!" she shouted at him once she was close enough. He turned and without warning she jumped up, wrapping her legs around his waist. He dropped his duffel bag and caught her effortlessly. He held her by her thighs and they were nose to nose as she whispered, "Remember the first time you held me in this position?" Maggie could have sworn Aidan growled as his eyes flashed with the memory. He tipped his mouth to hers and kissed her, more intimately than usual. It was almost tender.

"Well would you look at these two," a voice called from behind her. She knew that voice but couldn't quite place it. It would seem that Aidan had, though. Just as quickly as he had caught her, he released her. "What are you two up to that we don't know about? Apologies for interrupting" the voice called again as Maggie stumbled backward from the impact of being dropped so suddenly. She was shocked. Caught off guard. Embarrassed. She turned around after finally stabilizing herself and saw Jack and Max walking their way.

"You weren't interrupting anything," Aidan replied coolly. Maggie almost got whiplash from how quickly she turned her head back to look at Aidan. Was he serious right now?

"Mhmm, sure we weren't. Whatever. Are either of you interested in heading to the bar with us? Celebrate the long weekend?" Jack asked. Maggie was about to answer, but Aidan beat her to it.

"I can't man. I've got a thing I have to get to. Wish I could though," Aidan answered scratching the back of his neck. Maggie's jaw almost dropped from the shock. He was seriously going to deny their plans that blatantly. In front of her. What the actual fuck?

"I get it, I get it. What about you Maggie? You're always in for a good drunken night," Jack turned to her. Maggie was still staring at Aidan. She could see in his eyes the panic that maybe she wouldn't play along with his omission of the truth. That stung more than she expected. Slowly, she turned to face Jack and Max.

"I wish, but I have to get... home," she said, unable to come up with another lie as she stood there feeling embarrassed and slightly disoriented.

"Bummer. Have a good weekend, though. I'll see you on Tuesday night in elections class," Jack said as he walked past the two of them. Aidan turned as they walked past them, waving them off. When they were finally a good distance away he turned back to face Maggie. She was standing there with a look on her face that he had never seen before.

"Look Maggie–"Aidan started to say.

"Get your shit and let's just go. I wanna get there before it gets dark," Maggie cut him off and stormed past him. He grabbed his bag and jogged a few paces to catch up to her.

"Are you seriously going to be pissed right now, Maggie? Don't ruin our weekend away," Aidan grumbled as he picked up his pace to keep up with her.

"Pissed? I'm not pissed. Why would I be pissed?" she replied, tension rolling off of her.

"Maggie, stop," Aidan said, grabbing her arm and stopping her before he continued. "Why are you so mad right now?" This time Maggie's jaw did drop at the sheer audacity he had in asking that question. If there's one thing men had in spades, it was the fucking audacity. She stared at him a moment, failing miserably at calming down before she spoke again.

"What the fuck was that, Aidan?" she asked, trying to buy herself more time to muster up a calmer response.

"What was what?" he replied. Yeah, that wasn't helping her calm down.

"Why am I mad at you right now? You really want to know? Maybe because for weeks I've been trying to show you exactly how you deny my existence when we're around literally anyone we know. And you've denied that, telling me I was exaggerating or making it up. Maybe it's because I almost ate shit in the middle of a New York City sidewalk in front of my friends because you dropped me the moment someone we knew came around. Maybe its because I now get to drive in a car for at least two hours with someone I currently want to punch in the fucking face. Any of those reasons good enough for why I'm mad at you?" Maggie was on the verge of shouting by her last sentence.

"Why are you making something out of nothing right now? So what if I clammed up in front of our friends? I'm fucking shy alright," Maggie barked a sarcastic laugh and rolled her eyes as he continued, "I don't like people in my business. Fuck those guys. Don't ruin our weekend just because of that, please," he said, leaning towards her. Not this time. Maggie was not going to let him distract her with his touch this time. She pulled away as she pulled her arm from his grasp and turned back around.

"Well I hope you're shy enough to keep your mouth shut for the next two hours because there's not a single fucking part of me that wants to hear your voice right now," she said as she continued her march to the parking garage and heard his footsteps follow. She paid for her parking, they got in her car, and they drove to the Jersey shore in complete silence.

They had made good time on their drive. By some miracle they didn't hit any traffic and got to their hotel with enough time to check in and change before heading to dinner. The drive also gave Maggie enough time to quell her anger slowly but surely. By the time they were walking to dinner, she was starting to doubt herself. Maybe he was right and she was overreacting. But the way he had dropped her was so mortifying. Why couldn't he see or acknowledge what she was talking about?

As they waited to cross the street, Aidan reached for her hand and she finally let him interlace their fingers.

"I'm sorry for embarrassing you," he said, turning her to face him. "I really didn't mean to, Maggie. You need to know that." Maggie didn't know how to respond, and luckily the light changed so they could cross, saving her from having to come up with one. Maybe she was overreacting. It was the first time they had been caught by friends. Maybe it was reasonable that he froze like that. Maybe she was making something out of nothing.

Her anger continued to dissipate throughout dinner as she convinced herself he was right. She was just making a big deal out of nothing. She was exaggerating. By the time they got back to the hotel room, she was ready to start this weekend the only way they knew how. The same way their entire situation had started that night in the bathroom.

After that first night, their weekend had gone wonderfully. Maggie had to admit that it was nice being away with each other. She had packed the mint bathing suit from that party and decided to wear it the next day. Seeing her in that bikini raised the exact reaction she had hoped for. They didn't leave the hotel room until well after lunch.

Everything was back to exactly how she liked it with Aidan. They could joke and share intense looks. They could banter and scratch the surface of each other's lives. They could exist amicably.

On their last night before heading home, they sat watching the sunset together. He was seated in the sand with her in front of him, her back to his chest. The breeze on the beach had picked up, so Maggie had a towel around her shoulders that she pulled tightly across her chest. Maggie had always loved the sunrise and sunset, especially over the water. It was always so beautiful—the different colors the sun could make depending on whether it was rising or lowering. A perfect example of how darkness could be eclipsed by beauty on both sides.

Although she loved both, sunsets were always admittedly her favorite. The blends of oranges and pinks and purples reminded her of her favorite flower: birds of paradise. Her mom's favorite flower. Just like that for a moment she had let her guard down and the sadness spilled through her broken cracks straight to her core. The grief paralyzed her momentarily, causing her to stiffen against Aidan's back.

"Everything okay?" he asked, feeling the way she had tensed. No, it wasn't okay. Maggie wanted to feel anything else right now. And that's what Aidan had always done best for her: distract her. She couldn't acknowledge the pain that coursed through her so she denied it instead, asking Aidan to do what he did best.

In response to his question, she slid her hands down her chest to his thighs and used her thumbs to run small circles along his inner thighs. She could feel him start to harden at her touch and that eased her a bit. This. This is exactly what would do it. He would help her pretend she didn't hurt. He would numb the intensity of her pain as he always unknowingly had. Aidan slowly took the towel from around her shoulders and draped it across their laps like a blanket.

"It's still a relatively crowded beach, Maggie. You'll need to be quiet unless you want us to get caught. Understand?" Maggie nodded against his chest. Her only response before he slid his hand down the front of her body and under the towel and into her bikini bottoms. As he began working his fingers into her, he slowly worked his other hand around her, joining his first under the towel. She let her head drop back onto his chest as her breathing hitched. He worked the fingers of one hand in and out of her as the fingers of his other circled her clit with the exact amount of pressure he knew she liked.

They had done this so many times at this point, that he knew exactly how she liked him to move. He knew her body like the back of his own hand. He knew exactly what to do and it wasn't long before the pain that had just lanced through her was only a memory and she was instead now filled with lust. Lust had always been the easiest way to deny any of her other feelings. She could feel herself close as she turned her head slightly to whisper up to him.

"How about we finish this in the hotel room?" she asked quietly. Her eyes were closed, but she could feel him nod his agreement. Slowly he pulled his fingers from her and slid his hand up her body, dragging them slowly up her stomach and chest. It only made her want him more.

They walked hand in hand back to the hotel, both ready to release the tension in their bodies that they had created on the beach. They were waiting to cross the street, Aidan smiling at her when he noticed something behind her and immediately dropped her hand as if it were made of hot lava. Caught off guard, Maggie turned to see what could have caught his eye.

At first she didn't notice anything. She scanned their surroundings until she finally caught it. Not too far away but far enough she almost missed it. A few people they went to school with were packing up a car after spending the day at the beach. Her disappointment was overwhelming. It would always be the same with them. She would use him to deny the rest of the shit in her life and he would always deny her. Deny knowing her. Deny any of their intimacy. They were the physical embodiment of denial–both using the word in different ways.

The light changed and she started to cross the street wondering why he couldn't just let other people see them together. She couldn't figure out why this denial bothered her so much. It didn't just bother her, it infuriated her. Denial started to feel wrong for once, leaving a sour taste in her mouth.

They walked the rest of the way to the hotel in silence. Once they got to the room, Aidan turned around and pushed her against the closed door. He began showering her body with kisses. It would always be like this for them–only ever behind closed doors. As he worked his mouth down her body, she couldn't help but think about the numbness that came paired with denial. His touch, which usually roused her, felt cold now that she had accepted how it was for them. How he would always deny knowing her this intimately in front of anyone. How he would deny that he did so any time she brought it up.

The longer she thought, the more numb she became to his touch. She barely noticed when he picked her up and her body just automatically knew where to wrap her legs. She barely registered him carrying her to their bed while simultaneously untying her top. It was only when he had slid off both of their bottoms, put the condom on, and was about to slide into her that she froze. She put a hand to his chest stopping him and it was only then that he looked at her. She wasn't sure what expression he saw, but she saw his confused look.

"When we get back, will you please come to happy hour with our friends? With me? In a group?" the question felt pitiful coming out. But, she needed to see the extent of his denial. He looked at her for a long moment. Finally, he leaned down pressing a gentle kiss to her lips.

"Of course," he answered. For a second her heart skipped at his agreement. She hadn't expected that. When he pulled back up and she looked into his eyes, she could see it. The emptiness in the promise. He was lying.

Then, he slid into her as she accepted his lie and her truth. With each thrust, she began to release the only tether they had to each other–their denial. Her numbness was no longer a welcome friend. She had spent too long now hiding and denying away everything she should have been feeling. Seeing Aidan's final denial of her woke her from the coma she had chosen. The numbness wasn't working anymore. The distractions had worn off. And most of all, she didn't like the way denial felt.

As he continued to work his way in and out of her, she decided this was the last time. She didn't think she deserved much, but she knew she didn't deserve this. This was it for them. She would say goodbye to what had become her favorite distraction to numb the intensity of her pain. This would be their last night together.

And tomorrow? Tomorrow, she would finally wake up and live those first few blurred moments of bliss, where her mom was still alive and her entire existence didn't hurt. And then, when the fog wore off and she remembered and the grief started to settle on her chest, she would let it. She would feel it. She would allow the hurt to seep into everything and she would do her best to face it.

Would she survive it? She wasn't sure, but anything had to be better than what she had let encapsulate her entire being. As Aidan worked to send them both over the edge, and as she came, she came to the realization that she was tired of numbing out. She was tired of chasing these highs in order to stop feeling her lows. She would give herself this one last night of respite from the pain she had kept at bay these last few months. From everything she had ignored.

Tomorrow she would face it. Tomorrow she would feel again.

Anger

Playlist

Angry / Paravi

July / Noah Cyrus

Broken / Isak Danielson

Would've, Could've, Should've / Taylor Swift

Narcissist / Lauren Spencer Smith

3

Anger

It had been almost two months since Maggie's last night with Aidan. So far, she had mostly stuck to the decisions she had made that night. She ended whatever it was they had been doing on the drive back to the city. He didn't seem particularly surprised. In fact, he didn't seem very affected at all. She cut back on her drinking. She forced herself to feel the pain when it came, rather than using anything and everything to deny it.

As she did this, though, she learned that she could in fact feel even more miserable than she had ever thought possible. It felt like everything was attached to a memory of her mother. Maggie constantly felt like she was on the verge of a breakdown. Like at any moment something would send her emotions over the edge and she wouldn't be able to contain them like she used to.

This is exactly why when Rosa suggested they take up kickboxing on the weekends, Maggie jumped at the opportunity. Maybe being able to beat the shit out of a punching bag twice a week would be a healthy outlet for her emotions. At least she could hope.

As she strapped on her gloves for their very first beginner class, Maggie was ready to work it out. The class was not at all what she expected. There was a lot more moving and a lot less punching in the first portion of the class than she had thought there would be. She castigated herself for not working out more these last few months. Her legs felt as if they might actually fall off at any moment. When had she gotten so weak? She used to pride herself in her strength, but right now it felt like she was falling apart–not just physically either.

Finally, in the last twenty minutes it was time to practice some buddy work on the bag. Naturally, Maggie and Rosa paired up and Maggie let Rosa go first while she held the bag. This part of the class felt a little less structured so they used it as an opportunity to chat quietly and catch up. Maggie wanted to hear all about how Rosa was doing at work and what new projects she was taking on.

It was time to switch and now it was Maggie's turn to take her shots. She followed all of the instructor's tips and form descriptions and had at it. After her first three jab cross combos, Rosa's eyes widened.

"Okay Captain America, please remember the goal isn't to rip the bag here," Rosa joked as Maggie continued. Maggie laughed quietly but continued to focus on using this time to blow off some steam. She focused all of her hurt, her exhaustion, her frustration, and her resentment into her punching combinations. As if sensing something more was going on, Rosa for once stayed quiet and let Maggie do whatever it was she needed. Before Maggie knew it, the instructor was calling everyone back for a final cooldown and stretch.

Maggie had enjoyed that. It felt good to have a place to take out the feelings she forced herself to acknowledge every day.

"So you want to talk about it or not?" Rosa asked as they grabbed their stuff and walked to the parking lot.

"About what?" Maggie asked, not entirely sure what she was alluding to. The list of what she could've been referring to was endless after all.

"About your 'hulk smash' moment at the end of class there. There was a lot more behind those punches, Mags," Rosa clarified.

"There's nothing to tell Ro. I was just really into it, that's all," Maggie did her best to deflect.

"Bullshit Mags," Rosa refused to accept that half assed answer. "We haven't talked about what's going on with you in a while. How are you doing? What's been happening?" Her questions were grating. This is what the kickboxing was for. She didn't need to sit there and talk it out afterwards too.

"There's not much to tell," Maggie shrugged.

"Mags, fuck that. You're gonna have to do better than that. Give me something here. It's me," Rosa pushed.

"What do you want me to say, Ro? You want me to break down in the parking lot of a kickboxing studio because my mom is dead? Because I can see how she's missing in every aspect of my life every second of every day? Or because I broke the heart of a fucking phenomenal man? And that may forever be one of the worst things I've ever had to do. Or do you want me to go into how I proceeded to fuck myself silly with an utter piece of shit of a human in an attempt to deny what was happening in my life? Or would you like to hear about how every single day is fucking exhausting? Aching in a way I can't fix. There's no medicine I can take and all I do is carry it day in and day out and watch people carry on with their happy little lives while I'm stuck in this fucking nightmare. Is that what you want me to talk about? Is that what you want to get into? Is that fucking good enough for you?"

Maggie hadn't realized just how much she unloaded until Rosa nodded at her.

"There she is. There's my pissed off, mildly insane, I can carry it all by myself best friend. Anything else you'd like to unload in your misdirected rage?" Rosa said, smiling. Maggie couldn't help but think about how infuriating it was to have a best friend who knew you that well and loved you even more.

"Fuck you. And I'm sorry. You didn't deserve that. You did deserve that 'fuck you' for calling me insane, though," Maggie finally conceded.

"Bitch, you are insane and you know that. Plus, I said mildly. Want to grab some brunch and unpack some of that shit you've been keeping pent up in that brain of yours? I promise to just listen and keep all of my comments to myself," Rosa said, crossing her heart.

"Ro, I've known you for eight years and not once have I seen you be able to keep a comment to yourself. It's not in your nature. But yes, I really want to have brunch with my best friend. You're one of the few people I don't have to worry about tip toeing around. You get me. I can have blow ups like that and you know it's not about you. I appreciate you, even if you are a total pain in my ass," Maggie huffed in concession.

"And what a beautiful ass it is," Rosa winked. Maggie rolled her eyes playfully pushing her best friend as she led the way to their cars and brunch.

🌱 🌱 🌱

"Ho. Ly. Fuck. That was a lot," Rosa finally said after letting Maggie spend the last forty minutes unload some of the details she'd been carefully omitting from the last few months. Maggie had to admit that it felt good to finally let someone else in on the intricate web of mayhem and destruction that her life had become.

"Yeah," was all Maggie said in response, pushing around the breakfast potatoes on her plate. It had been a lot to carry on her own. And although she was still carrying the brunt of it, it felt good to have someone else at least *know*.

"Okay. First, you know I absolutely love you, right?" Rosa asked.

"Right," Maggie answered warily.

"Okay great. And you know it is never my intention to hurt you, right?" Rosa continued.

"Of course, Ro. Jeez, where are you going with this?" Maggie said.

"I just have to make sure because I am definitely about to say some shit that is probably going to hurt. But, you know if I'm anything, it's honest," Rosa continued. "Mags, I'm so sorry you didn't feel like you could tell anyone all of this, especially me. But now that I know, I have thoughts."

"What happened to keeping all your comments to yourself?" Maggie teased.

"I did keep my comments to myself–*while* you were talking. Now it's my turn for all of the comments," Rosa answered. The only response Maggie offered was rolling her eyes, so Rosa continued, "So, Aidan may have been a dumb mistake and an asshole, but I'm glad at least one of us was getting laid." Maggie threw the straw wrapper she'd been playing with at Rosa. "Okay, okay. Seriously. Aidan wasn't the end of the world. Sure, maybe it wasn't your most responsible choice or proudest moment, but you saw what you were doing and you saw how he was treating you and you ended it. That's some big girl shit! The pain you feel every day is entirely valid. You lost your *mom*, Mags. Your best friend. She was amazing and didn't deserve to go so soon. Fuck, I miss her and she wasn't even *my* mom. You'd be a robot to not hurt from that kind of loss." Maggie felt her eyes start to sting as Rosa continued, "But as for Kam... You're a fucking idiot and if I didn't care about you so much, I'd slap you for what you did to that man. I think that was a mistake you'll regret for the rest of your life. Why did you do it? That's one of the few things I don't understand from everything you just told me. Everything else makes sense to me given your situation, except that," Rosa finally finished, waiting for Maggie's response.

Maggie had no clue what to say. She had already admitted so much to her today, she didn't feel like admitting more. How do you tell your best friend who still looks at you with so much love and hope and caring and understanding that you feel like permanently damaged goods? That even on the good days, the only thoughts that rattle around your brain are how broken you are, how worthless you are, how no one will ever love who you've become.

"I just... I just couldn't handle it. I don't know. I'm still trying to make sense of it, honestly," Maggie offered in hopes it would be enough. The answer was partially true at least. By the look on Rosa's face, Maggie could tell she wasn't entirely buying it.

"We're revisiting the Kam thing at some point, but I'm glad you finally talked to me about all of this. Mags, you can't keep all this to yourself. You'll fucking explode," Rosa said, half sympathizing and half scolding.

"I know. I know. I'm just... I don't know how to share this shit until I'm absolutely forced to," Maggie said to her best friend with a sad smile. She had learned from a young age to hide the pain. To deal with everything herself. Relying on others wasn't in her wheelhouse.

"You know he's local now, right?" Rosa asked Maggie.

"What? Who?" Maggie had no clue what she was talking about.

"Kam. He's living with Jeff for a little while to see how he likes it here and to maybe even move to the city eventually. He's been here for like two months. I wonder what in the world could have motivated him to move closer," Rosa clarified. Maggie's throat went dry. Kam still called her once a week. Maggie never answered. She wasn't sure if it was the guilt that kept her away or the fact that she knew she'd let him in again if he tried, and she couldn't handle hurting him. Not again. But he was local now. Living with their mutual friend. Maggie wondered how Jeff had never mentioned it. She'd talked to him so many times. They'd even gone out a few times over the last month. What the fuck?

"Wait, how do you know this?" Maggie asked. She couldn't help but notice the guilt that crept into Rosa's expression.

"Well… I maybe, kind of still keep in touch with Kam," Rosa said, dragging out her response.

"Ro! What?!" Maggie shouted, drawing looks from the people seated near them.

"Okay, okay. I knew you two weren't really talking anymore. But Kam and I had kind of become friends. We bonded those first few weeks we spent supporting you and he's a really good dude. I figured this whole break you two were taking wouldn't be permanent. You always find your way back to each other. So I thought it wouldn't hurt to just maintain that friendship. It's not like we're besties or anything. We just update each other from time to time. He does make sure to ask about you any time we talk, just saying," Rosa admitted. For once, Maggie was speechless. This was the last thing she expected to hear today.

"Ro, I am *begging* you to please drop this. I'm glad he's here because he always talked about it. But, it wasn't for me. And even if it was, it would've been fruitless. I am no longer a part of his life. I plan on keeping it that way. If you want to keep that friendship, that's your choice and I'd never stop you. Please stop pushing this with me," Maggie emphasized those last words.

"Ugh. Fine. I don't believe that, but because you actually asked for once, I'll drop it. For now," Rosa answered. "Listen, I hate to have to leave, but I've got to help my mom with something, so do you mind if we grab the check and pick this up again some time later this week?"

And there it was again. The stabbing pain Maggie would feel when people talked about their moms. How could something someone says in passing so casually hurt so much? Would she ever be able to handle it? This was a good reminder for why she had left Kam's life. If her best friend helping her mom knocked the wind from her, how could she even consider spending forever with Kam and a family like his? A family not marred by death or pain. A family where they loved and laughed and still do so much together. She was right in leaving that day. She couldn't make him endure her pain. She wouldn't.

"For sure," Maggie nodded stiffly, once again keeping everything to herself.

"Amazing, thanks! Also, before I forget. I've decided to host a Halloween party at my house! Relive the old party in the garage glory days for a night. You have to come, obviously. After your night class of course. You're in, yeah?" Rosa said in parting.

"Garage party glory days? Of course I'm in," Maggie smiled. Trying to figure out what costume to wear would be a great way to temper the anger that was growing within her.

🌱🌱🌱

A few days later, Maggie was seated at the back of the room in her political science class refreshing her computer like a maniac and dressed like a cat. She couldn't imagine a more ridiculous scenario.

It was Halloween and she'd be going straight to Rosa's house after her night class, so she did what any other college senior would and spent the entire day in her costume. Her cat costume wasn't the most brilliant thing she had ever come up with, but it got the job done. She found herself in black jeans and a black boat neck, three quarter sleeve top. She pinned a black cat's tail to a belt around her waist to slightly enhance her bare bones costume. And then, in the most sophisticated of ways, she used black eyeliner to draw on a cat nose and whiskers.

She had spent the entire day like this. Her commute into the city. Her hours at work. And now, sitting in this classroom, retaining none of what her professor was saying and instead focusing on obsessively refreshing the screen in front of her.

Although Maggie had ended whatever had been happening between her and Kam just over six months ago, she had heeded his one constant request of her. She had finally finished all of her post grad applications. It had taken all of her effort, but she knew life would not stop just because it felt like hers had ended. So, she needed to at least have some options for after she graduated.

When she submitted her final application, Maggie decided that she was tired of making decisions. After submitting four post grad service applications, Maggie was certain that she would let the universe decide her future for her. Whichever post grad opportunity accepted her first, that would be what she would do and where she would go.

Which is exactly why she now sat in her night class fervently refreshing her screen. This was her fifth class with this professor and she had made sure to let him know ahead of time that she might be a bit more checked out than usual and why. Of course, the night of Halloween was when she would be getting the first response to one of those applications. She sat there dressed as a cat waiting to see whether or not her future had been decided yet.

Although Maggie had no clue what she actually wanted her future to look like, she did know it would involve service work. Service had become a major tenet in her life and she felt like she owed the world. She wanted to help people. Her mom had always been a giver and she wanted to continue that legacy.

As Maggie refreshed her screen for what must have been the fifty-fourth time, it finally changed. Staring back at Maggie were giant block letters that read, "REVIEW YOUR APPLICATION DECISION NOW." She had been waiting for this and yet actually clicking the button felt terrifying.

With one steadying breath, she dragged her cursor over the words and clicked. As the page loaded, her breath hitched. Then, as she read, "You've been accepted," she couldn't stop the smile that crept across her face.

"Fuck yeah!" Nor could she apparently hold back the words she shouted in the middle of her professor's lecture. He looked at her with an amused smile. He congratulated her on whatever she had been accepted to and asked her to give him an update at the *end* of class.

Of course this acceptance had each part of her future on a different page. She knew she had been accepted, but to do what and where were still unknown. Maggie clicked to the next screen. And the next. And the next.

On the final screen she finally had all of the pieces of the puzzle to what lay ahead. And so, it was in the back of a random fifth floor classroom and dressed as a cat, whiskers and all, that Maggie learned what her life after graduation had in store.

An hour and a half later, Maggie found herself in Rosa's driveway. She was equal parts excited and nervous to tell her best friend the news. She knew Rosa would be pumped for her, but she also knew it would be another goodbye. They had just gotten each other back, and now she would be moving away. Even so, Maggie knew this was what she was doing. Sure, she could turn the offer down, but she wouldn't. She had committed to letting fate decide for her and it had spoken.

As she walked down the driveway toward the blaring music coming from the garage, her phone began to buzz. She looked down and saw her brother calling. She had called him on the drive to Rosa's house because she figured he should be the first to know and then Rosa should be the second. She didn't think about who she had naturally wanted to tell third.

"Hey!" she answered.

"Yo. Sorry I missed your call. What's up?" her brother replied.

"So, I got a response on my first post grad app," she told him hesitantly. Her brother had been aware of her commitment to just go wherever she'd been accepted first and supported her choice–even if it wasn't the most enthusiastic support.

"And?" he prompted curiously.

"I was accepted!" Maggie yelped, dancing in her spot.

"Amazing sis! What will you be doing?" he asked.

"High school guidance counselor!" she offered.

"Awesome! That's exactly what you wanted, right?" he sounded excited.

"Yeah!" she replied.

"Where?" Her brother's final question made her nervous. Although she had been excited about her placement job, it was her placement location that had thrown her off. She honestly hadn't even remembered listing it as an option.

"Well..." she drifted in response.

"Mags. Where?" he prompted.

"...The Las Vegas Valley," Maggie said uncertainly. She waited for her brother's reaction. At first the line was quiet. Then, all she heard from the other end was an eruption of laughter.

"You? Of all people? In Vegas? That's ridiculous! Well, at least we all know you hate gambling!" he finally answered in between laughs.

"Glad to see you'll miss me," Maggie grumbled in response.

"Sis, come on. You know I'll miss you and if it were my choice you'd stay in Jersey forever. But Vegas? That's wild. Who even *lives* in Vegas?" he attempted at comforting.

"Apparently I will. Listen, I just got to Ro's for her Halloween party. I can barely hear you over the music. I'll call you tomorrow and we can laugh about my new location some more."

"Okay, Have fun! Love you sis," he said.

"Love you, too," she said before finally hanging up. Her family had never been a "love you" family. Until her mom got diagnosed that is. A cancer diagnosis has a way of highlighting the fragility of time and love. So they became a hugs, kisses, and "love you" kind of family. And once their mom had died, Maggie and her brother had committed to saying it more and more. Smiling gently at their goodbye, Maggie finally made her way the last twenty feet to Rosa's garage. Taking a deep breath, she went inside and greeted the party already raging before her.

"Look at all these fucking delinquents in one place," Maggie shouted jokingly as she walked through the garage door.

"MAGGIE!" everyone shouted back and she laughed in response. Maggie looked around, taking stock of who was there and who she would prefer to avoid. As she did so, Rosa came over with two drinks. Of course Rosa would have a drink waiting for her.

"Ro, you are seriously too good for me," Maggie said as her best friend handed her a red solo cup.

"Oh, I know it. Not sure why I stick around," Rosa said playfully. "You've already missed the flip cup tournament, but I'm sure we could start a new round if you really want to play."

"It's fine. I'm just here for my amazing best friend," at this, Rosa shimmied ridiculously and smiled broadly, "and to have a good time." Maggie could already tell she would have to wait until tomorrow to tell her best friend her news. Rosa was clearly a few beveraginos in and it would be a waste giving her the life update now. She looked around and saw that she recognized most of the people there. They had all mostly gone to high school together. Maggie was hoping everyone had drank enough that no one would want to get too deep into her life. She couldn't deal with the condolences and check-ins right now. She didn't want to. All she wanted for tonight was to have a damn good time.

Although the majority of the party was in the garage, Maggie found herself inside Rosa's house waiting for the bathroom and ready to move on to her next drink. She wasn't exactly sure what number drink this would be, but since she was sleeping at Rosa's did it really even matter?

"Those whiskers really suit you. It's almost like you were born with them or something," she heard someone say as she leaned against the kitchen counter, waiting for the bathroom to free up. She looked to her right and saw someone she didn't recognize coming to join the bathroom line. She couldn't deny that he was handsome. He was taller than her by at least a few inches. His eyes were a gorgeous hazel that had flecks of blue in them and stood out starkly against his deep, golden skin. His hair was close cut and she could tell it was freshly done with how crisp each line and fade was. She wasn't sure whether it was his looks or the whiskey, but she was intrigued by this stranger nonetheless.

"Mmmm. I do wish I could say these were natural but that would make me a liar. All fake, unfortunately," Maggie whispered the last sentence with mock seriousness. Her stranger played along, feigning surprise.

"I would have never been able to tell," he said.

"Oh, from far away it's hard to tell, but if you look really closely, it's clear as day. Fakes," Maggie said pointing to her drawn on whiskers as someone exited the bathroom, signaling her turn.

"Maybe at some point I'll be able to get a closer look," the stranger flirted as Maggie walked into the bathroom and locked the door behind her. She couldn't help the lazy smile that crawled across her face. She also couldn't help but admit that the flirting felt good. When she walked back out of the bathroom her attractive stranger was gone.

ᛉ ᛉ ᛉ

"You know I love you, right?" Rosa said as she wrapped her arms around Maggie's waist with a euphoric smile that only a drunken stupor could create.

"Obviously. I love you too, Ro," Maggie responded, wondering if it wasn't too early in the night for the drunken professions of love to begin. As her best friend snuggled deeper into her side, she couldn't shake the random glances of her bathroom stranger. "Question. Who is that playing beer pong with James?" Maggie tried to ask nonchalantly. Naturally, drunk Rosa swiveled her head in the most obvious maneuver possible.

"Oh that? That's Gabe! Hi Gabe!" Rosa shouted, waving one hand at the stranger who now had a name while the other clung around Maggie's hip. Maggie felt the blush that crept up her neck and rooted itself in her cheeks. Of course she couldn't rely on drunk Rosa to be any bit discreet.

"Ro, how do we know Gabe? I don't recognize him," Maggie said as she tried to get Rosa to focus.

"Oh, you don't know Gabe! At least it would be weird if you did. He went to my college. He graduated with me and I found out my last semester he lived in our area so I invited him," Rosa said as if it were the most obvious thing in the world. Maggie looked over at where Gabe stood playing with their friend James. Again, she couldn't deny how attractive he was. She had always been a sucker for a man with beautiful eyes and a great smile, and right now he was giving her both. Apparently although drunk Rosa couldn't figure out how to keep her voice down, she *could* notice how Maggie was checking Gabe out. "Wait, do you think Gabe is hot? Yes! This is perfect! Come on," Rosa drunkenly exclaimed as she dragged Maggie over to the beer pong table.

Fuck. Maggie knew she was about to be embarrassed as hell and there was simply no escaping it. She figured best case scenario this wouldn't end miserably. Worst case scenario and she could just blame Rosa's drunkenness.

"James, go away. Gabe has a new partner to play with now," Rosa said, shooing James from his spot. She continued, "Gabe, this is Maggie. Maggie, this is Gabe. You're both hot and could probably use your hotness to win this game or something. Enjoy!" Rosa finished turning on the spot and walking away before either of them could say anything else.

For a moment, Gabe and Maggie just looked at each other. After a split second they both started laughing hysterically. Gabe handed Maggie one of the ping pong balls and as she took it from him, she decided that tonight would be a great night. No matter what.

🌱 🌱 🌱

An hour and five consecutive beer pong wins later, Maggie found herself pressed between Gabe and the outside of Rosa's garage. In the middle of a sloppy, drunken kiss, Maggie pulled back to catch her breath. As she did so, she noticed something that made her laugh involuntarily.

"What?" Gabe asked, smiling.

"Remember when I said the whiskers were fake? Well, it would seem that you now have ridiculous black smudges on your face from my painted on nose," Maggie chuckled. He laughed in return leaning toward her to continue what they had started.

As they made out, Maggie couldn't help but think about how easy it would be to just leave with him. Spend the night with him. Let loose and just see what happens. Yes, it would be easy. But how would it feel? She couldn't help but think that leaving with him would just revert her back to the kind of shit she would do with Aidan. She didn't want to go back to that.

As these thoughts crossed her mind, someone began to open the side door of the garage–the door they had been making out next to. As the light filtered through the doorway into the dark night, Gabe and Maggie pulled apart abruptly and did their best to seem nonchalant. As if they had merely been chatting on serious topics out here. The snort James let out after looking at them, told them they had failed miserably in the nonchalance department.

"I'm out of here Maggie. It was good to see you, though! It was nice meeting you Gabe! Maybe we'll see more of you around here," James said, winking. He walked away and Maggie loosed a breath she didn't realize she'd been holding in. It slowly turned into a laugh again.

"Gabe, this has been..." Maggie was at a loss on how to finish her sentence.

"Phenomenal? Life changing? Ground breaking?" Gabe offered.

"Fun," Maggie supplied, rolling her eyes and laughing. She continued, "But I think this is where I should call it a night. I'm not really doing one night stands right now or planning on dating anyone, so I don't want to give you the wrong idea here."

"Who said that was what I was after?" Gabe asked her.

"I'm pretty sure my smudged kitty nose all over your face is some pretty solid evidence," Maggie joked. He laughed in reply. "Seriously, Gabe. It's been fun, but I'm going to tap out here and go check on Rosa. It was *really* nice meeting you," Maggie said as she started to walk away.

"Wait! Can I at least have your phone number?" Gabe asked hopefully. She turned to look at him. She wasn't dating. She wasn't looking for a fling. She definitely didn't have much she could offer him at the moment, so she was about to find an excuse not to, but…

But, the way he was looking at her–as if getting her phone number would be like winning the lottery–tugged at her heart. So, she took his phone, plugged in her number, and turned to go find Rosa. So what if she was also smiling like a fool as she walked away? That didn't mean a single thing.

🌱 🌱 🌱

Maggie woke up in Rosa's bed surrounded by french fries. Because of course at 2 AM the only thing they could drunkenly think about was feasting on a lifetime supply of french fries. Maggie rolled onto her side to take a look at Rosa and immediately started cackling.

Maggie had done her best to change her drunk best friend the night before, but Rosa had not been a willing participant. Which is exactly why Rosa was currently asleep in her bra, sheer tights, and a unicorn headband. She had one false eyelash still on and one off, and her lipstick had somehow managed to get smudged all the way to her eye.

"Can you fucking not right now," Rosa groaned as the bed started to shake from Maggie's laughter.

"I'm sorry. I'm sorry. You're just quite a vision right now," Maggie managed to contain her laughter long enough to respond. "I'm hungry so I'm going to pop over to the bagel shop. Do you want the usual?"

"Hmph," was all Rosa could muster as she rolled over, so Maggie assumed that was a yes. Maggie wiggled herself off the bed, threw on some sweats, and made her way downstairs. Thankfully, the house was relatively clean since most of the party had stayed in the garage. She was not looking forward to cleaning that later, but that was a later problem. Maggie grabbed her car keys and focused on her current mission. Bagels and coffee.

Twenty minutes later, Maggie was about to walk through the front door when she noticed a box on the porch. Using her many years of experience as a woman carrying a million things at once, she juggled the iced coffees, bagels, and mystery box as she unlocked the front door. When she walked through the main hallway and into the kitchen, she froze and almost dropped the coffees at the ridiculous sight before her.

Rosa hadn't bothered to handle her eyelash or lipstick situation before coming downstairs. In fact, all she had done was throw on a hoodie, which meant she was still in the sheer tights she had worn under her skirt last night. This meant that Maggie had a full view of most of Rosa's ass as she leaned over the sink, drinking water straight from the faucet.

Once again laughing like a fiend, Maggie kicked Rosa in the butt gently and started to unload everything she was masterfully carrying.

"Everything. Cream cheese. Tomatoes. Just how you like it," Maggie said, handing Rosa her coffee and bagel.

"An angel amongst mere mortals," Rosa said in exaggerated praise. "What's that?" she asked, nodding at the box Maggie had placed on the table.

"No clue. It was on your porch when I got back so I just brought it in," Maggie answered. Rosa paused her attack on her bagel to check the box.

"Mags. It's addressed to you," Rosa puzzled. That didn't make any sense. Who in the world would send something to Maggie at Rosa's house? Weird. Maggie got a pair of scissors and started to open the box. When she finally managed to get through the tape and the secondary box inside, she pulled out a beautiful bouquet of sunflowers. Maggie and Rosa exchanged a confused look. They both looked into the box again and noticed the card at the same time. Maggie prayed she would get to it first as she reached to grab it.

Of course not. Even hungover, Rosa's curiosity bested Maggie's reflexes any day. Rosa snatched the card before she could, pulling it out of its little envelope.

"Maggie," Rosa read from the card, "It was so great meeting you. Hoping these flowers light up your day like your laugh lit up my night. -Gabe" Rosa gaped at Maggie. "Did you suck him off or something Mags?"

"Ro! Why do you have to be so fucking crude all the time?" Maggie slapped Rosa's shoulder.

"Because I love seeing you blush and squirm," Rosa teased. "Seriously, though. Why is this man sending you flowers less than twelve hours after meeting you? What did you do to him?"

"We legit only made out Ro. I swear. I cut it off before we could take it any further and gave him my number. That's when I came and found you and tried and failed to get you changed for bed," Maggie told her best friend as she grabbed the card from her hand. She read it again to herself. She hadn't noticed her smile until Rosa commented on it.

"Oh fuck me. I am too hungover for this right now," Rosa complained.

"For what?" Maggie replied.

"For whatever that smile means. For whatever this shit between you and Gabe is about to be. I need my bagel. I need my coffee. I need to not puke. And, *we* need to clean the garage," Rosa ranted.

"Ro, this isn't going to be anything. I told him that last night. The flowers are just nice is all," Maggie answered, only half believing her own words.

"Yeah, sure. We'll revisit this later. Preferably when I'm not so hungover I'm knocking on death's door," Rosa said and took a bite out of her bagel. Maggie nodded her agreement as she went to open her own bagel, slipping Gabe's card into her pocket. The flowers were just pretty. That's why she was smiling. No other reason.

Two hours later, Maggie had done the brunt of the cleaning while Rosa did the brunt of the complaining. Luckily, the garage hadn't been left in too much disarray. It was mostly just collecting garbage and moving things back into place.

As Maggie washed her hands in the kitchen sink, she felt her phone buzz in her back pocket. She dried her hands and checked her notifications. She had two texts from an unknown number.

Hope you liked the flowers. I tried to find ones as pretty as you but realized that was impossible.

Followed by:

Any chance you're free to have dinner tonight? I'd love to take you out and talk some more.

Maggie smiled down at her phone and heard a groan from the doorway.

"Ugh. Let me guess. Gorgeous Gabe has finally put your number to use?" Rosa asked.

"What?" Maggie asked, a little flustered.

"Your smile," Rosa answered. "It's the same as the flowers smile. So I feel like it's safe to assume that flower man is the one texting you right now." Maggie knew it was futile trying to argue with her, so she just nodded and shrugged. Rosa looked at her for a long moment before she started talking again. "Listen Mags, you're my favorite person on the planet and I love you so much. But I know you and I know that smile. Although Gabe is absurdly attractive and charming, aren't you kind of avoiding this kind of thing right now? Doesn't this feel like a bit much for a guy you just met *last night*? It feels weird to me that he's already sending you flowers. I don't want to be a party pooper. I just want you to really think about this, especially after everything you opened up about a few days ago."

Maggie nodded at her best friend. Rosa wasn't exactly wrong. She had been actively avoiding men at the moment. But hadn't she told Gabe last night that she wasn't dating or anything right now? She had been clear. So maybe he wasn't expecting very much out of this either.

If Maggie was being entirely honest with herself, she was tired of feeling alone while everyone around her wasn't. It was easy for Rosa to point all of this out when she was constantly surrounded by her family and the friends they had gone to high school with. Maggie had started to feel more alone than ever these last few weeks. She barely crossed paths with her aunt because of their opposing work schedules. It was getting increasingly harder to see any of her friends who were either busy with new jobs or just as stressed as her about graduating.

If she were being honest, she kind of wanted someone to talk to and text. Someone to see here and there. She definitely wasn't looking for anything long term or serious. But, it would be nice to have someone she could text when she felt like it. She'd make herself clear with Gabe again and make sure he understood all of this before continuing too far.

They were beautiful, thank you. I've already got plans today. How about tomorrow night?

She looked down at the text she had sent him. She would make her intentions clear. She would make sure to tread carefully. She was moving to Vegas in a few months after all. There was a very clear expiration date to whatever they would do. Plus, it was just one dinner. What could it hurt?

It was with that mindset Maggie headed to the restaurant Gabe had picked. It couldn't hurt to be honest with where she was at and see what he thought of that in response. She was happy that he had picked one of her favorite restaurants. At least she knew she was in for some amazing food. When she got there, late as usual, he was already waiting at a table.

"I'm so sorry I'm late," Maggie said as she sat down.

"No worries. I'm just happy you came," he smiled at her. She liked his smile. Not only were his teeth immaculate, but it also felt warm. Real. It was the kind of smile you couldn't resist. It made you smile in return. So she did.

"I should warn you, I'm kind of a hot mess and tend to be late to life," she said as their waitress came over. She immediately recognized Maggie-she was a regular here after all. Knowing exactly what Maggie liked and typically ordered, she quickly took Gabe's order and then went to check on her other tables.

"I don't mind," Gabe answered once their waitress had walked away, "Someone like you is worth waiting for." The cheesiness of it almost made Maggie roll her eyes, but she didn't want to make fun of him just yet. They still didn't know each other well enough.

"I absolutely love this place," Maggie said across the table to Gabe.

"I know," he said. He tensed as if he hadn't meant to let that slip.

"What do you mean?" Maggie asked, angling her head slightly in confusion.

"I may or may not have asked Rosa what some of your favorite places were," he answered sheepishly. "Which brings me to this," he said as he lifted something from the corner of the table and handed it to her. It was a book. One she had been meaning to buy for weeks now.

"What-" Maggie started before he interjected.

"I thought flowers twice in one weekend might be too much, so I also asked her what else you liked. She mentioned you'd had this book on your TBR for a while now. I figured it would be better than another bouquet," he answered, tapping his fingers nervously.

Where had this guy come from? How was he already so considerate? She looked him over once more, a bit more thoughtfully this time. He was just as attractive as she had remembered, but this kindness and care enhanced the effect his looks had on her. She nodded and smiled again, more fully this time.

"This is amazing, thank you," she finally said. At her response, she could visibly see his nerves ease. She noticed how much she enjoyed being able to calm him. How much she already cared about putting him at ease. She wasn't sure what collision course had set him on her path, but she decided at that moment she was really curious to see exactly where it would lead.

Dinner went perfectly and Maggie was really doing her best to find any flaws she could in this man. The entire evening he had been funny and smooth. He listened attentively to everything she said and gave thoughtful responses. He had taken everything she said about what she was going through and how she wasn't looking for anything serious right now like a champ. He said he was okay with simply seeing how things go and deciding as they move forward. He was extremely kind and respectful to the servers, covered the entire bill, and tipped them *really* well. You could tell a lot about a person based on how they treated restaurant staff. He was doing everything right and she spent most of the night waiting for the other shoe to drop.

After they were done eating, they decided to walk in the park that ran along the river's edge across the street from the restaurant. This park was part of the reason Maggie loved this restaurant so much. She loved coming here afterward and watching the headlights of the cars driving on the highway across the river. There was something soothing about watching the chaos that was happening across the river from the quiet calm of a bench at the park.

"So I have to ask you something, and I don't want you to take it the wrong way," Gabe said as they took a seat on her favorite bench.

"Oh boy, here we go," she joked.

"Do you have any flaws? I've spent almost the entire night trying to figure it out. You're beautiful and smart and funny and kind and resilient and giving and a great friend. What is it? Really bad toe fungus or something? I need to know," Gabe asked.

Maggie couldn't help the snort she replied with. She was very far from perfect. Sure, Gabe had mentioned some of her best qualities, but he still didn't know her well enough to know all of her worst ones. The bad far outweighed the good. Eventually, he'd grow to be as disgusted by her as she was with herself.

"I could ask you the same question, sir. Here's this attractive, warmhearted, generous, funny guy, who took me to my favorite restaurant and brought me a *book*. How am I not supposed to swoon?" Maggie did her best to deflect.

"Oh, this is just me showing off. You'll see I'm not as amazing as this first date would have you believe. Sure, I may be all of those things, but I also have a terrible snore," he joked. "So there's my character flaw. What character flaw does the perfect Maggie have?"

If only he knew all of the answers she could give. There would be no second date after that. She searched for anything to say but the truth as she stared out over the river. She looked for a joke response like the one he had offered. Nothing came to her. She finally turned her gaze from the river and looked at Gabe. The way he was looking at her made her still. The look in his eyes. Their rawness. Their openness. As if she could say anything and he could handle it. So she gave it a shot. If he ran for the hills, so be it. She wasn't looking for anything beyond some companionship at the moment anyway.

"I'm broken," she started at a volume just barely above a whisper, turning back to the river. "I'm broken, maybe beyond a point of any repair. My grief has consumed me, chewed me up, and spat out the mauled pieces. I don't think I'll ever be the person the world used to know before my mom died. I don't think I'll ever be able to put myself back together. I don't think a whole version of me will ever exist again." As she finished, she sighed at the truth she had just spoken into the world.

She waited for it. For him to make up some excuse and make as swift of an exit as he could. Who would want to stick around after that brutal level of honesty? Especially after only one date. She felt his hand wrap around hers and she couldn't contain her surprise as she looked at their interlaced fingers. He used his other hand to tilt her face toward him, bringing her eyes to his. She looked into them and was overwhelmed with the gentleness she saw. The understanding.

"Maggie," he said quietly, "that doesn't make you any less perfect. It just makes you human." She took a breath, overcome by his words. Then, he leaned in and kissed her. A tender kiss. One that felt full of promise and patience. One that made Maggie wonder if someone could potentially tolerate the broken person she'd become. Not love. She'd given up on that a while ago. She couldn't expect anyone to love her when she didn't even love herself. Maybe Gabe could offer her something close enough to it. With that thought and with his kiss, she felt a small glimmer of something she hadn't felt in months: potential.

The holiday season flew by in a blur. In November, Maggie got a chance to meet Gabe's parents while she joined him in some of their favorite holiday traditions. They were good people, but she never felt entirely comfortable around them. They clearly came from old money and that set Maggie on edge. It made her feel like an outsider who would never be good enough for their son.

His parents had never given her any reason to feel this way. They had always been welcoming and warm. For anyone on the outside looking in, it looked like they loved the girl Gabe had brought home. Maggie couldn't wash it off, though, the feeling of falling short of the kind of person their son deserved.

The more she learned about Gabe, the more perfect he continued to feel. He had an amazing job, which meant he never let her pay for anything. He had recently gotten an apartment in the city which was immaculate. Maggie had started spending more and more nights there because of how much time it took off of her commute. His roommates–who were also some of his best friends–were awesome and she loved being around all of them. He was always surprising her with some small gift or bringing lunch by her work. It all felt too good to be true. Like she had stepped into some cheesy Hallmark holiday movie and she was finally getting the small town guy who treated the female lead like treasure.

They spent December strolling the various holiday markets that popped up around New York. They drove around looking at Christmas lights and tried new restaurants every week. He treated her to all of it. He told her she deserved it for how happy she made him.

He had even gone as far as making her an advent calendar out of books. Twenty four books he had taken the time to pull from her TBR pile, wrapped, and left at his apartment for her to open each day. He joked that it was his way of selfishly making sure she had to come over every day. She couldn't ignore it. How cared for he made her feel. She couldn't help but realize that he made her feel like maybe her life wasn't entirely fucked. Like maybe she wasn't a lost cause after all.

༊ ༊ ༊

"Guess who has two thumbs and just got all As on every single one of her finals," Maggie said, spilling through the front door of Gabe's apartment.

"Hell yeah!" she heard his roommates shout back from the living room as she walked over to where Gabe was standing in the kitchen. She got up onto her tiptoes to kiss him and noticed he tasted like peppermint and chocolate.

"Any chance a girl can get in on this hot chocolate action here? Tastes delicious," she winked playfully at him. Gabe smiled at her and went to grab another mug.

"I'm proud of you, Maggie," he said as he turned away.

"I'm just happy I can relax and try and enjoy the holidays now," she sang in response as she hopped up to sit on the kitchen counter. "I'm a little sad we won't be able to see each other more, though."

"I know, but my family takes a trip for the holidays every year. It's tradition," he said, coming back to where she had propped herself. "But seriously, congratulations. One step closer to graduating cum laude. Glad I could help make it happen," he said, planting a smiley kiss on her lips. Maggie's brows furrowed.

"What do you mean?" she asked.

"By what?" he said, tilting his head.

"You said you were 'glad you could help make it happen' about my final grades for the semester. I don't get what you mean," she said.

"Oh, well... I mean obviously *you* did the work itself. I'm not taking that away from you Maggie. But, be honest with yourself. Would you have been able to do it without me?" he replied. At first she thought he was messing with her, but when he turned back to her with the mug of hot chocolate he had just made, she could tell he was absolutely serious.

"Gabe, I'm the one who did the work. These grades are my own. This accomplishment is mine," she said slowly. She tried to work through what he could've meant.

"Well yeah, Maggie. You did the work itself. But how much time have you saved by staying with me here instead of commuting all the way to your aunt's house? And how much more have you been able to focus without stressing about money since I make sure to pay for everything? You can't deny those things didn't play a role in this." She teetered between offended and shocked. She had always taken pride in what she accomplished given her circumstances. How could he sit there and try to take some of that away from her?

"Are you serious right now?" she couldn't help the question.

"As a heart attack. Maggie, you would not have been as successful without my help. I can't believe you don't see that," he said, clearly frustrated. Well, Maggie was frustrated too. What bullshit was he on right now?

"Gabe, there is no denying that the time and money you have helped me save have been valuable. But I need to be clear, I would have been this successful with or without you. I had already done it before you came into my life. I appreciate all you give and do for me, but I did this on my own. I need you to understand that.

It's important to me that you do–accomplishing things even with everything that's happened in my life is important to me. I've never needed anyone and although I care about you and you've definitely made my life better, I did not need you to get these grades." Maggie saw his eyes narrow ever so slightly. Was he really upset about this?

"I understand," was all he said, more tersely than she'd ever heard him speak. She gave him an uncomfortable smile. She really didn't want this to turn into an argument. They hadn't had many so far but of the ones they had, Maggie already knew that Gabe had a tendency to overreact on occasion.

He looked at her for a long moment. Then, he turned away before continuing, "I understand that you like your independence. You like to accomplish things on your own and you like that feeling of success." As he spoke, Maggie could feel herself relax. He got it. He understood her. "I learned that about you early on Maggie. But what I never noticed until now apparently, is how ungrateful you are," he continued as he poured the hot chocolate he had just made for her into the sink.

She felt her muscles tense and her throat tighten. She swallowed. She couldn't figure out why this was turning into such a big deal.

"And," Gabe continued, "how delusional you must be. How could you *actually* believe your pitiful self could have gotten those grades without the extra help." The words felt like a physical blow. He had never spoken to her like this. He had never used anything but kind words to describe her before. He had always sympathized with her and built her up. Pitiful? Did he really think that?

"Gabe–" she tried to insert.

"I'm not done Maggie," he said before she could get more than just his name out. "Sure, you're relatively smart for a pretty face, babe. You've obviously shown that you can handle some shit situations. But what do you really think you're capable of on your own? How good do you really think you could be?"

"Good enough to get perfect grades," she finally interjected. She wasn't going to stand for this bullshit. How dare he speak to her like that?

"Oh really?" he almost purred. She couldn't help but think he may have been getting some satisfaction out of her hurt. "Is that what you actually think? Be honest with yourself. We both know the truth. The things you whisper when we're alone in bed. How you'll never be good enough. How you're a disappointment. Don't you remember?"

"I'm good enough to do this," Maggie said breathlessly as a single tear fell down her cheek. He was using her own words against her. Late night confessions she had given him in moments of vulnerability. She was almost too stunned to believe it.

"Oh! Interesting. Well, if that's the case then you'll also be good enough to make your own hot chocolate. And buy your own dinner tonight. And for that matter, since you don't need me at all, how about you find somewhere else to sleep tonight?" he said, his voice like ice.

Maggie was startled into silence. They had small arguments before. Gabe had overreacted to a few irrelevant things over the last few weeks, but this was entirely different. He had never been so mean to her. So cold. So indifferent to her feelings. She had no clue what to say, so she didn't. She slid off the counter and put her jacket back on. As she was about to walk out of the kitchen, he grabbed her by the wrist and spun her back to face him.

"Maggie, don't bother coming back here until you understand your place in my life. Until you're ready to stop lying to yourself and finally admit that you've never been good enough to do anything without some help. Especially mine," he finished, releasing her and turning to walk to his bedroom. She stood there frozen for a few moments. After a few steadying breaths, she grabbed her bags and headed back the way she came. She ignored his roommates and half ran down the stairs to her car.

She had no clue what to do. How had something so simple spiraled so out of control? In the comfort of her car, she let her tears fall freely. What the fuck was that? Gabe wasn't like that. He wasn't cruel or malicious. He wasn't conceited and mean. She had no clue who she had just dealt with, but it wasn't the man she had grown so fond of these last few weeks.

She also had no clue where to go. She had been staying with Gabe more and more these last few weeks that going back to her aunt's house didn't feel right. She didn't want to scare her aunt by being there when she got home from work late.

"Think Maggie, think," she said to herself. The more she thought the more upset she got. She was angry at him for speaking to her like that. She was sad about not being able to celebrate with him tonight. She was frustrated by feeling like she had nowhere to go. She was angry at herself for not knowing what to do right now. She looked out of her car window and up at his apartment. She froze when she saw him standing in the window with a smug smile on his face. He knew she wouldn't know what to do.

Maybe he was right. Maybe she wouldn't have been able to do this on her own. Look at her right now. She had no clue what to do and where to go. Maybe she did need him more than she had realized. The longer she looked at his smug smile, though, the angrier she got. How fucking dare he? She refused to concede. To let him win. So wiping the last few tears from her face, Maggie turned on her headlights, put her car in drive, and pulled out of her parking spot.

She knew she wasn't done with Gabe, but she also knew she couldn't handle seeing him again tonight. He had hurt her and she needed space. She had no clue where she was driving to but that was something she would figure out as she went. She could figure this out. She had to.

Forty minutes later, Maggie found herself parked in Rosa's driveway. Other than her aunt's house, she had no idea where else to go. She wasn't ready to deal with Rosa's questions, but she also couldn't sleep in her car. She grabbed her bags, breathing deeply and prepared to put on an act. She racked her brain for any excuses for why she'd need to spend the night here. As she walked across the yard to the front door, Maggie thought she saw a car she recognized parked out front. It couldn't be, though. Impossible. She unlocked the front door and started making her way to the kitchen where she was almost always guaranteed to find Rosa.

"Honey, I'm home," Maggie did her best to shout in a sing-song voice she prayed sounded happy.

"Fuck," Maggie heard Rosa say in a half shout, half whisper. Weird. Maggie had no clue what that could be about. And then, as she stepped into the doorway of the kitchen, she realized exactly what that *fuck* had been about.

She looked into the kitchen and saw Rosa and Kam sitting at the table having *tea* of all things. What alternate universe did she just walk into? The shock hit Maggie like a lance through the heart. Maggie had known Rosa and Kam stayed in touch. Rosa had mentioned it enough to make certain of that. She had never thought they actually got together. She sputtered as she tried to find anything to say to them. Anything to recover from the endless shock of tonight. She tried and tried, but both Rosa and Kam took one look at her and shot to their feet. They spoke at the exact same time.

"What happened?" Kam asked.

"Mags are you okay?" Rosa panicked. As the initial shock of seeing the two of them together began to wear off, she realized what they were reacting to. Her. She hadn't thought to look in the mirror before getting out of her car. She had collected her emotions, but she hadn't collected herself. In the reflection of the dark window across the kitchen, she got a peek into what they were seeing. Her hair was a complete mess. Her eyes were puffy, nose red, and cheeks still tear stained. Her mascara was a lost cause. To summarize, she was a total fucking mess.

She took a breath. She needed to say something but had no clue what. She had mentally prepared herself for Rosa but not for Kam. They all stood there and stared at each other. Not a word coming from anyone for a few moments.

"Mags, what happened?" Kam asked again. Her eyes shot to his. She could see his concern–even after what she had put him through. She was reminded once again of how much she didn't deserve him. Gabe's reminder of how she would never be good enough clanged through her. She felt the hurt of it all constrict around her heart. She couldn't manage to speak as the live wire of emotions she was feeling smothered her. Rosa walked over to her slowly. Almost as if she were afraid any sudden movements would scare Maggie off.

"Mags, are you okay?" her best friend said softly while putting her hands on Maggie's shoulder. Maggie's eyes finally moved from Kam to Rosa. She took a deep breath.

"I need somewhere to stay tonight," Maggie said meekly. Kam looked at her with an expression she had never seen from him. It was a mix of confusion and pain and a hint of...anger? She had had enough of anger for tonight. So she looked back at Rosa.

"Of course," Rosa answered immediately. "But are you okay Mags?"

"I'll be upstairs," was all Maggie said before turning around and walking back the way she came and up the stairs. She set her things in the corner of Rosa's room and just stood there. Tonight had been too much. It was as if her brain couldn't compute everything she had heard and seen and felt. Maggie wasn't sure how much time had passed as she just stood there letting her thoughts bounce around her brain like a pinball machine. Eventually she heard two sets of footsteps coming up the stairs. She heard a knock on the door but didn't bother answering. Only Rosa came in, closing the door behind her. Maggie turned around and saw her best friend standing there smiling gently. Lovingly.

"Talk to me Mags," Rosa almost whispered. It was her tone that finally made Maggie break down. The tenderness. The caring. The *love* inherent in Rosa's voice. Maggie closed the distance between them, flung her arms around Rosa, and began to sob. She started to crumple to the floor and Rosa moved with her, softening her fall.

"It'll never be enough will it?" Maggie managed in between sobs. "No matter how hard I try. No matter what I do. No matter how long passes. No matter anything. It'll *never* be enough," Maggie sobbed and raged as Rosa rocked her gently.

"What won't be enough?" Rosa asked, her voice pained as she watched her best friend shatter all over again.

"*Me.*" It was the saddest word Maggie had ever uttered. She saw it now. How her life wasn't the problem. She was. She continued to sob as her best friend held her, stroking her back soothingly. She sobbed and sobbed, finally showing Rosa every ounce of frustration and pain she had been holding onto.

They sat on the floor of Rosa's bedroom for a long while. She wasn't sure what she would do in the morning. She wasn't sure what the point of any of it was anymore.

She was sure of her anger, though. She hated this life of hers. She hated her choices. She hated the loss that had ruined her. She hated her brokenness. She hated herself.

She sat there sobbing and raging at her own self loathing. She was so wrapped up in her own rage, she failed to realize the love of the best friend in front of her. Had Maggie taken a moment to step away from her anger, she would've seen the love in Rosa's eyes and felt it in her gentle touches. Had she taken a moment to listen closely, she would've heard the quiet sobs on the other side of the door. The cries that matched her own in frustration and pain. She would've heard the caring in those cries. And, she would've heard the footsteps that led that love back down the stairs, out the front door, and away from her.

Maggie had already been awake for hours before she felt Rosa stir. She had spent the entire morning thinking about last night. About how a night she thought would be so joyful could turn out so terribly. She couldn't stop thinking about letting Kam see her so distraught and the pain she was still causing him.

Even more, though, she couldn't stop thinking about Gabe and everything he had said to her. Although his timing and intentions were cruel, she couldn't deny there was truth to some of what he had said. She had said most of it herself already. He had simply parroted her own words back to her. She was broken. She was constantly disappointing those around her. She wasn't good enough anymore. Maybe before her mom died she had been but not anymore. Not this new monster she had become.

She had no one she could be mad at anymore. No one but herself. She felt the freshness of this anger. The realization that this was entirely her fault settled into her. She was the one fucking everything up.

Maggie's thoughts were interrupted by a knock on the front door. A few moments passed before Rosa got up and she heard the front door open.

"What do you want, Captain Douche Nugget?" she heard Rosa say.

"Is she here?" she heard Gabe's voice. She sat up abruptly. She hadn't expected him to come looking for her. She had already planned to go back to his apartment later today. This twist of events took her entirely by surprise.

"Depends on what you want," Rosa answered. Her best friend. Always so fierce and so protective.

"I just want to talk to her, please, Rosa," he pleaded.

"Try testing out what you're going to say on me first and then I'll let you know if she's here," she heard Rosa fire back. Maggie took a steadying breath. She knew this would go nowhere, so whether she wanted to or not, it was time to face their blowup from last night. She grabbed a hoodie and made her way downstairs.

"Ro, it's okay. I'll talk to him," Maggie said gently from the bottom of the stairs. Rosa turned to look at her, surprise flashing her features. Maggie hadn't told Rosa much. All she had managed to tell her after her breakdown was that her and Gabe had a fight. No specific details. After doing one more look over Maggie, Rosa finally turned back to Gabe.

"Fine, but I'll be right down the hall in the kitchen if you need me. Handling knives. Very sharp knives," she said, flexing one more time at Gabe. Maggie couldn't help the small smile that flashed across her face. Her tiny protector. It was almost comedic. Almost.

As Rosa turned to walk toward the kitchen, Maggie moved the final few feet to the doorway. She grabbed a jacket from one of the hooks on the wall and stepped outside, closing the door behind her. Gabe looked over her entire body, finishing with her face. She could see the sorrow and regret in his eyes. It must've matched her own.

"It looks like you got about as much sleep as I did last night," Gabe finally said after a long stretch of silence. She watched the cloud his breath created in the cold air. His words swirling as he spoke them. She didn't say anything, though. She wasn't entirely sure where to begin. He stared at her a moment longer before dropping his forehead to hers.

"I'm so sorry," he whispered. "I didn't mean any of it. I've just been so stressed at work and dealing with some shit. I have no clue what came over me. You know I think you're absolutely perfect. You're smart and funny and gorgeous. I was an ass. I overreacted to something that didn't warrant any reaction at all." He waited for her to say something. Anything.

"I know," she finally said. "And... I'm sorry too. You weren't entirely wrong about *everything* you said. I shouldn't have pushed it when we were both clearly getting upset. I didn't help the situation either." At her response he took a deep breath and visibly calmed. She still loved being able to be the one who put him at ease. It made her feel like she was actually doing something right for once, rather than screwing everything up as usual.

He leaned forward and planted a gentle kiss on her lips and then leaned down far enough to rest his head on her shoulder. It was only with his head down that she noticed the messy lump on the porch swing behind him. She tilted her head trying to make out what it was. Her movement brought him back to the moment and he followed her gaze.

"Oh yeah, that..." he said sheepishly. "I wanted to do something nice for you, but I may have done it in the messiest way possible." He walked away to pick up whatever it was and brought it back to her. Maggie looked it over. There were books and fake flowers and plastic leaves surrounded by tissue paper and ribbon. For the life of her she could not figure out what it was meant to be. She quirked a single brow at Gabe. He shrugged.

"It's supposed to be a book bouquet. I saw a video of one and thought it would be perfect. Apparently, they don't just sell them. I had to get all the stuff and put it together. I tried my best to make it look like a bouquet, but clearly my creative best didn't work." She looked at him and the lump in his hands and laughed. It was so ridiculous. She could imagine him trying to put this together and the image of it was almost too much. She laughed even harder.

"Your best was absolutely perfect," she said, placing a gentle hand on his cheek. He leaned into her touch. "Listen, I need to go back inside and talk to Ro. After breakfast with her, I'll pack up my stuff and head over to your place. Maybe we can just have a chill movie day or something? What do you think?"

"That sounds like the perfect Saturday," he said. He looked into her eyes and she could see that he really did care about her and he really was sorry for what he had said and how he had acted. He pressed a single kiss to her forehead before turning and heading back to his car. She watched him walk away and was overwhelmed by his care for her. He had cared enough to come find her. He had cared enough about hurting her that he wanted to make it right. He didn't care that she was broken and messed up and damaged. He tolerated her, flaws and all. And really, wasn't that all someone like Maggie could ask for?

Maggie walked back into the house with Gabe's attempt at a book bouquet and a goofy grin on her face.

"Absolutely not," Rosa's voice snapped Maggie back to reality. She looked up and saw Rosa fuming from the kitchen doorway.

"What?" Maggie questioned.

"Absolutely not Mags! You can't be serious right now! That man said whatever he said to you last night that made you *that* upset... upset enough to feel the need to escape to my house and breakdown... and all he has to do is show up here with a nice smile and whatever the fuck *that* is... and you just forgive him? Just like that? Absolutely not," Rosa seethed.

Maggie understood where Rosa was coming from. Rosa had always felt a fierce desire to protect her. She was seriously overreacting here, though. She was making a big deal out of what was probably just Gabe and Maggie's first real argument.

"Ro, I get where you're coming from. But really, it was nothing. We had a fight. Couples fight all the time. It was our first real argument and now we know what to expect when we disagree on something. He said some things he shouldn't have, which he didn't even mean. And I escalated the situation by bickering. It's not like he hit me or something. We just made each other... mad. And then my mad turned to sad, that's all. Really," Maggie explained.

Rosa took a few steps toward Maggie. The look on her face was a mix of rage and disbelief.

"Mags, you shouldn't be around people who make you feel that way. You shouldn't let anyone make you feel the level of hurt you felt last night," Rosa tried to reason.

"People hurt us all the time, Ro. You're seriously making this a bigger deal than it needs to be. Come on, people fight all the time," Maggie replied, exasperated.

"Kam would never have made you feel that hurt. Not even in an argument," Rosa flung back at her. The comment stung and Maggie had to take a breath to keep herself from raging at her best friend.

"Well, Kam isn't here. He–" Maggie started.

"He would be if you let him," Rosa interrupted Maggie before she could continue. "I still don't fucking get it Mags. You have an amazing person who would treat you like the sun shines out of your ass and instead you're bouncing around with these losers who hurt you more and more. I love you so much, but it's fucking infuriating to watch. You say you don't want a relationship and then you end up in these situationships with these random guys anyway. Guys who are clearly making you hurt more than you already do. It doesn't make any sense to me. The Maggie I know would never tolerate this kind of trash," Rosa insisted.

"Well, then maybe I'm not the Maggie you know anymore." The words were out of Maggie's mouth before she could stop them. She saw the moment they landed. Rosa took a step back as if

Maggie had physically struck her and stared at her in stunned silence. When Maggie didn't offer anything else, Rosa nodded and turned to walk back into the kitchen without another word.

Maggie grabbed her stuff from Rosa's room and walked out to her car. She turned it on and blasted the heat. She stared at Rosa's house. How did she manage to ruin everything? Maggie used to be a hurricane of joy and light. Now, it seemed all she brought everyone around her was pain and ruin. She hated herself for what she had said to Rosa. She hated herself even more for how much it hurt her. She hated herself most for being too afraid to own her actions and apologize.

"Fuck!" Maggie shouted slamming her hands against the steering wheel. "Fuck! Fuck! Fuck! FUCK!" she raged. Maybe that was all that was left of Maggie after everything she had been through. Maybe her entire life had reduced her into one festering bout of rage. Maybe this was all that she could offer the world these days. With that final thought, she put her car in reverse and pulled out of the driveway.

Maggie had learned early in her grief journey that celebrations were the hardest for her. Holidays. Birthdays. Anniversaries. Really, anything that got a big group of people together. Christmas it seemed would be no exception.

Maggie came from a huge extended family and they always got everyone together on Christmas Eve. It was tradition. Normally, Maggie would have been the one helping with all the planning and cooking, but this year she barely had the desire to show up.

It wasn't the idea of being around a big group of people that she dreaded. Maggie had conquered that struggle back in April. She knew how to turn on her personality to give everyone the life of the party they loved to see. If only she had pursued an acting career earlier she would have been damn good at it.

No, it was the relationship dynamics she'd see in this particular group. It was her family after all–aunts, uncles, cousins. She knew that one of the times she was struck with the most pain was when she would watch her cousins with her aunts. It was hard watching them laugh and joke and hug. The joy they would naturally bring to each other. The kind of joy and warmth she'd never have again. No matter how much family she had. No matter who loved her.

It also didn't help that watching her cousins with their moms–her aunts–reminded her of that day back in April when she saw Kam's mom and sister dancing in the kitchen. The day she decided for good she needed to leave them. To let them live their lives without her. They stood a better chance at happiness without her around.

Needless to say, Maggie was dreading Christmas Eve dinner at her aunt's house. She knew she could turn on the smile she'd need to force, but did she have the stamina to maintain it?

"What are the chances you want to stop somewhere so we can get some beers before we get there?" Maggie asked her brother who was driving.

"I'm down. We're already late anyway. What's ten more minutes? Isn't there a shop right by their house?" he answered.

"Yeah. I can run in and grab them," she offered. His little "hmm" was all he needed to do to show he agreed. Maggie turned to look back out the passenger window into the dark night. The sun set so early in the winter, she felt like she never saw the light anymore. Or maybe she was just projecting.

❧ ❧ ❧

"The party has arrived!" Maggie and her brother shouted as they walked through their aunt's front door. They held up the case of beer and the handle of Johnny Walker they had bought on a whim and were welcomed with a chorus of "hey!" and "hell yeah!" It looked like they had arrived just in time for the traditions to start.

First up was the tradition where everyone walked around "breaking bread." It was a Polish tradition they had done every year for as long as Maggie could remember. Everyone gets a piece of a wafer that's been blessed and you walk around wishing each other well for the coming year. Once the wishes have been shared, you break off a piece of each other's wafers and eat. Maggie came from a large family, so this part tended to take a while.

Normally, Maggie didn't mind this tradition. As she had gotten older, the wishes became more comical. She would get wishes for lots of money or to find a good man. This year, though, it took all of her strength to sit through. While her other cousins still got the somewhat silly wishes, Maggie noticed hers had become more serious and somber. Her aunts and uncles were wishing for her to find peace and healing. They wanted her to be happy and strong. *Blah blah blah.*

Maggie almost rolled her eyes at their wishes. The tears that sprang into some of their eyes. What did they know about her happiness and strength? What did they know about her peace and healing? Bullshit. She couldn't stand their tears. Their attempt at consoling. She needed this shit to end and quickly.

By some miracle, Maggie made it through her last few family members without exploding. Next it was time for them to all sit around the table for the prayer. After prayer, they would eat the traditional Christmas Eve dishes and then it would be time for presents. Maggie and her brother already agreed that they wouldn't linger for too long after gifts were exchanged.

Maggie was surprised by how quickly dinner passed. Some of her frustration had even started to melt away at this point. All she had to do was get through gifts and she was in the clear. She decided to check her phone before gathering around the gifts with the others. She only had two notification, one of which was a text from Gabe:

I know parts of tonight might be hard for you, but you've got this. I can't wait to see you when I get back.

She couldn't help her smile. It was sweet of him to check in on her. Her smile faltered slightly when she saw the other notification. She had a missed call from Kam. Weird. He had stopped his weekly calls back in November. She started to wonder if there was anything she should worry about, but her thoughts were interrupted by one of her cousins. Melany looped her arm through Maggie's elbow and dragged her off into the living room. Maggie only needed to survive presents. She could do this.

꙰ ꙰ ꙰

Maggie found out a half hour later that she could in fact not do this. It was too much being in such close quarters with everyone. Seeing their smiles and their genuine happiness. It felt wrong. She knew she shouldn't be, but she couldn't help being angry with all of them. Or not really with them, but with the time they still had.

With the moments they still got. With the memories they still had the chance to make.

She could feel her anger starting to boil over and the smile she had plastered on start to falter. Her patience was thinning and she wasn't sure how much more she'd be able to take.

It was at that very moment, while Maggie felt like a pot that was on the verge of boiling over, that one of her aunts walked over to her with a gift.

"Your mom bought this for you. She wanted to save it for your graduation, but I thought you might want one more Christmas gift from her." Maggie's entire body seized and she felt as if there was no air left in this room. This house. This world. She grabbed the small boxes from her aunt and held them for a moment. She tried to stop the tremor of her hands, but her attempts were futile. She stared at the boxes and after a noticeable pause finally began to unwrap.

Her final gift from her mother was a stunning necklace and earring set. It was exactly what she loved–her mom knew it. White gold with small diamonds. Enough to give a shimmer but not so much to be gaudy. Just how Maggie preferred her jewelry. Her mom must have worked and saved for so long to afford this.

Maggie felt a roaring in her ears and she was overwhelmed by every thought swirling through her. She was suddenly aware of most of her family looking at her. Watching her reaction to the gift. Gauging. She knew she wouldn't be able to maintain the joyful facade she slapped on for her family for much longer.

"It's absolutely beautiful," she finally said with a small, tight smile. "I'm going to go to the bathroom to put them on." Maggie stood on shaky legs, unsure where she was finding the strength to move. Everything hurt. Her grief manifesting as physical pain. She moved as quickly as possible, not entirely certain how long she'd be able to keep herself upright.

She made her way out of the living room, dropping the jewelry in her bag along the way. She passed the bathroom and walked straight through the front door. She stood in the yard still covered in snow from the storm they had been hit by yesterday.

She dropped to her knees and screamed, barely registering the frigid temperature. It was a ragged sound, one that had been clearly repressed for too long. It was full of rage and despair and hopelessness. Everything that now swirled through Maggie on a daily basis. Her mom's last Christmas gift. She dropped her head to her knees, curling in on herself, and screamed one more time.

She didn't hear the front door open and close. She didn't hear the footsteps that came toward her down the stairs. She didn't hear the crunch of snow under someone's feet. It wasn't until she felt someone grabbing her shoulders, moving to pull her up that she realized she was no longer alone.

Her first instinct was to push them off of her. As she tried, their grip tightened and she finally turned to see her brother.

"Let go of me," she raged, trying and failing to get her shoulders out of his grip.

"No," was all he said.

"Let fucking go of me," she shouted in his face. He just looked at her and moved closer. She slammed her hands against his chest trying to push him back and away from her. He only moved closer, tightening his grip. Her rage finally spilled over to a point she couldn't contain.

"*LET GO! LET GO! LET GO!*" Maggie pounded on his chest over and over and over again, repeating the two words until she had nothing left. Until she finally gave up. Until she finally stopped screaming and was left sobbing in her brother's arms as they sat in the cold snow.

For a long time the only sounds were the muffled sobs she pressed into his chest. Until even her sobs became whimpers that eventually turned into silence.

"It's not fair," she said, void of any emotion.

"I know," he replied.

"It's bullshit," she said just as emptily.

"I know," he answered.

"Why do they get to keep their moms and we had to lose ours?" she whimpered, feeling the pain of saying it out loud.

"I don't know," was all he mustered in response.

"She's gone. And I can't help but hate everyone who still gets to have their mom. I resent them and their happy little lives. Because I don't get to call mom or laugh with her or buy her presents. I don't get to live with her anymore. And I'm not sure how I'm supposed to live without her," Maggie finally admitted. She could feel her brother's nod in response. "I'm just *so mad.*"

"Me too," he answered. "Want to go home?" She nodded against his chest in reply. "I'll get our stuff and say bye to everyone. You can just go straight to the car," he said, standing and helping her up in the process. He unlocked his car and Maggie walked across the driveway to get inside. As she watched her brother go back in the house, she couldn't help but think about how grateful she was for him. He understood the hurt of it all. He felt a similar pain to hers. They may not have talked about it often but they understood the burden they shared. He finally came back out with her bag and all of their gifts.

"Let's go home and watch a movie," he said, offering Maggie a small smile. Again, all she could muster in response was a nod. Because his statement had reminded her of another sad fact: she no longer had a home. She had nowhere she could just go. She had nowhere to fall back to and rely on. She had nowhere she belonged. The pain of that realization shattered the last bit of her resolve.

She was tired of living in this bullshit world. She was tired of feeling sad and weak in a life that was tearing her down. She was tired of the tears and the hurt. She was tired of the pain. So, as she turned to look back out the passenger window, Maggie decided she was done with sadness. She was ready to let a new emotion take its place.

The new year came and went and Maggie was ready to get back to work and classes. She was ready for Gabe to come back from his family trip. She was ready to celebrate his birthday. They weren't actually a couple or anything. She had made it very clear she didn't want a label, especially since she'd be moving in July. But they were very clearly *something*.

A week after his return, Maggie felt a shift. She noticed subtle adjustments in the nuances of their interactions. Gabe, normally a very physical person, had been really hands off with her. She noticed he was commenting on her outfit choices more often and how they were fitting. He had brought up more than a few times that one of her resolutions should be more time at the gym. Small comments were made about the fine details of her existence.

Although it bothered her, she didn't read too much into it. They were still having sex after all and mostly enjoying each other's company. Maybe they were just out of the "honeymoon" phase. Maybe this was just them settling into a new routine. She did her best to excuse it all and not let it bother her. Until the night of his birthday party.

"Is that all you brought with you?" Gabe asked as she slipped into the little black dress she had decided on for his birthday party. His roommates were regrettably out of town for his birthday weekend—both on work trips. Gabe had decided he still wanted to have his party this weekend even without them in attendance. They decided to host a small gathering at his place and then he and Maggie would have the entire apartment to themselves the rest of the weekend. It would almost be like a romantic staycation he had told her.

"It's all I have that's party worthy," Maggie replied. "Why?"

"It just doesn't look great, honestly. I've seen you look better," he said plainly. Maggie froze where she was putting in her earring. The earring her mom had gotten her. Her last gift from her mother.

She thought she had curated the perfect outfit. It was a little black dress that she had thought fit her curves perfectly. She had paired it with sheer black tights that had a slight shimmer to them and over the knee heeled boots. Her only accessories would be a gorgeous ring Gabe had brought back from his trip for her and the earrings and necklace from her mom. She thought it was classy and tasteful.

"What's wrong with what I'm wearing?" she turned and asked him.

"Like I said, I've seen you look better. It just looks a little tight. The fit isn't flattering," he said callously. Maggie was taken aback. She was so used to receiving flattery from Gabe that she couldn't tell where all of his recent comments were coming from. She felt a flare of annoyance.

"Well, this is all I have. So unless you'd rather I walk around naked in front of all of your friends, suck it up," Magge said, clearly irritated.

"Damn, calm down. I just didn't want you to embarrass yourself looking like a slob in front of everyone," he said.

"Embarrass myself? A slob? You're fucking delusional," Maggie said, raising her voice. Gabe shot up from where he was sitting on the edge of the bed and threw his shoe down on the ground. The loud, unexpected thump it made caused Maggie to jump. She just stared at Gabe in the mirror where she stood entirely still.

"Never call me delusional," he seethed. "You're the deluded one, remember?" He grabbed his shoe and walked out of the room. Maggie finally let out the breath she'd been holding. She took another long look in the mirror trying to figure out what Gabe was seeing. She thought she looked great. Sure, her dress was a little snug, but it was meant to be fitted. And sure, she knew she had a few pounds she could lose but it was nothing to blow up over.

Maggie took her time putting on her necklace and her boots. When she finally came out of Gabe's room, it was about fifteen minutes before guests would start arriving. She looked out into the rest of the apartment and saw Gabe on the couch, drinking a beer and watching sports highlights. She made her way over to the kitchen and started pulling trays out of the fridge and oven.

They had decided on a low key party with just finger food for people to pick on. There wasn't much to set up, but she still had hoped Gabe would help. She looked over to the couch and could tell from his body language that he had no intention of doing anything of the sort. He was radiating annoyance and frustration.

It was as if her simply being there irritated him. She didn't want to make him more upset on his birthday, so Maggie silently went to work setting up the rest of his party.

The party was in full swing by the time Maggie finally had a moment to breathe. Everyone seemed to be enjoying themselves, so she made her way over to Gabe's side and joined his conversation. He was in the middle of a story with a group of friends and Maggie could tell by his stance that he was about to deliver the punchline.

3… 2… 1… and everyone erupted in laughter. She joined their laughter even though she had only heard the tail end of the story. She wrapped herself into Gabe's side, putting one arm around his lower back and placing the other on his chest. He put his arm around her waist, but his touch felt foreign somehow. She almost felt like he was forcing himself to hold her.

"So, you must be the marvelous Maggie that we keep hearing about on our lunch breaks," someone she didn't recognize said to her. She chuckled.

"It's just Maggie. But yes, that's me. I'm assuming you all work with Gabe?" she asked, extending her hand in introduction.

"That's us. I'm Mark. This is Reyna and Kevin. And this is… actually, I'm so sorry I forgot your name," Mark said as Maggie shook all of their hands.

"Sarah," the final stranger offered as she took Maggie's hand and shook. "I actually don't work with these guys," Sarah offered Maggie in explanation. "I've just known Gabe for a while. We go way back." The way Sarah said this raised silent alarms in the back of Maggie's mind.

She shook it off because she had no concrete reason to be suspicious of this stranger. Who wasn't actually a stranger but a drop-dead gorgeous old friend of Gabe's. An old friend she'd never heard about before. She noted that tidbit in the back of her mind but vowed to leave it alone for tonight. It was Gabe's birthday and she wanted everyone to have a great time. Her curiosity and insecurities could wait.

The conversation continued naturally and Maggie found that she enjoyed Gabe's coworkers. Reyna was extremely interesting. Kevin was clearly extraordinarily intelligent and knew random facts about everything. Mark had to be one of the funniest people she'd ever met. She stuck around their group until she felt obligated to check on some of their other guests. Maggie couldn't help but notice that Gabe's friend Sarah had kept a keen eye on every point of physical contact Gabe and Maggie shared. Strange. She'd made a mental note to ask Gabe about it later.

彩 彩 彩

It was well past 1 AM and the party was finally starting to wind down. Many of the guests had gone home with only a few stragglers left behind. Two of Gabe's friends had enjoyed themselves a little *too* much and were now passed out in one of the spare rooms. Mark and Kevin had also overindulged and were now arguing with Gabe about whether they were sober enough to navigate the subway back home.

Maggie was over in the kitchen packing up leftovers. She laughed to herself as Gabe argued that the two men would probably pass out on the subway and end up riding it all night. As she turned to move a tray from the counter to the fridge, she was startled by Sarah standing right behind her.

"Oh! I'm sorry, I didn't mean to startle you. I just wanted to see if you needed any help," Sarah offered innocently.

"That would be amazing actually. I would love to get this done. Thanks," Maggie replied. As the two proceeded to consolidate plates and cover them up, Maggie felt like this was a great opportunity to learn more about Sarah.

"I have the worst memory. Can you remind me how you know Gabe?" Maggie asked, aiming for casualness.

"We've known each other a while. We're old family friends. Our parents have been friends for ages, and so we got roped into it. I was actually just in Colorado with them," she said sweetly.

"Oh! Do your families do joint holiday trips?" Maggie asked.

"Oh no," Sarah laughed. "It was just me. My family likes to be home for the holidays, but when Gabe invited me I just couldn't resist. His family is just the best, aren't they?"

"Yeah... they are," was all Maggie could say as her brain started spinning. Pieces falling into place and connections being made with the few details she had collected so far. "Listen, do you think you could get this last tray in the fridge for me? I'm going to try and help Gabe in his battle against Mark and Kevin," Maggie said, forcing a honeyed smile onto her face.

"Of course!" Sarah said, grabbing the last tray off the table. Maggie could've sworn that the smile Sarah now wore had switched from sweet to smug. She didn't like the feeling that now coiled in her gut as she walked over to where Gabe and his coworkers were standing.

"Okay fellas, as the unofficial lady of the house, I'm ordering you to stay in the other room. I'd much rather not hear about you two falling asleep on the train and waking up with all your clothes gone," Maggie joked as she pushed the two men toward the other bedroom. Gabe mouthed a silent *"thank you"* to Maggie.

She laughed to herself and continued to usher the two drunk men toward the spare room. After a few minutes she finally got them inside and was headed back to the living room. She froze as she saw Sarah and Gabe at the front door. She couldn't hear them, but the kiss on the cheek Sarah gave him and her grip on his waist as they hugged their goodbye felt too intimate for casual, old friends. As Sarah turned to finally leave, she gave one last smile to Maggie. That smile told her everything she needed to know. That motherfucker. Maggie saw red.

🌱 🌱 🌱

Once everyone had left and their drunk guests were tucked in, Maggie poured two glasses of champagne. It was finally only her and Gabe. She walked over to where he was folding some chairs and handed him a glass.

"To another year. May this one be full of love, *honesty*, joy, and *friendship*," Maggie said, raising her glass. He raised a curious brow at her somewhat strange toast and tone but clinked his glass to hers and drank. Maggie downed the entire flute of champagne in one and then turned and walked away.

"Everything okay?" Gabe asked cautiously.

"Why wouldn't it be?" she replied. "Did you enjoy your party?"

"Yeah… It was really great getting to see everyone. And I'm glad you got to meet everyone you haven't yet," he answered as if he was walking on eggshells. Gabe wasn't sure what was wrong, but he wasn't stupid and he could tell something was bothering her. "Are you sure everything is okay?"

"I really loved getting to meet everyone too! Your coworkers are hilarious. I can see why you love working with them. You know who I found really *fucking fascinating*?" Maggie prompted.

"Who?" he took the bait.

"Sarah," Maggie said. She noticed the small way his hand tensed around his glass. As if she had hit a nerve. Or, had caught on to something she wasn't supposed to know. "Yeah. Sarah was a well of information. I heard your families go way back! Weird that you don't do family trips together. Except for Sarah. Apparently, she gets to come with your family. She told me how much she enjoyed Colorado."

"Maggie—" Gabe started, but Maggie wasn't done and her anger was only growing the more she looked at him.

"Do you really think I'm that fucking stupid, Gabe? That you could invite her to your birthday party and nothing would come out?" Maggie was starting to shout.

"Keep your fucking voice down," was Gabe's only answer.

"Don't fucking tell me what to do. Do you know what kind of embarrassment you just put me through? Having to talk to the woman you most likely fucked? To look her in the eye and be sweet as sugar cane and then have to sleep with you tonight? You're a fucking asshole," Maggie's voice continued to rise.

"Maggie, shut–"

"Did you fuck her? Yes or no?" she bristled.

"Maggie–"

"It's a simple question, Gabe. *Did you fuck her?*" Maggie's hands were shaking from her rage. How had she been so stupid? She should've seen it sooner. The way he was talking to her and treating her. The way he'd been acting. She knew the answer before he said it.

"Yes." Maggie's blood boiled. Before she realized what she was doing, the champagne flute was flying out of her hand and across the room at Gabe. He ducked just in time and the glass shattered against the wall behind him. He sprang back up with pure shock that quickly turned to unfiltered rage on his face.

"What the *fuck* is wrong with you?" he shouted at her.

"You fucked another woman while away on a family trip, Gabe. You fucked her and then paraded her around in front of me. That's what's *fucking* wrong with me. I'm done, Gabe. With whatever we've been doing here. I'm done," Maggie replied in a lethal calm. Gabe closed the space between them forcing her backwards until she was flat against the wall behind her, his face a mere inch from hers.

"Where the fuck are you going to go Maggie? Back to Rosa's? Even she's disappointed in you these days. To your aunt's house? It's only a matter of time before she gets tired of you. To your brother's? Please, we both know he can barely look at you because you remind him too much of your mom. Face it, Maggie. I'm the best you've got," he snarled at her.

"I can do *so much* better than you, Gabe," she spat back at him. Maggie saw the pure rage flicker across Gabe's face. Her own rage quickly dissipated, replaced by fear.

"No Maggie, you can't. We both know that. Who else is going to put up with your shit? Who else is going to deal with your mood swings that border on psychotic? Who else is going to coddle you and your sad little life with your dead mom?" his voice had become a cruel tease. "You were right that night of our first date, Maggie. You're broken. I don't see any way of fixing you. You think someone else is going to want damaged goods? To have to listen to you cry and whine about how miserable your life is? Poor Maggie. Get a fucking grip. No one else will love you like I do. Most people don't even want to deal with you."

Damn him for using her own words against her. For taking those confessions she made in confidence and turning them on her. She couldn't control the fury that came over her once again, abating her fear as she looked him in the eyes and slammed her hands against his chest with all her force.

If she thought she had seen anger on his face before, it paled in comparison to the look he now wore. It was an icy glare staring back at her. Pure fury and malicious wrath.

She saw the fist he raised and flinched instinctively. Eyes closed and face turned away from him, she felt his fist collide with the wall directly next to her head. Felt the small breeze that rustled her hair in the process. She felt him grab her chin, his fingers pressing into her jaw so tightly it hurt, and turn her face to his. She didn't open her eyes, but she could feel his nose on hers, his breath on her face.

"Now, you're going to shut the fuck and clean the rest of this apartment. Pick up all the glass your crazy ass shattered. Wipe everything down. Then, you're going to come to bed and I'll forgive your little outburst," he whispered, kissing her roughly before finally releasing her. She heard his footsteps as he walked away and the small click of his bedroom door as he closed it behind him. She made herself count to ten before opening her eyes. Her hands were still shaking but no longer with rage.

She looked around the apartment. At the mess. What had she become? What had her life become? She walked over to where the pieces of her shattered champagne flute were scattered. As she began to pick up each piece, she couldn't ignore the words that popped into her mind.

Broken. Disgusting. Alone. Unloveable. Damaged. Worthless.

As she continued to pick up each piece of glass, a new word joined the collection in her mind with it. She couldn't help but feel like Gabe was right. She had nowhere else to go. She only had a broken love to offer. How could she ask for more than a broken love in return?

※ ※ ※

Over the next few months Maggie had grown accustomed to Gabe's patterns. She could tolerate his outbursts as he tolerated her existence. The comments on her weight and appearance. The verbal lashings he would unleash. *Stupid. Damaged. Useless.* She had already known all of this about herself. She learned to sit and bear it. She could tolerate his anger as he tolerated her brokenness. She learned she could tolerate his fits of rage in exchange for all of the good he brought to her life.

They had worked their way into a dysfunctional flow. Maggie would trigger Gabe's anger, typically by simply existing when he was in a bad mood. He would lash out and say any hurtful thing he could think of. Maggie would rage back at him until she was too tired to argue or his rage grew too large to contain. Then he'd apologize with a book or a plant or a fancy dinner or a weekend trip. He'd blame the stress at work or how much he had to drink. Maggie accepted it. His anger met hers.

She was just thankful he still cared about her even with everything that was wrong with her. She was thankful his venom was his voice and not his hands.

※ ※ ※

It was now March and Maggie had grown bitter. She resented the world for what it was and what it had become for her. She resented how others could go on with their lives normally while *this* is what she got stuck with. Imagining what her life could have been had her mom never died, who she could have loved, where she could have ended up made her rage more.

She found herself picking fights with Gabe more often, letting his external anger become the manifestation of what she felt internally. It felt good to argue. It felt good to be reminded of her worth, or lack thereof. It felt better than simmering in her own resentment. And all of this was better than the pain.

Even with the fights, there were some nights Maggie simply hurt. Maybe it was the nights her soul was too tired for anger. Or nights she despised the taste of her own bitterness. Or maybe it was the fact that they had just passed the first anniversary of her mom's death. It was hard to tell, but there were simply some nights that Maggie's heart was overwhelmed with the grief of losing her mother. Those were the nights Maggie couldn't stop the tears no matter how hard she tried.

Tonight was one of those nights. The pain strangled her heart as she made her way to Gabe's bathroom. She turned on the faucet, hoping it would mask the sounds of her sobs and sat on the floor. Gabe had been in a mood before bed and she didn't have the energy for one of their fights tonight. It took all of two minutes before Gabe appeared in the doorway.

"Can you not do this right now? I have a really important meeting in the morning and I don't have time to comfort you tonight," he said plainly. Maggie wondered when her pain had become a chore for him. A task to deal with like taking out the trash.

"I just need a minute. I'm sorry," Maggie heaved in between sobs. Gabe sighed in annoyance. He walked over and sat on the toilet right above where she was situated on the floor and started stroking her hair. Maggie was surprised. She could tell he was annoyed with her, so she hadn't expected him to actually offer her any comfort.

"It's okay, Maggie. I'm here. You're not alone," he attempted soothingly. Except, she was alone. He had made that very clear on so many occasions. Her mom had been the only person who made Maggie her number one priority. She knew other people cared for her, but they had their own lives with their own people and concerns. She wasn't one of them, not like she had been for her mother.

This thought spiral made Maggie sob harder. She tried to reign it in but tonight she simply couldn't. She felt Gabe's hand tense on her head.

"Fucking shit, Maggie. Can't you save this shit for tomorrow? I'm trying here and instead you're going to start crying harder? Get a fucking grip. I get it. Your life is sad. You're sad. No one loves you and you can't figure out what to do to make it better. Your mom is dead. So fucking what," he gripped her hair pulling so that her head was tilted up and facing him. She flinched at his grip, pulling hard enough she felt her scalp sting. "People die Maggie. You're going to have to get over it because these late night sobbing fits are getting old. Now, I'm going to need you to shut the fuck up so we can go to bed. Do you understand me?"

Maggie tried to nod, but couldn't without causing more pain where he gripped her hair. As she looked up half staring at Gabe and half staring at the ceiling, she couldn't help but wonder how her life had gotten to this point. How she had gotten to a place of hating herself and resenting the world so thoroughly.

So thoroughly that she was now sobbing on a cold bathroom floor in front of a man she was convinced only loved to hate her. The thought of what she had made of her life and what an embarrassment she would be to her mom hit her, and she shuddered as she released another uncontrollable sob.

Gabe looked at her with pure disgust in his eyes. He tightened his grip on her hair and flung her aside as if she were nothing. Maybe to him she was nothing. As she fell from the force with which he had released her, she knocked the side of her head against the bathtub. She immediately restabilized herself and reached for her forehead.

"Fuck, Maggie. Look what you made me do," Gabe sputtered. "Hold on," he said as he got up and walked out of the bathroom.

She sat there frozen. What just happened? She was so confused. So caught off guard. Had he really just pushed her like that? Or had she lost balance when he released his grip on her hair? She was still trying to figure it out when he came back in with an ice pack.

"I'm sorry," he said as he gently held the ice pack to where the pain on her forehead was growing.

He looked at her, all annoyance and disgust gone. He gave her the look that reminded her of their very first date. Of the night when she admitted to being broken and he had reminded her that she was only human.

As he held the ice pack in place looking at her like that, she finally stopped sobbing.

The next day Gabe surprised Maggie with Broadway tickets and dinner at a restaurant she had been wanting to try for weeks.

April came around and Maggie and Gabe had yet again settled into their dysfunctional rhythms. Although Maggie still spent most of her time either angry herself or tempering Gabe's anger, she had to admit that she had started to wonder. She wondered what her life could have been like if she had made certain choices and done certain things differently. Her rage was still there, but she could feel it starting to wear down. As if her anger was just as tired as she was.

Unfortunately, the same could not be said of Gabe. His fuse seemed to be shorter than ever and Maggie found herself treading as lightly as possible whenever she was around him. She made sure to keep everything exactly how he preferred and avoided anything that could set him off. She had managed to avoid many blow ups this way.

Tonight, they were staying in and watching some movies that had been on their list for a while. The Thai food they had ordered had just been delivered and Maggie was setting down some plates and utensils while Gabe grabbed the food. He had told her about how much stress he was dealing with at work. He seemed tense but not angry. She knew she would be walking a fine line with him tonight.

She hoped a calm night together while his roommates worked late would keep his anger at bay.

She turned from the table to grab them some beers when she saw him, and her body instinctively tensed. She could see he was upset about something but couldn't tell what. She walked over to where he stood with their food.

"Everything okay babe?" she said, attempting to sound cheerful and calm.

"You ordered the food like always, right?" he asked, revealing nothing.

"Yeah! I have our orders saved in the app. I plugged them in the way we always do," she answered, aiming for casualness.

"Then why the fuck is my food wrong? There are onions in here. You know I hate onions," he said.

"What? Oh no! The restaurant must have forgotten. I can order another one. Or, I can take all the onions out for you," Maggie tried her best to problem solve before this escalated unnecessarily.

"The restaurant never messes up. *You* must have fucked up my order. How fucking stupid are you? It's not rocket science. No onions Maggie, like every single other time we order from this place," he said, his voice rising.

"I know. I'm sorry. I swear I put in no onions. I can grab my phone and show you," she stuttered as she started moving away. She could immediately tell that had been the wrong thing to say.

"Are you calling me a liar? Just fucking accept that *YOU. MESSED. UP.* Just like you mess everything else up," he bellowed, throwing the open container of food at her. She flinched but didn't dare move otherwise.

"I'm sorry. You're right. I'll make sure to resave it and make sure it's right next time." she said, her feet covered and surrounded in fried rice. She was too afraid to move, unsure of what to do next.

"Next time doesn't help me right now Maggie. What the hell am I supposed to eat right now? Riddle me that." She knew there was nothing she could say that would appease him. Knew that no matter what she said or what she did, he would find a way to make it her fault. It was always her fault. Everything was. So, she stood silent and stared at the ground.

"What? No solutions for me now?" He took four steps toward her. She felt her muscles lock more with each thud of his foot fall. Once he was only a few inches from her face he asked again, "What the fuck am I supposed to eat now?" His voice was pure venom. She needed to find a way to back up–to create space between them.

"I'll go to the restaurant and get your order myself after I clean this up," she said as she took a step away from him.

"Don't you dare turn away from me while we're talking," he said and grabbed her arm with so much force that it threw her off balance. She was now back in between the couch and the coffee table where she had been setting up their plates. She teetered a moment before falling sideways onto the couch.

"I'm sorry," she said faintly as she stood back up. "I'll clean this up and go get you another order. I'll make sure it's right this time." She resented how pitiful she sounded. She resented what accepting this kind of love had turned her into.

She made to take a step forward, but was stopped by Gabe's arm.

"How the hell am I supposed to trust your dumbass to get it right this time?" he said with a vicious smirk. She stared at the wicked gleam of his smile that she had once found warm. Was this what the rest of her life would become? She knew she could never give or have the kind of love she had once dreamt of, but this? This couldn't be it.

"I'm not stupid," Maggie whispered, barely audible.

"What was that?" Gabe asked. Maggie finally tilted her face up to his. Her rage finally matching his once more.

"I said, I'm not fucking stupid," she seethed. Gabe looked at her with genuine surprise. She had stopped talking back a while ago. He had worn her down. This lash was unexpected.

His shock was quickly replaced with icy cold rage as he backhanded her across the face. The force of it knocked Maggie backward, her body twisting slightly as she fell. Before she could fully comprehend what was happening, she was lying on the table. Her elbow was bleeding from shattering a plate and glass and her head was spinning from hitting the edge of the table. She didn't have any time to recover or react before she felt Gabe's foot against her side, pushing her off the table.

She crumpled on the floor gripping her side, coughing and trying to catch her breath. She didn't have time to make sense of what just happened before Gabe was in her face again.

"Maggie, you have chicken shit for brains. Now because you fucked up my order, I'm going out to grab some food. Make sure this is all cleaned up by the time I get back," and before she could even roll onto her back to respond, he was already out the door.

Slowly, she sat up taking stock of what hurt the most. Her brain was racing. How had that escalated so quickly? She had done everything right. She couldn't make sense of any of it. She stared at the shattered plates and felt the blood from her elbow trickle down her arm. What the fuck had happened?

She had learned how to tame her own fury. She had learned how to temper his rage. It still did her no good. She looked at the broken plates one more time and came to a sobering realization. She'd die if she stayed with him. It would kill her. As much as she didn't necessarily want to live, she now knew for certain she did not want to die either.

It was as if that one realization flicked a switch in her brain. She grabbed a garbage bag and headed straight for their bedroom. Her hands were shaking, but she worked as quickly as she could to put all of her clothes in the bag. She grabbed anything that felt important off her nightstand and their dresser. She was overwhelmed by how much of her crap was here. She had effectively moved in, she now realized. She couldn't remember the last time she had stayed at her aunt's house. She couldn't remember the last time she had seen friends that weren't his. He had boxed her in. He had done this on purpose.

Her anger returned. She let it fuel her motions as she grabbed anything of any value to her and crammed it into another bag. She needed to be quick. She knew she needed to be gone before he got back. If he got back and saw her packing he would either convince her to stay or his rage would reach a level she had not yet seen. Neither were options she could survive.

She did one last scan around the apartment and decided that anything else could be left behind. With a final look at the shattered plates splattered with her blood, she turned around, walked out the door, and promised herself she'd never return again.

She ran down the stairs, garbage bags in hand just as she had all those months ago when she ran from their first fight. She should've known then. Rosa had seen it. Why hadn't she listened?

As she got to her car, shoving the bags in her trunk, she hauled herself into the driver's seat. Her elbow and side began to throb as the adrenaline wore off. Every injury was starting to surge with pain, but she needed to get out of here before she could take stock of what was wrong. She couldn't risk him coming back and finding her like this. So, she started the car, turned on the headlights, put it in drive, and pulled out of her parking spot. This time, unlike their first fight, she didn't bother turning to look back at his apartment and she had no intention of ever returning.

She had been aimlessly driving for thirty five minutes now and still had no clue where to go. She couldn't go to her aunt's house in her current state. She needed to get cleaned up before going back there. She thought of Rosa's but felt too embarrassed. She knew her friend loved her and wouldn't care, but she personally couldn't face the shame. She couldn't face what she had allowed for the last few months. She definitely couldn't go to her brother's. He'd murder Gabe.

She continued down the highway as tears started to streak down her face. The pain had become unbearable as it throbbed in various parts of her body and she felt more alone than ever. Where the hell could she go this late? She ran through her options again. Would she really end up spending the night in her car in some parking lot?

As she racked her brain, she remembered something. There was somewhere she could potentially go. It wasn't a good option and she wasn't entirely sure it would work, but it was her best option for tonight. It wasn't fair, but it was all she had left. So, she swallowed her sobs and some of her pride and drove on, now knowing exactly where she was headed.

Twenty minutes later, she was parked outside of Jeff's house. It was dark and none of the exterior lights were on, but she could see the lights inside through the windows. Someone was home. She took as deep of a breath as she could with her throbbing side and walked up to the front door. She rang the doorbell and waited.

The seconds felt like hours and she almost turned to go back to her car when she heard a familiar voice.

"Are you expecting anything because I'm–" she heard a man call out as the door swung open and he saw her. "Oh." Kam stood there. "Do you need Jeff? I can go grab him?" Kam said as he started to turn away.

"Kam, wait! No, ah–" Maggie had moved to grab his arm, but she had done it with the sliced elbow and she winced in pain. It was then that Kam took a second to really look at her. He opened the door wider and stepped out a little further, letting the light from inside filter out and onto Maggie. Whatever he saw made him pale as he took her hand, leading her into the house and gasped, "Mags, what happened?"

It would seem that the very last ounce of adrenaline coursing through her had faded. As if her brain knew she was finally safe and she no longer needed to move and be on alert. Because as soon as Kam grabbed her hand, her entire body gave out and she sobbed as she crumpled to the ground.

"Mags, what happened," Kam said, coming down to the floor and holding the side of her face ever so gently. "Who did this to you?"

Maybe it was the strain in his voice or the pain in his eyes. But looking at him, Maggie rallied enough strength to stand back up and let him half carry her into the house. She looked into his eyes and for the first time since her mom died remembered what home felt like.

Bargaining

Playlist

blame's on me / Alexander Stewart

Your Daughter / Chase McDaniel

Devil Doesn't Bargain / Alec Benjamin

Daddy's Eyes / Zoe Wees

champagne problems / Taylor Swift

I'll Be Waiting / Cian Ducrot

4

Bargaining

Maggie didn't speak for the first hour she was at Kam's house, no matter how much he asked and tried to make her. Whether she was too tired or simply wasn't capable anymore, she wasn't sure. All she had managed to conjure so far were nods, shrugs, and shakes.

"I still think we should go to an emergency room or something," Kam said as they sat in his bathroom. She shook her head, too aggressively, causing her pounding headache to worsen. She winced. She hadn't realized how many cuts she had gotten as she fell on top of the table and then fell off of it. Wait, not fell. That would've made it an accident. Or her fault. She was slapped and then kicked. He had done this. She could no longer take the blame for Gabe's anger. As the scene replayed in her mind, her body began to tremble uncontrollably.

"Hey, you're here. You're safe. I've got you," Kam said, unsure of what else to do. She looked at him and she knew he meant it. She knew she had come to the right place. She knew he wouldn't make her explain anything tonight if she didn't want to. She knew he would help her. She knew he would offer her some steadiness.

She knew it wasn't fair of her to ask this of him after what she had done to him. She also knew she had no clue what else to do.

Once she had clarified that she had not been in an accident and that no one else was hurt, Kam had eased up on the questions and let her just sit. She realized as she sat there on the edge of the bath tub that this was the first time in months she wasn't on edge. That she wasn't worrying about what to say or what to do. Or rather, worrying about how someone would react to what she said and did. She looked up at Kam one more time and started to cry. This time because of what she had let go and what she had accepted.

Kam placed a gentle hand on her head as her face fell and she sobbed. She flinched at the touch–unable to avoid the memory of the last time someone had put their hand on her head as she sobbed in a bathroom. Kam's face hardened as he noticed her involuntary reaction. He wasn't stupid and after all, up until she had left him, he had known her best. He looked at her and glum realization settled on his features.

He nodded, more to himself than to Maggie, and grabbed her hand. He walked her to his bedroom, handed her a tshirt, hoodie, and a pair of his shorts, and walked out giving her space to change.

She didn't move from where he left her and as she heard his door close, she fell to the floor again. She winced at the pain in her side. Her knees. Her elbow. Her face. Her body was now an amalgamation of bruises and lacerations. Her skin now reflected all of the feelings she had kept so carefully leashed within.

She couldn't figure out how she felt so much pain while simultaneously feeling so much nothing. She cried at the truth she had always known. The truth that was now blatantly staring her in the face–she had never deserved him, even at her best. Kind Kam.

She had broken him and yet here he was, willing to help her put herself back together. Again.

She finally managed to pull herself off the floor and start changing. She wasn't sure how long she had sat there, but she knew a good while had passed. She had heard Jeff check in with Kam and say goodnight.

Maggie had just finished putting on the shorts and was changing into the shirt when she heard a knock on the door.

When she didn't answer, Kam walked in and froze as he saw her sliding his shirt over her head. When she looked at him he was staring at her stomach. He stormed across the room and lifted the shirt back up. She had no clue what he was looking at.

"What the *fuck* did he do to you Mags?" she tensed at the rage mixed with hatred in his voice. He saw it and took a deep breath before continuing, "Mags, look." He pulled her over to where his mirror stood.

She could see what had made him so upset. Across her side, there was a very clear bruise starting to form around a multitude of small cuts. She knew it would be painful and dark when the bruise finally set and knew it would take a long time to go away. She already dreaded having to see that reminder every day for however long it would last.

"I need you to answer two questions for me, Mags," Kam finally spoke, still staring at her stomach in the mirror. "First, are you *sure* you don't want to get looked at by a doctor? There could be more wrong here," he asked. She shook her head. She would take stock again tomorrow if anything, but she felt too tired and overwhelmed to be looked at today.

None of her injuries felt serious enough, anyway. They would hurt like hell, for sure, but not kill her. He nodded. It was a terse and frustrated gesture, but he would always let her make her own choices and accept them–even if it was begrudgingly.

"Okay. Fine. I don't agree, but it's up to you," he said, taking another deep breath. "Second, I need to know... was it Gabe?"

Shame slammed into Maggie. She would have to admit it eventually, but she wasn't sure how. She couldn't bring herself to answer yet, but avoiding Kam's eyes was all the confirmation he needed.

She could almost feel the rage rolling off of him. As if it were a tangible thing she could hold onto. For the first time in months, though, this rage didn't scare or overwhelm her. For once, the fury wasn't coming from within or wasn't being directed at her. It was an anger fueled by protection. By caring. By love. *For her.*

Maggie sighed and dropped onto the edge of his bed, wincing as she went to put on his hoodie. She was so sore all over and she knew it would only be worse tomorrow. As she finally got her head through, she could see Kam pacing back and forth at the foot of the bed where she sat.

She took a moment to take in the sight of him. He was still as handsome as ever. She couldn't help noticing that he looked a little more grown. His hair was a little longer and he had finally found the perfect amount of stubble to make him look simultaneously rugged and put together. She could see more muscle definition peeking out of the sleeves of his shirt. Their time apart had served him well.

She looked around his room and it felt so *Kam*. There was minimalist art hung around the walls and a massive bookshelf that had books crammed messily in every possible crevice. She noticed a photo booth strip taped to the edge of the bookshelf next to one of her favorite books. It was from the day they had gone to the bookstore together. Her heart squeezed.

"I'll fucking *kill* that piece of shit," he finally fumed as he turned to walk away. This brought her back to the present moment.

"Kam, stop," she said weakly–her voice raspy. He froze. Those were the first words she had said since she arrived on his doorstep. He turned and looked at her. As he looked her up and down, she saw his demeanor change from fury to devastation. Kind Kam, who always wanted to help and always had to be doing something but had no clue what to do here. She knew it would infuriate him. That he would feel useless. He wasn't. He had already done more for her tonight than he'd ever acknowledge.

"Mags, I can't just sit here and–"

"You can, Kam. You can and you will," Maggie said. Even she was surprised that she had found the composure and strength to say it so firmly. He looked at her and nodded once, walking over to where she sat. The mattress shifted as he sat down next to her.

She could feel his pent up, chaotic energy. His knee bobbed at a speed she didn't think was physically possible. He picked at his cuticles—his number one stress habit—and looked around the room, shifting his gaze constantly.

"Kam, thank you," Maggie said, putting her hand on his knee to stop its bobbing. He froze entirely and stared at her hand. "I'm sorry I showed up and put this on you. It's not fair to you after what I did and how I left. I just... I just..." Maggie struggled to find the words. "Nowhere else felt right. I'm not sure how to explain it," she finished, shrugging.

"You are the last person who should be apologizing tonight," Kam started. "Maggie, I don't mind helping you. Shit, stay forever if you need. But, Maggie..." he looked away briefly, "I do want to know what happened. I *need* to know," he said, balancing sounding both firm and gentle.

She looked at him and she could see the deeper meaning behind what he was asking. He didn't just mean tonight. He wanted her to go back. Back to the night they had together. Back to the day she left him stunned in his driveway. To the day she had broken the promises she had made to him for the first time ever. She nodded.

She spent the next few hours sitting on his bed and telling him everything. She did her best to explain why she left him there and went no contact. She told him about Aidan and the denial she went through. She told him about Christmas and her resentment. She told him about Gabe and his anger laced with bouts of sweetness and grand gestures.

She cried and blushed. She talked and talked until she finally got to tonight. To the fight that she now realized she had no hope of ever avoiding, no matter how hard she tried. To her mad dash to leave. To her aimless driving. To how she finally made it to his front door. To this moment.

Kam sat next to her soaking in every word. She didn't miss the stray tears he would let slip. She saw every nuance of his expression as it changed. She saw his pain and understanding. She saw his frustration and caring. She saw his disgust at what she had accepted as affection. And behind it all she saw his love. And as she finished her tall tale, she couldn't help but think about how he still loved her. She knew it was there, but was it the same? Or had it changed? And if so, into what?

As she looked at him listening to her intently with zero judgment or pretense, a thought flashed across Maggie's mind. For just a split second. Maybe, she thought, Kam's love actually *could* save her. That one word rattled through her as they finally started to fall asleep. *Maybe.*

The next morning felt weirdly natural. Both Maggie and Kam had called in sick to work, so they slept in. Maggie woke up second and crept to the kitchen unsure of how the morning would go. From down the hallway she could hear Kam half shouting and half whispering, clearly trying his hardest to keep his voice down.

"You should be thanking whoever the fuck you pray to that we haven't convinced her to press charges. Never call her again. Never text her again. Don't even fucking *think* of her again. And if you come near her, I will make it my personal mission in life to ruin yours. Everyone will know what you did. I'll make sure everyone around you knows what a despicable piece of shit you are," he fumed. She walked in as he hung up and saw that he had been on *her* phone. He turned and smiled as he saw her. It was his forced smile. The one she hated.

She nodded. What else was she supposed to do? He handed her the phone. She checked her home screen and almost vomited when she saw she had 63 texts, 32 missed calls, and 18 voicemails from the night before. All from Gabe. She put her phone face down on the counter and walked over to help Kam with breakfast.

They sat in a mostly comfortable silence and it wasn't until Maggie started loading their dishes into the dishwasher that Kam finally spoke.

"Why didn't you go to your aunt's?" he asked, as he walked over to help. Of course he had noticed her discomfort at bending over. Kam would.

"I didn't know if I'd be able to clean myself up, and if so, if I'd do it in time. I didn't want her seeing me like this," Maggie offered in response.

"And why not Rosa's?" he followed up.

"Rosa *was* my initial thought, honestly," she sighed as she continued, "but I felt too ashamed. She had asked me to stop seeing Gabe after our first fight. She had told me I was tolerating too much. I know she'd never actually say I told you so, but I couldn't help feeling ashamed that I hadn't listened. That I'd instead distanced myself from her and in a sense chose him." She hated herself for that now, but there was no going back. She couldn't change what she had done, only what she would do moving forward. Kam nodded in understanding.

"You know you're going to have to tell her, right? She's like a hound with secrets. You'll never keep it from her," he said. Maggie smiled at how well he knew her people, her life.

He was right. If there was anyone who would get to the bottom of everything, it was Rosa. She would figure out how to tell her everything. And apologize. Eventually.

"Why didn't you go to your brother's?" he asked as she sat back down at the table, moving noticeably more slowly than usual. She could see where his questions were leading, but she wasn't sure she was ready to answer what he truly wanted to know.

"I thought about it, but I knew he'd kill him. I already have a dead mom. I don't also need a brother in prison," she joked. He bristled at how casually she had mentioned her mom's death. Just another testament to how much time had passed and how much they had changed. He hadn't been around to watch her develop a tolerance to her grief. She hadn't let him.

"I wanted to kill him," he answered simply.

"I know. I figured you would. But, I also knew I could talk you down. Convince you to stay. With me," she fidgeted with her rings in discomfort at the words. She felt the blush in her ears at how awkward she felt admitting that.

"But you wouldn't be able to with your brother?" he clarified.

"You've met my brother, right? We're talking about the same person here?" she joked. At this, he laughed. It was his full Kam laugh. She ignored the sting from the cut on her lip as she smiled broadly, still loving how she felt being able to make him laugh like that.

"Okay, okay. Makes sense. But I still don't understand. Why..." he trailed off.

"Why you," she offered. He nodded. She looked at him and realized that he not only needed to know, but deserved to know. Even if she wasn't entirely sure what her answer was. She would do her best to explain it, and where words failed her hopefully honesty wouldn't.

"I..." she fiddled with her rings again as she tried to organize her thoughts. "I ran through my list of people the same way you just did. In that exact order, actually," she chuckled a bit. "I got desperate. I was hurting and felt so alone again. I honestly thought I'd have to sleep in my car or something. Clean myself up at a gas station and then find a relatively safe parking lot." His expression was a combination of frustration with her own pride, anger that she'd even considered that option, and sadness at her loneliness. Her inability to see and accept how much her people loved her. "I was racking my brain for any other possibility I hadn't considered. Driving around aimlessly. Then I remembered Rosa mentioning you had moved in with Jeff. I'm not entirely sure what sparked that line of thought, but once I started my brain spiraled. I knew it wasn't fair. I knew it was selfish and cruel to put this on you.

I knew it made me a horrible person. I knew it just highlighted how useless and miserable I am. But, I also knew you wouldn't judge me. I knew you'd be patient. I knew you'd help. I knew you'd give me the space and time I needed just like you always have. Or maybe, I didn't know for sure. Maybe I just hoped. I don't know," Maggie finished, shrugging.

He looked at her for a long time and neither of them said anything. Her anxiety started to creep up. Had she made any sense? Had she explained it all wrong? Had she been *too* honest?

"I don't know how many times you've heard all of that to make you say it so casually, but you are not cruel," he started, sounding angry. "You are not useless. You are not miserable. You're not a horrible person, Mags," he shook his head before he continued. "You're just a pain in my ass. But it's okay. I'm a masochist and your pain in my ass is my favorite," he smirked at her. Her laugh came out as a bark before she wheezed in a pained breath and winced.

"I didn't even know you knew big words like masochist," she joked back.

"Oh, it's been a year Mags. I've done so much reading in that time. You'd be *shocked* by the extent of my vocabulary these days," he winked at her, but her smile faltered. A year. Had it really been that long already?

"A year…" she whispered, trailing off. He nodded, realizing where her mind had wandered. It was now April. She had run from him a year ago. How had that much time passed already? How had she done nothing with it other than squander her life? How was he still so *Kam* after all this time? How was he an even better version of the man she had known? How was she even more broken than she had been before? How in the *fuck* had it been a year?

"I went to church, you know," he said, interrupting her internal spiral. At her confused look, he continued, "On the anniversary of her death. I went to church and lit a candle. Felt like something she'd appreciate." Kam had never been religious. In fact, he had always joked that if he ever entered a church, it'd probably spontaneously combust.

"You went to church... and it didn't explode or anything?" Maggie finally replied. It was her feeble attempt at a joke. He took the bait, knowing she needed the distraction. Knowing, kind Kam.

"I was just as shocked as you are. Now, come on," he said, grabbing her hand and pulling her back toward his bedroom.

"What? Where are we–" she started.

"We need to get dressed and go tell your best friend what you've been dealing with. Ro deserves to know. And you *need* to tell her. But if my memory serves me correctly, you'll avoid it as long as possible. So, we're telling her. Today." Maggie stopped so abruptly that it jolted Kam to a halt. He turned around and looked at her. He saw her fear and the overwhelming anxiety. He knew this would be hard to relive for her, especially with Rosa. But he also knew of all people, Maggie was absurdly capable of doing hard things.

"I don't–" she started.

"Mags, you have to do this. You can't avoid it or it'll eat you alive. You need your best friend. And she needs you. Honestly, I'm ready to give up my foster time with her. When you pushed her away I filled the gap. She's great, but holy shit is she a lot. I will happily hand her back to her forever home," he tried to make light of their situation.

"Okay," Maggie agreed weakly, even though it was the last thing she wanted to do right now. He was right. He had even gone so far as to step up when she had stepped out. Oh Kam. What had she done to deserve him? Nothing, she realized as the thought sank like a boulder, dropping to the pit of her stomach.

A year had passed but not much had truly changed. She was still a disarray of poorly taped together shattered shards and he was still kind, knowing Kam. She still didn't deserve his love and wasn't sure she ever would. As he grabbed her hand smiling and turned back to walk them the rest of the way to his bedroom, she couldn't help the flutter she felt. *Maybe.*

An hour later, they were outside Rosa's house with bagels and coffee. She was working from home and Maggie felt her anxiety build as Kam parked out front. He walked around to open her door and help her out of the car. Once outside, she immediately froze. Maybe it was too soon for this. Maybe Rosa was too busy for her right now. Maybe–

"She won't care about any of it," Kam said, interrupting her building panic. "She'll just be happy you're okay and to have her best friend back. I'll be happy to let you two consume each other's time with your shenanigans and not mine," he finished with a joke.

"You love our shenanigans," she said, avoiding thinking about what she was about to do. *Needed* to do.

"You two are absolute shit shows and I am aging at an incredible rate from the stress it causes," he said, guiding her up the porch steps. Before she could turn and run, as Maggie desperately desired to do right now, he knocked on the front door.

A few moments later Rosa appeared, surprised to see the two of them together. She looked first to Kam, whom she had become significantly closer to these last few months–both from missing Maggie and from concern for her. Then she looked at Maggie.

Maggie looked down but Rosa stepped forward and pushed Maggie's chin back up. She looked at the cut on her lip, the cut on her forehead, and the bruises no doubt now darker than when Maggie last saw them.

Rosa inhaled sharply and looked at Kam. In her peripheral vision, Maggie could see Kam nod once and Rosa's eyes flared with outrage. Had they talked about the possibility of this? Had Maggie been that blind to what was happening? Maggie shook her face free of Rosa's grip and looked down at her feet again, even more embarrassed.

"Fuck. Him," Rosa spat, crouching down so that Maggie was forced to look at her. "Fuck him, Mags. Fuck him and anything he did. You are not allowed to be ashamed right now. *He* should be. Do not continue to give him power right now. I'm your *best friend*," Maggie's heart hurt at the crack in Rosa's voice when she said those last two words. "I'm your *sister*, Mags. I refuse to let you let that fucking twat waffle make you feel ashamed because of his actions." Maggie hadn't realized she had started crying. She swiped at a tear as she chuckled.

"I missed your colorful cussing, Ro," Maggie sniffled.

"I missed *you*," Rosa replied, and Maggie saw she too was crying. "Now, get your asses inside with those bagels and coffee. I want to hear anything you're willing to tell me right now. And don't think we're just going to ignore whatever the *fuck* this is," she said, pointing back and forth between Kam and Maggie. They hadn't realized they were holding hands.

Maggie laughed. Kam groaned. But they both walked into the house with small smiles. As Maggie looked around and followed

Rosa into the kitchen, she once again couldn't help but think...
Maybe.

Maggie spent the next two weeks staying with Rosa. Kam and Jeff had brought her car and things over that first night, giving Maggie a chance to tell her everything. If Maggie had been concerned about her brother's potential rage, she then realized she had massively miscalculated and should've been more concerned with Rosa's. How could she have so drastically underestimated the fiery love of her very best friend?

Gabe had made the mistake of calling her one more time that first night. This time while she was with Rosa. Rosa answered and rapid fired her rage in Spanish at him. Maggie's Spanish was rusty but she had gotten the gist of what Rosa had shouted. There was the threat of castration and setting something on fire and shoving it up his ass. Although her threats were most definitely more colorful than Kam's, they sent the same message. Leave Maggie alone.

The next two weeks went as smoothly as Maggie could have hoped. Gabe for the most part left her alone. It was clear to her now that he cared more for his own reputation than he ever had for her. He didn't want people to know the truth that sat behind his picture perfect facade. He was afraid Kam and Rosa would follow through on their threats. He sent her one last text before radio silence.

I wish you hadn't made me do what I did. It shouldn't have ended like that. We could've been happy.

It somehow was still her fault. It had been ridiculous of her to think she'd get any form of apology from him. She had hoped, but Maggie was quickly realizing that maybe hoping had become her downfall. Maybe she hoped for too much compared to what life was willing to give her.

Maggie somehow eased back into the old rhythm of her life. She eventually moved back in with her aunt. She dove back into all of her work projects with a newfound fervor. She had committed to weekly friend dates with Rosa and Kam.

Maggie was surprised to see how close Rosa and Kam had gotten over the last few months. They had become true friends and it overwhelmed her heart. They had always mostly liked each other, but never fully bothered to foster a friendship beyond their connection to Maggie. It made her happy to see how her two favorite people had come together. It was at one of their friend dates that Maggie decided to drop something she'd been ruminating on.

"I'm thinking of reaching back out to my dad more," Maggie said as their conversation hit a natural lull. The shock sprang to both of their faces before either of them could school their features.

It was no surprise to anyone that Maggie had a rocky-putting it very kindly-relationship with her father. Her parents had separated when she was young and divorced shortly after. He was an alcoholic who had finally hit a point her mom couldn't take anymore. Her mom's priority had always been her and her brother, so she made him leave.

Her dad meant well most of the time, but the road to hell is paved with the best intentions. Her childhood had been full of missed pickups and excuses. There were the drunken phone calls no child should have to answer. And, her least favorite of all, how he would try to make her mother sound like the big bad in every situation.

Maggie became overly observant from a young age. She taught herself how to read rooms and moods. She learned how to pay attention to details most people ignored. She learned how to take in as many clues as possible, come to her own conclusions, and adapt accordingly. Which is exactly why her dad's attempts at shit talking her mom never worked.

Anyone could see who the more committed parent was. She worked overtime. She showed up to every school and sporting event. She held their hand through every heartbreak and bandaged every scraped knee. He was just the guy who *sometimes* sent child support and showed up when he said he would even *less* often. Even with all that, Maggie's mom always encouraged her to keep giving her dad chances. She always encouraged her to call and make plans. It was her dad who ruined his image in her mind entirely on his own.

"Are you sure you want to do that?" Rosa finally said, glancing at Kam. They both knew Maggie's situation with her dad intimately. Their unease was understandable. Their skepticism was reasonable when they would be the ones helping to pick up any more pieces he broke.

"I think so," Maggie continued slowly, sipping her drink. "I can't help but think about how maybe this could be our chance. Yes, I lost one parent and it fucking sucks and I'm still dealing with the grief of it. But, he's still alive? What if this is our chance to try and repair some of our relationship? What if although I lost one parent, I can maybe have a chance with another one?" At the look Kam and Rosa shared, she continued her attempt to try and make them see. "Listen, I know he's probably still not a great person. He'll never be my mom. But, he is my dad. I'm not saying it's going to be rainbows and unicorns and we'll be a happy family. What if we can try to be *something*? What if maybe he can help?" She picked at her food as she anxiously waited for their response.

"If you want to try, we won't stop you, but we want you to be sure. We know him, Mags. Sure, *maybe* he could make things better…" Rosa started.

"We also know how much *worse* he has the potential to make things," Kam grumbled, finishing for her. He was clearly much less on board with this idea.

"I know. I'm going to go in slow. Start small. Give him a chance to try and be a dad. See where it goes. Keep it low stakes. If it works out, I'll have a relationship with the only parent I have left. If it doesn't, no harm done," she offered to appease them. They muttered some agreement, but it wasn't hard to see they weren't sold. Maggie had never been a low stakes, low key person. Rosa and Kam worried about what mayhem Maggie's father would create and what messes he'd leave behind for them to clean up.

🌿 🌿 🌿

A week later, Maggie found herself at her dad's house having lunch. She always found things a little awkward with him. She just wasn't entirely sure how to interact with him. Everything was always so effortless with her mom; it was a challenge to maintain the same casual flow with her dad.

She told herself it would get easier. More natural. They just needed some time. They needed a chance to get to know each other. She was convinced that if only they took the time and put in the effort, everything would work out.

With May came graduation. Maggie was honestly shocked to find herself grabbing her cap and gown. She couldn't stop the memory of her mom always telling all the nurses and doctors that she had to keep living. She had a daughter she needed to see graduate college. She didn't want to ruin her makeup, but she couldn't help the tear that made its way down her cheek.

Today would feel sad, she knew that. But, she also thought that maybe if she focused on everyone who *would* be there, she wouldn't feel as sad. She knew all of her aunts were coming, her brother, her brother's best friend who was basically family, Rosa, Kam, and even her dad. She would focus on that.

"One Dunkin' iced coffee for the soon to be college grad," she heard her brother say as he came through the front door. She was getting ready at his house since a bunch of them had decided to carpool to her graduation. She pulled herself together and walked out to the living room.

Maggie loved her brother, Colin, but it was moments like this when she was truly grateful for him. He was the kind of big brother who wanted the best for her. He wanted her to be happy, and she knew he hated that he got so many more years with their mom than she did. Their age gap had always kept a reasonable distance in their relationship, but now that they were older and had been through what they had together, they weren't just siblings anymore. She counted Colin as a friend now.

He had gone out of his way to get coffee for everyone who would be driving in his car today. He had even coordinated most of it so that Maggie wouldn't have to stress. He wanted her to feel loved and not feel as much of the pain of what she was missing. For him, she'd try today.

She had barely pulled her iced coffee from the drink carrier when she heard more footsteps coming up the stairs. Rosa and Kam came through the door her brother had just closed.

"Look at this beautiful, talented, edumucated GRADUATE," Kam said, shouting the last word. Maggie curtseyed with every compliment, giggling like a fool.

"Well, *almost* graduate," she replied.

"I'm proud of you mama," Rosa said, coming in for a hug. "I've got something for you–well us," she continued as she pulled two travel size bottles of Jack Daniels out of her purse.

"Hey! None for me? Not cool," her brother said by way of greeting.

"You're driving! You can wait," Rosa laughed, swatting Colin on the shoulder. "You need this more than the rest of us," she said more quietly, turning back to Maggie. Rosa opened the lid to Maggie's iced coffee and poured one of the bottles in. She then repeated the same process with her own.

"None for you, then?" Maggie asked, turning to Kam.

"Not today. Someone has to step up and be the designated chaos coordinator. I'll wait until later," he answered. Just as he finished, Maggie could hear another set of footsteps coming up the stairs. This had to be Nate–Colin's best friend and Maggie's big brother by extension.

"Maggie!" his voice boomed, "Damn you're getting old! Graduating college already! Shit," he said. She laughed as she walked over to hug him in greeting. This would be their car today: Maggie, Colin, Nate, Rosa, and Kam. She looked around at her people and smiled. She could feel who was missing, but she also felt so *loved* in who was here. It was overwhelming.

"I just want to thank all of you for coming today. It really means a lot to me. The last year has fucking sucked, but I think even on the worst days, deep down I always knew I could count on all of you through any of it. I definitely wouldn't have made it to graduation without y'all. So, thank you! Genuinely. Now, let's go get a bitch graduated!" Maggie cheered.

"Alright, does anyone need anything else before we get in the car and head over to the ceremony? I'm not turning around," Colin said to the group. They all looked at each other and nodded their heads in affirming 'good to go' motions. After a few more moments of silence, Maggie began to take her first steps out of the house.

"Shots?" Nate asked before she could get very far. She rolled her eyes and laughed. Maybe Kam was right. Maybe they would need a chaos coordinator.

🌿 🌿 🌿

Had Maggie originally thought they would *maybe* need a chaos coordinator? She was quickly shown that they would *definitely* need one. Unbeknownst to Maggie, Rosa had many more of those tiny bottles of Jack in her purse. Also unbeknownst to Maggie, Rosa had poured another one into Maggie's coffee and *then* asked if she wanted to take one as a shot. They stopped for breakfast bagels and then headed into the city so that Maggie could at least try and come close to being on time for her own graduation.

Maggie could perfectly envision her mom shaking her head warmly at the shit show this crew had become. They had crammed into the car—Colin and Nate up front and Rosa, Maggie, and Kam in the back. Maggie was riding in the middle, but she didn't mind if it meant sitting in between two of her favorite people. Rosa and Nate were arguing over something ridiculous and unimportant. Colin simply inserted comedic commentary sporadically. Maggie was laughing like a fool and Kam was just looking out the car window.

"Whatcha thinkin' over there big shot?" Maggie asked, leaning into Kam. He angled his head slightly to look at her and smile.

"I'm thinking about how far we've come–you've come. You're doing it Mags! You're graduating. Even after all the shit you've been through," he started quietly so only she could hear. Not that anyone would be able to hear them at a normal volume over Nate and Rosa's bickering. She smiled goofily as he continued, "You are the most astounding person I know. You leave me in awe and most days it's hard for me to believe you're real. It's even harder for me to believe you'd choose me. Everyday," he grabbed her hand and held it in his before he kept going. "And I just need to tell you–"

"Hey!" Nate said, slapping Maggie's hand out of Kam's and nearly knocking over her iced coffee in the process. "No holding her hand! None of those lovey dovey eyes either! She's not allowed to date until she's got a master's degree!" Nate yelled at Kam.

Although she was definitely much tipsier than she should've been, and the chaos indeed continued at the ceremony as Maggie's brother hurdled a security barrier to get her the rest of her breakfast bagel, her graduation went surprisingly smoothly. She sat through the speeches, munching on her bagel. She walked across the stage and got her diploma. She met up with her family for pictures afterward.

Her dad had showed up. He was actually there. She couldn't help but think he could do this for her. If only he could keep showing up, she could have a semblance of what she used to have. Even a fraction of what she used to have with her mom would be good enough for her. It could help make her feel even a tiny bit in control of something in this tangled, turbulent future of hers.

A few hours later Maggie found herself on her brother's couch leaning into Kam's side. Everyone was mid laugh after something Nate said. They were all multiple beers and shots deep and Maggie was in the midst of that fuzzy level of drunkenness where everything is just right. She had a lazy, goofy grin on her face and felt like maybe the majority of her sadness was over.

If only she could keep life feeling like this, her future could look closer to what she once thought it would be. Her future. This was the first time in a long time Maggie had let herself bargain with her own thoughts about any future. If only this could continue, she could maybe have a future again. *A future.*

At the thought, she angled her head to look up at Kam and of course he was already looking down at her. As if he was always aware of her next move. The look in his eyes made her wonder if he was reading her mind. He was looking at her with wonder and love, joy and promise, pride and just a hint of fire. Most of all, the look in his eyes held a question. *Maybe?* He could feel it too.

Maggie's stomach flipped. She wasn't sure if it was the whiskey or that look in his eyes. Maybe she was ready to realize some potential for herself but admitting that to Kam? That was an entirely different story. Her future was currently hinged upon a lot of what ifs and if onlys. She couldn't bear breaking Kam for a second time.

She gave herself one last moment to soak in the love in his eyes. To soak in the feeling that it was directed at her and how that warmed her chest. Then, she looked away, diffusing the feelings raging within her the only way she knew how.

"Shots?"

The next morning Maggie woke up on her brother's living room floor crammed in between two bodies. She felt the hangover she'd no doubt have all day start to build. She slitted open her eyes and saw that it was Kam's chest she was laying on, with his arm wrapped around her tightly. As if even in sleep he was still afraid of her running off again. She frowned at the fear she had instilled in him–even if it was entirely warranted. She turned her head to confirm that it was Rosa's butt right on top of hers.

She turned to nestle back into Kam's chest and the movement caused him to stir and start to wake up. She closed her eyes to feign sleep not wanting to ruin this moment. In this moment she could remain in the what ifs and if onlys.

"Stop faking. I know when you're actually sleeping. I've watched you sleep more times than I'd like to admit," Kam whispered. She should've known he'd know. She should've known better. He always did. She reopened her eyes and smiled up at him. He pulled her in tighter and kissed the top of her head, as if this was entirely normal for them.

He immediately tensed, realizing the intimacy of the moment. An intimacy neither was sure they shared anymore. An intimacy that felt awkward given their confusing history and their lack of any clear future.

"Sorry," he whispered.

'It's okay," she whispered back. They remained there a while longer in a more comfortable silence. She pulled herself even closer to him, scratching lazy circles into his chest as he mindlessly moved his thumb up and down where his hand rested on her hip. Eventually, Maggie dozed off again and was startled awake by Kam's alarm.

"Fuck, I need to get going so I can get to work on time," Kam grumbled. Reluctantly, he removed his arm from where it was wrapped around her and she rolled out of his hold. He moved to get ready for work, since he'd be going straight in, and Maggie remained sprawled on the hard floor, staring at the ceiling.

What the fuck was she doing? She still loved Kam, she knew that. She was almost entirely certain she always would. Her future was already dangling by a thin thread. If only she could get her relationship with her dad in check. If only she could regain some control of her spiraling life. If only she could know for sure that her hurt was subdued and not waiting to lurch back into her heart and strangle the life out of her.

Most of all, as much as she loved Kam, she knew there was another emotion she tethered to his presence in her life: fear. She wasn't afraid of Kam, of course. He wouldn't ever knowingly hurt her. She was afraid of what a future with him would entail. He'd force her to be honest. He'd force her to face her shit. He'd force her to be real with herself, rather than living in what ifs. He'd make her feel again. Everything. More than anything else, she feared the control he had over her. Of what losing him would do to her.

Not that he was fully aware of it or would ever use it maliciously, but it was there nonetheless. She was just in the process of regaining a semblance of control in her life. She was bargaining her life in a way she could keep neat and organized after a tsunami of chaos. As much as she loved Kam, their relationship had always been complex, even if much of that was on her.

She was tired of complicated. As much as she was working to gain control, he'd make her lose it in the one place she couldn't afford to–her heart. Maggie definitely wasn't ready to give up all of the control she was negotiating back into her existence.

"Walk me downstairs?" Kam's question disrupted her swirling thoughts. He held out a hand to help her stand up. It was a simple gesture, but Maggie felt like accepting his hand would mean more somehow. So in her full stubborn headed way, she rolled and used the couch to rise instead. Confusion crossed Kam's face momentarily, but he shook it off and smiled at her. His real smile. The full and brilliant one he always reserved for her. The one that always devastated Maggie's heart.

They walked downstairs in silence, Kam leading the way out the front door. It was a gorgeous day–cloudless and that perfect end of May temperature the East Coast always manufactured this time of year. Maggie closed her eyes and turned her face toward the sun, soaking in its gentle warmth.

When she finally reopened her eyes, without looking at him, she knew Kam was staring at her–soaking her in the same way. Taking in all of the good and ignoring all of the bad. Soaking up her gentle warmth while ignoring her harmful rays. Ignoring the way she could burn him.

"I'm taking you to dinner tonight," he finally said. Maggie whipped her head in his direction.

"Wh-What?" she stuttered.

"I'm taking you to dinner. Tonight. You know? The meal where you eat delicious food at some point in the evening. Drinks are sometimes involved," he quipped.

"Yes, I've heard of the concept. But you have work," she replied.

"I'll come back after work. I'll pick you up from here and we'll go to dinner," he pushed on.

"No," was all she answered.

"Yes," he rebutted.

"No," she said more forcefully.

"Yes," he replied, matching her tone.

"What if I don't want to?" Maggie glared at Kam.

"Oh you want to. I know that for sure. I'll pick you up at 7:30. Be ready, or I'm throwing you over my shoulder and we're going to dinner in whatever you're clothed in when I show up," he said over his shoulder as he made his way down the stairs smirking.

"I fucking hate you," she shouted playfully.

"No, you don't," he sang in reply.

"No, I don't," Maggie whispered somewhat sadly as she looked after him, feeling her control slipping with every word.

🌱 🌱 🌱

Kam was true to his word and showed up exactly at 7:30, looking more dapper than Maggie had ever seen him on any of their dinners before. She was thankful she went with a simple fitted dress that accentuated all of her curves and a pair of heels that elevated the look slightly but were still comfortable. It was an outfit that could work in multiple settings. She still had no clue where he was taking her after all.

"You really know how to make a man want to stop and stare, you know that Mags," he said as he took her hand and guided her down the stairs. She rolled her eyes, but couldn't help the smile and blush that crept into her cheeks. As much as she didn't like the lack of control Kam made her feel, she couldn't resist what almost felt like an innate desire to impress him.

He played the part of the perfect gentleman. He opened the door, helped her into the car, and even had flowers waiting for her. She smiled at the bouquet with its single bird of paradise flower at the center. She looked at him as he got into the driver's seat, her eyes softening. Kind Kam. Thoughtful Kam. He could be *her Kam.* She shut the thought down as quickly as it came. Not yet. She couldn't put him through her yet. Maybe in time. She looked down at the flowers. Immediately, he put his hand on her chin and gently forced her to look up again. At him. She couldn't help her gasp at the intensity in his gaze. He was a man on a mission. She knew exactly what that mission was: *her.*

"We should probably get going, right?" she said, hoping to break the moment and move forward. He gave her a single nod and put the car in drive. Maggie knew one thing for certain from that look of his: she was absolutely fucked.

Kam parked in a parking lot she knew very well. Maggie's entire body strained. It was her favorite restaurant. He knew that. The last time she was here, though, had been on her first date with Gabe. He also knew that.

Sensing her tension, Kam dragged a slow knuckle down her arm until reaching her hand, where he interlaced his fingers with hers. He waited until she finally turned to look at him. He could see it. All the hurt that motherfucker had caused her rising to the surface. He had expected a reaction like this. He hated that the piece of shit had the power to make her fear a place she had once loved.

"It's just you and me tonight, Mags," he whispered. Her nod was small and tense.

"The last time I was here..." her voice faded.

"I know," was all he said in response and waited. When she said nothing else he offered, "We can go somewhere else." He saw it in her eyes. She was thinking and processing. Weighing the hurts she was willing to bear and the ones she was hoping to release. Then, like a storm, resolve entered her gaze.

"No. Like you said, it's just you and me tonight. No one else gets to ruin things for me," she said with enough determination to convince almost anyone. Kam knew her better than most, though. He heard the note of apprehension. Even so, pride swelled in his heart. Maggie had always been a fighter. He was afraid she had given up for a while, but he could see her strength again. Her ability to conquer everything that came her way was what initially made him fall for her. He couldn't comprehend how anyone could look at her and not be in awe. How anyone could look at her and not fall at least a little bit in love.

A similar determination had been in her eyes the first night they met. He remembered that night clearly, even years later. They had been at a party celebrating a friend's birthday. He had just ended an argument with his freshly minted ex-girlfriend and needed to get away from the group for a few minutes. He knew the perfect spot where no one else would be. There was a small roof that overlooked the front door of the house. He made his way to his friend's room, whose window led right out onto his favorite hiding place. He noticed the already open window, thinking it strange, but shrugged and started to climb through anyway.

That was the moment he saw her for the first time, hunched in the window with one leg on the roof already and the other still on the floor back in the bedroom. He froze. Looking back now, maybe he should've known then that it wasn't the shock of seeing someone else on the roof that made him gasp, but rather the girl he found. She hadn't noticed him yet and he took a few moments to take her in.

She was in shorts and a tattered hoodie with her hair unbound. It was waist length back then and the blonde was a golden hue on one side from the streetlight and a silver hue on the other from the moonlight. She had her knees pulled to her chest with her arms wrapped around them. It was almost as if she were trying to make herself as small as possible. There was a beer bottle in her hand that she kept swirling as she stared off into the street. The look was one he knew well because he'd worn it himself more than enough times. It was a combination of disappointment and sadness. The look of someone who was tired of experiencing the same hurt over and over again.

He knew he should turn around and just leave. Find another corner of the house to take a breather in. There was just something about this girl that made him want to know her, know what had happened. Something inside him wanted nothing more than to make her smile and laugh. Knowing nothing about her, he somehow knew her laugh would be his favorite sound. So ignoring what he knew he should do, he followed the invisible tug that pulled him the rest of the way out of the window and toward this total stranger.

"I could bring the party out here to you, but I feel like it would get a little crowded," he humorously attempted. She didn't startle at his voice which surprised him. She did look a little irritated, though. He was about to double back into the house as her tension seemed to ease and she nodded at the spot next to her. He didn't even know her name, but he felt with an intense persistence that he needed to know everything about her as soon as possible. He walked the few steps to the edge of the roof and took a seat next to her.

She held out her beer bottle to cheers, which they did, and drank. They sat in silence for a few moments and it was killing him not to try and ask her a million questions. Or, at the very least figure out where to start the conversation with this girl who clearly had no desire to talk to or know anything about him.

"Do you ever think about how fucked it is that the people who are supposed to love us the most just don't sometimes? That they can be the ones who hurt us the most?" she asked without looking at him.

Of all the things he had expected her to potentially say, that was not one of them. As she stared at the street below, he stared at her. What the fuck was he supposed to say to that? That was some intense shit. He didn't know a single thing about her and she was just casually opening up one of the deepest conversations he'd ever had.

Or maybe it wasn't casual, he thought as he continued to stare at her. She looked too young to be asking these kinds of questions. He was only seventeen and she looked like she was a year or two younger. Then again, life never cares how old you are when it decides to start breaking you down. He thought about deflecting the question with a joke since that was his norm. Somehow he knew it wouldn't work with her. His norm would disappoint her further and he desperately wanted to avoid that.

"Sometimes," he finally offered her. A million dollar response clearly. He was floundering but had no clue what the hell to say. It felt better than saying nothing.

She turned to him surprised, as if she hadn't expected him to answer. It was only brief, before that disappointment flooded back in, as if it were overwhelming her. He needed to make her laugh, that was his only thought. It was as if even then he knew he would always be willing to drag her out of any depth.

"What are we supposed to do with that kind of love? Or is it even really love at that point?" she asked and took another gulp of her beer. She was truly something else. He was already in awe of her. The pretty girl with a sharp mind who seemed to materialize out of nowhere in his life. He needed desperately to not sound like a total idiot right now.

"I think there's more to love than just the good. I also think maybe some people just aren't capable of giving us the kind of love we need," he finally offered her. She looked at him as if she were just now sizing him up–trying to decide whether he was worthy to continue this conversation.

For reasons he couldn't figure out, he felt as though being deemed worthy was the most important thing in his life right now. After a few moments where Kam held his breath awaiting her approval, she grunted and then turned back to the street. They sat in silence for a while, or as much silence as a Brooklyn street could offer.

"My dad called me twenty minutes ago to remind me for the third time this week that women, myself included, have chicken shit for brains and I'll never amount to anything because of it. You would think always being top of my class and getting into one of the best high schools in the state would convince him otherwise, but I guess not," she shrugged, downing the rest of her beer. Kam tried to hide the shock on his face. With no clue what to say, he opted for a silent presence, nodding and leaning back on his elbows, letting his feet dangle over the edge of the roof.

"Bet you weren't expecting this conversation when you came out here to clear your head," she said, resting her head on her knees, angling it so she faced him.

"It's much better than the one I was just having downstairs," he answered.

"Let me guess... Girlfriend felt like you haven't been giving her enough attention, so y'all broke up and now you're up here with a complete stranger wondering how you ended up in the depths of my melodramatic teenage despair," she offered. Kam almost choked on his beer because that is *exactly* what had happened.

"How– Wha–" Kam blustered.

"You two had your argument directly below me. I wasn't eaves-dropping; she was just yelling," she winked, a small smile pulling at the corners of her mouth. Kam couldn't help but chuckle.

"Yeah, that's the gist of it. Except for the depths of your melodramatic teenage despair. I don't think you're being melodramatic, I think your dad is an asshole. And I don't think you're in despair at all," he said confidently.

"Oh really?" she wondered, reaching her hand out for his beer. He handed it over without hesitation.

"Yeah," he shrugged before continuing, "A dad shouldn't do that to his child. It's pretty fucked."

"And what about my despair?" she asked. He felt like his answer was important to her for some reason. That she cared about what he had to say even if she didn't know him at all.

"You're not in despair. I can see it in your eyes. You've been hurt by someone who is supposed to love you for sure. But there's something else there. I think you're someone who is used to proving people wrong. Telling the world to suck it. You have a look that tells me you'd never let a piece of shit move like your dad just pulled put you into despair. Instead, I think you're determined."

"Determined? To do what?" she asked, leaning towards him.

"To overcome," he offered simply. At this she nodded slightly and downed the rest of his beer before laying back on the roof next to him. She pulled her hair over one shoulder and turned on her side, resting her head on her hand.

He could see it clearly then: the fire in her eyes. This girl before him had been born to overcome, to fight, to keep going. Even with the fire, though, he could see her smile was still sad and felt like he needed to do something about that immediately.

Without giving it much thought, he asked for her phone. She looked a bit confused but handed it over anyway. She couldn't see what he was doing and looked even more confused as he handed her phone back to her.

"You said your dad called you three times this week?" he asked.

"Yeah..."

"Okay, pick up on the third ring!"

"Huh?"

Before she could ask more her phone was ringing. She looked at the number she didn't recognize and then back at him. She let it ring once, twice, and then answered on the third ring.

"Hello?" she said tentatively.

"Hey! This is Kam. The annoyingly handsome guy sitting next to you," at this her eyes crinkled in what he knew was the smile she was doing her best to suppress. "I just wanted to say that your brain has been the most impressive thing I've had the opportunity to experience in months and in no way resembles chicken shit." At this she finally allowed herself to smile broadly. Kam found it heartstopping.

"Oh yeah?" she smiled into the phone.

"Absolutely. And one more thing. FUCK YOUR DAD!" He wasn't sure if it was the unexpectedness of it or the way he shouted it into the empty Brooklyn street, but she started laughing without restraint. His prediction was right. Her laugh was his new favorite sound and he'd do anything to hear it over and over and over again.

"Thanks Kam," she said, hanging up.

"Anytime," he answered.

"Oh yeah?" she teased.

"Yeah. You need a reminder like that, you just call me up, and I'll answer on the third ring every time," he said, looking at her in a way he hoped conveyed how much he meant it.

"You can call me too, you know. I'll answer on the third ring too. It can be our thing," she offered.

"Promise?" he asked.

"Promise," she answered with a certainty that told him she never broke her promises. She sat up and rested her head on his shoulder finally adding, "My name is Maggie, by the way."

🌿 🌿 🌿

The memory hit him like a freight train. He remembered how they sat on that rooftop talking all night. They didn't go back inside until the sun was rising and party goers were passed out all over the house. As they searched, Maggie realized her ride had left her.

Naturally Kam offered to drive her home without knowing that this would become their routine. Not knowing that to the rest of the world Kam and Maggie would become a *they*. That to each other, they would become a *we*. That they would grow unyieldingly intertwined as their lives became seamlessly interwoven.

For the next few years, he repeatedly got to watch her prove him right. She was not someone to underestimate. He had seen that same blazing determination in her eyes so many times throughout their friendship. The same burning resolution he was seeing right now as they sat parked outside her favorite restaurant that Gabe had managed to ruin for her. But she wouldn't let him because deep down that's who Maggie was. It was one of the things that awed him most–her tenacity and her continued gentleness toward the world after so much pain and sorrow.

"I love—," he caught himself before he finished an admission that would almost certainly send Maggie running, covering up his almost slip with a cough. "I love this place and I know you do too. I wanted to remind you of its goodness, instead of letting some asshole ruin it for you forever."

"Thank you," she said, squeezing his hand gently. He had forgotten they were holding hands. Apparently she had too, because she looked down and immediately released their hold and started turning toward the car door.

"Freeze!" Kam half shouted, hopping out of his seat and running across the front of his car to open her door. As they walked into the restaurant, her hand resting in the crook of his elbow, Kam knew two things for certain. First, he loved this woman more than he had ever imagined possible. Second, he had loved her from that very first night and had just never let himself realize it.

Dinner went flawlessly. The food was delicious. The sangria was flowing. Kam had Maggie laughing so hard she was crying and by the end of the night her cheeks hurt from the perpetual smile she had been wearing. Kam had hazarded an attempt to hold her hand across the table, and to his surprise she let him without any hesitation.

After dinner, they made their way out of the restaurant and Maggie made to turn toward the parking lot, but he tugged her gently. He nodded his head to the little park across the street. The one with the bench she loved to sit on. Again, she froze.

The last time she had visited her favorite bench was that first night with Gabe. The things she had shared that night. She couldn't help but wonder how she had been so stupid to let him in so quickly. She shook her head and hoped Kam would acknowledge that it would be too much in one night for her.

Instead of following her pull to the car, Kam quirked a brow, held up one finger asking her to hold on, turned around, and squatted a bit.

"Kam, no," she said, knowing exactly what he was doing.

"Hop on," he said, motioning for her to jump on his back for a piggy back ride. Just like he had at Mitch's party when her anxiety had peaked. He waited a moment before looking over his shoulder at her. Damn him for the way he looked at her. The determination. The spark. The *hope*.

Hope had always been the curse in Maggie's life. Hope for her was like the sea kissing the shoreline during a storm. You could rely on it to come and go but never in a steady rhythm. Damn Kam and his hope and the way it gripped her heart, dragging her in against all of her best senses. Without another word, she gave Kam a small nod and hopped on his back. Would hope be a caressing wave or a destructive tsunami tonight? Maggie had no clue.

They sat on the bench staring at the highway across the river. Maggie rested her head on Kam's shoulder while he held her hand in his lap. It was a comfortable silence, neither feeling the need to fill it for the longest while.

Maggie thought about what life could have been like if her mom had never died. Specifically, what life with Kam could have looked like. She was certain it would have been filled with lots of nights like tonight. Nights that felt good. Nights that made her feel a little more alive again. If only.

What if he was willing to wait for her? What if he gave her some time? What if she could reconstruct a relationship with her dad that looked a fraction like what she had with her mom to fill that gap? What if she could use the time she was committed to work in Vegas to do a little more healing? What if she could have Kam after all of that? If only.

Meanwhile, Kam's thoughts had him entirely convinced that Maggie and him could work out. Immediately. He knew she was moving, but they could make that work. Distance had never been an issue for their relationship before. Plus, she'd be coming back. He knew she had a lot of things she was working on, but he was ready to walk through it all with her. Step up where she needed and step back where she didn't. This felt too right to ignore. It felt good. It finally felt like she was his right person at the right time.

We could do this.

"What?" Maggie asked. Apparently he hadn't just thought the last part. Somehow it had made its way through his mind and out of his mouth. He looked down at Maggie, who was looking at him, waiting. He wasn't entirely sure how this would go, but he might as well try. He was never one to wait and tended to throw caution to the wind.

"We could do this," he said more clearly, looking at her and assessing her reaction. At first he saw confusion, warranted as he had given her no context. Then, as she looked back and forth between their intertwined hands and the look in his eyes, clearly conveying his meaning, he saw the flash of panic. His disappointment was immediate. Panic was not the response he had been hoping for. He was ready to start back tracking, but before he could start, Maggie spoke.

"I was just thinking about the same thing," she whispered. At first Kam was elated. For once, they were on the same page, but it was the way she had said it that didn't feel quite right. Her voice was small. Her shoulders slumping slightly. Her eyes looking away from him. His elation deflated.

"But...?" he prodded.

"But, not right now," she offered him slowly, as if it hurt her as much to say as she knew it would hurt him to hear.

"What do you mean?" he couldn't stop the question as it tumbled from his mouth. If not now, then when? What was there to wait for? Shit, hadn't they already wasted enough time waiting? He wasn't sure where this sense of urgency was coming from. Maybe it was the memory of the first time they met. Maybe it was how perfect this night had felt. He felt in his bones that it had to be now and he had to make her see that.

"I mean," Maggie sighed, "not right now. I'm moving to Vegas Kam. Of course, I'll be back, but I'll be there for a while and–"

"Distance has never been an issue before," he interjected before she could continue.

"I know that, but this isn't just a long drive. This is time zone differences and long flights. We've never done *that* before. I was thinking... I was thinking what if I used that time to heal more? To get better for you?" she asked shyly.

"Mags, you're already perfect for me. Why can't you see that? I don't need to wait two years for you to become what you deem as better. I want to walk with you for those two years becoming better together. I'm tired of waiting. We can *do* this," he offered her. She heard the urgency mixed with a hint of desperation and a bit of frustration. She could tell that what had started as a perfect dinner may just become another turning point in their relationship. She wasn't sure yet which way it would turn.

"That's not the only thing," she said.

"What?" Kam asked. She wondered how to phrase what she was hoping would come of her relationship with her father. Kam hated the guy and she knew he wouldn't want to hear about him in the context of their relationship. She pulled her hand from his and steeled herself as she spoke before she could second guess herself.

"I was thinking, what if we waited until I could figure things out with my dad? What if he could be better too? What if he could fill a small fraction of the gap that losing my mom has left? If only I could heal a small portion of that pain, I could offer you so much more," she said, crossing her hands in her lap and bracing for his reaction. Kam was silent for a long time. Too long. She finally found the courage to look over at him and saw the anger he was doing his best to hold back. She opened her mouth to try and explain more, but Kam started before she could.

"Asking me to wait two years for you to come back from Vegas is one thing," he started, "but asking me to wait around for something that's *never* going to happen is another thing entirely."

She tensed. At him. At his words. At his tone. Did he really think it was that impossible? She felt like it was logical. A good way to regain some of what she had lost. How could he not see what she was trying to do? How could the man who had always understood her not understand?

"What–" she started.

"He's never going to change, Mags. I know you want to believe that he can so you can have a hope of filling in some of the holes your grief has created, but your dad isn't the man for the job. He never has been and he never will be."

"But he could," Maggie started, her voice rising. She was annoyed by his inability to budge when it came to her father. These last few weeks he'd been trying. He'd shown up to every meeting they planned. He was sober at all of them. He had just come to her graduation. They were talking on the phone regularly. He was doing it.

"No, he can't," Kam said. For the first time in all the years she had known Kam his voice was cold. She had heard this tone a few times before but never directed toward her. She was hit with an initial wave of shock that turned immediately into rage. How had their night taken such a drastic turn so quickly?

"Yes, he fucking can, Kam. In case you haven't noticed, he already is. He's working on it. He's showing up. He's drinking less–at least around me. He's trying to be my *dad*. Do I know he'll never be my mom? Of course. I'm not a moron. No one could ever be my mom. But he could be something. Something I might need right now. Why can't you give him a fucking chance, Kam? I don't get it," she had stood up and was almost screaming by the time she was done.

"Why do you give him SO MANY chances, Mags?" Kam shot back, also rising to his feet.

"Because chances with him are all I have left in my life," she said sadly. Kam knew her pain should've squashed his rage, but his emotions had entirely overtaken him. How many chances was he going to give her? How many times was he going to give her the power to break him? How many times was he going to keep letting her run back into his life and his heart? How many times was he going to keep running in circles, ending up in the same place with her every time?

"So you'd rather chance it with him than know for sure with me?" he asked, still half shouting.

"That's not what I'm saying, Kam," she said, entirely deflated. Normally, Kam would rush to comfort her. He would find the right thing to say. The right thing to do. Tonight, though, he didn't feel like doing any of that. He loved this woman in front of him. He knew that with every fiber of his being, but he couldn't keep letting her hurt him. He couldn't keep feeling like this. Maybe it was like what he had said to her the first night they met. *Maybe some people just aren't capable of giving us the kind of love we need.*

Maybe that was the problem with him and Maggie. Hadn't she said exactly that to him when she left him in his driveway? Maybe, her warning was valid. Maybe the Maggie that was left in the wake of her grief wasn't capable of giving Kam the kind of love he needed. And maybe, he wasn't capable of giving her the kind *she* needed. Maybe his hope for their future had blinded him to this truth. Maybe she was the right person, but maybe it would just never be the right time.

"Kam," Maggie continued. "I love you, you have to know that. More than I've ever thought possible. More than I ever thought I'd love someone. But, I'm just starting to enter a place where I can regain some control in my life. I want to be able to focus on that without being distracted by–" at the look on Kam's face, Maggie knew she had just said the entirely wrong thing.

"So I'm a distraction?" Kam said, voice like ice.

"No, that's not what I–" Maggie started.

"Yes, it is. You know what Mags, whatever. If you want to waste your time with your piece of shit father, be my guest. I can't keep wasting my time. I can't keep hoping that one day you'll be ready. The hope will kill me. Or at the very least start to sour the love I feel for you. I'm here. Right now. Ready to love you like you deserve. Ready to walk through fucking fire with you. Ready to make you laugh and love and *live* again. Ready to fill those gaps you're talking about. But, if you want to spend your time focusing on a man who has hurt you more times than I can count, go for it. But you can't keep running back to me. So go ahead and choose. Me–right in front of you and ready for everything life together could entail. Or your dad. The man who constantly forgets you exist. Who drinks more than he breathes. Who will not be there for you. Who doesn't love you the way he should. Who you will never be good enough for. Who tells you that you have fucking chicken shit for brains," Kam fumed, his breathing ragged by the time he was done.

Maggie flinched as if he had physically struck her. That was all it took to entirely diffuse his anger. He instantly knew he fucked up. Although he had mostly meant everything he just said, he knew using her father's words against her was a mistake. He had promised her once that he would never use anything she opened up about in any future arguments. Enough people had done that to her before. That's exactly what he just did. Her extremely honest and personal admission from the first night they met had just become his leverage against her dad.

"Take me home," Maggie whispered.

"Mags," Kam started, reaching out for her.

"Take me home," she shouted this time. He could see the glassiness of her eyes. The tears she'd never cry in front of him.

"Mags," he said, the gravity of what just happened finally hitting him.

"Take me the fuck home, Kameron," she seethed. Although his words had been grounded in truth, the way he chose to express that truth wasn't fair. He had hurt her. He had used her past against her. He knew there was nothing he could say or do right now. So he simply nodded his head sadly and turned back toward the parking lot.

How could a day that had started with Maggie in his arms end with a distance between them he wasn't sure they'd ever be able to close? How had this all happened in what felt like the blink of an eye?

A month passed. Maggie kept true to her plan of rebuilding some kind of relationship with her father. They continued to consistently meet up and talk on the phone. He was still showing up and he was always sober. He never drank around her and she could feel the hope of what this could become over time. He'd never fill the chasm losing her mom had created, but he could offer her something. Something for Maggie was better than nothing.

Maggie, Rosa, and Kam continued their friend dates, but they began feeling forced and uncomfortable. Kam started showing up less consistently until he stopped showing up altogether. Kam and Maggie continued to talk here and there, mostly through text. The conversation was forced in a way it never had been before.

The only thing that felt like it had remained the same was their promise to answer on the third ring. Although the calls were significantly less frequent, if she called him, he would still *always* answer on the third ring. She always did the same. Although it seemed they had given up on what could have been between them, they still hadn't given up on each other entirely.

Another month passed and with it came her mom's birthday. This was always a hard anniversary for Maggie. Yet another reminder of all the birthdays her mom had been robbed of because of her cancer. She always remembered her mom's last living birthday. The tears her mom cried as Maggie and her brother sang happy birthday to her over a cupcake while crammed in their tiny kitchen. The tears caused by the simple joy of being able to see another birthday. Being able to live long enough for one more.

This was a day that Maggie tried to spend alone wrapped in only her grief. She wasn't ready to face the world on these kinds of anniversaries. She'd usually post something on social media to excuse her absence, heart any texts from friends, and then stay in bed all day. Most people knew to leave her to her own devices. She'd wallow and then be ready to face the world again the next day.

She always thought about how many other birthdays would be happening on the same day. About how many weddings might be happening. About how many good anniversaries might be happening. About how many babies might be born today. She always found it fascinating that one of the worst days of her life could be the absolute best day of someone else's.

As she pondered this, her phone rang. Weird. Everyone knew to leave her alone today. Who could be calling her? She picked up her phone and saw "INCOMING CALL FROM DAD" flash across the screen. Although she didn't really feel like talking to anyone, maybe talking to him would help.

"Hello?" Maggie said, half greeting, half question.

"Hello, my daughter. My blood. My love," her dad responded. Maggie's heart sank to her stomach. That greeting and the way he said it was all she needed to tell that he was drunk. If she had to guess, he was absolutely plastered and it was only ten in the morning.

"Dad?" she offered.

"That's me. Your father. The one who gave you life," he rumbled back. This was hopeless. Maggie knew that deep down. When he got like this, it was inevitable that he would say something hurtful. When he got this drunk, her dad would strike out for blood. It looked like today she was his victim of choice, as she had been so many times before. And yet, some tiny part of her hoped today would be different.

"What are you up to?" she asked, hoping to try and control the conversation before he could say anything hurtful.

"A little of this and a little of that. What about you, my daughter?" he asked back.

"Just at home. I don't usually do much today. Mom's birthday is usually a little hard for me," she answered.

"Heartless bitch," he bickered. This shocked Maggie to her core. Was he calling her a heartless bitch? Or her mom? Neither was a good option, but where had this come from?

"What?" she asked, clearly shocked.

"Your mom. She was a heartless bitch. She always told you all these lies about me. To keep you away from me. To make you hate me," he continued spouting vitriol as Maggie dazed out of the conversation momentarily.

What the fuck was he talking about? Her mom was far from heartless. If anything, she had felt things a little too fully at times. Her mom was the reason there was any ounce of a relationship to restore with her dad. Her mom had been the one to constantly encourage her to give him another chance. Her mom was the one who had always told her to call him. Her mom always made sure Maggie didn't give up on him entirely. Her mom was the reason Maggie had even thought her dad had a chance at stepping up in her mom's absence. Drunk or not, this was low–even for him. By the time her thoughts finished spiraling and she tuned back into the conversation, minutes had passed and her father was still spewing hate at her mother. Maggie snapped.

"Shut the fuck up," she said with years of pent up rage.

"Excuse me? Who do you think you're speaking to?" her father raged back.

"I'm speaking to a drunk, pathetic fool who wants to blame everyone else for his own bullshit behavior," she met his rage with her own.

"I'm your FATHER," he shouted into the phone.

"No, you're not. You're a sperm donor. The only reason you can even try to call yourself a *father*," Maggie said with absolute distaste, "is because of the woman you're calling a heartless bitch. She was the one telling me to always give you another chance. She was the one always trying to convince me that you loved me the best you could. She was the one always telling me to call you and hang out with you. Had it been up to me, I would've given up on you a long time ago. It was mom who tried to make me hate you less. Looks like it was all for nothing," Maggie was shouting.

"You're a little bitch just like her," he spouted back, "You two deserved each other. You deserved to lose her. She deserved to die," he said as if it were nothing. It felt as if every ounce of air had been ripped from Maggie's lungs. How had she forgotten he could be so hurtful? How had she let herself be so blinded by the potential of him that she forgot the reality of him?

"Go fuck yourself," she said coldly into the phone, void of any real emotion and hung up. The plan she had so carefully crafted crumbled. The deal she had made with herself was belly up. The control she thought she was gaining spiraled out. Before she could take another breath, sobs overtook her. How could she have been so fucking stupid?

She wasn't sure how long she had stayed in bed sobbing, but eventually her tears stopped. Or maybe she just ran out of tears to cry. As the sobs subsided, she felt the urgent need to talk to someone. Anyone. First she phoned Rosa, who she knew was working. She wasn't surprised when she didn't answer–she couldn't. She tried her brother next. He answered, but the conversation left her feeling equally empty and out of control. Their conversation consisted mostly of her sobbing again while he vowed to kill their dad. Not helpful.

She sat in bed staring at the wall across from her. Even with all of her bargaining and planning and trying, she still ended up in the same place. Hurting and alone.

She didn't want to be alone right now. So she made one more call. Of course he answered on the third ring, sounding a little surprised. They made a plan to grab a drink in an hour. Kam had been right the entire time and she felt compelled to tell him.

Compelled to be near him. She was doing exactly what he had accused her of that night in the park: running back to him. It wasn't fair and she knew it. With one plan crumbling she started making another in her mind. She was done bargaining and operating on what ifs.

Before she started getting ready, she knew she needed to do something. She had always been trash at expressing herself when it came to Kam. She always said the wrong thing or chose her words poorly with him. She turned to the one strength she had always been proud of–her writing. She sat and wrote two letters to Kam. Two letters for two potential outcomes. One for if things went the way she hoped, and one for if things went the way she feared they might.

༝ ༝ ༝

An hour later Maggie found herself nervously tapping the side of her glass of beer while waiting for Kam. For probably the first time ever, Maggie was early. Given her late to life nature, she wasn't used to being the one waiting for the other person.

After fifteen impatient and anxiety filled minutes, Kam walked in. Apparently, he was also so accustomed to her being late that he was shocked to see her already there. He walked over to the high top she was seated at and Maggie wondered if she would ever get used to the feeling that rushed over her whenever she saw him. The way having him near always settled her.

He looked her over and furrowed his brows. She knew he could tell she had been crying, but things had been so tense between them recently, he wasn't sure how to proceed. Their waitress came over, took his drink order, and their uncomfortable silence continued. They both stared at each other, neither knowing what to really say. Since she had been the one to ask for him to meet her, Maggie figured she should dive right in.

"How are you?" he asked.

"You were right," she said simultaneously. Shock streaked his features. If there was one thing Kam knew Maggie hated, it was admitting someone else had been right and she had been wrong. He just stared at her, mouth slightly agape.

"You were right," she said again, looking down and fidgeting with the napkin in her hands. "You were right and I was wrong. I was so fucking dumb." It wasn't until Kam saw a tear drop onto the table that he realized she had started crying. He knew today was her mom's birthday and that it was a hard day for her. That's why he was so surprised she had called at all. She usually hermitted herself away on days like today. He somehow knew these tears weren't about the anniversary. They were about something else entirely.

"What are you talking about?" he asked softly.

"My dad. You were right. I should've listened to you. He's never going to be what I need. He just isn't capable of changing. Not entirely at least. I needed you to know that you were right. I needed you to know that–" she stopped abruptly, doing her best to hold back a sob.

"I'm sorry," Kam offered as she composed herself. "I really didn't want to be right. Even with what I said, which I shouldn't have, I really wished you could have what you were hoping for with him." She nodded sadly and it hurt him to see her so resigned. Like she had entirely given up.

"I'm sorry, too," she said. And he saw the shift happen–from resignation back to that fire. A shift he'd witnessed dozens of times. It was small and mixed with doubt, but the fire to overcome was still there. The look he loved. His girl was a fighter.

"Admitting I was right *and* an apology all in one day. Is hell freezing over?" he asked jokingly. A smile tugged at her lips as she rolled her eyes, but even his joke couldn't get rid of the anxiety that was written all over her. What had her so nervous?

"Don't you want to know what I'm sorry for?" she asked, not quite looking at him but staring off at the space just past him.

"Only if you want to tell me," he answered.

"I'm sorry because I should have chosen you. I should have *always* chosen you," she said, finally looking into his eyes. He could see she meant it. Her eyes were riddled with a mix of regret and pure love. Kam felt his breath catch. He had waited so long for this. Not long ago he had been desperate for her to finally choose him over everything else–her dad, her chaos, her grief. But now, he wasn't sure what to say. As he stared at her in stunned silence, Maggie reached across the table to grab his hand. He looked down at where she held his hand. He had wanted this for so long, but...

"There's someone else," he finally said quietly, giving her hand a gentle squeeze before pulling away. Maggie nodded slowly as if she weren't entirely surprised, her mouth pressing into a line. "I'm sorry Mags. It wasn't something I expected. I was just so frustrated and tired. She came out of nowhere and I decided to give it a chance. It's not serious, but I think it could be if I give it the opportunity."

"You have nothing to apologize for, Kam. I'm the one who fumbled our potential. You deserve to be happy," Maggie said as she plastered on a smile. The smile he hated. The fake one she used to try and convince everyone around her that she was fine. He hated that he could be the root of any pain for her, but he wasn't lying when he said this had been unexpected. He also wasn't lying when he said he saw the potential for more. The kind of potential he used to hope Maggie would be willing to work toward with him.

"You don't have to fake it with me Mags," he said.

"I'm not," she replied, "I really am happy for you. You deserve to be so loved. I'm sorry I didn't step up for you sooner. I want more than anything for you to have a real chance at love in your life. A love you deserve that isn't challenging and hard. If you're happy, I'm happy," she said, but her smile was sad and didn't quite reach her eyes. With that, she downed the rest of her beer and pulled an envelope from her bag. She handed it to him as she stood to leave.

"What is this?" he asked.

"I've never been good with telling you things, Kam. So I tried writing them down this time instead. Don't read it today, please. It'll probably just make you frustrated or confused if you do. Hold onto it though. One day sometime in the future, if you're thinking of the potential of us again, that's when you should read it. Or maybe if you're ever reminiscing on what we had or could've had. But not now. I love you, Kam. Be happy," she explained, leaning down and gently kissing his cheek.

Before Kam could say another word Maggie was walking toward the exit. Kam couldn't help but wonder if she wasn't just walking out of this bar, but also out of his life. He also couldn't help but wonder if this time when she was walking away, it was forever.

Depression

Playlist

loml / Taylor Swift

Numb Little Bug / Em Beihold

Inside Her Head / Bryce Savage

Just Because I Called You / Will Linley

if depression gets the best of me / Zevia

5

Depression

A year had passed since that final conversation with Kam. Maggie had mostly settled into her new life across the country. In that year, she got a puppy, started her new job in education, and tried to make the best of what life had given her.

She had new routines and found that her breakdowns happened less and less. That being said, although the frequency of her breakdowns had decreased, the intensity of them grew exponentially. She found herself in the middle of one of those breakdowns right now.

She had been driving home from a day of casual shopping when she looked over at her passenger seat. A thought crossed her mind before she could stop it: mom should be sitting there. As soon as the thought hit, so did the sobs. She knew she looked insane to anyone who drove by her, but when she was struck by one of these bursts of grief she simply could not stop them. She had learned in her year living on her own that all she could do was wait them out. Endure them. Survive them.

As she sobbed, she made her survival plan for this one. She would stop at some fast food drive thru, pick up a bottle of wine, and then sit on the couch self soothing with her food and booze.

This was a routine she had slipped into all too comfortably. Was it the healthiest? No. Did it at least work? Also no. Maggie just convinced herself it did.

Although the move hadn't necessarily been her choice since she had been placed in Vegas, she was thankful for the distance. Life felt easier, in a way, being so far away from her friends and family. She of course still stayed in touch with everyone, but she had been much more low contact since moving across the country. People would come to visit and she answered calls and texts, but she didn't particularly instigate communication. She preferred being alone and on her own. It was easier to avoid her grief when she was so far away from it. Except when one of these moments hit, but at least with the physical distance this only happened once every so often compared to almost every day.

Her first year in education had been overwhelming. Hell, life in general had been overwhelming in the last year. At least she had a knack for education. She was good with kids. She understood them and could build authentic trust with them. They respected her and she respected them. It made working with them significantly easier and made the kids more likely to listen. She had found at least one thing in her life that she could do well. She was almost excited to go into her second year. At least as excited as she had managed to be about something in her life in a while.

Life itself still felt overwhelming and heavy most days. Adult responsibilities came with adult problems and Maggie had already had enough of those before she had even graduated college. In the last year, she'd made some local friends and met a few people, but she had never really moved on from that last meeting with Kam.

Damn her heart. Her breath caught at just the thought of him. Would that feeling ever go away? She could still remember the look in his eyes and the pain in his voice when he had to tell her there had been someone else. As always, right person, *wrong* time. She wondered if he was still dating them. Had it gone anywhere? Gotten to the level Kam had always hoped for?

They still talked every so often, but their friendship had been somewhat strained since that last meeting and her move. Their conversations typically stayed surface level. Work. Her dog. Vegas life. Life back East. They never pushed any further and usually kept the conversations short. She preferred it this way. Keeping everyone at a distance was an easier way to live. A safer way to live.

Was Maggie sad? Not particularly. Was she happy? Not really. She tended to live in the in-between of feelings. In a place where you didn't really feel much of anything. She liked it there. It was in the in-between that she could avoid the overwhelm and confusion. It was in the in-between she could not necessarily live, but at the very least survive.

Another year passed with Maggie living in much the same way. Wake up as late as she could and still be on time. Go to work. Come home alone. Go to sleep as early as possible. Repeat.

Sometimes she would sprinkle in a bottomless brunch or boozy night out. Anything where she could potentially end up black out. Avoiding everything was her modus operandi, whether it was through sleep or too much alcohol, it didn't matter–she was ready to stick with it.

It wasn't a particularly interesting life, but it got her to the next day and that was truly her only goal. Stay alive and survive until tomorrow. She didn't want to die, but she didn't particularly want to be alive either. So she survived. For her family and friends. So they wouldn't have to experience the same pain that she did in losing her mother.

She started reaching out to people less and isolating more. She preferred being home with just her and her dog. Bingeing whatever was on hand. A TV show. A cheeseburger. A bottle of wine. It didn't matter as long as she had too much of it in order to block out her own emotional overwhelm.

Maggie was supposed to be moving back East, but she had decided not to. Her two year commitment was up, so she technically could leave without any issues, but had decided to stay in Vegas. Being away from everyone was easier. Being in a place that didn't carry memories of her mom in every nook and cranny made it simpler to avoid the missing her that had plagued her for so long. She had learned that isolation and avoidance were tantamount in her survival.

She couldn't promise her family and friends the Maggie they had always known, but she could promise she would survive. It was better for them to not know what survival looked like in her life these days. So she stayed in Vegas. She didn't need her people in her business and judging the means by which she kept herself alive, which she knew they would. They wouldn't understand it. They wouldn't understand the need to calm the overwhelm through whatever means worked for her. It was easier this way. Better.

¥ ¥ ¥

It was early August and Maggie found herself at a professional development conference before starting her third year in education. She had expected the hoards of teachers and the loads of professional development books they'd be handing out. What she hadn't expected was the unhinged behavior of the massive purple cow mascot in front of her. Whoever was inside that costume was definitely not getting paid enough.

The purple cow was there to advertise some literacy program to support students, but not a single person was paying any attention to the handouts and books on the table. Everyone was instead watching this mascot as it twerked and attempted (without success) to do cartwheels. Maggie had to admit, the person in the cow costume was great at getting everyone's attention. You couldn't help but look at them. But, she doubted anyone had a single clue what the mascot was actually there to advertise.

"Do you think he does private parties?" Maggie heard a voice ask beside her. Since she had come alone, she was a bit startled by the random conversation. She looked over at the man who had spoken to her and took him in for a moment.

He was just barely taller than her with deep brown hair that she felt would shift between auburn and chestnut depending on the way the sunlight hit it. His eyes were a pale shade of brown and transfixed her. His smile shone against his olive skin and she noticed she liked the way it looked. It was a shy smile that she caught herself staring at.

After a few moments, she realized she had been staring for too long without responding. She also realized she had entirely forgotten what he had asked.

"What?" she fumbled, sounding far from eloquent while blushing slightly. His shy smile grew a fraction warmer.

"I had asked if you thought the cow did private parties? Clearly it has a talent for entertaining. I think he'd be great for my grandma's 75th birthday party," he joked.

"I can try and sneak in there and get a contact for you, but I prefer to avoid injury by twerking cow. I'd hate to have to explain that one to my insurance," Maggie quipped back. At this, he laughed deeply. His laugh made Maggie feel something she couldn't quite put her finger on. She had locked her feelings away for so long that she had started struggling to even name them. She could tell that it would never be her favorite laugh in the world but she liked it enough.

"Rafael," the stranger said, holding out his hand.

"Maggie," she offered, shaking his outstretched hand.

"Well Maggie, as riveted as I am by this cow, I think I'd much rather buy you a cup of coffee. Something tells me that you'll be much more captivating. What do you say?" he asked, his eyes hopeful. She should say no. She had said no so far to everyone else who had asked her out in the past two years. But something in his laugh and his eyes had her nodding her agreement before she realized what she was doing. And so, off she walked with him, breaking her true isolation for the first time in two years.

❦ ❦ ❦

An hour later, Maggie found herself laughing so hard her stomach hurt. She learned that Rafael, who went by Raf, worked in a middle school and they had spent the last hour swapping war stories. Kids were truly ridiculous. As her laughter died down, she checked her watch. She should get going so she could let her dog out, but she had to admit she was enjoying herself. As if noticing her apprehension, Raf spoke first.

"Listen, I'm having a blast, but I need to get going. I promised a friend I would help them with something and need to leave soon to get there on time. Is there any chance I could get your phone number and we can plan a time when I could take you out?" he asked. Again, Maggie knew she should say no. She knew he didn't fit into her survival plan. She knew better, and yet... she found herself writing down her phone number on a napkin and sliding it across the table to him.

"I'll text you later," he said, getting up and leaving the coffee shop. Once he was gone, the overwhelm kicked in. What the hell was she doing? She had her routines. She had her ways. She had her survival method. She didn't know what had come over her, but she did know that Raf was guaranteed to interrupt whatever cycles she found herself in. She wasn't sure if that terrified her or excited her. Or maybe it was a little of both?

Two weeks later Maggie was on Zoom with Rosa catching up on life. Rosa was the only person Maggie let break her self isolation. If she were being honest, though, she'd admit she had even started to keep Rosa at an arm's length. She hated herself for it, but she was convinced she was better off alone. Rosa was in the middle of updating Maggie on her new project when her phone pinged. Maggie checked it quickly, at least she thought she had.

"Oh for fuck's sake! You're smiling at his texts now? You're in trouble girlfriend," Rosa joked through the computer screen.

"What? No!" Maggie half shouted back in a panic. She had told Rosa about Raf—as much as there was to tell at least. Which wasn't much. They had only gone on three dates since the day they met.

"Bullshit! I just watched you. I know that smile Mags. It's the smile you get when a person you're interested in texts you something so mundane, but it feels so special coming from them. So, unless that's Harry Styles and you failed to mention that you and him are now in a budding romance. It's Raf. You like him," Rosa argued.

"No, I don't," Maggie said exasperated.

"Yes, you do. But you don't want to admit it because you're in this little bubble you've created that no one can enter. And that's fine. For now. I'll let you believe what you want. But, someone has got to be honest with you if you won't be honest with yourself," Rosa ranted. Maggie just rolled her eyes. Rosa was right, of course. She had always been right when it came to Maggie's relationships. Maggie was far from willing to admit she was slowly letting someone back into her life. She wasn't even sure she had the capacity to let anyone in anymore.

She figured she shouldn't get ahead of herself, it had only been two weeks after all. Raf would grow out of caring for her. She was too messy and heavy. How could he, or anyone for that matter, ever want to love her once they saw all of her? She didn't even want to love herself.

⁂

"Are you seeing anyone else," Raf asked as they sat on Maggie's couch watching a movie. Two more weeks had passed and Maggie and Raf had been spending a lot more time together. A lot of it felt like things you would do with a friend. A quick coffee stop. A new hike. A baseball game. They had never done anything particularly intimate.

"What?" the question caught Maggie off guard. "No, why?" she sputtered.

"I was just wondering," he said. Maggie nodded and turned her attention back to the movie. "I'm not seeing anyone else either," he added after a few moments had passed. He seemed tenser than usual. Nervous.

"Okay..." Maggie said slowly, looking over at him. As soon as her eyes locked with his, she understood his intention. She felt so stupid for not understanding sooner. A month had passed and this was his way of asking her to be exclusive, however people did that these days.

Her breath caught in a panic. She hadn't entirely expected this. Then again, what had she expected? They had been spending increasing amounts of time together and that typically had one outcome. Somehow she had hoped they would avoid this altogether–that maybe he wasn't actually interested in her and they would just be flirty friends.

Looking at him now, though, she knew that her line of thinking was entirely wrong. He was interested in her and he was doing his best to express that, even if it was coming out a bit awkward. She needed to decide now what she would do. Would she continue whatever this was or kill it before it could go any further?

As they stared at each other, she realized that although she loved her isolation, she didn't want to be entirely alone right now. Maybe she could have a bit of both. Maybe she could still maintain a semblance of keeping herself closed off, while giving him just enough of what he needed.

So, before fear or rational thought stopped her, she shifted on the couch so she was facing him. She leaned forward and kissed him, slowly. She could feel his initial shock, but then all of his tension eased as he put a hand on either side of her face and kissed her back. He kissed her with purpose. As if at any moment she might change her mind and he needed to convince her otherwise. Poor Raf. He had no clue the mess he was entering with this kiss.

Their kiss deepened as purpose turned into desire. Maggie found herself moving before she could stop herself. One moment she was beside Raf and the next she was straddling him on her couch. In the process his hands moved from her face to her shoulder blades and down her back. She slid her hand up his shoulders and around to the back of his neck, running her fingers into his hair.

She had missed physical contact like this. She missed being wanted. She missed being desirable. She missed being touched. She wanted *more*.

She felt her body moving of its own accord. She broke their kiss and Raf's disappointment was obvious. She winked at him, pressing a quick, gentle kiss to his lips before she pulled her shirt over her head. The feel of his fingers on her bare skin sent a shiver down her spine as she arched into his touch. She forgot how good it felt to be touched like this.

She brought her eyes back to his and saw nothing but desire. Before he could say anything, she brought her face to his and this kiss was full of urgency. She wanted him badly and she wanted him to know that.

As she deepened their kiss, still on his lap, she started grinding against him. Her hips moved with a fluidity she had forgotten and the friction felt amazing. As she moved, his hands slowly made their way to grip her hips. He squeezed as she continued to grind on him. She could feel him growing harder beneath her. It was a glorious sensation–both physically and knowing she could still make a man feel like this–which she had forgotten in the last two years.

Feeling his erection growing, she dragged her hands slowly down his chest and started on the button of his jeans. Immediately, he moved one hand from her hips to stop her. She froze.

"I... I struggle with intimacy," he offered her. Maggie nodded and started to move off of him when he continued. "But I don't want to stop right now. I just don't want to go there. At least not tonight," he said almost apologetically.

"I understand," Maggie said with a soft smile. She leaned forward kissing him again and started slowly moving her hips once more. His groan was guttural as she continued what they had started. She continued moving, picking up the pace, and he gripped her hips tighter, forcing her against him harder. She felt his erection fully. She felt equal parts elated and ridiculous. Was she really dry humping this guy on her couch like they were teenagers? She couldn't deny that it felt exciting to be desired again, even if the scenario felt a little ridiculous. Lost in her thoughts, Maggie almost didn't notice Raf's grunt and the jerkiness of his movements until...

"Did you just..." Maggie asked, almost in disbelief.

"Yeah," Raf answered sheepishly. Maggie tried not to be shocked, but she couldn't help how high school this felt. He had just come in his pants from making out and dry humping?

"You can go to the bathroom to clean–" she started.

"It's probably best if I just go home," he interrupted her.

"Okay," she said. She could tell he was embarrassed and she wanted to be sympathetic to that. So she gave him one more gentle kiss before sliding off of him and walking him to the front door. He left quickly, leaving Maggie to her thoughts.

What the fuck was that and what the fuck was she doing? That felt like some teenage fever dream. She could understand his embarrassment, but also wondered if that was common for him?

It had only been a few moments and they stayed almost fully clothed. Not to mention this conflicted with her self isolation plan. She shouldn't have fed into this. She should've cut it off before it even started.

She figured she would just let this one play out. Maybe he would be too embarrassed to continue seeing her and she wouldn't even have to be the one to pull the plug. She was overwhelmed with confusion, so she did the one thing she had learned to do best. She followed her survival plan and grabbed a bottle of wine–no need for a glass.

❦ ❦ ❦

Three months later and she was still seeing Raf, if that's what you could call it. It was by far the strangest relationship Maggie had ever been in. Which for Maggie was saying something given her dating history. She struggled to even call it a relationship. They spent a lot of time together going on dates or spending nights in, but everything felt just slightly off with him.

Raf wanted a level of emotional intimacy that Maggie refused to give him. She preferred to keep everyone at an arm's length–still within reach, but never too close. While she refused him the emotional intimacy he desired, he refused her the physical intimacy she desired. Any time she tried to push things along a little further, he stopped. This led to a few repeats of their first makeout session and left Maggie to do the work of finding her release on her own.

She respected his wishes of course. She understood better than most that everyone had their past and their own traumas. She simply wished he would give her the same courtesy. Where she always stopped when he asked, he instead was constantly pushing her to open up and tell him more. When she wouldn't, he would get upset and leave her to her own devices. It annoyed her, but to be entirely honest, she didn't mind it much. She preferred her alone time, spending hours on the couch or in bed, streaming one show or another where she could live in a different world while slamming fries and wine.

Having Raf around was nice enough, but she was tired of the mental energy it took to appease him. Her norm had become time with herself doing nothing but existing. When she was around Raf, she had to put in effort. She had to smile and joke and contribute to the conversation. She had to put all of her energy into faking that she believed life was a blessing and a beautiful gift, like he did. She had to pretend she wasn't tired of being alive.

"I just don't get why you always freeze up when I try to know more about you," Raf said with a hint of accusation in his tone. Maggie was used to this argument. This one had already happened a dozen times and it always went the same way.

"You know enough, Raf. I share things when I'm ready and you know what I've been ready to share," she said back into her car phone. She knew she sounded annoyed, but she didn't have the energy to be kind today.

Today had been a harder day than expected. For some reason, no matter what she did, she couldn't escape the thoughts of her mom. Working in education, she didn't have the luxury of taking the day off. Nor did she have the luxury of showing her foul mood at work. When you work with kids, whatever you have going on in your personal life gets left at the door. Especially when you're the counselor that they're coming to with their own personal struggles. It had been exhausting to push it all down all day and act like nothing was going on. All she wanted to do was stop at a drive thru for some fast food, get home, grab a bottle of wine, and crawl under her blankets in bed with her dog. Raf had called on her drive home, though, and now she was dealing with this bullshit. She was over it.

"Well, I want more," he replied.

"Yeah? Well, sometimes so do I! But you don't see me pushing you to do more than you want, so stop doing that shit to me," she fumed. A shocked silence came through the speakers. She had never expressed this frustration before. This was new.

"I didn't realize–" Raf had started, but Maggie was fired up now.

"No, you didn't, Raf. Because everything is always your way. We do what you want, when you want. I force myself to share things I don't even want to tell you because you push and you push. You do it continuously until you wear me down. You never respect when I want to stop, but I *always* respect when you do. It's not fair," her voice was a snarl by the end. She knew she was taking her mood out on him. She acknowledged there was probably a better way of saying what she had, but it needed to get said one way or another.

"I didn't know this was such a big issue for you," he said quietly.

"It's been almost 5 months and we still haven't done *anything* Raf. I know you have your past, which you also refuse to share with me, I might add. But it's unnerving. I feel like a teenager making out on my mom's couch until you get off fully clothed and leave. It's frustrating and creates a level of self doubt. But I never push you! And yet, you always push me. It's like a bullshit double standard. I have to give you everything you want, but you don't have to do the same for me. It's exhausting," she was out of breath by the end of her tirade.

"I just want to know you," he said, sounding small.

"I know, but part of that is listening to me and knowing when to fucking stop, Raf," was all she offered.

"I do listen to you," he said.

"No, you don't. You listen to YOU and do what YOU think is best for me," she fired back.

"Oh, so just because I haven't fucked you, that means I don't listen to you?" he stormed.

"That's not what I'm saying. I'm trying to give you an example of how I respect your wishes and boundaries but you don't respect mine," she explained.

"No, that's exactly what you're saying. I didn't realize sex was the end all be all here. Silly me for wanting to get to know more of you before moving forward with anything else," he fumed.

"You're not hearing me Raf," she pushed, exasperated.

"No, I hear you loud and clear. Have a great night Maggie. I'll talk to you tomorrow if anything," he said and hung up on her. What the fuck? Sure, Maggie knew she hadn't phrased what she meant to say in the best way, but for him to disregard the message she was trying to send entirely was unfair.

Whatever. She had enough on her mind today. Just add this to the pile of heavy thoughts. Was he right? Was she putting too much of an emphasis on being physically intimate? It still felt strange to her that he refused to have sex with her after five months. Especially since she had already shared more with him than she had originally planned to.

She parked and grabbed her fast food as her foggy thoughts spiraled, ping ponging from one negative to the next. As she entered her apartment, looked around, and sighed heavily, one thought that had recently been constant in her mind came to the forefront yet again: *I'm so tired of being here.* It cleared every other thought away.

She was so tired of having to pretend she was happy at work. She was so tired of whatever the hell she was doing with Raf. She was so tired of simply going through the motions day in and day out. She was so tired of going through each day with coming home to do nothing as her only goal. She was so tired of all of it. The exhaustion of her existence was bone deep.

She couldn't stop the sobs as they started. Her life wasn't supposed to be so fucking hard. She wasn't supposed to feel so fucking empty. Her life wasn't supposed to be so fucking heavy. She slowly slid down the counters to the floor, holding onto a drawer handle for support. As she slid, the handle broke clean off the drawer, because of course that would happen to her at this exact moment.

She had no clue what to do with the tornado she was feeling, so she chucked the handle across the room with all her strength. Seeing her tears, her dog came barreling at her and started to lick them away. Maggie wasn't sure how long she sat there. All she knew was that her life would be a lot easier if she weren't in it anymore.

✻ ✻ ✻

Two more months passed but not much changed. Maggie and Raf continued whatever it was they were doing. She continued to withhold emotional intimacy and he continued to withhold physical intimacy. Maggie continued to rely on copious amounts of wine and whiskey. She spent more time in bed and struggled more each day to pull herself out of it. Life was quiet. Life was empty. Life was heavy. Life was exhausting.

On a random Friday evening, Maggie found herself staring at her tv, but not quite taking in the episode of Game of Thrones she was on. She had started zoning out a lot recently. She wasn't sure when it had started, but it helped. She liked not thinking about anything. She liked not existing in the moment. It sped up her days–marginally, but she would take what she could get.

Her quiet was disturbed by a knock on her front door. She wasn't expecting anyone and the noise startled her. She slowly unraveled from the fluffy comforter she had wrapped herself in and made her way to the door. She looked around at the pile of dishes she had let sit for too long in the sink and the mess all over the kitchen island that continued to accumulate each day. She knew she should be embarrassed about letting someone in with the current state of her apartment, but she couldn't find it in herself to care.

Finally making it to the door, she saw Raf through the peephole. She didn't have the energy for anything today, let alone Raf. She had just texted him an hour ago that she was having a quiet night in, so she couldn't pretend to not be home.

Taking a deep breath, she opened the door and said nothing. She didn't have it in her to fake it today. He smiled wide waiting for her greeting which never came. She shrugged, turned around, walked back to the couch, and rewrapped herself in the comforter. She vaguely heard the front door close and something thunk on the kitchen island. Then she felt the couch cushions shift slightly as Raf sat next to her.

They sat there silently for nearly twenty minutes before Raf finally spoke.

"Is this what you do? When you say you're just hanging on your own for the night? Do you just sit here like this?" he asked slowly, as if trying not to offend her.

Her only response was to pull the comforter tighter at her chin and turn her head slightly to look out the window instead of at the tv. He wanted to know more of her? Well this was all there was to her these days. The quiet heaviness.

To his credit, Raf let Maggie sit there silently. He didn't try to get her to talk. He didn't try to hold her. He just sat there watching tv as she stared off. After about an hour, she finally said out loud the one sentence she'd been thinking more and more, but had been too afraid to speak into reality.

"Most days, I don't want to be alive," she said, her voice just barely louder than a whisper. It was now she turned to Raf. She wanted to see his reaction. If he wanted to run, which she was half hoping he would, now would be the time.

As she turned to look into his eyes, she saw a mix of emotions. She could tell he cared for her deeply, maybe more deeply than she had realized. But behind every emotion he was expressing with his eyes, she saw one she hated most–pity. She loathed that look.

He moved closer to her, putting his arm around her shoulders and pulling her into his side. She let him. She didn't have the energy to fight it. Instead, she let him hold her while she sat there feeling entirely empty. She felt nothing, and she wasn't sure she'd ever really feel anything ever again. She wasn't entirely sure she ever wanted to.

The next morning she woke up in bed. She must have fallen asleep on the couch and Raf had carried her in here. She started to roll over when she realized she wasn't alone. She turned her head and saw Raf sleeping next to her. She carefully got up so she wouldn't wake him and was unsuccessful. As she started to rise from the bed, she felt his arm wrap around her waist and pull her back down into him. She knew she should playfully giggle, so she did. She knew she should nuzzle into his touch, so she did.

That was what her life had become. A series of knowing what was expected of her in situations and doing them just because she knew she should.

"We have Katie's barbecue today and it looks like we're already getting a late start. Want to get ready, then swing by my place so I can change, and then head over together?" Raf's voice rumbled sleepily behind her. She checked her phone. He was right. It was already 12:30. She had never slept that late before. She nodded and slowly got out of bed.

Today would be a long day. At least she had gotten used to doing what she knew she should. She knew today she'd be acting like the life of the party again. She knew that role well because she used to love it. Now, she knew better. Life was anything but a party.

Six hours later, Maggie was in the passenger seat of Raf's car and they were headed back to her place. She hadn't said anything since they left the barbecue other than offering the occasional grunt or mhmm to show she was listening to Raf. She was staring out the window as they drove down the wide, winding Vegas roads.

"Is this what life with you is like?" Raf asked.

"Hmmmm?" Maggie had been listening but not actively participating in the conversation. The question caught her off guard.

"This. The silence. The brooding. The void. Whatever you want to call it. Is this what your life is like?" he pushed.

"I guess," she said indifferently.

"But I don't get it," he said.

"Get what?" she asked.

"You were *just* fine. I literally just watched you laugh and dance and drink and have fun with our friends. Then once you're alone with me, you're back to this sad, mopey rain cloud. You were just *fine*," he explained.

"I wasn't fine," she started without looking at him, "I was faking it. I've learned what people want to see and I've learned how to be that person in any given situation. I know how to hide how I'm really feeling. I've learned how to function when I'm out in the world, even if this is what I'd rather be doing all day," she offered in explanation.

"So this is it? This is your life?" he followed up.

"I guess. If that's what you want to call it," she answered. The car was silent for a while.

"It's depressing," he finally said after some time.

"Well, maybe I'm depressed," she whispered to the window.

"But I don't get it. You were just fine. You were more than fine. You were happy. You can't be depressed," Raf said as if trying to make it make sense for himself. All Maggie could do was shrug.

A week had passed since that conversation and one thought had plagued her that entire time. Was that what this was? Was she depressed? Sure, she had been sad in the years since her mom died but depressed felt like an entirely different level. She had never put much thought into it since she always accredited these feelings to her grief, but over the last week she had fallen down a rabbit hole of research. She kept reading article after article explaining lists of symptoms.

- loss of interest in activities once enjoyed
- continuous low mood or sadness
- fatigue or low energy levels
- feeling hopeless or helpless
- having low self esteem
- feeling irritable and intolerant of others
- finding it difficult to make decisions
- feelings of guilt, worthlessness, or self loathing
- finding it difficult to do daily care tasks like showering
- feeling anxious or overwhelmed
- having no motivation or interest in things
- difficulty getting out of bed or starting the day

Well fuck.

Days began to blur into weeks and before she knew it she had been with Raf for eight months. She could tell her depression annoyed him. Every so often he made it clear that he didn't entirely believe her. He always told her how fine she seemed whenever they were in public and that it was hard to believe she was really that sad in reality. On occasion he would even accuse her of faking for attention or to win arguments with him. Today had been one of those occasions.

She didn't have the energy to disagree anymore, so she always just shrugged and walked away. It would seem she had lost all of her fight. She used to love her fire. Her determination. Now, she barely remembered that girl. Now, she was unrecognizable.

Sure, she would turn it all on when she talked to friends and family. That was just her faking for their sake. Her reality was something entirely different from the scraps she would offer them.

Maggie was just pulling into her assigned parking spot after a trip to the liquor store when her phone started buzzing. She figured it was Raf attempting to continue their argument. She didn't even have the energy to listen to him today and was about to send the call to voicemail, when she looked at the caller ID. Jeff?

Other than the occasional text here and there, she hadn't really talked to Jeff since her last visit back East. It would be midnight there. What the hell was he calling her about? Immediately, she panicked. Had something happened to Kam? They did still live together. Although her and Kam hadn't talked much over the last year beyond a few texts, she still cared about him. As much as she could these days anyway.

"Hello?" she answered as a question.

"MAAAAAAGGIEEEEEEE," Jeff shouted into the phone. He was drunk. She rolled her eyes as she got out of the car and headed for her bags in the trunk.

"That's me," she said.

"I miss you friend. You need to visit again soon," he slurred.

"I'm doing my best to get right on that," she answered.

"It wasn't supposed to be like this, you know? You were supposed to live here still. We were all supposed to be happy and be grown ups together. Now it's all just fucked, isn't it?" he continued, dragging some words and stumbling over others.

"Is it?" she asked, starting to smile. Drunk Jeff was one of her favorites. He went full contemplative when he was drunk but could barely ever get the right words out. It was highly entertaining. He was about to continue when Maggie heard a commotion. It sounded like the phone had dropped to the ground as someone cussed in the background. She chuckled to herself and waited for Jeff to pick up the phone and get back on the line.

"Mags." Her heart stopped. She knew that voice all too well and she hadn't heard it in all too long. She couldn't breathe for a moment. How did he still manage to make her react like this?

"Kam," she finally said once she regained some of her ability to breathe.

"I've missed you," he said.

"I've missed you too," she said back. Then, the line was quiet for a while. She had no clue what to say to him. She also had no clue how drunk he was. She waited for him to say something first.

"You should be hereeeee," he finally said, sounding both frustrated and whiny. Oh, he was drunk alright.

"But I'm here," was all she offered.

"But you were supposed to move back," he said, sounding like a toddler who was just told they couldn't have dessert before dinner. She imagined him sitting there, brows scrunched and lower lip pouting in frustration. The image made her laugh and the laugh was out before she could catch it.

"What are you laughing at? This isn't funny," he continued in full tantrum mode.

"You sound like a baby right now, Kam," she told him in between giggles.

"Well, I'm upset," he pouted.

"Sure sounds like it," she responded.

"MAAAAAAGGIEEEEE," she heard Jeff's voice screaming in the background. "Just come back already! We want you–oh fuck!"

"Hold on, Jeff just tumbled over a side table. Give me a second," Kam said in explanation. Maggie waited as she unbagged the wine she had gotten at the liquor store and poured herself a glass. She could hear a bunch of grumbling and commotion on the other end of the phone but nothing clear. She chuckled to herself as she sipped her wine and imagined what could possibly be happening on the other side of the phone.

"Okay, Jeff is all tucked in on the couch. It's just us now," Kam finally said, coming back to the phone sounding significantly more sober all of a sudden.

"How is he?" she asked.

"He's alright. He'll have a nasty bruise and headache in the morning, but he'll survive," Kam said.

"How are you?" she asked.

"I'm okay," he said, going quiet.

"So to what do I owe the pleasure of this phone call?" Maggie asked.

"It was random. We were drinking and you came up. Both of us realized we hadn't talked to you in a while so we decided to call. You're not busy are you?" he sounded shy.

"Talking about me? I hope only good things," she joked.

"Oh no, only the worst. Especially about that nasty mole you have on your ass," he joked back. Maggie smiled at his reference to their past.

"It is an excellent ass after all," she said back, remembering the conversation.

"Don't I know it," he mused. For a second the silence was awkward. Only for a second, though. Then they both burst out laughing uncontrollably. As if no time had passed and as if they did not have the history that they did, they talked like they once had. About everything and nothing. The conversation was never forced and Maggie actually *wanted* to contribute. She felt an energy thrum through her that she hadn't felt in a long time.

Before she knew it an hour had passed and she was starting to get tired as it was past her usual bedtime. Even so, she didn't want the conversation to end. They were in a comfortable lull and she had to admit to herself that she missed this.

"I love you," Kam said softly. Maggie stilled.

"I love you too," she couldn't stop herself from saying.

"No, you don't understand Mags. I *love* you," he said, frustrated as if she weren't getting his point.

"Believe me Kam. I do get it. I love you too," she said seriously. His sigh was the only response he offered.

"HEEE LOOOOVES YOUUU," she heard Jeff shout in the background.

"Oh for fuck's sake," Kam said and Maggie giggled.

"Listen, you go deal with Jeff and if anything we can talk another time. I'll be here," she said.

"But you won't be *here*," Kam sounded sad.

"No, I won't," she replied with equal sorrow.

"This was nice Mags," he said wistfully.

"It really was," she said and hung up. She couldn't remember the last time she had spent so long smiling and laughing without forcing it. Without faking it. Her happy bubble was immediately popped as she saw she had 7 new messages from Raf.

9:02 - Want to do something?

9:07 - I guess you're "sad" tonight? Like always.

9:19 - What the hell, Maggie? Answer me!

9:28 - This is bullshit. If you can fake it so well, why not do it now? For me?

9:32 - Bitch

9:44 - You're exhausting. Just get over it.

9:57 - Go to fucking therapy or something.

He was exhausted *by* her and she was exhausted *being* her. He wasn't necessarily wrong on that last one, though. Therapy would probably work some wonders in her life. She knew she should call him and try to figure out what was going on. Talk him down. Maybe hang out and fake it as he suggested. She thought of all she could do. All she should do. Instead, though, she decided there was something else she *must* do.

Let's get drinks tomorrow. Talk then.

It was all she replied before setting her phone on do not disturb and going to bed. She needed to rest to have enough energy for tomorrow.

 ψ ψ ψ

The next day passed painstakingly slowly. She spent most of it in bed with the covers pulled up and curtains pulled down. It would seem the high of her phone conversation last night with

Kam had drained her entirely. She stayed in bed, only getting up to let her dog out onto the patio every so often. She waited until the very last moment to finally drag herself out of bed and get ready for drinks with Raf.

She felt empty today. She felt as if you were to shake her body, her bones would clang about like loose change rattling around an old can. She knew her mood would annoy Raf, so she decided on the drive there that she would take his suggestion and fake it. She would be bubbly and flirty and fun. She would be functional for at least the next few hours.

When she arrived at the bar, she was late and he was already there. She sat next to him and offered him exactly what he had not so kindly asked for the night before. She made all the right jokes and all the right comments. She leaned toward him and always kept some physical contact. For all Raf knew, the night was going perfectly as they left the bar to stroll around the green right beside it.

He took her hand as they walked silently. Lights were strung across the green in a zigzag pattern illuminating it dimly. It was late, so there weren't many other people sharing the space. He looked at her and he was *happy*. She could see it in his smile. In the way it reached his eyes, causing them to crinkle.

It was his happiness that confirmed for her what she needed to do. He had no clue she was faking it. For all he believed, this was who she truly was and her quiet depression was just a quirk he had to tolerate. He didn't realize that this persona was a full time job for her, and it was exhausting. She pulled him over to a bench and took a seat.

"I think we need to break up," she said, bracing for his response.

"Wh- Wh- What? Why?" he sputtered.

"Raf, you have to see that we aren't right for each other. Don't you?" she asked.

"Is it the texts I sent last night? Maggie, I already told you I was drunk. I didn't mean them," he protested, voice rising. As if being drunk excused what he had said. How he had said it.

"It's more than those texts, Raf. It's–" she started.

"Is this because I won't fuck you?" he shouted, rising from the bench and gaining them looks from the few others milling about.

"Raf, this has nothing to do with that–" she tried to explain.

"The fuck it does. I know it bothers you, so you're going to leave me over sex? That's low Maggie," he fumed.

"Rafael, this is not about the sex. I'll admit I find it bizarre, but me wanting to end this has nothing to do with your unwillingness to '*fuck*' me. Look at me and tell me honestly that you're genuinely happy with what we have," she pushed.

"I am! I'm happy. You are too! I could see it tonight!" he said. She wasn't sure if he was trying to convince her or himself.

"No Raf, I'm not. Tonight was an act. You couldn't even tell. I had to drag myself out of bed just to get ready and show up. That is my life, Raf. I wake up. I'm sad that I woke up. I force myself to survive the day. I go to bed. I know it's no way to live, but it's how I survive. It's not how you should have to live," she forced.

"But I'm happy," he said, sounding defeated and sitting back down next to her.

"No, you're not," she said gently.

"You're my other half," he whispered, staring at his hands and twisting his fingers. They sat in silence. For so long, he wasn't sure that she'd heard him at all, until she finally spoke.

"I can't be your other half," she answered hollowly. He looked up and saw the sadness streaking across her features. She stared straight ahead, but her eyes were empty. Her lips curved down ever so slightly. Her cheeks flat, devoid of the rounded cheer her smiles typically formed.

"I can't be your other half," she continued just as emptily, "because I'm barely a tiny piece of myself right now. I'm still broken and shattered, with pieces flung everywhere. Barely keeping one piece held to another. And every time I think I've collected enough pieces to maybe start putting myself back together again, they start slipping right through my fingers. I'm perpetually falling. Perpetually catching pieces of myself. Perpetually dropping them again without meaning to. You can't make your other half out of shattered shards. All they'll do is cut and hurt you."

With those parting words, Maggie stood and walked away.

Reconstruction

Playlist

How I'm Feeling Now / Lewis Capaldi

Back To December / Riot House, Jack the Underdog, ENZI

A Lot More Free / Max McNown

Fearless (Taylor's Version) / Taylor Swift

WHAT I HAVE / Kelsea Ballerini

6

Reconstruction

A year and a half had passed since the night Maggie left Raf. She had spent that entire time exactly how she had once described it to him:

Wake up.

Be sad that she woke up.

Force herself to survive the day.

Go to bed.

Some nights she'd let alcohol speed the sleep process. She'd reply to just enough text messages and phone calls to make sure people didn't worry too much. Kam hadn't been among those messages. In fact, they hadn't spoken at all since that last phone call. Good. She wanted him to keep living his life and move on without her.

She'd post just enough on her socials. She'd go to just enough events to make sure she was saving face, which is exactly how she found herself walking into this new bar in town for a quick drink with some coworkers. As she pushed the door open, Maggie took a deep breath. She could smile and laugh and fake her way through one more hour. Then, she could go home, change, and just get into bed until it was time to repeat the process tomorrow.

She was the first to arrive, so she made her way across the room and grabbed the three seats at the corner of the relatively empty bar. It was early in the evening and still quiet. Just how she liked it. She was turned toward the door with her back to the bar, checking to see if her coworkers had arrived as she slid into her seat. Head still turned away, she felt a touch hit her knee and start to tap up her leg.

"What the f–" she began, whipping her head back to the bar.

"Shit! I'm so sorry! I wasn't trying to do anything, I swear!" said a man in all black who looked only a few years older than her.

"You know, usually I at least make someone buy me dinner first," she joked halfheartedly.

"Well, it's a good thing I'm the bartender and can buy you dinner AND a drink in this case," he winked back, walking away to head back around to the other side of the bar. Maggie reluctantly noticed that he had a nice smile. It paled in comparison to her favorite smile, but it seemed kind and playful.

"What *were* you doing anyway?" she asked as he walked over with a drink list.

"We're planning to put in hooks along the bar for bags and coats. I was supposed to be measuring the distance to see how many we needed but got distracted and turned away. I wasn't looking and must've gotten to your spot as you were sitting down. Seriously, I'm sorry. I'm not a creep and would never do something like that to anyone." She could tell he meant it. His discomfort from the accident was palpable as he waited for her to decide what she wanted to drink.

"Well, as long as you get me that drink–a Basil Hayden neat with a ginger back–we'll be square," she smiled in response to ease his worry. He smiled, nodded, and walked away. As he made her drink, she found herself staring at the bartender. His smile was bright against his deep, warm skin tone. His eyes were a dark brown that twinkled with a combination of mischief and confidence. He was muscular in a way that told you he worked out but wasn't obsessive over his routine. She liked the look of him. He looked like the kind of man who put people at ease.

In the midst of her perusal, her coworkers arrived and she blandly listened to whatever it was they were talking about. Internally, she was counting down the minutes to when it would be socially acceptable to excuse herself and head home.

As she counted time and nodded periodically at their stories, she couldn't help but glance over at the bartender occasionally. Every time she looked, he already had his eyes on her and that smile on his face. She couldn't help but think it was a smile she wouldn't mind seeing again. The thought startled her since it had been so long since she had *wanted* to do *anything*.

Finally, enough time had passed. She asked for her check and told her friends to stay without her. She needed to get home to tend to... something. When her check came, the grand total was a whopping $0.01 and at the bottom was a phone number with a scrawled note, "IOU. Call it in whenever you'd like." Her smile was small and when she glanced up, he was already looking at her with a smile that spelled promise. Of what? She wasn't entirely sure.

As she walked to her car, Maggie had one final thought, "*Why am I such a fucking sucker for smiles?*"

"Mags, when was the last time your skin saw the sun?" Rosa asked through the computer screen a few days later. Their monthly video chats were the one consistent in Maggie's life.

Well, that and her utter desire to do absolutely nothing all the time.

"Just means I won't wrinkle as fast as you will," she attempted at a joke. It fell flat. Rosa was expressing genuine concern but Maggie couldn't be bothered to care.

"Mags, you have to go do something. Even if it's just some lizard lady time in the sun. Your apartment complex has a beautiful pool. Use it! You pay for it after all," Rosa argued.

"I'll consider it," Maggie said noncommittally.

"Any good books to recommend to me this month?" Rosa attempted. Maggie knew what she was doing. She was fishing to see if Maggie had done anything other than go to work or curl up in bed since their last video chat. She hadn't. Just like the month before. And the month before that.

"Not really," Maggie shrugged. There was a pause where no one said anything. Maggie stared at the screen, half in a daze and half wondering why she couldn't muster up a single thought for her very best friend in the world. A longer stretch than normal passed before Rosa spoke again.

"Maggie. I'm going to do something I didn't think I'd ever do with you," Rosa finally said. Maggie did not at all like the words nor the tone she said them with. "I'll preface this by saying that I have been more patient with you than I would have been with anyone else on this planet. I don't want to do this, but I can't keep watching you fade away. I can't keep watching you live a life with nothing in it. Literally NOTHING. You do nothing. You say nothing. You give nothing. You try nothing. I can't keep allowing you to let your life be nothing because *you are not nothing to me.*"

Rosa paused for a moment to allow Maggie to respond, but she didn't. What could she say? Rosa was right. And even worse, Maggie didn't care enough to deny it. Or, do anything about it.

"So I'm going to threaten you, because at this point I'm not sure any other motivator will work on you. You have one month from now–until our next video chat–to do three things on your own. They could be *anything*. Go to a coffee shop. Take a walk somewhere. Bake something. I don't give a shit what they are. You just have to do them and message me with proof," she explained.

"And if I don't?" Maggie asked. The words were empty. No hint of challenge or dispute, just bland consideration.

"Then I will get my ass on a flight on a random day, at a random time, with no warning, and simply show up at your doorstep," she answered. The smug smile that spread across Rosa's face told Maggie that the panic she felt at the threat was evident. In her current state, this was her worst nightmare. Having someone show up unexpectedly, without her having time to prepare herself to expend the energy to socialize. Having someone she knows see the state her apartment was in. Having Rosa there every moment of every day to see first hand the expansive nothingness her life had become.

"You wouldn't," Maggie whispered.

"Bitch, have you met me? Of course I would. I have the money. I have the time off. And, I have a best friend that I'm losing to a silent battle more and more each time I see her. I won't stand for it. So yes, if I don't hear about your three things, I'm coming to Vegas baby," Rosa said triumphantly leaning back in her seat. Waiting.

Ugh, how did this friend of hers manage to be simultaneously the absolute best and the absolute worst? What choice did Maggie have? Rosa had found her motivator and would be true to her threat if Maggie didn't do three things in the next thirty days. Such a simple task, and yet, it felt as if she were about to attempt climbing Everest.

"Fine."

A week had passed already and all Maggie could think about were these three damn things she was supposed to do. What could she do with minimal effort that had super low stakes? She was picking up a massive pile of laundry, just in case Rosa did show up anyway, racking her brain for ideas.

The more she thought, the more frustrated she became with herself. Why was this so hard? She literally just had to do *three* things. Anything. She used to do dozens of things a week–hell, a day. When had it become so hard to do three things in a month?

She was checking the pockets of all her pants before throwing them in the washing machine when she felt a piece of paper. Opening it, she saw the bartender's phone number on the receipt and remembered his smile. The mix of mischief and kindness it held. As she stood, staring at the slip of paper, a single thought came to her. *Fuck it.*

She grabbed her phone and sent him a text.

Hey! It's bar hook girl. When is a good time to cash in that IOU?

She pressed send before she could think of a million reasons not to. She put her phone down and finished getting the current load of laundry into the washing machine. As she poured the detergent in, her phone buzzed. She grabbed it to check her notifications, pressing start on the wash cycle.

**You'll be happy to find out that we've installed
our bar hooks and will no longer accidentally
feel up people's knees!**

Followed almost immediately by a second text.

Can I take you out this weekend? Saturday at 1:30?

He was suggesting a time early enough where Maggie could
still get home and just rot the rest of the day. Plus, she could count
this as two things! Meeting someone new and going to the park.
Perfect. She replied:

That works for me! Just tell me where and when.

His reply came quickly:

**The main entrance to Sunset Park. I'll send you a pin
just in case too. Oh, and my name is Karsen. So you
don't have to save me in your phone as "hot bartender"**

The chuckle was out before she realized it. When was the last
time she had laughed, even a small one, while alone at home? She
couldn't remember.

**My name is Maggie, but you're welcome to save
my contact as "bar hook girl"**

Maggie took a screenshot of the conversation and sent it to Rosa with a simple message that said, "here is your proof." Rosa's response was almost immediate.

Your proof will have to be a picture while you're actually there. Screenshotted plans can be canceled. And no, you can't count this as two separate things. Seeing "hot bartender" at the park is one thing in my book. My game, my rules. Deal with it.

Damn Rosa for knowing Maggie's schemes. She locked her phone, threw it and herself onto the bed, and mentally prepared herself for Saturday.

Before she knew it, Saturday had come and Maggie was walking toward the entrance of Sunset Park that Karsen had pinned. She was already overwhelmed and tired. The sun felt too bright and she could feel the beads of sweat forming on her skin. Every sound felt piercingly loud as she did her best to breathe and at the very least show up. She took a picture of the park entrance and sent it to Rosa.

She put her phone in her bag and looked around trying to spot Karsen. As she searched, she tried to push down the intense sensation of overwhelm. After almost two years of essentially going to work or isolating in her apartment, this park was a lot.

She was getting ready to cut bait and run back to her car–at least she can count coming to the park as one of her things with Rosa. Even if it would be shitty to essentially stand Karsen up.

Who cared? She was getting ready to turn and walk back the way she came when she heard jogging footsteps coming toward her.

"Maggie, hey! You made it! We're over this way at the volleyball courts. I'd hug you hello but I'm fucking gross at the moment," she heard Karsen say from behind her. We? Volleyball? What? What the hell had Maggie gotten herself into here? She turned toward the voice and immediately noticed that Karsen was in fact gross and dripping in sweat. He grabbed her hand and pulled her alongside him toward where she could see a group of people in an intensely unserious game of volleyball.

"Karsen, I hope you don't expect me to play. I may be tall, but I absolutely suck at volleyball. Just ask my middle school team coaches. I didn't even make the practice squad," she rambled as he just smiled at her over his shoulder. "Seriously, it's embarrassing how bad I am."

"Then you'll fit right in," was all he said before shouting an introduction between Maggie and everyone already on the court. They all smiled and waved as she stood there trying her best to look normal, but knowing she probably looked more like a deer in headlights.

"Seriously, I'm mortifyingly bad," she threw at Karson, panic in her tone. He looked at her with what looked like genuine concern for a moment before throwing back on his most charming smile.

"We're all shit, I swear. We just think it's fun. But, if you want, you can sit along the side and just watch. I'm almost sweaty enough to take my shirt off. That's when the real show will start," he offered her. His friends made gagging noises behind him, poking fun at his shirtless comment.

They all laughed while Karsen stared at Maggie, waiting for her response. His look was nervous, almost cautious. As if she would be easily scared away. When had she become someone people looked at that way? Someone who was so easily scared off? Someone you tiptoed around? Someone who sat on the sidelines of everything? She looked at the sand volleyball court one more time before turning back to Karsen.

"Fuck it," she said, throwing her bag on the ground and her hair into a ponytail. Karsen beamed at her and she couldn't help the wide smile she offered him in response. When was the last time she had smiled without forcing or faking it? That was something she'd ponder another time. Right now? She had some volleyball to suck at.

¥ ¥ ¥

Forty-five minutes later and Maggie was covered in sweat at the front of the net. Bent at the waist, she looked over her shoulder at Karsen who was getting ready to serve. This would be game point if their team actually managed to score since everyone had to call it quits after this round. Maggie had learned that everyone in the game was in the service industry and would need to leave to get ready for work.

He winked at her, served, and her eyes followed the ball as it flew over the net. Everyone was locked in and this was probably the only moment where they were all finally taking the game seriously. After a few volleys back and forth, she saw the ball being lobbed right over where she was standing.

"Fuck it," she whispered. This seemed to be Maggie's mantra since meeting Karsen. Drawing all the strength she could muster in her legs, which she frustratingly noticed throughout this game had grown extremely weak, she jumped as high as she could. Praying she could display any semblance of hand eye coordination in this moment, she spiked the ball with all the force she had left.

By some miracle, it landed right in between the two people who had simultaneously dived for the spike and hit the ground.

Her team erupted in cheers. The next thing she knew, she was chest bumping the woman next to her and being swept off her feet. Looking down, she saw it was Karsen who had wrapped his arms around her thighs and hoisted her up. She couldn't help the laughter that followed as the rest of their team circled around them, chanting her name.

Slowly, Karsen lowered her back to the ground and she found her hands on his shoulders and her eyes level with his torso. His very shirtless torso. She looked up and saw the wild smile on his face and cursed herself yet again for being such a sucker for smiles. As she started to pull away, he pulled her closer.

"What are you doing tonight?" he asked. Maggie was shocked to find that her answer of nothing felt wrong. For the first time in a long time, she really wanted to do *something*.

That is exactly how Maggie found herself–showered and cleaned up–five hours later at Karsen's bar. When she walked in the place was packed, much more so than the first time she had been there. Even with almost every table occupied and an entirely full bar, Karsen managed to notice her the moment she walked through the door. He waved her over to the seat at the very end of the bar, removing a little reserved placard as she sat.

"Give me a few minutes to get some orders and I'll be right back," he said smiling broadly. Somewhere in the middle of mixing drinks and taking orders, Karsen dropped two glasses at Maggie's spot. She took a look and a sniff. Basil Hayden neat with a ginger back. Of course he remembered. She smiled and looked up at him.

Although he leaned forward listening to an older woman, she saw his quick wink and smirk in her direction.

A few hours passed and Maggie found that she didn't mind this. Not at all if she were being honest with herself. Karsen would come over and chat with her in the pockets of time between mixing drinks and chatting with customers. His actual work station was right in front of her seat so she could watch him craft away–forearms flexing beneath his rolled up sleeves. Shit, when had forearms become sexy?

He was charming, she had to give him that much. He knew exactly how to make the ladies bat their lashes and blush and the men laugh at whatever he was saying. She enjoyed watching him work. She enjoyed that she didn't have to actively participate the entire time. That she could sit back and people watch. She'd occasionally engage with the woman sitting next to her, but for the most part she was free to simply *be*.

After a few more hours had passed, it was nearing last call and closing time. Maggie truly couldn't remember the last time she had been out of the house for this long for something that wasn't work. The woman sitting next to her, Molly, seemed to be in her sixties and was a few glasses of wine deep. She was also shamelessly flirting with Karsen and he was charming her right back. Maggie couldn't help but smile. He was making this woman's night. When he walked away to check on the other side of the bar, Molly turned to Maggie.

"He's quite the sweet talker, isn't he?" the woman asked.

"He is indeed," Maggie answered, giggling.

"I'm so sorry, sweetheart," Molly said.

"Sorry? Sorry for what?" Maggie asked, clearly confused.

"I'm just over here flirting up a storm with your boyfriend while you're sitting right there! I don't mean anything by it! At my age, the attention is just fun," Molly said, blushing slightly.

"Oh! He's not my boyfriend," Maggie smiled back.

"Not yet at least," Karsen said cheerfully as he zoomed by carrying two ice buckets. Maggie shook her head and smiled while rolling her eyes.

"I could have sworn you two were together! The chemistry, the eyes, the banter. That's not nothing, honey. Take it from someone who has been around a lot longer than you have. A smile like that doesn't come around very often," Molly preached, downing the last of her wine and gathering her things to leave.

"No, it doesn't," Maggie said so quietly, as if the response was only for herself. Her mind wandered as she started thinking of another smile. She shook the thought from her mind almost as quickly as it appeared. What a useless train of thought.

After being out of the house longer than she'd been in years, Maggie found herself being walked to her car. The day had been warm, but the night was cool and breezy. Neither of them spoke as they strolled through the parking lot. When she got to her car door, she turned to look at Karsen. He leaned against her car, hands in his pockets and shoulders slightly raised. It almost seemed like a shy stance. What a weird dichotomy with the man she just watched work the bar for hours. He pulled one hand out of his pocket and scratched the back of his neck.

"So, what are you doing next week?" he asked. Expectant. Hopeful. Unsure.

And just like that, with a smile and an inkling of curiosity, Maggie started doing things again.

Her apartment looked almost unrecognizable from what she had let it become. Maggie had made a list of all the things she'd let go to hell in her life and started creating realistic solutions for each. She decided even if it took the rest of her life, she'd slowly work her way back to not feeling like total shit. First on the list: the absolute disgustingness that she had let her place become. She hired a cleaner and made a cleaning schedule for herself. This way, each week she worked on a small piece of the apartment and wouldn't let the entire thing go to hell again.

She took a picture of the cleaning schedule and spotless apartment and sent them to Rosa with the message, "One of my three things for this month." Although it had been three months, Rosa had maintained her threat of an unexpected visit if Maggie didn't do her three things.

Maggie could admit that the first month of doing things had been exhausting. Karsen was not one to just sit around, so he easily found things for them to do. After so long of doing nothing, Maggie felt herself drained at the end of any day that first month. Now, though, the exhaustion had transitioned into a tolerable tiredness. It would seem that Maggie was rebuilding her stamina for the world. For life.

The cleaners had impeccable timing. They wrapped up and left right as Maggie grabbed her bag to leave for her now weekly volleyball game with Karsen and his industry friends. Although her favorite was just sitting at the bar while he worked, she quickly learned that this man always had something up his sleeve. They went hiking and to see new shows in town. They tried new restaurants and had movie nights at home. They took short road trips and got library cards together. He had even convinced her to do the zip line down the Fremont Street Experience.

They had been together for a few months now. Maggie had even been impressed by how he handled the relationship conversation. After quite a while of Maggie explaining vaguely and poorly why she didn't want a relationship, they agreed that they were exclusively dating each other, but didn't necessarily need the boyfriend/girlfriend title.

She appreciated his patience because at this point she was primarily focused on piecing herself and her life back together, not creating a life with someone else. As she looked around her clean apartment on her way out, she couldn't help but think that this was a wonderful starting point for reconstructing her life.

$$\text{✿ ✿ ✿}$$

"Would you be willing to meet me at closing time tonight? I want to show you something," Karsen asked Maggie as they were packing up after another intensely unserious volleyball game.

"Sure! Anything I need for this particular adventure?" she smiled at him.

"Nope! Just you. Maybe a hoodie in case it gets cold," he said, kissing her casually and grabbing her hand. They walked back to the parking lot together, and Maggie couldn't help but notice how good it felt to do something in her life again. Maybe one day she'd even want to do something *with* her life again.

꙳ ꙳ ꙳

It was just past 2 AM when Maggie pulled up next to where Karsen was parked outside of his bar. He motioned for her to follow him as he pulled out of his spot and in front of her car. She still had no clue where they were going or what they were doing. And that... excited her. She was amazed by how much could change in just a few months. Three months ago she couldn't even imagine handling scheduled plans. Now, she was following blindly into the unknown.

Except Maggie knew how quickly things could change. How someone can be in your life and at the center of your world one day and then gone the next. That ache she knew so well crept back into her chest and had a viselike grip on her heart. She struggled to breathe for a moment, letting the tears come but not overtake her entirely. She was thankful they were driving separately, even if Karsen could probably see her crying in his rearview mirror with how closely she was following him.

Before she knew it, Karsen was turning into a tiny parking lot she never noticed before along the side of the airport. She parked next to him and saw that he had a blanket and pillows that he was setting up on the hood of his car, smiling. That smile. She loved it. And yet, she couldn't help but feel like it was *so close*, and yet not quite.

She admonished herself for comparing him to someone she needed to leave in her past. Karsen was a good man and deserved to be measured on his own scale. Not compared to a perfect ideal that no longer existed for her. Great smiles and K names–at least she had a type.

She hopped out of her car and walked over to Karsen. Without warning, he grabbed her, spun her, and dipped her. Kissing her deeply as airplanes taxied nearby. She just smiled up at him.

"I thought tonight we could just sit and watch the planes land and take off... and talk." For a second, Maggie's heart dropped at the way he said the word talk. Was he over her indecision and indifference toward a long term relationship? Was this some elaborate way to gently break off whatever it was they were doing? Sensing the panic in her tensed muscles, he quickly continued, "Nothing bad, Mags. I just want to get to know you. Listen, I love doing things with you. And the sex? It's otherworldly. But... you don't really talk about... well, you don't really talk about anything. I feel like we're always *doing something* but I don't actually know anything about you." He looked at her longingly. Hopefully.

She knew that look. She had repeatedly broken the heart of a man who had looked at her with such similar eyes, but not quite. She nodded and climbed onto the blankets.

For a long while neither of them said anything. They simply watched as the airplanes taxied, took off, and landed. She was terrified of telling him anything, but he was right. She'd blatantly avoided sharing anything about herself and he deserved better. He deserved to know.

"There's a reason I avoid talking about my life," she said quietly.

"I figured as much. I just can't figure out what it is," he said, turning his head to look at her.

"I just... I just really like the way you look at me. Like I'm normal. Like I can lasso the moon for you. Like you *want* me. Like I'm not absolutely out of my mind. Once you know the calamitous mess my life has been, most of the time because of my own making, I'm afraid of how you'll look at me," she admitted.

"What if I just don't look at you while you tell me? Blindfold me if you have to, Mags," he said. Her laugh came out as a particularly unattractive snort. Of course Karsen would find the work around and the way to make her feel just a bit more comfortable doing something that made her feel so supremely uncomfortable. She looked over at him and he was already covering his eyes with his hands. At this, she laughed fully. One of those throw your head back and make your eyes water kind of laughs.

"Okay," she said. "Okay," she repeated, bracing herself and staring off at the airplanes in the distance.

She told him everything. She went all the way back to her mom's cancer and death. How had it been so many years already? She told him about Rosa's fierce love. She told him about the shock of breaking Kam's heart. About her denial with Aiden and what she now recognized as his gaslighting bullshit. About Gabe's anger and how she waited so much longer to leave than she should have. About her brother and graduation and bargaining with her dad. About the second time she broke Kam's heart and when her father broke hers. She told him about moving here and meeting Raf and her depression spiraling so low she wasn't sure she'd ever see the top again. She told him about Rosa's ultimatum and meeting him. She talked about how she still couldn't see the top of the mountain she had fallen so far down, but now it at least felt like she had a set of stairs carved into the side to slowly climb back up. One step at a time. One piece at a time. And about how he had helped her feel this way.

To his credit, Karsen stayed quiet, only interrupting to ask clarifying questions. She never looked at him while she spoke, but having been with him a few months now she could sense his emotions at various parts of her story. By the end, she was almost too afraid to look over at him. She was tempted to hop off his car and run into hers and speed away. She had to know, though. Slowly, she turned to him and saw that...

...he wasn't even looking at her. He was staring off at the airplanes starting and ending their journeys in front of them. He couldn't even look at her, he was that disgusted. She knew it. She knew telling him would ruin everything. He saw her for what she was now. Damaged goods. Broken. Useless. Worthless.

"It's okay if you think I'm certifiable and want to run for the hills. We can part ways here and I'll at least have a new awesome spot to wallow in thanks to you," she said, slowly scooting away. Karsen grabbed her arm, halting her motion.

"I don't think you're certifiable. And I'm sure as shit not running. I think you're someone who was dealt a shit hand and had to learn how to deal with it whatever way you could. I don't think any less of you just because your grief was... *is* messy. I'm just thinking about a connection I noticed that I'm surprised you haven't," he said steadily. She turned to look at him again and this time their eyes locked. She saw it. He was deep in thought, but somehow even after hearing the entirety of her tale, she could see the sparkle in his eye. A gleam that told her he still thought the best of her even after hearing the worst of her. She inhaled deeply, freely.

"Connection?" she asked.

"Part way through your story, I couldn't help but make an observation..." he trailed off.

"Don't worry, I can take it! Hit me," she replied, noticing his wince. Maybe a poor choice of words after sharing her time with Gabe with him. He took a deep breath before speaking.

"Think about it, Mags... the shock of Kam and the denial of Aiden. Gabe's anger and bargaining with your dad. The dep–" he started.

"Holy shit! You're right!" she interrupted him. "Shock, denial, anger, bargaining, depression. The stages of grief," she whispered. He smiled at her.

"I think you unconsciously coordinated your grief journey with the relationships in your life," Karsen started again. "From how you told your story it sounds like you've been hoping to find healing in someone else, when really it has to come from you. Another person is never going to do for you what you have to do for yourself when it comes to grief. You're so worried about everyone around you that you stopped considering yourself in your own life."

He was right. Maggie just kept jumping from one person to the next hoping they could love her just enough but not too much. Because she didn't want to face the pain of losing someone she loved as much as she loved her mom again. And somehow, every time she skipped to the next person they mirrored what she was feeling internally, but refused to acknowledge until it was time to move on to the next.

"Are you sure you're only a bartender? Because you just fucking nailed that," she finally said looking back at him.

"Maybe I missed my calling," he joked. "Seriously, though, hearing and acknowledging this, what are you feeling?" A loaded question for two people who had essentially pulled an all nighter.

"I think... I don't know. I think I'll have to think about it more. Process. I think therapy might need to move up on my 'piecing myself back together' priority list. And I think..." she paused chewing on the inside of her cheek nervously. "I think it also means I'm going to have to start doing more things alone," she looked at him sadly. He just nodded. Of course he'd understand.

With that, she leaned back into him, resting her head on his shoulder. They watched the airplanes in a comfortable silence, both realizing their journey no longer crossed paths. Neither wanting to say it and instead choosing to simply enjoy this moment.

ᛉ ᛉ ᛉ

"I signed up to run a half marathon," Maggie said to the screen in front of her. Rosa's fork froze halfway to her mouth as her jaw dropped even farther in shock. Laughing, Maggie rolled her eyes and continued, "I need something to focus on that's easy to keep track of and not too complicated to plan for. With running, I can just do it."

"Mags, when I told you I needed you to start doing at least three things a month, I didn't mean for you to make one of them torturing yourself," Rosa finally answered, mouth full.

"It's just running, Ro. I'll be fine... ish. I'm not really in the best physical shape right now. I think it'll be good for me. Plus, I already registered and paid. They have my money so there's no backing out now!" Maggie attempted to explain and sound excited.

"Why a half marathon specifically? I feel like I should be *more* concerned about you now. Remember, I ran the mile with you in high school. Every year. We hated it. Do you have a death wish?" Rosa asked.

"I don't know. It just felt like something hard that I could try to do," Maggie mumbled, shrugging.

"It *is* hard, Mags. 13.1 miles is such a ridiculous distance. Obviously I'll come cheer you on no matter what, but I'm trying to figure out why you'd choose the torture of running of all things? There are lots of things you could do to meet my quota every month without putting yourself through burning lungs, sore legs, and boob sweat," Rosa continued, perplexed.

"I just want to see if I can still do something hard by myself. I'm afraid I've lost all of my fight," Maggie whispered, but Rosa heard her. Nodding slowly, as if finally being able to look past the torture of running, Rosa understood what Maggie needed. She needed proof that she could attack life the way she used to before grief destroyed every shred of belief she had in herself.

"First of all, Mags, you have done something hard by yourself every day for years now. You have continued to survive after being dealt a blow that was staggering. But if you can't acknowledge that then I guess I'll tolerate this half marathon masochism," Rosa dry heaved on the words 'half marathon' making Maggie laugh. "What do you need from me?"

"I really want to be the one to do this on my own and prove to myself that I can. So really, all you'll have to do is listen to me bitch about running. I've already got a training plan in place and bought some running shoes. I start training next week. I downloaded some audiobooks to listen to while I run and have accepted that it's going to be hard as hell. You're totally welcome to come out for the race itself, but not at all necessary since I know it'll take me forever. I'm not really looking forward to all the running, but honestly... I'm kind of excited, Ro," Maggie was rambling and it was the most animated Rosa had seen her in months. She couldn't remember the last time she rambled like this. Maggie smiled at the thought of finally looking forward to something and it felt like a piece of herself clicked back into place.

"Famous last words bitch," Rosa deadpanned, turning Maggie's smile into an all out cackle.

"Run a half marathon Maggie."

"It'll be fun Maggie."

"You'll feel so good afterwards Maggie."

"You need professional help Maggie."

"How in the fuck did you think this was a good idea Maggie?"

This was how Maggie's internal monologue went on every single run. It had been a month of training so far and every run still felt like the biggest struggle of her life. Well, second biggest. Dead mom trumps most struggles, naturally. As she huffed her way through today's 6 miles, she began the thought spiral that always hit her at about the halfway point on her runs. What if the running never got easier? What if this first challenge she had picked for herself was in fact too hard? What if she wasn't strong enough anymore? What if she had actually lost all of her fight?

NO.

Maggie almost stumbled as the voice in her head shouted the word at her. No? No. No, the running wouldn't get easier? Or, no she hadn't actually lost all of her fight? She waited and of course, the voice in her head chose to stay quiet instead of offering any clarity.

"Training for a half marathon and hearing my own voice yell at me. Somebody sedate me," Maggie huffed out loud to herself, turning a corner. As she kept running, though, she noticed that although the running most definitely did not get easier, her thoughts didn't plague her as they just had.

She just kept going. Although her legs were burning beyond belief, her steps somehow felt lighter. A small kernel in her chest lit up as her footfalls felt stronger. Maybe she should let that voice in her head yell at her more often. As she continued her run, a small piece of who Maggie was clicked back into place.

Two months into training and as Maggie predicted the running *did not* get any easier, but she did get stronger. Her schedule revolved around work and running, and planning something she wasn't quite ready to tell anyone else about yet. Karsen and her had decided they could continue to be friends, but that Maggie should back off from any romantic relationships for the time being. As if she had time for one anyway. Between work, running, and just maintaining the basics of life, there weren't enough hours in the day anymore.

Maggie couldn't help but chuckle as she thought about how just a few months ago, time felt like something that would never pass. And now, she was struggling to find enough of it. Before, she'd just sit in bed and wait for the day to end. Now it ended before she was ready for it to be done. As she grabbed everything she needed to soak her muscles in a bath, Maggie looked around her apartment.

It was chaos incarnate but in an entirely different way than it had been a few months ago. Before, she let the messes pile up because she had no will to deal with them. She didn't care enough and it just felt like it was too much to handle.

Now, there were boxes all over the place. Art work was propped on the floor and no longer hung on the walls. Everything she owned was staggered in piles of organized chaos. It looked like she had lost her mind. Maybe she had. Or, maybe she was just finding it again. Shrugging, she headed to her bathroom to soak her muscles and make a list of all the things she still had left to do in this last month.

A month later, Maggie found herself driving with Rosa and Colin to the park where her half marathon was taking place. She had tried her hardest to convince her best friend it was unnecessary to come out for this one race, but her attempts were fruitless. No matter what she said, Rosa didn't care. She had decided she was coming and that was final. Someone had to be the stubborn one in their relationship.

Maggie was excited her brother was there, even if his visit had technically been planned for another reason that Maggie had yet to tell Rosa about. They drove in comfortable silence, sipping iced coffees, and still waking up. Maggie had signed up for one of the earliest heats available and neither Rosa nor Colin were particularly happy about that choice. Having done mostly morning training runs, the early start didn't bother Maggie one bit. As they drove, Maggie couldn't help but hum along with the radio, tapping the steering wheel to the beat.

"You look better mama," Rosa said unexpectedly from the backseat. Maggie looked at her in the rearview mirror and finally admitted to herself what she never thought would be possible.

"I am better mama."

❦ ❦ ❦

Running along, Maggie felt exhilarated during the first mile of the course. Between the music and the excitement of all the runners around her, she was almost amped about running. She smiled as she trotted along and was shocked when her Apple watch buzzed, signifying she had completed her first mile and saw she'd run her best mile pace yet.

At the third mile, it felt like she had found her stride. Sure, she wasn't exactly relaxing, but after so much training 3 miles didn't feel as hard as it once had. She noticed the crowd of runners start to thin as those who only signed up for the 5k portion finished their race. Still, she was feeling good and fresh, even if she was slightly jealous of the runners who got to stop while she still had so much course left to cover.

It was at mile seven that Maggie began to question every life choice she had ever made up until this point. The group of runners was now extremely small as those who only signed up for the 10k portion of the race had already covered their distance. Although she wasn't at her max level of exertion and tired yet, she could feel her legs starting to drag. She'd gone further than this in training, so rationally she knew she could keep going, but she wasn't entirely sure she *believed* she could.

As she rounded a bend, she saw a section of the course where spectators could stand and cheer runners on. She knew she was red as a beet and had zero desire to fake a smile as she ran past Rosa and Colin, trying to pretend she wasn't dying internally. As she got closer, she saw something bouncing in the air. Scratch that, she saw two of something bouncing in the air but couldn't make out any details. It just looked like two giant ovals bouncing over the crowd.

Finally coming into clear view of the crowd, Maggie couldn't help the laugh that burst out of her–even if it sounded more like a pained gargle in her current state. In the crowd she saw Rosa and Colin holding massive cutouts of her head that said, "bad bitch" across the forehead. She ran by giggling and waved at them as they cheered for her as if she were running in the Olympics. Passing the crowd, she shook her head, felt her second wind kick in, and locked the fuck in. Six more miles? She could absolutely do this.

At mile 12.1 Maggie realized she absolutely could *not* do this. Her training had only ever made her go as far as 12 miles and this last mile was uncharted territory for her. Her legs felt like they were emancipating themselves from the rest of her body. Her lungs were in a perpetual state of not having enough air. As her heart raced, she couldn't help but wonder if this is what heart attacks felt like. She could feel the disappointment kick in as she considered stopping, frustrated that this last mile is what would keep her from accomplishing the goal she set three months ago.

"I can't do this," she whispered to herself. Her lips quivered as she tried to keep in the tears and her legs wobbled as she struggled to continue moving forward.

"*Run! Faster!*"

Her muscles locked and her steps stuttered as she heard the voice shoot like lightning through her mind. This wasn't the voice that had told her "no" months ago on that training run. This was another voice she recognized immediately but hadn't let herself think about in years.

"Come on! Faster! Run damn it!" she heard it shouting at her again. Just like her mom had shouted from the sidelines during years of middle school and high school sports. Her mom, who never missed a game even if her teams weren't all that great. Her mom, who was the loudest on the side lines of every game to the point of terrifying her teammates and getting ejected by refs. Her mom, who was always there… but wasn't able to be *here*. But that voice. It would be enough. Maggie made damn sure of that.

She couldn't stop the tears as they came now. But she found her legs also refused to stop at the chorus of her mom's yelling. The yelling that used to frustrate and embarrass her, was the only thing keeping her going now. The woman who would never tolerate her giving up. Fueled by her mom's voice, Maggie found a final kernel of strength and propelled herself forward.

As she saw the finish line come into view, Maggie knew she looked like a mad woman. She was somehow simultaneously laughing, crying, and gritting her teeth from the pain and exhaustion. She saw Colin and Rosa screaming and flailing their arms. She heard her mom screaming at her in her head. She felt another piece of herself click back into place.

🌱 🌱 🌱

"You are utterly insane sis," Colin said to Maggie as she stood under the finish line banner holding her finisher medal. She laughed as she felt a new fire blaze within and flipped him off with both hands. He snapped pictures of her, bright red face and all. Rosa joined in at some point. Then passing the phone to a stranger, Colin joined in. Maggie couldn't stop smiling and laughing. Even as Rosa and Colin tried (and failed) to lift Maggie onto their shoulders in victory. She smiled the entire time she limped back to her car. She smiled the entire drive home. She smiled the entire rest of the day. She smiled until her cheeks were almost as sore as her legs. *Almost.*

Maggie barely moved for almost a full 24 hours after the half marathon. Thankfully, Rosa and Colin were there to cater to her as she recovered from the massacre she just put her body through. A day later and she was still sore as shit, but at least she could walk. She had no time to waste. Today would be exhausting for an entirely different reason. Colin had left about an hour ago to pick something up while Maggie prepared to tell Rosa the third thing she'd be doing this month to meet Rosa's quota.

"Mags, this place is bare bones. Are you tight on money or something? Did you sell all your shit? It doesn't even look like someone lives here at this point," Rosa called over from the kitchen of Maggie's apartment.

"Ro, come over here. I wanna tell you my third thing for this month," Maggie called her over.

"You just ran a half marathon yesterday. I think I can let you off the hook," Rosa joked as she plopped on the couch with her coffee.

"Well, I already have this one planned. I've been planning it for a few months actually and there's no backing down now," Maggie answered, smirking. Rosa narrowed her eyes, curiosity consuming her. As Maggie opened her mouth to speak, Colin burst through the front door.

"I've got the truck! You ready sis?" he shouted, holding up the key to a U-Haul. Maggie looked at Rosa and could see her eyes bouncing around like pinballs as her brain worked furiously to catch up. She looked at the almost empty apartment, Colin holding the U-Haul key, Maggie's suspicious smile, and gasped.

"You sneaky bitch! You're moving!" she shouted.

"I'm moving," Maggie answered, grinning mischievously. She could see the hopeful gleam in Rosa's eyes.

"You're coming back East?"

"I'm coming back East."

"But you ran away," Rosa said softly. Maggie could see the hurt her best friend had carried from being essentially abandoned as Maggie tried to outrun her grief.

"I did. I ran away. I never stopped running. Until recently," Maggie answered.

"You're coming home?" Rosa asked, holding her breath, as if trying her best not to pop her bubble of hope.

"I'm coming home," Maggie said with certainty. For the first time in a long time, the word 'home' didn't make her chest hurt or her mind rattle. The word home felt true. Rosa flung herself into Maggie's lap, wrapping her arms around her neck. There was screaming. There was crying. There was laughing. Eventually Colin broke up the emotional celebration with a little tidbit that Rosa had yet to realize.

"Yeah, yeah, yeah. Mags is coming home. We're all excited as shit. Unfortunately Rosa, this means you and I are the ones packing the U-Haul because *somebody* decided moving right after running a half marathon was a good idea," Colin said, plopping onto the couch across from them. Maggie looked at her best friend, shrugging and smiling as innocently as she could.

"*You sneaky bitch,*" Rosa fumed with faux fury. All Maggie could do was laugh as another piece of herself clicked back into place.

Acceptance

Playlist

invisible string / Taylor Swift

Love I Got Left / Max McNown

Electric Touch (Taylor's Version) / Taylor Swift, Fall Out Boy

Where You're Coming From / Vincent Lima

Homeward / Dermot Kennedy

7

Acceptance

Kam despised being late. It was one of his biggest pet peeves. Today had been one giant clusterfuck of chaos that kept pushing his day back more and more. So much for Fun Friday; more like Fuck it Friday. As he got out of his car to head into the remarkable venue his friends Jax and Jenna had rented for their engagement party, he struggled with his tie. It was crooked and the knot looked wrong, but at this point he didn't care. You would think after years of attending events where he had to wear a tie, he would have mastered the skill by now. Nope.

"Who has a black tie engagement party anyway?" Kam whispered to himself, walking through the front doors. This event already looked more like a wedding. Looking around at the absurdly extravagant venue they chose for their engagement party, Kam couldn't help but wonder how over the top their actual wedding would be.

Looking around the main entrance, he finally saw the black and gold sign that highlighted which ballroom Jax and Jenna's event was in. Attempting one last time to turn his mood around, he took a cleansing breath and entered the party with his fake, charming smile on. Fake it till you make it had become his survival method these last few years.

He worked with Jax and figured more of their staff would be here. Glancing around, he couldn't see anyone he recognized yet–granted this place was massive so he'd have to do way more than just a cursory sweep. The open bar was probably a great place to start knowing his coworkers. There was a cluster of people already surrounding the bar, but he couldn't quite see if he recognized anyone yet.

Walking across the room to at the very least get a drink, his feet stuttered, his breath caught, and he froze mid stride as he heard a sound that he'd recognize in any room. Any space. Any lifetime.

A laugh.

A laugh he hadn't heard in years.

A laugh he had spent years trying to invoke.

A laugh he almost didn't believe was real. Maybe he was hallucinating. Maybe his long day was finally catching up to him.

As if in reply to his disbelief, the crowd around the bar slowly parted and he saw *her*. He shook his head thinking he must officially be going insane. Rubbing the exhaustion from his long day out of his eyes, he looked again. She was still standing there.

He decided against tempting fate to question how she was here and whether this was real. Her head was thrown back as she laughed fully and heartily. She was leaning with one arm against the bar, drink in hand, as her other hand went to her chest. That laugh was the sound that replayed in his favorite dreams. That laugh had been the sound he played in his head on his hardest days. That laugh was everything to him.

Loosing a breath, he took a moment to take her in. She looked fucking amazing. Granted, Kam had thought she always looked amazing but this was different. She seemed even *more* somehow.

She wore high waisted, wide leg black pants that just kissed the top of her obnoxiously tall heels. He had always thought it was so sexy that she didn't let her height dissuade her from wearing heels. Her top was long sleeved but made entirely of sheer lace with a deep V neck that came down to a point halfway between her chest and her belly button. Her hair was shorter now, just barely grazing her shoulder blades.

She was radiant.

Kam realized his memory had failed him. Because no matter how many pictures he saw on social media or how many times he had conjured an image of her in his mind, she had never looked like this. There was a light and exuberance emanating from her that he'd never experienced before. There was a healthy happiness that surrounded her. He could feel the magnetic pull that clearly drew people to her. He saw who she had grown into, or was it *healed* into in her case? He could see the charismatic, confident, creative woman she'd become. He was looking at a woman who seemed naturally at ease in the circle that surrounded her. She radiated a love of life he once thought she had lost. Was she actually *glowing*?

"Maggie," he said so quietly it was barely a whisper. His voice must have traveled on some phantom wind, because although he was still halfway across the room her head whipped in his direction. As if the sound of her name on his lips beckoned her.

Their eyes locked and he learned he could still read every expression on her face. First, shock. Then, confusion. Finally, happiness. Her green eyes crinkled in a smile and without willing his body to move, his legs began to carry him to her. This invisible string always pulled them together. He never had a choice when it came to her.

The next thing he knew, he was looking down at her as she smiled up at him and waved goodbye to whoever she had been speaking to. No one said anything for a few moments, the two of them just drinking each other in. As if afraid speaking would break the spell of this moment.

"What can I get ya?" the bartender asked, pulling Kam out of their moment and back into the massive ballroom he was standing in with hundreds of people. Seriously, who had an engagement party this big?

"The same thing that she's having," Kam said, without taking his eyes off Maggie. He couldn't think of anything to say. His mind was succumbing to the shock of seeing her in person after so long, that the singular brain cell he had left after a long day was short circuiting. What was the point of having a single brain cell left if it wasn't even going to work?

"Which side are you here for?" Maggie finally asked.

"I work with Jax. Who are you here for?" he replied gruffly. It would seem every emotion he was feeling at the moment was stuck in his throat and making it difficult to speak.

"I work with Jenna," she answered, smiling even wider. It took him a moment to process what she had said.

"Wait. You *work* with Jenna. That means... that means you live here again," he said it as a statement that sounded more like a question.

"I do," she said shyly, looking down. As she looked down, she noticed something that made her outright laugh again. She reached forward, adjusted his collar, loosened the knot on his tie, and pulled it over his head. He couldn't help but notice that she had done it all so carefully that she avoided touching him the entire time. Sliding the tie over her own head and retying it like she had dozens of times in the past for him, she chuckled as she said, "I see ties are still not your strength."

How the fuck did she make tying a tie look sexy? Where the hell was the bartender with his drink? He needed something else to focus on. He'd take anything to distract him right now. The knot she was working on fell perfectly into the V on her chest. He swallowed, his Adam's apple bobbing, and looked away quickly, blushing as he realized that he was blatantly staring at her boobs. She clocked his entire sequence of actions and giggled as she finished redoing his tie.

"It's okay to look, you know. I didn't wear this shirt for nothing," she joked as she went to replace the tie around his neck. This entire exchange reminded him of the first time they met. Another night where he had no clue what in the hell to say or what to expect. He was still at a loss for words as she tightened the tie, readjusted his collar, and gently patted the knot she had made. Her touch lingered as her hand slipped down his chest a bit. Her touch was gentle, but her finger tips sizzled on his skin and his eyes whipped back to hers. Was that *longing* in her eyes?

"Maggie! You met our friend Kam already! You take all the fun out of everything! I was excited to be the one to introduce you two," Jenna, the woman of the night, said as she sauntered over with her new fiance.

"Wait… Kam is the friend you wanted to introduce me to?" Maggie asked, laughing as if this were some kind of inside joke. What in the actual fuck was happening right now and was this real life? Kam pinched his own leg, hard, and winced. Yupp, this was real.

"Well, yeah," Jenna replied, bewildered.

308 | NICOLE CHMURA

"This is the friend you were so excited for me to meet because you were sick of my vow to swear off men and thought he'd be perfect for me?" Maggie asked, beaming.

"I don't think I phrased it that way," Jenna huffed in response. Maggie laughed as everyone else just stared at her. Jenna and Jax stood there totally confused but also engrossed by this entire interaction. They're confused? Kam was fucking confused.

"The universe is one funny bitch," Maggie said, wiping away tears of laughter from the corner of her eyes. "Jenna, I hate to break it to you but I've known Kam for over a decade. So you don't get any points for trying to find me a guy and making the 'introduction of the century' as you called it. But, I do agree that he'd be absolutely perfect for me," she smiled sweetly up at Kam.

"What in the hell is going on?" Jax finally spoke.

"Second that," Kam grumbled, finally getting his drink.

They stared at Maggie as if she held the answer to everything and could explain this all neatly. She rolled her eyes and Kam couldn't help the smile that spread across his face at the seemingly normal gesture of hers that he had missed so much.

"Short answer: We know each other already and that history is a *long* story. One that I can tell you at brunch tomorrow Jenna since tonight is about you and Jax. Then, you can relay the details to Jax since men are shit at details and I'm sure Kam will fuck up telling it somehow," Maggie winked at Kam as she gave the most basic answer ever to describe the anthology that was their history.

"Hey! I would not fuck up telling it," he jokingly scolded her, reaching around her to pinch her side playfully. He knew exactly where she was ticklish and she jumped as he got her in the exact spot to cause maximum reaction. So what if he then left his hand resting on her waist instead of pulling it back? And so what if she let him? Jax and Jenna stared at them, jaws dropped.

"I've literally never seen you be so ... *playful,*" Jax said to Kam.

"You hate being touched," Jenna said simultaneously to Maggie.

"I know," Maggie and Kam responded in tandem.

"No really. You won't even let *me* side hug you," Jenna continued, absolutely flabbergasted, staring at where Kam's hand rested comfortably on Maggie's hip.

"I know," Maggie sighed sadly, leaning even more into Kam. It was as if she needed his touch to ground her, which was at odds with what Jenna was saying. She didn't like to be touched at all? He knew she wasn't a fan of physical contact in general but not tolerating it at all was new. What was that about? He made a mental note to ask about it later. There would be a later.

"My mind is absolutely blown right now," Jenna said.

"Jenna, Jax please go mingle and say hi to your eight million guests. I will explain everything I can at brunch tomorrow. Now leave me be with the former love of my life," Maggie ordered.

"Former?" Kam raised a brow sarcastically.

"Oh please, get the fuck over yourself, Kam," Maggie laughed, swatting his chest.

"Jesus Christ this just gets weirder and weirder. I literally cannot with you two right now. I need a fucking drink and to not look at whatever the hell this is," Jenna huffed, walking past them to the bar.

"Sorry to burst your dream of being the matchmaker of the century," Maggie joked as she passed. Jax followed his fiance staring between Kam and Maggie like he was staring at some kind of oddity.

"Okay, but seriously, Mags, what the fuck is going on? I've had quite a day, and my mind truly cannot wrap itself around whatever is happening right now" Kam asked, guiding them away from the bar and to one of the open seating style tables around the room.

"I think this is one of those times where the universe decides it wants to be a meddlesome bitch and stir the pot for the plot because she's bored," Maggie offered, smirking. Kam stared at her deadpan.

"You live here again?" he asked for the second time.

"I live here again," she answered with a single nod.

"How long?" he continued.

"Almost a year…" she trailed off, blushing.

"A year?!" he exclaimed and then remembered he was at his friend's engagement party and lowered his voice. "A year, Mags? How? Why didn't Rosa say anything? Why didn't anyone say anything? Why didn't *you* say anything?"

"I asked her not to. I asked everyone not to tell you. I heard you were doing well and were happy. I didn't want me being back to somehow mess that up for you," she responded bashfully. "I figured we'd bump into each other eventually with how many of our circles overlap. I never thought it would take this long, and I definitely didn't think it would happen with two people I didn't even meet until after I moved back East.

Of course Maggie kept herself away. Because Kam was happy. Well, at least he made it seem that way to anyone on the outside looking in. He knew if Maggie had been here, she would've called bullshit within minutes. Maybe even seconds. She would've been able to tell that his life was fine. But that was it. Not great. Not joyful. Not amazing. Not happy. Just fine.

"Wait, you are happy, right?" Maggie asked as if reading his mind and scrunched her brows in concern.

"Yeah, of course," he smiled. She stared at him for a few seconds as if a staring contest would tell her everything she needed to know.

"Bullshit," she scoffed bluntly. Apparently a staring contest *would* tell her everything she needed to know. Saving him from having to answer, he felt his phone buzz in his chest pocket. Pulling it out, he checked the text message that came through and ran a hand along his face in frustration.

"Listen, I have to call work real quick but don't you dare move. This conversation is not done. I will be right back and you will not run away this time," he said a little more sharply than he meant to. The only response Maggie offered was a dazed nod with her mouth parted from a quiet gasp. As he got up to walk away, Kam wondered what had caught her so off guard that she hadn't even bothered with some snarky retort. As he made it to the front door of the venue already dialing his work line, it hit him.

His fucking lock screen.

His fucking lock screen.

Maggie sat staring at the seat Kam had just been occupying. She should've been surprised to see Kam here, but after all the curveballs life had thrown at her over the years, she just took it in stride and laughed. She had learned to accept that life could be both chaotically confusing and wildly wonderful, and she had no control over which it selected to be and when. Seeing Kam's lock screen, though. Now *that* had surprised her.

It was a picture of her. Not of them or a group. Just of her. Not just any photo of her either. It was one of the pictures she took after finishing her half marathon. The one where she was flipping off the camera with both hands while laughing under the finish line banner. She had posted that one to socials with a few others, but never thought she'd see it as Kam's lock screen.

She sent a silent "what the fuck are you doing right now," to the universe and grabbed her phone to text Rosa.

> **BITCH. Will I have the story of a lifetime for you tomorrow. The universe is just continually throwing me around like she's a mechanical bull and I'm some bitch wasted off of $2 drinks on ladies night holding on for dear life.**

Rosa's response didn't take long.

> **That is such a weirdly specific scenario to relate to, but I'm foaming at the mouth with the chisme I know is coming my way tomorrow. Have fun tonight!**

Maggie laughed. She had given up her obsession with being in control a few months ago thanks to the therapist she found immediately after moving back East. As she pondered what game the universe could be playing tonight, Kam returned to the seat next to her.

"Where were we?" he asked, sitting down.

"I called bullshit and you were about to tell me why you're not as happy as I thought you were," Maggie stated as fact.

"I'm pretty sure you were about to tell me about you moving back here and why I'm just learning about it a year later," he countered.

"My story is longer, so you first," she didn't budge. Kam sighed. Even after all this time, he knew that look. He wasn't going to win this battle.

"There's not really a story to tell Mags. Life is... fine. I'm not unhappy, but I'm also not over the moon ecstatic with things right now. But really, everything is fine. I'm not miserable or anything. Life just is..." he let the sentence trail.

"So your life has essentially turned into a half erect dick? Almost there, but not quite? That's unfortunate" she said frankly. For a moment he just stared at her. Then, he broke out into the loudest, deepest laugh. He forgot he could laugh this fully. It had been so long.

Maggie smiled broadly at her ability to still make him laugh and reveled in the way his laugh made her feel. The sound flowed over her skin in a warm embrace. He laughed so loudly and for so long, shoulders shaking, that people started looking at them. She even noticed Jenna and Jax staring at them, both with a single confused and curious brow raised.

"Yeah, I guess you could phrase it like that," Kam finally responded, composing himself. "Your turn Mags."

"Okay, so in the name of transparency, my story isn't actually longer. I just wanted my answer first," she said as Kam shook his head and grinned. "I decided to move back after realizing running away didn't solve all the problems my grief caused. I asked everyone not to say anything to you because I didn't want to ruin your life for the eighteenth time. But I'm just here. Working, running, going to therapy, and facing my shit."

"Therapy, huh? How did the Polish aunties handle that one?" he asked, genuinely surprised.

"They think I'm a little bitch for going to therapy, but they've stopped saying it to my face. I just love that immigrant mental health stigma. Because keeping it all locked up inside and swept under the rug was clearly going so well for me," she fumed.

"Also, you never ruined my life," he said quietly.

"Oh kind Kam, you give me too much credit," she started. "Maybe I didn't ruin your life, but I definitely didn't make it any better. I hurt you over and over and over and over and over and over–"

"Okay okay, I get it. You hurt me," he cut her off before she could continue a sequence of the word over that would never end. "I was there, remember? But, I wasn't perfect either–"

"Yes, you were," this time it was Maggie's turn to interrupt him. "You *were* perfect Kam. You were patient and kind. You showed up and you took care of me. You loved me. And I... well, I was a broken, hurting person who made shit choices and decided you were better off without me," she said with a sad smile.

"I wasn't, you know... better off without you," he said, his gaze burning into her. They sat in tense silence that was full of everything that had been left unsaid between them. Or now that the universe had somehow flung them back together, was it everything they still had left to say to each other?

"So, your lock screen," Maggie finally wondered aloud.

"I was hoping you hadn't noticed that," he said, pulling out his phone and putting his lock screen back on display.

"How would I not notice a horrible picture of myself looking like an absolute disaster and redder than Satan's nutsack?" she asked sarcastically.

"Where the hell do you come up with the shit you say?" Kam laughed.

"I get struck with colorful descriptors randomly and keep them all in the chaos that is my notes app," she replied with mock seriousness.

"Well, I don't think the picture is horrible. I honestly love this picture of you. I feel like you can almost see actual fire in your eyes. That look you get after proving the world wrong and telling it to suck it for ever doubting you. It's my favorite look of yours. It reminds me most days that I need to live the same way," he explained.

"It wasn't the world I was trying to prove it to," she said faintly.

"I know," he nodded, understanding what she was trying to convey. "Is it creepy that it's my lock screen? Now that we're talking about it, I feel like it's creepy. I'm officially a creeper," Kam rambled. Maggie knew a rambling Kam was a nervous Kam and nervous Kam always made her giggle.

"I'd say if it were literally anyone else it would be creepy, but it's us. Plus, if you're a creep, then I'm a creep," she pulled out her phone as a blush crept up her face. He noticed her lock screen was a picture of her and her mom.

When she unlocked her phone, though, her home screen was a picture of the two of them. Not just any picture. A picture of them he had never seen before. It was a selfie they had taken on the very first night they met as the sun was rising. She was leaning into him and smiling at the camera. His face was angled toward her and he was looking at her in a way that he now realized only one word could describe: *love.*

"I've never seen this one," he whispered, staring at her home screen in awe.

"I know. I never shared it. Anywhere. With anyone. This picture has always been just mine. It got me through a lot over the years. It was nice to have one picture where someone looked at me like–" she stopped abruptly, shaking her head as if she had already admitted too much.

"Like what?" he questioned, staring at her until she answered.

"Like I was *everything* to them," she admitted wistfully.

And there it was. The truth they had both spent the entire time they'd known each other skirting. From the night they met some invisible force had kept pulling them back to each other. No matter how many relationships they got into to ignore it. No matter how many times they tried to convince themselves they were just friends. No matter how messy and painful and chaotic their story had been, the story was just that: *theirs.* Together. His life was infinitely intertwined with hers and Kam realized then that it always would be. He realized why his life had been just *fine* and not more. It was her. It had always *been* her. He had felt more alive in the last hour than he had in years.

From the night they met his heart realized something his mind took until now to catch up to: she had always been and would always be his *everything.* Right now, Maggie was looking at him like he might just be her everything too.

"Dance with me," he said, holding out his hand. She looked at his hand, then him, before smiling in a way that made his chest tighten and time stop. As she put her hand in his and he guided them to the dance floor, he couldn't stop from wondering which deity he should pray to for bringing back the piece of him he thought he had lost forever.

When they got to the dance floor, he pulled Maggie in close, letting her head rest on his chest and his hand slowly sweep down her spine. When he finally rested his hand on her lower back and felt her melt into his touch even further, he made a vow. He vowed to write a personalized thank you note to every single deity in existence because it must have taken all of them collectively to bring his girl back to him.

Maggie wasn't sure whether they had spent minutes or hours on the dance floor, but she was sure of one thing. If he was willing to let her, she was never leaving this man again. As they swayed to whatever slow song was playing, they stared at each other smiling relentlessly.

"You look good," Kam leaned in, whispering in her ear.

"I am good," she said with certainty. Well, mostly good. There were still bad days and she still had a LOT of therapy ahead of her, but for the most part she could feel good about life again. She had learned to live with her grief and was ready to keep living.

Kam pulled her in tight again, and Maggie realized how badly she needed him. Wanted him. How often she'd hope to randomly run into him just to find out what his life was like these days. This man dancing with her was different from the last time they spoke–they both were–but he was still *her* Kam.

"Take me home," she said, leaning back to look up at him. She smiled at the surprise in his eyes.

"Take *you* home or take *us* home?" he asked, making sure he understood her intentions.

"Us," she said simply.

"What about your vow swearing off men?" he playfully jested.

"You're not just any man Kam. Plus, it's been over a year for me and seeing you again has made me realize how long a year without sex actually is. It's a long time. And the way you keep looking at me keeps blazing right through me and making me want to climb you like a fucking tree. So unless you'd like me to hop on in front of the seven million people at this massive engagement party, if you're interested I recommend taking us home," Maggie said in a flurry. Like the hurricane he remembered she had once been. He lost track of how many times he laughed tonight. He pulled her in closer before dipping her low and leaning down to kiss her deeply. A kiss that attempted to start making up for lost time.

"Let's go," were his last raspy words before he pulled her off the dance floor and back into his life.

Walking up to her front door, Maggie could feel the tension but not a trace of nerves. Kam had made her feel many things from the day they met but rarely nervous. She unlaced her fingers from his to get her keys while he stood behind her and pressed soft kisses into the side of her neck. For a moment she leaned into his touch even deeper before unlocking and swinging her front door open.

As they made their way into the house, Kam couldn't help but try and take in every detail he could manage. He wanted to learn everything he could about this new version of Maggie. She was the same and yet so different. Still funny and bold and unfaltering in her determination when she wanted something. But she was also more. Surer. More confident. Grown. Changed, but in a way that made it feel like she had accepted what life had thrown at her and finally chose to live fully anyway. His girl was a fighter. He always believed that, even when she hadn't.

"So this is me now," Maggie said tentatively, twining her fingers anxiously and shifting her weight. Kam looked around the living room and kitchen space. Her style had definitely changed over the years, but this home still felt like her. It was like walking into a warm embrace but with pops of color all over. It was the kind of space that made you feel comfortable while still having small, unexpected surprises peppered throughout.

He took in the emerald couch and iron art work hanging above it. The intricate design counterbalanced the simple medium of the art stunningly. The couch looked elegant and well worn. He could easily make out the spot where Maggie spent the most time. It was the cushion just beside an intricately designed flower lamp. He could imagine her curled up with one of the hundreds of books that he knew she had squirreled away somewhere in this house. Then he noticed a massive wall of picture frames.

"I need to go let my dog out, but I'll be right back," he vaguely heard Maggie mention as she walked out of the room.

He walked over to look more closely at the photos she deemed most important to display. Dozens of pictures in different sizes were scattered along the wall in mismatched frames. Maggie with her brother and mom. Maggie with Rosa. Maggie with friends he didn't recognize but was determined to learn about. He couldn't stop the stab of jealousy he felt as he saw a picture of her with a man he didn't recognize looking a bit too comfortable with each other.

It was gone as quickly as it came when he noticed another picture. Larger than most of the others and blurry. It was of them; a candid from that party he forced her to go to forever ago. They looked so young. She was still on his back after he had given her a piggyback ride. She was in the middle of a laugh with her head thrown back while holding onto him for dear life. Meanwhile, he was looking sideways over his shoulder at her with a smile he knew he had always reserved for her.

"This one reminds me on the hard days that even at my lowest and when I really didn't want to, I was able to find moments of joy and light. Especially when surrounded by the people I–," she stopped suddenly and Kam jumped at her voice. He had been so engrossed in the picture, he hadn't realized she had come back and was standing next to him. Her voice was shy as she spoke. As if she were nervous he was judging this new person she had become. As if he could ever believe she was anything less than perfect.

"The people you what?" he encouraged.

"Love," she turned to face him fully, staring directly into his eyes. Her gaze held a challenge and a question. He already knew his answer. It had always been her and it would always *be* her.

In a single moment he had her pressed against the wall they had just been looking at, his mouth slamming into hers. This kiss felt like lightning. Hungry. It was full of need from the time they had lost with each other.

Her hands slid from his chest to his shoulders, pushing his jacket down as they slid down his arms. She then went to work on the buttons of his shirt, moving slowly but deliberately–a devilish gleam in her eyes. After moving at a painstaking pace, she finally placed her hands on his bare chest. He had to bite back his groan from how the skin to skin contact sparked where her hands rested.

"Damn, you *really* grew into yourself Kam. You were always attractive, but now you're...," she whispered, her words trailing. Her gaze supplied the adjective she was failing to come up with. It swept over the muscles he knew were new to her along his upper body. He let her explore with her fingers as her touch gently swept down his arms.

Her touch was then replaced by soft kisses. Starting with one shoulder and moving to the other. Even in her heels, she had to stand on her tiptoes to reach. She fluttered gentle kisses along his chest, before adding in a little scrape with her teeth. The sensation was almost too much and Kam had to steady himself with both hands against the wall behind her. A feline grin spread across her face at his reaction.

"Oh Kam, you're never going to last if this is already driving you to the edge. You're so fucked," she laughed as she continued to pepper kisses down his torso.

"Actually, I'll be the one doing the fucking. But yes, I can't resist when it comes to you. You could wear a fucking worm costume and I'd still somehow find it to be the sexiest thing ever," he gritted out as she made it to the space just below his belly button and stilled. He looked down to where she was crouched in front of him, hands on the v that dipped into his pants. She looked up at him and started laughing sweetly. Like what he had said was the funniest thing in the world and like he wasn't on the edge of throwing her over his shoulder and fucking the daylights out of her.

Looking at her laugh so freely struck a chord in his heart and it lurched. He didn't want to just fuck her. He wanted to love her. He wanted to care for her and protect her. He wanted to support and empower her. He wanted to share the good and the bad of life with her. He wanted to lean on her and learn from her. He wanted to continue to be amazed by her every single day. He wanted to share the rest of his life with her.

As her hands reached for his belt, he grabbed them and yanked her up to stand. She gasped at the abruptness of the motion as he pinned her hands over her head and locked her into place with his thigh between her legs. Her breathing was ragged as she stared into his eyes.

"If we do this, we do this Mags," he said and she nodded in reply. "Say it," he ordered.

"If we do this, we do this Kam," she said.

"No running away tomorrow," he rasped.

"No running away tomorrow," she agreed.

"We love each other," he whispered.

"We love each other," she breathed back to him. Releasing the grip on her hands, he reached down for her thighs, lifting her up as she instinctively wrapped her legs around his waist.

"Now where the hell is your bedroom? I have no desire to fuck you against a wall right now, but maybe tomorrow if you're a good girl," he whispered into her ear. She barked out a laugh, but kept her bratty response to herself.

Following her directions, he carried her to the bedroom and Kam couldn't help but notice how right things felt with Maggie. He didn't need to fake it or overthink with her. Loving her had always felt effortless and it still did even after all this time. Loving her had never been the problem–it had always been life that kept them apart. As she stared at him biting her bottom lip, he couldn't help but wonder if maybe life was finally done screwing with their chances.

He sat down on the edge of the bed with her still wrapped around his waist. For a moment, they just looked at each other. It was as if neither of them could believe they had finally found their way back to each other again. As if they both couldn't believe they were finally each other's right person, right time.

"You know, I might have a worm costume in my closet if that'll do it for you," Maggie sassed.

"Fuck you," Kam chuckled.

"That's the goal here," she retorted. In one moment he was rolling his eyes and in the next he was up, turning, and tossing Maggie onto her back on the bed. She laughed as she bounced gently and Kam was once again taken aback by the sight of her. Still clad in all black, golden hair, and laughing like she had never known sorrow.

"Look at you. Perfect," he whispered in awe. He saw her eyes flare at the praise. At least he could still rely on her praise kink as he rediscovered everything else Maggie loved tonight. "You are wearing way too many pieces of clothing still," he growled.

"That sounds like a you problem," she smirked. He rolled his eyes at her again and reached for her feet, undoing the straps of her shoes as she continued, "That's twice now I've made your eyes roll since we entered this bedroom. You've yet to make my eyes roll a single time." Placing a gentle kiss on her inner ankle he rolled his eyes at her again. "Oop! That's three Kam," she teased.

"Well, it looks like I have some catching up to do in that case," he said, pulling her to the edge of the bed so that his knee was in between her thighs. He looked down at her before leaning forward and pushing her shirt down her shoulders.

Before she could come up with another smart remark, he fluttered gentle kisses along her jaw. Then down her neck and collarbone before finally taking one of her nipples into his mouth. She immediately arched into him, her reaction feeling just as desperate as he was for her.

As he played with her using his tongue and teeth, he brought his hand to her other breast and teased that nipple between his thumb and forefinger. He twisted it in a way that made her moan and a wicked smile crossed his face. She started to grind along his thigh, needing more friction and more of his touch. She needed more of everything right now.

"More. Kam please, more," was all she could muster between breathes. He chuckled and she could feel him nod along her chest. Slowly, he made his way down her body and she lifted her hips obediently so he could more easily take her pants and bodysuit off.

"No more snarky remarks?" he asked, placing her thighs on his shoulders. Before she could even try to sneak one in, he leaned forward and began to work his tongue into her.

"Oh fuck you," she moaned.

"That's the goal," he used her own words against her, before continuing his antagonizing pace with his mouth. She slid her fingers into his hair, unable to get enough. She tried only once to move her hips, to which he placed a steady hand just under her belly button holding her firmly down. Using her moans and gasps as his guide, it wasn't long before Maggie felt the tension build and with one last expert flick of his tongue, her eyes rolled back and stars exploded in her vision as she shouted his name. She felt herself pulsing around nothing as she came and wished for nothing more than to have all of him inside of her. It wasn't just a wish, it was a need. Urgent and burning.

"That's one," Kam said smugly.

Still breathing heavily, she threw her legs off his shoulders and sat up abruptly. Tipping his face to hers, she kissed him while making quick work of his belt and the button at the top of his pants. It only took a matter of seconds to strip him down to the same nothing she was wearing. She stood up in an attempt to match his height and looked once more into his eyes.

A love like theirs had been years in the making. No, making wasn't the right word. Their love had been forged. It had been through fire and hell, beaten, pressed, rolled, and hammered. And yet, it survived. She had survived. *They had survived.*

Her heart exploded as she leaned up to kiss him again, softer than before. She reached down for his hand and placed a gentle kiss on each of his knuckles. He just watched her gentle tour of his body and allowed her all the time in the world. Because they finally had all the time in the world, or at least as much time as this life would gift them.

He picked her up once more, her legs again instinctively wrapping around his waist. and he laid her down more gently this time, bracing his weight above her. Earlier was full of need and urgency. Now, the moment had turned tender. They looked into each other's eyes while feeling every single point of contact along their bodies.

"Are you ready?" she asked. A simple question, but the look on her face told him she was asking about so much more than this moment.

"I've always been ready. I was just waiting for you to catch up," he smiled down at her.

"Condoms are in the nightstand. Bottom drawer," she nodded.

He unraveled himself from between her legs to roll toward the nightstand she had indicated and grabbed a condom from the bottom drawer. He was quick with the wrapper, slid it on, and rolled back into her embrace, joking, "For someone who had sworn off men, you seem pretty prepared to be ravished at any moment." Her chuckled response held a hint of embarrassment.

"I had hoped," she said, her gaze boring into his.

"Hoped for what?" he asked, once again bracing his weight just over her body.

"I hoped for you," she admitted. They spent the rest of the night lost in hope and each other and most of all, love.

With her head resting on his chest and their legs intertwined, Kam stroked gentle circles around her back as a question came back to him.

"Jenna said you don't like to be touched at all anymore?" he wondered aloud, gesturing to every point where their bodies were currently connected.

"Yeah," she started sheepishly. "We're still working through my Gabe era in therapy and I've been forced to fully actualize what happened with him. It's triggered some new involuntary reactions to physical touch." Kam's jaw clenched hearing Gabe's name again.

"What else don't I know about you anymore, Mags?" he asked, wanting desperately to know all of her again. Feeling once again like that kid on a roof all those years ago.

"You've missed a lot," she teased.

"Tell me everything," he said seriously.

Maggie did her best to in fact tell him everything. She told him about Rafael and the deep depression she struggled with before, during, and after that relationship. If you could even really call what they had a relationship. She explained the ultimatum Rosa forced upon her to get her to start doing just about anything again. She flew through her time with Karsen and how he helped her start to laugh and live again. She explained that their time together had helped her start to see glimmers of the good in life. Kam never thought he'd be thankful for another man who had dated his girl, but if he ever met Karsen, he was buying him a damn steak dinner for helping her start her journey of coming back to life.

Maggie then explained training for the half marathon and coming to the realization that she could never outrun her grief. She talked about hearing her mom's voice during the last mile of the race—at which point they both cried. She told him about the ridiculous road trip back across the country with her brother and Rosa. She told him about everything she'd started doing in the last year as she finally faced her grief head on so she could accept it. She maintained an exercise routine and went to therapy. She started talking about it more with Colin, rather than both avoiding it as if their mom wasn't dead. She started hosting at her house and trying new things at least once a month, which Kam learned is where her new found passion for bread baking stemmed from.

She talked and he listened, as he had so many times before. This time, though, he felt like this wouldn't be the last time. This felt like the first of many times where he would listen to her long winded story telling with endless tangents, expressive use of her hands, and colorful language. He smiled at her as she shifted to rest her chin on his chest and look up at him.

"Are you sick of me yet," she asked jokingly, but he could sense the hint of anxiety behind her words. She was worried everything she'd just admitted would make him want to run—would make him think less of her. And why wouldn't she? So many others already had. He knew it would take a lot of time and a lot of reassurance before she fully believed how much she meant to him.

"I don't think I could ever be sick of you," he said, leaning down to gently kiss her. "Especially not when I just got you back. Mags, when you explained your home screen picture earlier and said I looked at you like you were everything to me, it's because you *are* everything to me. A part of me knew it then, but the rest of me needed time for the realization to sink in. *Everything you are is everything to me*," he hoped she believed him.

She stared at him for a long while with a strange look in her eyes before nodding and resting her head back on his chest. He pulled her in tighter and made it his life's mission to show her that those weren't just empty words. She would believe him. He would make sure of it.

The next morning, Kam was in Maggie's kitchen making breakfast. Her dog was resolutely staring up at him in hopes that even a tiny piece of bacon might accidentally find a way onto the floor. It was late, but if he remembered correctly Maggie loved breakfast any time of day. As if his thoughts conjured her, Maggie came bustling through the kitchen in a flurry. She was fully dressed, with her hair and makeup done, confusing Kam. When he woke up before her, he figured they'd have a calm day. He was ready to just soak in any moment he could with her.

Had she changed her mind? Was she freaking out? Maybe last night was too much like it had been the first time? His anxiety started to spiral as he thought about her running away from him yet again.

In the midst of her hurricane to get ready and out the door, she saw Kam tense and frown as he stood at the stove making eggs. Her heart broke because she knew exactly what he was thinking. She had been the one to instill this particular fear in his heart.

"I'm not running Kam," she said sadly, walking over to him and wrapping her arms around his neck. She leaned up on the tips of her toes to kiss him deeply and slowly. "But I am running late," she said, pulling away. "I'm supposed to be at brunch with Jenna and some of the girls in 5 minutes, which means according to Google Maps I'm going to be 20 minutes late."

"I'm going to have to get used to being late to things again, aren't I?" he chuckled, holding onto Maggie's waist.

"Yupp" she said, popping the p for emphasis. "Also, after brunch we're going to a late lunch/early dinner with Ro. *Both* of us. There's not a singular chance I'm sitting through a whole meal trying to explain everything that happened yesterday to that chismosa alone. You are my back up."

"Just text me where and when and I'll be there," he said, looking her up and down. "You look amazing," his voice was husky as his eyes heated with the words. He stared at where her dress stopped precariously high around her thighs. The thigh tattoo peaking out was new. It was a cascade of lightning with branches streaking out all across the upper half of her thigh. "This tattoo is amazing," he mused, running his fingers along each lightning streak.

"That one was for you," she said hesitantly. His head whipped up and he stared into her eyes before she looked down embarrassed by her own admission. His hand moved from her thigh to lift her chin so their eyes met again. He noticed she was chewing the inside of her cheek–her nervous tick.

"Tell me," his whisper was a plea.

"You've always been lightning to me Kam," she whispered back. Their faces were so close that he felt her breath with each of her words. "Your touch. Your laugh. Your presence. I never knew when or where in my life you were going to strike, but I always knew that when you did you'd light up everything around you. It's never been a spark or a blaze with you. It's always been a lightning strike. I got it to remind myself that a love like that had existed in my life once before and to keep hoping that it might exist again."

"Astonishing," Kam brushed the word against her mouth as he leaned forward and kissed her. She pulled away begrudgingly and saw the desire fueled resolve in his eyes.

"Kam, I'm already going to be 20 minutes late. Absolutely no–" before Maggie could finish, Kam had lifted her onto the kitchen island and was standing in between her legs.

"I'm going to be more than 20 minutes late, aren't I?" she asked.

"Dumb question," he said, already starting to lower to his knees in front of her.

"30 minutes late?" she asked, her voice already getting breathy as he kissed each branch of her lightning tattoo. He shook his head looking up at her from between her thighs.

"Let me just text Jenna that I'm running late and will be there in–*holy fuck*," Maggie groaned as Kam showed her that it'd be a miracle if they managed to even leave the house today. She threw her phone to the side forgetting what she had even been doing with it. Forgetting about brunch entirely and getting lost in the love of her life.

Maggie spent 30 minutes that day profusely apologizing to Jenna for missing brunch and scheduling a lunch she vowed to be at no matter what the next day. Dinner with Rosa had gone well, even if she had sat there with a smug "I told you so" smile on her face the entire time. Maggie couldn't deny it. Rosa had in fact told her so when it came to Kam. She'd let her have this win. They were heading back to Maggie's house with Kam driving. Maggie had been wondering something since last night.

"Did you ever read my letter?" she asked. She saw his hands tense around the wheel for a flash of a second and then he sadly shook his head. She nodded and looked back out her window more than willing to leave it at that.

At the next red light she heard Kam shuffling next to her and turned to see what he was doing. He had his hips raised, trying to get something out of his pocket: his wallet. He flipped it open and pulled out a folded up piece of paper.

"I took it out of the envelope but was always too afraid to read it for some reason. I folded it up so it would fit in my wallet and have carried it with me every day since you gave it to me. I hoped

I'd read it one day, but my anxiety always won out," his voice was just barely a whisper.

"I think you should read it when we get home," she nodded, understanding. He tensed again but nodded back.

Fifteen minutes later they sat on her back patio as Kam fiddled with the folded up letter in his hand. He had sat like this many times before and had always let his apprehension win. He wasn't exactly sure what about the letter made him so nervous.

"I promise you'll like it. Well, most of it," Maggie said from beside him with a secretive smile. With that promise as his tether, he opened the letter he had held onto for years but never read. As he faced the words she had written to him so long ago, his breath caught as he noticed smudges from what were clearly tear stains on the paper. He looked over at Maggie and she nodded encouragingly. He turned back to the letter and read:

Dear Kam,

I hope when you read this letter it is the perfect time and place for everything I'm about to say. I also hope I find the right words for you. Hope. I haven't hoped for much recently but I do hope for you. I hope your life is everything and more. I hope you live and laugh (your real laugh, not your fake one) and love. Ferociously and without limitations. I hope you get the love you deserve, and Kam you deserve the love story of the century. I'm sorry for not being able to give that to you.

You have given me... everything. You have cared for me more than I think anyone ever has and ever will. When you considered your life and your actions and your choices, you always considered me with them. I'm not entirely sure if it was a conscious thought or just habit. You always considered how you would affect me and what I was dealing with. Feeling that thought of and seen has been a gift I'm not sure I actually deserve.

You did so many little things that I took for granted over the years. Always keeping ketchup at your house for me even though you hate it. Teaching yourself latin dances for that wedding so I could spend the entire night on the dance floor. Keeping my favorite lotion in the glove compartment of your car. Giving me your real smile. Always answering on the third ring. Always making sure I wasn't alone at a party. Keeping the pens I prefer to write with on your desk at all times. Never wearing yellow because it makes me weirdly anxious. Letting me sleep on your side of the bed because it's also my side of the bed. Never getting upset with me for making us late places even though I know how much you hate being late. Loving my mom and making her laugh with your antics all the way to the end. Showing up to everything no matter how insignificant. Never leaving a single message unanswered. Piggyback rides to ease my nerves or when I was too scared to move on my own. Looking at me and seeing me—truly—and never thinking less of me no matter what you saw.

No wonder all your ex-girlfriends hated me so much.

So many little things that were so easy to miss in the moment but that make my heart ache looking back now. But I guess that's where we find true love after all. Everyone thinks love requires grand gestures and sweeping professions. Looking back on us, I can see how false that is. Love has always been in the little things.

And I can say with certainty Kam that I am in love with you. I honestly think I've been in love with you since the very first night we met. I'm not too big to admit that I fell first, but the jury is still out on who fell harder. From the moment a boy with hard eyes and gangly limbs stepped onto a roof and didn't think my blunt honesty was too much. When you looked at me with curiosity and not caution. When you looked at me like I was everything.

But I'm not everything Kam. Not anymore at least. I'm struggling and broken and most days it feels like I'm fighting for my life. I'm not everything anymore because I barely feel like a fragment of anything most days.

But you Kam? You're everything. Even if you won't admit it with your self-deprecating humor and nonchalance toward the world. You are kind and caring. You are patient. You are joyful and loving. You are smart and tenacious. You are somehow loud and chaotic while simultaneously being my calm, grounded home base. Kam you are absolutely everything and everything you are is everything to me.

I wrote two letters for today for two potential outcomes. I think a part of me expected there'd be someone else. Somehow my soul always knows when it comes to you. I don't think life would ever beat us in a fair fight but our story hasn't been fair, has it? So I hope in your future you are happy and loved and as brilliant as ever. I hope you're able to read this letter and remember us as we were and not necessarily as we are right now. I hope I get to hear about how wonderful your life is.

And on the off chance your life isn't? I'll be waiting.

Love always,
Mags

Maggie watched Kam as he read. He laughed and scoffed and rolled his eyes. He'd tense at moments and she could see the muscle in his jaw flex occasionally. With each reaction, she could tell exactly where in the letter he was. Which is why when he gasped, she knew he had read the line that made her assume last night he had read this letter long ago.

"Everything you are is everything to me," he whispered. She nodded and let him finish the little that was left. When he was done reading he said nothing. They both stared out into her yard silently. Naturally, Maggie began overthinking and spiraling and catastrophizing–something she was working on with her therapist but still had a long way to go. She must've been so wrapped up in her own thoughts that she nearly jumped out of her own skin when she felt her phone buzz. She looked down at the screen and then quickly at Kam, who had his own phone pressed to his ear. Smiling, she counted.

Ring.

Ring.

Ring.

"Hello," she answered, giggling just as much as she had when he had pulled this stunt back when they were teenagers.

"Hey Mags, I was wondering if you could help me out with something," Kam said into his phone while looking directly into her eyes.

"What's that?" she asked.

"Would you be willing to check out that gnarly mole you know is on my ass?" Maggie couldn't help but throw her entire body back in her chair laughing, recalling that conversation they had what felt like a lifetime ago. Kam reached over grabbing her hand and pulled her toward him.

"Yeah, I think I can do that," she answered as she climbed out of her chair and into his lap.

"Oh, and one more thing," he started.

"Two favors might be too many, Kam," she joked.

"Will you finally stay with me and be everything that you are so I can love you for the rest of forever?" He looked at her with an intensity she had never seen before. Although a piece of her still felt like screaming and running for the hills, the rest of her wanted to stay right here, wrapped in his arms.

"The rest of forever is a long time, Kam. Are you sure about that?" she wondered aloud. She looked into his eyes and saw the resolve of the man she loved.

"The rest of forever isn't anywhere near long enough for me," he whispered against her lips.

Maggie looked into his eyes and thanked whatever cosmic force had brought Kam back into her life. The rest of forever sounded amazing to her, and for the first time in a long time, she was excited to live it.

Epilogue

4 YEARS LATER

Playlist

Simply The Best / Billianne

I Think He Knows / Taylor Swift

You're Still the One / Teddy Swims

Epilogue

As Kam stood in front of the room waiting for the ceremony to start, his cheeks ached from smiling. Could your heart hurt from being too happy? He was pretty sure his heart hurt from being quite literally overjoyed. It took Kam a long time to convince Maggie to marry him. They had moved in together almost immediately but the rest took what felt like forever. Thankfully, he was a patient man.

Over the last four years they had gotten to know each other again, as they both had changed in their time apart. They traveled and experienced the world together. They worked to start Maggie's non-profit organization together. They got another dog together. And another. And another. Kam had asked her to marry him repeatedly, and she said no *repeatedly*. Thankfully, he was patient *and* persistent.

He understood her hesitation toward marriage. Between her parents divorce, her dad being who he was, and her fear of losing someone she loved so much again–he got it. Thankfully, Maggie kept going to therapy and even Kam had started with his own therapist so that they could both continue to grow together. It took two and half years of asking before she finally said yes.

Thinking of everything they had survived and done together and of all the times they separated just to reunite, he smiled even wider. They made it, and he'd make sure they'd continue to make it.

He saw motion at the back of the room and stilled. Rosa came around the wall blocking off the bridal party with a mischievous gleam in her eyes. Oh sweet baby Jesus, what were they up to? Before he knew it, she pointed to the musicians and they faded out of the instrumental they had been playing and pressed play on something on their computer. Confusion hit him full force.

Maggie and Kam had agreed to two things: their first dance would be to Teddy Swim's cover of "You're Still the One" and the wedding party would walk down the aisle to an instrumental version of "Simply the Best." Apparently not.

As the music started, he immediately knew what was playing. Of course she had somehow found a way to go behind his back and sneak fucking Taylor Swift into their wedding ceremony. She decided *she* was walking down the aisle to "I Think He Knows."

His laugh bellowed across the room and their guests looked at him puzzled. Maggie just smiled from behind the wall at the laugh she loved so much, proud that after all this time she was still able to get it out of him.

"This was *not* the song the two of us had agreed upon. My wife, well very soon to be wife, is full of surprises for us today," he said loudly enough for everyone to hear. As he looked to the back of the room again, Rosa had already danced half way down the aisle with an exuberant smile. Was she passing out shots of Jack while she walked down the aisle? Of course she was. At this point why was he even surprised by any of this?

As the second verse started, he saw Colin come into view. His breath caught as Maggie finally shifted into his line of sight. He couldn't help the raw emotion that filtered through him and the tears he felt forming in the corners of his eyes.

They looked at each other for a long moment and then Maggie with a Cheshire cat grin and pure mayhem in her eyes mouthed along with the music while staring directly at him, "*he's so obsessed with me and boy I understand.*" She then had the audacity to wink at him before starting her walk toward him. Toward the rest of their forever. Their guests laughed as he just watched her, shaking his head and beaming. How could one heart experience so many feelings at once and still survive?

Finally getting to him, he grabbed her hand asking loud enough for everyone to hear, "Any more surprises for us today, Mags?"

"Listen Kam, it took us 15 years and 7 stages of grief to get here. I was going to make sure everyone knew how obsessed with me you were that entire time. What better way to show it than with a Taylor Swift song?" she joked back.

"And love," he said. He saw her initial confusion at his statement and noticed the exact moment she understood his meaning.

"Yes. 15 years and 7 stages of grief and love," she nodded, as a tear trickled down her cheek. "But also, of course there are more surprises everyone. It's *me* after all," she said over her shoulder, to which everyone laughed. "Remember Kam, you asked for all of this for the rest of forever."

"I did. And all of this is everything to me, Mags." The look in her eyes told him that she *finally* believed him.

Note from the author

**Things I wish people hadn't said to me after my mom died
and what I wish they had said instead:**

"How are you doing?"
*You must be feeling so many things right now. I'm here if you want
to get some of it off your chest.*

"What can I do to help?"
*Can I help with (come up with a task already)? OR, just do some-
thing you know can be helpful (cooking meals, collecting donations, etc.)*

"They'll always be with you."
*What's one thing you'll really miss doing with them? (And then if
you're able, do that thing with the person in the future on occasion.)*

"You're handling this so well. You're so strong."
*I'm amazed at how you're handling all this, but you know you don't
need to feel like you have to be strong around me, right? It's okay to not
be okay.*

"It'll get better in time."
*I know it hurts right now, so make sure to take as much time as you
need to process and heal.*

"I know it's sad, but be grateful for the time you had with
them."
Tell me about one of your favorite memories with them.

Acknowledgements

It feels absolutely surreal that we have made it to the end of my first novel. I have spent so many years toying with this idea and letting it go unfinished that I almost can't believe we're here. I firmly believe I made it this far thanks to so many of you.

Thank you to my brother, Chris, who has always supported every outlandish idea his little sister has come up with. From the time I wanted to be a personal trainer to the jokes about stealing elephants, I thank you for your constant, steady presence in my life. Your support of me has never wavered no matter how insane you think my ideas are. I couldn't have asked for a better big brother.

Rita, thank you for being *you*. Thank you for growing up with me and loving me through what I know were my less favorable phases of life. Thank you for believing in this book before a word had ever been written. Thank you for believing in me and for always keeping the promises you made my mom. Thank you for being the kind of best friend that people pray for. I'll never be entirely convinced I deserve you, but I'll keep you all the same.

Sami, thank you for taking my chaos and running with it. Your beta reading reactions gave me the strength to keep going when I wanted to scrap, burn, and delete this project entirely. Thank you for taking the time to encourage me and even threaten me when I suggested not finishing this book. You are the little sister I never had, and I am so thankful the universe crossed our paths so chaotically.

Sandra, thank you for being the MVP Capricorn in my life. Thank you for your steady earth sign presence that forever counterbalances my wild water sign waves. I will forever love our chaotic text thread and the fact that I never know what I'm going to get when I see a notification pop up from you. Thank you for your creative work on this book. Thank you for never letting me stop and for your persistent–if a little unhinged–pep talks that continuously propelled me forward. Your faith in me has never gone unnoticed and I will be eternally grateful for the confidence you have helped me develop.

Tasha, thank you for calming my page break panic with your unwavering kindness and support. I know I'm a chaotic presence in your life, but I thank you for loving me anyway. Thank you for always showing up for whatever outlandish idea comes next and thank you for being willing to answer the birds of paradise beacon within minutes.

Elysa, thank you for never allowing me to linger in my own self doubt and wallowing for long. I'm not sure you realize just how much that means to me. Your care has helped me survive the last decade. Thank you for helping me stay alive long enough to publish this book and for being an amazing friend along the way. I'll stop saying nice things because I know how much you hate it. Get in loser, we're doing shots!

To my group chats that never fail me: Bills Bitchachos (Lalita and Kristen), Shrek Shawties (Heather and Dallas), and my Gaming Girlz (Rachel, Makayla, Melissa, and Megumi) thank you for being the kind of friends that help make my world go round. Thank you for the support and excitement about this book to counterbalance my persistent anxiety and nausea about publishing. Thank you for being aggressively supportive and never allowing me to doubt that I'd be anything but successful. Thanks for never making me feel like the single friend and including me as you build your lives.

Charity, thank you for helping me find the right adjectives when I was uncertain and for at least trying to be better about answering my texts. Thank you for finding my humor to be your brand of humor too. Thank you for being amazed by me even when some of it is unwarranted. I hope I found the right words in this book. Now go check your phone because there's probably a text you haven't answered there.

To my Pickle Promo Baddies (or whatever the hell we're calling ourselves by the time this book has been published), thank you for believing in me and this project even when there was minimal context. Thank you for the utterly unhinged IG group chat that made me laugh and question my own sanity. Thank you sharing this book with your worlds for me. I appreciate your faith in me and I really do hope I get to front that retreat to the UK one day.

To the rest of my inner circle, village, coven or whatever you want to call yourselves, thank you for being the first in line to order my debut novel. Thank you for always building me up and being there for whatever I needed. Whether it was a beer on a Friday night, watching Mamma Mia with sangria, or helping me move houses in the heat of May, you my friends have always been there for me and I will never forget that. Thank you for loving me as much as you love reading and I hope this book made you proud to call me your friend.

Solange, thank you for your creative work on the cover art. Thank you for somehow making sense of my poorly drawn stick figures and rudimentary descriptions. Thank you for working with me on bringing my vision to life.

To every shitty date I've ever been on or heard my friends talk about, thank you for giving me more than enough inspirational material to work with for this book.

To the men who have actually treated me well, thank you for showing me what glimmers of love could look like. Thank you for helping me combine imagination and experience to create a dreamy MMC for this novel. Thank you for being good to me in a world that has been particularly cruel at times.

Readers, thank you for giving this book and me a chance. I know it's my first and it may not be my best, but it is the most precious to me. This idea will always be the one that started my journey. Thank you for giving Maggie and Kam a chance. I hope you love them almost as much as I do.

And last but never least, thank you to my mom. Thank you for loving me so deeply that losing you cut even deeper. Thank you for being the kind of mom that some people wish for. Thank you for believing in me and pushing me to always be and do more. Thank you for showing up to every dance competition, soccer game, and winter concert. Thank you for loving me so deeply that I would give just about anything for one more minute. Thank you for being a light in my world for the twenty years I had with you. I wish you could be here to see this and read this book. Okay, maybe not read *all* of this book. Thank you for your unwavering belief in my success. Thank you for loving me so much that grieving you created this story to share with the world. Miss you. Love you, mean it.

Nicole Chmura is a debut author and former educator. She is an avid reader, animal rescuer, and occasional recipe sharer. Originally from New Jersey, she is a first generation American now residing on the West Coast. In her spare time she can usually be found trying out a local bottomless brunch, exploring with her dogs, or enjoying time with her found family. Go Bills!

CONNECT WITH NICOLE ONLINE
www.readsandrescues.com
@readsandrescues on Instagram and TikTok

www.ingramcontent.com/pod-product-compliance
Lightning Source LLC
Chambersburg PA
CBHW030236120726
47903CB00005B/1502